Koizumi Edition
THE WRITINGS OF LAFCADIO HEARN

LIFE AND LETTERS OF LAFCADIO HEARN
INCLUDING
THE JAPANESE LETTERS

EDITED BY
ELIZABETH BISLAND

VOLUME I

WILDSIDE PRESS

www.wildsidepress.com

COPYRIGHT, 1906 AND 1910, BY ELIZABETH BISLAND WETMORE
COPYRIGHT, 1922, BY HOUGHTON MIFFLIN COMPANY

ALL RIGHTS RESERVED

The Riverside Press
CAMBRIDGE · MASSACHUSETTS
PRINTED IN THE U.S.A.

PREFACE

IN the course of the preparation of these volumes there was gradually accumulated so great a number of the letters written by Lafcadio Hearn during twenty-five years of his life, and these letters proved of so interesting a nature, that eventually the plan of the whole work was altered. The original intention was that they should serve only to illuminate the general text of the biography, but as their number and value became more apparent, it was evident that to reproduce them in full would make the book both more readable and more illustrative of the character of the man than anything that could possibly be related of him.

No biographer could have so vividly pictured the modesty and tender-heartedness, the humour and genius of the man, as he has unconsciously revealed these qualities in unstudied communications to his friends. Happily — in these days when the preservation of letters is a rare thing — almost every one to whom he wrote appeared instinctively to treasure — even when he was still unknown — every one of his communications, though here and there regrettable gaps occur, owing to the accidents of changes of residence, three of which, as every one knows, are more destructive of such treasures than

PREFACE

a fire. To all of his correspondents who have so generously contributed their treasured letters I wish to express my sincere thanks. Especially is gratitude due to Professor Masanubo Otani, of the Shinshu University of Tōkyō, for the painstaking accuracy and fulness of the information he contributed as to the whole course of Hearn's life in Japan.

The seven fragments of autobiographical reminiscence, discovered after Hearn's death, added to the letters, narrowed my task to little more than the recording of dates and such brief comments and explanations as were required for the better comprehension of his own contributions to the book.

Naturally some editing of the letters has been necessary. Such parts as related purely to matters of business have been deleted as uninteresting to the general public; many personalities, usually both witty and trenchant, have been omitted, not only because such personalities are matters of confidence between the writer and his correspondent, a confidence which death does not render less inviolable, but also because the dignity and privacy of the living have every claim to respect. Robert Browning's just resentment at the indiscreet editing of the FitzGerald Letters is a warning that should be heeded, and it is, moreover, certain that Lafcadio Hearn himself would have been profoundly unwilling to have any casual criticism of either the living or the dead given public record. Of those who had been his friends he always spoke with tenderness and respect,

PREFACE

and I am but following what I know to be his wishes in omitting all references to his enemies.

That such a definite and eccentric person as he should make enemies was of course unavoidable. If any of these retain their enmity to one who has passed into the sacred helplessness of death, and are inclined to think that the mere outline sketch of the man contained in the following pages lacks the veracity of shadow, my answer is this: In the first place, I have taken heed of the opinion he himself has expressed in one of his letters: "I believe we ought not to speak of the weaknesses of very great men" — and the intention of such part of this book as is my own is to give a history of the circumstances under which a great man developed his genius. I have purposely ignored all such episodes as seemed impertinent to this end, as from my point of view there seems a sort of gross curiosity in raking among such details of a man's life as he himself would wish ignored. These I gladly leave to those who enjoy such labours.

In the second place, there is no art more difficult than that of making a portrait satisfactory to every one, for the limner of a man, whether he use pen or pigments, can — if he be honest — only transfer to the canvas the lineaments as he himself sees them. *How* he sees them depends not only upon his own temperament, but also upon the aspect which the subject of the picture would naturally turn toward such a temperament. For every one of us is aware

PREFACE

of a certain chameleon-like quality within ourselves which causes us to take on a protective colouring assimilative to our surroundings, and we all, like the husband in Browning's verse,

> Boast two soul-sides, . . .

which is the explanation, no doubt, of the apparently irreconcilable impressions carried away by a man's acquaintances.

Which soul-side was the real man must finally resolve itself into a matter of opinion. Henley, probably, honestly believed the real Stevenson to be as he represented him, but the greater number of those who knew and loved the artist will continue to form their estimate of the man from his letters and books, and to them Henley's diatribe will continue to seem but the outbreak of a mean jealousy, which could not tolerate the lifting up of a companion for the world's admiration.

Of the subject of this memoir there certainly exists more than one impression, but the writer can but depict the man as he revealed himself throughout twenty years of intimate acquaintance, and for confirmation of this opinion can only refer to the work he has left for all the world to judge him by, and to the intimate revelations of thoughts, opinons, and feelings contained in his letters.

E. B.

CONTENTS

INTRODUCTORY SKETCH	1
I. BOYHOOD	3
II. THE ARTIST'S APPRENTICESHIP	36
III. THE MASTER-WORKMAN	97
IV. THE LAST STAGE	127
LETTERS, 1877–1886	151

ILLUSTRATIONS

FOUR GENERATIONS OF THE HEARN FAMILY   6

MRS. HEARN AT HER WRITING-DESK   110
From a photograph by Burton Holmes.

MRS. HEARN, HER OLDEST SON, KAZUO, AND HER DAUGHTER, SUZUKO   120
Photograph by Nonomiya, Tōkyō.

IWAO AND KYOSHI, THE SECOND AND THIRD SONS OF HEARN   148
From a photograph.

LAFCADIO HEARN FROM A PHOTOGRAPH TAKEN ABOUT 1873   154

H. E. KREHBIEL   270
From a photograph by Underwood & Underwood.

LIFE AND LETTERS OF LAFCADIO HEARN

INTRODUCTORY SKETCH

LIFE AND LETTERS OF LAFCADIO HEARN

CHAPTER I
BOYHOOD

LAFCADIO HEARN was born on the twenty-seventh of June, in the year 1850. He was a native of the Ionian Isles, the place of his birth being the Island of Santa Maura, which is commonly called in modern Greek Levkas, or Lefcada, a corruption of the name of the old Leucadia, which was famous as the place of Sappho's self-destruction. This island is separated from the western coast of Greece by a narrow strait; the neck of land which joined it to the mainland having been cut through by the Corinthians seven centuries before Christ. To this day it remains deeply wooded, and scantily populated, with sparse vineyards and olive groves clinging to the steep sides of the mountains overlooking the blue Ionian sea. The child Lafcadio may have played in his early years among the high-set, half-obliterated ruins of the Temple of Apollo, from whence offenders were cast down with multitudes of birds tied to their limbs, that perchance the beating of a thousand wings might break the violence of the fall, and so rescue them from the last penalty of expiation.

LAFCADIO HEARN

In this place of old tragedies and romance the child was born into a life always to be shadowed by tragedy and romance to an extent almost fantastic in our modern workaday world. This wild, bold background, swimming in the half-tropical blue of Greek sea and sky, against which the boy first discerned the vague outlines of his conscious life, seems to have silhouetted itself behind all his later memories and prepossessions, and through whatever dark or squalid scenes his wanderings led, his heart was always filled by dreams and longings for soaring outlines, and the blue, "which is the colour of the idea of the divine, the colour pantheistic, the colour ethical."

Long years afterward, in the "Dream of a Summer Day," he says:

I have memory of a place and a magical time, in which the sun and the moon were larger and brighter than now. Whether it was of this life or of some life before, I cannot tell, but I know the sky was very much more blue, and nearer to the world — almost as it seems to become above the masts of a steamer steaming into equatorial summer. ... The sea was alive and used to talk — and the Wind made me cry out for joy when it touched me. Once or twice during other years, in divine days lived among the peaks, I have dreamed for a moment the same wind was blowing — but it was only a remembrance.

Also in that place the clouds were wonderful and of colours for which there are no names at all — colours that used to make me hungry and thirsty. I remember, too, that the days were ever so much longer than these days — and every day there were new pleasures and new

BOYHOOD

wonders for me. And all that country and time were softly ruled by One who thought only of ways to make me happy.... When day was done, and there fell the great hush of light before moonrise, she would tell me stories that made me tingle from head to foot with pleasure. I have never heard any other stories half so beautiful. And when the pleasure became too great, she would sing a weird little song which always brought sleep. At last there came a parting day; and she wept and told me of a charm she had given that I must never, never lose, because it would keep me young, and give me power to return. But I never returned. And the years went; and one day I knew that I had lost the charm, and had become ridiculously old.

A strange mingling of events and of race-forces had brought the boy into being.

Surgeon-Major Charles Bush Hearn, of the Seventy-Sixth Foot, came of an old Dorsetshire family in which there was a tradition of gipsy blood — a tradition too dim and ancient now to be verified, though Hearn is an old Romany name in the west of England, and the boy Lafcadio bore in his hand all his life that curious "thumb-print" upon the palm, which is said to be the invariable mark of Romany descent. The first of the Hearns to pass over into Ireland went as private chaplain to the Lord Lieutenant in 1693, and being later appointed Dean of Cashel, settled permanently in West Meath. From the ecclesiastical loins there appears to have sprung a numerous race of soldiers, for Dr. Hearn's father and seven uncles served under Wellington in Spain. The grandfather of Lafcadio rose during the Peninsula Campaign to the position of lieutenant-colonel of the Forty-Third Regiment, and commanded his regiment in the battle of Vittoria. Later he married Elizabeth Holmes, a kinswoman of Sir Robert Holmes, and of Edmund Holmes the poet, another member of her family being Rice Holmes, the historian of the Indian Mutiny. Dr. Charles Hearn, the father of Lafcadio, was her eldest son, and another son was Richard, who was one of the Barbizon painters and an intimate friend of Jean François Millet.

It was in the late forties, when England still held the Ionian Isles, that the Seventy-Sixth Foot was ordered to Greece, and Surgeon-Major Hearn accompanied his regiment to do garrison duty on the island of Cerigo. Apparently not long after his arrival he made the acquaintance of Rosa Cerigote, whose family is said to have been of old and honourable Greek descent. Photographs of the young surgeon represent him as a handsome man, with the flowing side-whiskers so valued at that period, and with a bold profile and delicate waist. A passionate love affair ensued between the beautiful Greek girl and the handsome Irishman, but the connection was violently opposed by the girl's brothers, the native bitterness toward the English garrison being as intense as was the sentiment in the South against the Northern army of occupation immediately after the American Civil War. The legend goes that the Cerigote men — there was hot blood in the family veins — waylaid and stabbed the Irishman, leaving him for

Four Generations of the Hearn Family
Robert T. Hearn, Daniel J. Hearn
Robert Bush Hearn, Lafcadio Hearn

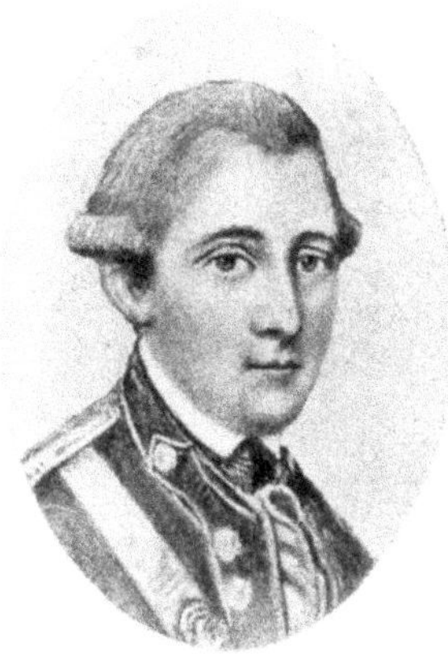
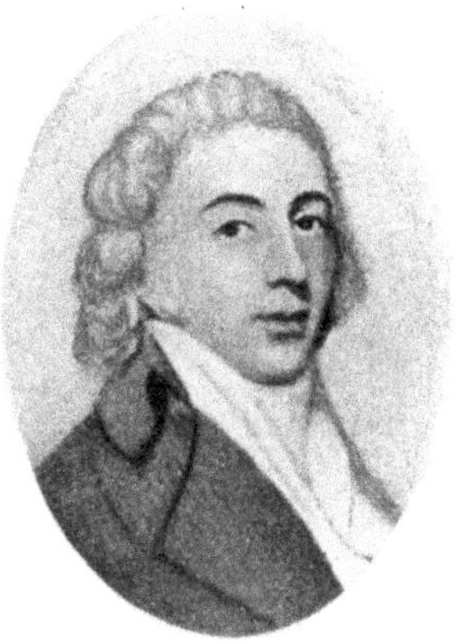
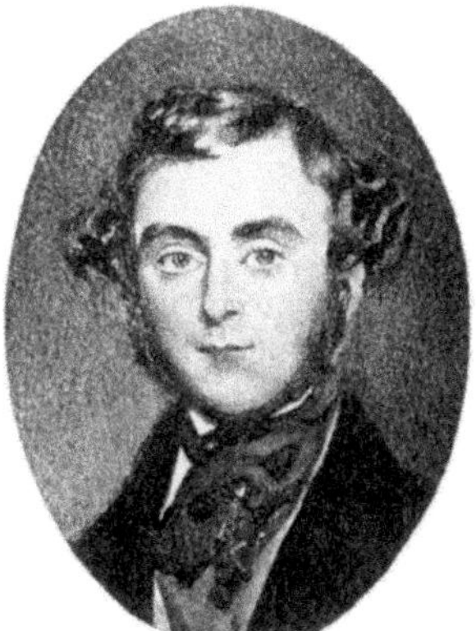
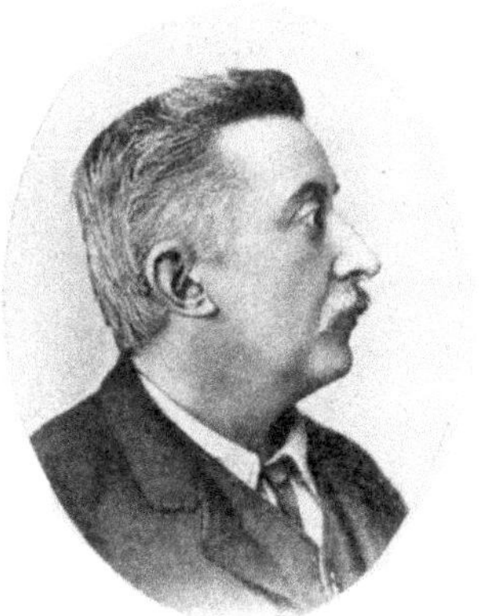

BOYHOOD

dead. The girl, it is said, with the aid of a servant, concealed him in a barn and nursed him back to life, and after his recovery eloped with her grateful lover and married him by the Greek rites in Santa Maura. The first child died immediately after birth, and the boy, Lafcadio, was the second child; taking his name from the Greek name of the island, Lefcada. Another son, James, three years later in Cephalonia, was the fruit of this marriage, so romantically begun and destined to end so tragically.

When England ceded the Ionian Isles to Greece Dr. Hearn returned with his family to Dublin, pausing, perhaps, for a while at Malta, for in a letter written during the last years of his life Lafcadio says: "I am almost sure of having been in Malta as a child. My father told me queer things about the old palaces of the knights, and a story of a monk who on the coming of the French had the presence of mind to paint the gold chancel railing with green paint."

The two boys were at this time aged six and three. It was inevitable, no doubt, that the young wife, who had never mastered the English tongue, though she spoke, as did the children, Italian and Romaic, should have regretted the change from her sunlit island to the dripping Irish skies and grey streets of Dublin, nor can it be wondered at that, an exile among aliens in race, speech, and faith, there should have soon grown up misunderstandings and disputes. The unhappy details have died into silence with the passage of time, but the wife seems to have believed her-

LAFCADIO HEARN

self repudiated and betrayed, and the marriage being eventually annulled, she fled to Smyrna with a Greek cousin who had come at her call, leaving the two children with the father. This cousin she afterwards married and her children knew her no more. The father also married again, and the boy Lafcadio being adopted by Dr. Hearn's aunt, a Mrs. Brenane, and removing with her to Wales, never again saw either his father or his brother.[1]

The emotions are not hard to guess at of a pas-

[1] The following version of the story is reproduced from a letter written by Mrs. Hearn in reply to a request for any knowledge she might have gained on this subject from her husband's conversations with her during their life together in Japan. Its poignant simplicity is heightened by the transmutations through two languages.

"Mama San — When about four years old I did very rude things. Mama gave me a struck on my cheek with her palm. It was very strong. I got angry and gazed on my Mama's face, which I never forget. Thus I remember my Mama's face. She was of a little stature, with black hair and black eyes, like a Japanese woman. How pitiable Mama San she was. Unhappy Mama San; pitiable indeed! Think of that — Think: you are my wife, and I take you with Kazuo and Iwao to my native country: you do not know the language spoken there, nor have any friend. You have your husband only, who prove not very kind. You must be so very unhappy then. And then if I happened to love some native lady and say 'Sayonara' to you, how you would trouble your heart! That was the case with my Mama. I have not such cruel heart. But only to think of such thing makes me sad. To see your face troubled just now my heart aches. Let us drop such subject from our talk."

"Papa San — It is only once that I remember I felt glad with my papa. Yes, on that occasion! Perhaps I was then a boy like Iwao or Kiyoshi. I was playing with my nurse. Many a sound of 'gallop-trop' came from behind. The nurse laughed and lifted me high up. I observed my papa pass; I called him with my tiny hand — now such a big hand. Papa took me from the hands of nurse. I was on horseback. As I looked behind a great number of soldiers followed on horseback with 'gallop-trop.' I imagined myself that I was a general then. It was only on that time that I thought how good papa he was."

BOYHOOD

sionate, sensitive boy of seven, suddenly flung by the stormy emotions of his elders out of the small warm circle of his narrow sphere. To a young child the relations of its parents and the circle of the home seem as fundamental and eternal as the globe itself, and the sudden ravishment of all the bases of his life make his footing amid the ties and affections of the world forever after timid and uncertain.

A boy of less sensitive fibre might in time have forgotten these shocks, but the eldest son of Charles Hearn and Rosa Cerigote was destined to suffer always because of the violent rending of their ties. From this period seems to have dated his strange distrusts, his unconquerable terror of the potentialities which he suspected as lurking beneath the frankest exterior, and his constant, morbid dread of betrayal and abandonment by even his closest friends.

Whatever of fault there may have been on his mother's part, his vague memories of her were always tender and full of yearning affection.

To the brother he never saw he wrote, when he was a man:

And you do not remember that dark and beautiful face — with large, brown eyes like a wild deer's — that used to bend above your cradle? You do not remember the voice which told you each night to cross your fingers after the old Greek orthodox fashion, and utter the words — Ἐν τὸ ὄνομα τοῦ Πατρὸς καὶ τοῦ Υἱοῦ καὶ τοῦ Ἁγίου Πνεύματος, "In the name of the Father, and of the Son, and of the Holy Ghost"? She made, or had made, three little wounds upon you when a baby — to place you, according to her childish faith, under the protection of those three powers, but especially that of Him for whom alone the Nineteenth Century still feels some reverence — *the Lord and Giver of Life.* . . . We were all very dark as children, very passionate, very odd-looking, and wore gold rings in our ears. Have you not the marks yet? . . .

When I saw your photograph I felt all my blood stir — and I thought, "Here is this unknown being, in whom the soul of my mother lives — who must have known the same strange impulses, the same longings, the same resolves as I! Will he tell me of them?" There was another Self — would that Self interpret This?

For This has always been mysterious. Were I to use the word "Soul" in its limited and superannuated sense as the spirit of the individual instead of the ghost of a race — I should say it had always seemed to me as if I had two souls: each pulling in different ways. One of these represented the spirit of mutiny — impatience of all restraint, hatred of all control, weariness of everything methodical and regular, impulses to love or hate without a thought of consequences. The other represented pride and persistence; — it had little power to use the reins before I was thirty. . . . Whatever there is of good in me came from that dark race-soul of which we know so little. My love of right, my hate of wrong; — my admiration for what is beautiful or true; — my capacity for faith in man or woman; — my sensitiveness to artistic things which gives me whatever little success I have — even that language-power whose physical sign is in the large eyes of both of us — came from Her. . . . It is the mother who makes us — makes at least all that makes the nobler man: not his strength or powers of calculation, but his heart and power to love. And I would rather have her portrait than a fortune.

BOYHOOD

Mrs. Brenane, into whose hands the child thus passed, was the widow of a wealthy Irishman, by whom she had been converted to Romanism, and like all converts she was "more loyal than the King." The divorce and remarriage of her nephew incurred her bitterest resentment; she not only insisted upon a complete separation from the child, but did not hesitate to speak her mind fully to the boy, who always retained the impressions thus early instilled. In one of his letters he speaks of his father's "rigid face, and steel-steady eyes," and says: "I can remember seeing father only five times. He was rather taciturn, I think. I remember he wrote me a long letter from India — all about serpents and tigers and elephants — printed in Roman letters with a pen, so that I could read it easily. . . . I remember my father taking me up on horseback when coming into the town with his regiment. I remember being at a dinner with a number of men in red coats, and crawling about under the table among their legs." And elsewhere he declares, "I think there is nothing of him in me, either physically or mentally." A mistake of prejudice this; the Hearns of the second marriage bearing the most striking likeness to the elder half-brother, having the same dark skins, delicate, aquiline profiles, eyes deeply set in arched orbits, and short, supple, well-knit figures. The family type is unusual and distinctive, with some racial alignment not easy to define except by the indefinite term "exotic"; showing no trace of either its English origin or Irish residence.

LAFCADIO HEARN

Of the next twelve years of Lafcadio Hearn's life there exists but meagre record. The little dark-eyed, dark-faced, passionate boy with the wound in his heart and the gold rings in his ears — speaking English but stammeringly, mingled with Italian and Romaic — seems to have been removed at about his seventh year to Wales, and from this time to have visited Ireland but occasionally. Of his surroundings during the most impressionable period of his life it is impossible to reconstruct other than shadowy outlines. Mrs. Brenane was old; was wealthy; and lived surrounded by eager priests and passionate converts.

In "Kwaidan" there is a little story called "Hi-Mawari," which seems a glimpse of this period:

On the wooded hill behind the house Robert and I are looking for fairy-rings. Robert is eight years old, comely, and very wise; — I am a little more than seven — and I reverence Robert. It is a glowing, glorious August day; and the warm air is filled with sharp, sweet scents of resin.

We do not find any fairy-rings; but we find a great many pine-cones in the high grass. . . . I tell Robert the old Welsh story of the man who went to sleep, unawares, inside of a fairy-ring, and so disappeared for seven years, and would never eat or speak after his friends had delivered him from the enchantment.

"They eat nothing but the points of needles, you know," says Robert.

"Who?" I ask.

"Goblins," Robert answers.

This revelation leaves me dumb with astonishment and awe. . . . But Robert suddenly cries out:

BOYHOOD

"There is a harper! — he is coming to the house!"
And down the hill we run to hear the harper.... But what a harper! Not like the hoary minstrels of the picture-books. A swarthy, sturdy, unkempt vagabond, with bold black eyes under scowling brows. More like a bricklayer than a bard — and his garments are corduroy!

"Wonder if he is going to sing in Welsh?" murmurs Robert.

I feel too much disappointed to make any remarks. The harper poses his harp — a huge instrument — upon our doorstep, sets all the strings ringing with a sweep of his grimy fingers, clears his throat with a sort of angry growl, and begins:

> Believe me, if all those endearing young charms,
> Which I gaze on so fondly to-day...

The accent, the attitude, the voice, all fill me with repulsion unutterable — shock me with a new sensation of formidable vulgarity. I want to cry out loud, "You have no right to sing that song!" for I have heard it sung by the lips of the dearest and fairest being in my little world; — and that this rude, coarse man should dare to sing it vexes me like a mockery — angers me like an insolence. But only for a moment!... With the utterance of the syllables "to-day," that deep, grim voice suddenly breaks into a quivering tenderness indescribable; then, marvellously changing, it mellows into tones sonorous and rich as the bass of a great organ — while a sensation unlike anything ever felt before takes me by the throat.... What witchcraft has he learned — this scowling man of the road?... Oh! is there anybody else in the whole world who can sing like that?... And the form of the singer flickers and dims; — and the house, and the lawn, and all visible shapes of things tremble and swim before me. Yet instinctively I fear that man; — I almost hate him; and I feel myself flushing with anger and shame because of his power to move me thus. . . .

"He made you cry," Robert compassionately observes, to my further confusion — as the harper strides away, richer by a gift of sixpence taken without thanks. . . . "But I think he must be a gipsy. Gipsies are bad people — and they are wizards. . . . Let us go back to the wood."

We climb again to the pines, and there squat down upon the sun-flecked grass, and look over town and sea. But we do not play as before: the spell of the wizard is strong upon us both. . . . "Perhaps he is a goblin," I venture at last, "or a fairy?" "No," says Robert — "only a gipsy. But that is nearly as bad. They steal children, you know."

"What shall we do if he comes up here?" I gasp, in sudden terror at the lonesomeness of our situation.

"Oh, he would n't dare," answers Robert — "not by daylight, you know."

[Only yesterday, near the village of Takata, I noticed a flower which the Japanese call by nearly the same name as we do, Himawari, "The Sunward-turning," and over the space of forty years there thrilled back to me the voice of that wandering harper. . . . Again I saw the sun-flecked shadows on that far Welsh hill; and Robert for a moment again stood beside me, with his girl's face and his curls of gold.]

Recorded in this artless story are the most vivid suggestions of the nature of the boy who was to be father of the man Lafcadio Hearn, the minute observation, the quivering sensitiveness to tones, to expressions, to colours and odours; profound passions of tenderness; and — more than all — his nascent interest in the ghostly and the weird. How great a part this latter had already assumed in his young

BOYHOOD

life one gathers from one of the autobiographic papers found after his death — half a dozen fragments of recollection, done exquisitely in his small beautiful handwriting, and enclosed each in fine Japanese envelopes. Characteristically they concern themselves but little with what are called "facts" — though he would have been the last to believe that emotions produced by events were not after all the most salient of human facts.

These records of impressions left upon his nature by the conditions surrounding his early years open a strange tremulous light upon the inner life of the lonely, ardent child, and from the shadows created by that light one can reconstruct perhaps more clearly the shapes about him by which those shadows were cast than would have been possible with more direct vision of them.

The first of the fragments is called

MY GUARDIAN ANGEL

> Weh! weh!
> Du hast sie zerstört,
> Die schöne Welt!
> FAUST

WHAT I am going to relate must have happened when I was nearly six years old — at which time I knew a great deal about ghosts, and very little about gods.

For the best of possible reasons I then believed in ghosts and in goblins — because I saw them, both by day and by night. Before going to sleep I would always cover up my head to prevent them from looking at me; and I used to scream when I felt them pulling at the bedclothes. And I could not understand why I had been forbidden to talk about these experiences.

But of religion I knew almost nothing. The old lady who had adopted me intended that I should be brought up a Roman Catholic; but she had not yet attempted to give me any definite religious instruction. I had been taught to say a few prayers; but I repeated them only as a parrot might have done. I had been taken, without knowing why, to church; and I had been given many small pictures edged with paper lace — French religious prints — of which I did not understand the meaning. To the wall of the room in which I slept there was suspended a Greek icon — a miniature painting in oil of the Virgin and Child, warmly coloured, and protected by a casing of fine metal that left exposed only the olive-brown faces and hands and feet of the figures. But I fancied that the brown Virgin represented my mother — whom I had almost completely forgotten — and the large-eyed Child, myself. I had been taught to pronounce the invocation, *In the name of the Father, and of the Son, and of the Holy Ghost;* — but I did not know what the words signified. One of the appellations, however, seriously interested me: and the first religious question that I remember asking was a question about the *Holy Ghost*. It was the word "Ghost," of course, that had excited my curiosity; and I put the question with fear and trembling because it appeared to relate to a forbidden subject. The answer I cannot clearly recollect; — but it gave me an idea that the Holy Ghost was a *white* ghost, and not in the habit of making faces at small people after dusk. Nevertheless the name filled me with vague suspicion, especially after I had learned to spell it correctly, in a prayer-book; and I discovered a mystery and an awfulness unspeakable in the capital G. Even now the aspect of that formidable letter will sometimes revive those dim and fearsome imaginings of childhood.

BOYHOOD

I suppose that I had been allowed to remain so long in happy ignorance of dogma because I was a nervous child. Certainly it was for no other reason that those about me had been ordered not to tell me either ghost-stories or fairy-tales, and that I had been strictly forbidden to speak of ghosts. But in spite of such injunctions I was doomed to learn, quite unexpectedly, something about goblins much grimmer than any which had been haunting me. This undesirable information was given to me by a friend of the family — a visitor.

Our visitors were few; and their visits, as a rule, were brief. But we had one privileged visitor who came regularly each autumn to remain until the following spring — a convert — a tall girl who looked like some of the long angels in my French pictures. At that time I must have been incapable of forming certain abstract conceptions; but she gave me the idea of Sorrow as a dim something that she personally represented. She was not a relation; but I was told to call her "Cousin Jane." For the rest of the household she was simply "Miss Jane"; and the room that she used to occupy, upon the third floor, was always referred to as "Miss Jane's room." I heard it said that she passed her summers in some convent, and that she wanted to become a nun. I asked why she did not become a nun; and I was told that I was too young to understand.

She seldom smiled; and I never heard her laugh; she had some secret grief of which only my aged protector knew the nature. Although handsome, young, and rich, she was always severely dressed in black. Her face, notwithstanding its constant look of sadness, was beautiful; her hair, a dark chestnut, was so curly that, however smoothed or braided, it always seemed to ripple; and her eyes, rather deeply set, were large and black. Also I remember that her voice, though musical, had a peculiar metallic tone which I did not like.

Yet she could make that voice surprisingly tender when speaking to me. Usually I found her kind — often more than kind; but there were times when she became so silent and sombre that I feared to approach her. And even in her most affectionate moods — even when caressing me — she remained strangely solemn. In such moments she talked to me about being good, about being truthful, about being obedient, about trying "to please God." I detested these exhortations. My old relative had never talked to me in that way. I did not fully understand; I only knew that I was being found fault with, and I suspected that I was being pitied.

And one morning (I remember that it was a gloomy winter morning) — losing patience at last during one of these tiresome admonitions, I boldly asked Cousin Jane to tell me why I should try to please God more than to please anybody else. I was then sitting on a little stool at her feet. Never can I forget the look that darkened her features as I put the question. At once she caught me up, placed me upon her lap, and fixed her black eyes upon my face with a piercing earnestness that terrified me, as she exclaimed:

"My child! — is it possible that you do not know who God is?"

"No," I answered in a choking whisper.

"God! — God who made you! — God who made the sun and the moon and the sky — and the trees and the beautiful flowers — everything!... You do not know?"

I was too much alarmed by her manner to reply.

"You do not know," she went on, "that God made you and me? — that God made your father and your mother and everybody?... You do not know about Heaven and Hell?"

I do not remember all the rest of her words; I can recall with distinctness only the following:

"— and send you down to Hell to burn alive in fire

BOYHOOD

for ever and ever!... Think of it! — always burning, burning, burning! — screaming and burning! screaming and burning! — never to be saved from that pain of fire! ... You remember when you burned your finger at the lamp? — Think of your whole body burning — always, always, always burning! — for ever and ever!"

I can still see her face as in the instant of that utterance — the horror upon it and the pain.... Then she suddenly burst into tears, and kissed me, and left the room.

From that time I detested Cousin Jane — because she had made me unhappy in a new and irreparable way. I did not doubt what she had said; but I hated her for having said it — perhaps especially for the hideous way in which she had said it. Even now her memory revives the dull pain of the childish hypocrisy with which I endeavoured to conceal my resentment. When she left us in the spring, I hoped that she would soon die — so that I might never see her face again.

But I was fated to meet her again under strange circumstances. I am not sure whether it was in the latter part of the summer that I next saw her, or early in the autumn; I remember only that it was in the evening and that the weather was still pleasantly warm. The sun had set; but there was a clear twilight, full of soft colour; and in that twilight-time I happened to be on the lobby of the third floor — all by myself.

... I do not know why I had gone up there alone; — perhaps I was looking for some toy. At all events, I was standing in the lobby, close to the head of the stairs, when I noticed that the door of Cousin Jane's room seemed to be ajar. Then I saw it slowly opening. The fact surprised me because that door — the farthest one of three opening upon the lobby — was usually locked. Almost at the same moment Cousin Jane herself, robed in her familiar black dress came out of the room, and advanced toward me — but with her head turned upwards and sidewards, as if she were looking at something on the lobby-wall, close to the ceiling. I cried out in astonishment, "Cousin Jane!" — but she did not seem to hear. She approached slowly, still with her head so thrown back that I could see nothing of her face above the chin; then she walked directly past me into the room nearest the stairway — a bedroom of which the door was always left open by day. Even as she passed I did not see her face — only her white throat and chin, and the gathered mass of her beautiful hair. Into the bedroom I ran after her, calling out, "Cousin Jane! Cousin Jane!" I saw her pass round the foot of a great four-pillared bed, as if to approach the window beyond it; and I followed her to the other side of the bed. Then, as if first aware of my presence, she turned; and I looked up, expecting to meet her smile.... She had no face. There was only a pale blur instead of a face. And even as I stared, the figure vanished. It did not fade; it simply ceased to be — like the shape of a flame blown out. I was alone in that darkening room — and afraid, as I had never before been afraid. I did not scream; I was much too frightened to scream; — I only struggled to the head of the stairs, and stumbled, and fell — rolling over and over down to the next lobby. I do not remember being hurt; the stair-carpets were soft and very thick. The noise of my tumble brought immediate succor and sympathy. But I did not say a word about what I had seen; I knew that I should be punished if I spoke of it....

Now some weeks or months later, at the beginning of the cold season, the real Cousin Jane came back one morning to occupy that room upon the third floor. She seemed delighted to meet me again; and she caressed me so fondly that I felt ashamed of my secret dismay at her return. On the very same day she took me out with her for a walk, and bought me cakes, toys, pictures — a multitude of things — carrying all the packages herself.

BOYHOOD

I ought to have been grateful, if not happy. But the generous shame that her caresses had awakened was already gone; and that memory of which I could speak to no one — least of all to her — again darkened my thoughts as we walked together. This Cousin Jane who was buying me toys, and smiling, and chatting, was only, perhaps, the husk of another Cousin Jane that had no face.... Before the brilliant shops, among the crowds of happy people, I had nothing to fear. But afterwards — after dark — might not the Inner disengage herself from the other, and leave her room, and glide to mine with chin upturned, as if staring at the ceiling?... Twilight fell before we reached home; and Cousin Jane had ceased to speak or smile. No doubt she was tired. But I noticed that her silence and her sternness had begun with the gathering of the dusk — and a chill crept over me.

Nevertheless, I passed a merry evening with my new toys — which looked very beautiful under the lamplight. Cousin Jane played with me until bedtime. Next morning she did not appear at the breakfast-table — I was told that she had taken a bad cold, and could not leave her bed. She never again left it alive; and I saw her no more — except in dreams. Owing to the dangerous nature of the consumption that had attacked her, I was not allowed even to approach her room.... She left her money to somebody in the convent which she used to visit, and her books to me.

If, at that time, I could have dared to speak of the other Cousin Jane, somebody might have thought proper — in view of the strange sequel — to tell me the natural history of such apparitions. But I could not have believed the explanation. I understood only that I had seen; and because I had seen I was afraid.

And the memory of that seeing disturbed me more than ever, after the coffin of Cousin Jane had been carried away. The knowledge of her death had filled me, not with sorrow, but with terror. Once I had wished that she were dead. And the wish had been fulfilled — but the punishment was yet to come! Dim thoughts, dim fears — enormously older than the creed of Cousin Jane — awakened within me, as from some prenatal sleep — especially a horror of the dead as evil beings, hating mankind.... Such horror exists in savage minds, accompanied by the vague notion that character is totally transformed or stripped by death — that those departed, who once caressed and smiled and loved, now menace and gibber and hate.... What power, I asked myself in dismay, could protect me from her visits? I had not yet ceased to believe in the God of Cousin Jane; but I doubted whether he would or could do anything for me. Moreover, my creed had been greatly shaken by the suspicion that Cousin Jane had always lied. How often had she not assured me that I could not see ghosts or evil spirits! Yet the Thing that I had seen was assuredly her inside-self — the ghost of the goblin of her — and utterly evil. Evidently she hated me: she had lured me into a lonesome room for the sole purpose of making me hideously afraid.... And why had she hated me thus before she died? — was it because she knew that I hated her — that I had wished her to die? Yet how did she know? — could the ghost of her see, through blood and flesh and bone, into the miserable little ghost of myself?

... Anyhow, she had lied.... Perhaps everybody else had lied. Were all the people that I knew — the warm people, who walked and laughed in the light — so much afraid of the Things of the Night that they dared not tell the truth?... To none of these questions could I find a reply. And there began for me a second period of black faith — a faith of unutterable horror, mingled with unutterable doubt.

I was not then old enough to read serious books: it was only in after years that I could learn the worth of

BOYHOOD

Cousin Jane's bequest — which included a full set of the "Waverley Novels"; the works of Miss Edgeworth; Martin's Milton — a beautiful copy, in tree-calf; Langhorne's Plutarch; Pope's "Iliad" and "Odyssey"; Byron's "Corsair" and "Lara" — in the old red-covered Murray editions; some quaint translations of the "Arabian Nights," and Locke's "Essay on the Human Understanding"! I cannot recall half of the titles; but I remember one fact that gratefully surprised me: there was not a single religious book in the collection.... Cousin Jane was a convert: her literary tastes, at least, were not of Rome.

Those who knew her history are dust.... How often have I tried to reproach myself for hating her. But even now in my heart a voice cries bitterly to the ghost of her: "*Woe! woe! — thou didst destroy it — the beautiful world!*"

In the paper entitled "Idolatry" he reveals, as by some passing reflection in a mirror, how his little pagan Greek soul was hardening itself thus early against the strong fingers endeavouring to shape the tendencies of his thought into forms entirely alien to it.

IDOLATRY

*Ah, Psyché, from the regions which
Are Holy Land!*

THE early Church did not teach that the gods of the heathen were merely brass and stone. On the contrary, she accepted them as real and formidable personalities — demons who had assumed divinity to lure their worshippers to destruction. It was in reading the legends of that Church, and the lives of her saints, that I obtained my first vague notions of the pagan gods.

I then imagined those gods to resemble in some sort the fairies and the goblins of my nursery-tales, or the fairies in the ballads of Sir Walter Scott. Goblins and their kindred interested me much more than the ugly Saints of the Pictorial Church History — much more than even the slender angels of my French religious prints, who unpleasantly reminded me of Cousin Jane. Besides, I could not help suspecting all the friends of Cousin Jane's God, and feeling a natural sympathy with his enemies — whether devils, goblins, fairies, witches, or heathen deities. To the devils indeed — because I supposed them stronger than the rest — I had often prayed for help and friendship; very humbly at first, and in great fear of being too grimly answered — but afterwards with words of reproach on finding that my condescensions had been ignored.

But in spite of their indifference, my sympathy with the enemies of Cousin Jane's God steadily strengthened; and my interest in all the spirits that the Church History called evil, especially the heathen gods, continued to grow. And at last one day I discovered, in one unexplored corner of our library, several beautiful books about art — great folio books containing figures of gods and of demigods, athletes and heroes, nymphs and fauns and nereids, and all the charming monsters — half-man, half-animal — of Greek mythology.

How my heart leaped and fluttered on that happy day! Breathless I gazed; and the longer that l gazed the more unspeakably lovely those faces and forms appeared. Figure after figure dazzled, astounded, bewitched me. And this new delight was in itself a wonder — also a fear. Something seemed to be thrilling out of those pictured pages — something invisible that made me afraid. I remembered stories of the infernal magic that informed the work of the pagan statuaries. But this superstitious fear presently yielded to a conviction, or rather intuition — which I could not possibly have explained — that the gods had been belied *because* they were beautiful.

BOYHOOD

... (Blindly and gropingly I had touched a truth — the ugly truth that beauty of the highest order, whether mental, or moral, or physical, must ever be hated by the many and loved only by the few!)... And these had been called devils! I adored them! — I loved them! — I promised to detest forever all who refused them reverence!... Oh! the contrast between that immortal loveliness and the squalor of the saints and the patriarchs and the prophets of my religious pictures! — a contrast indeed as of heaven and hell.... In that hour the mediæval creed seemed to me the very religion of ugliness and of hate. And as it had been taught to me, in the weakness of my sickly childhood, it certainly was. And even to-day, in spite of larger knowledge, the words "heathen" and "pagan" — however ignorantly used in scorn — revive within me old sensations of light and beauty, of freedom and joy.

Only with much effort can I recall these scattered memories of boyhood; and in telling them I am well aware that a later and much more artificial Self is constantly trying to speak in the place of the Self that was — thus producing obvious incongruities. Before trying to relate anything more concerning the experiences of the earlier Self, I may as well here allow the Interrupter an opportunity to talk.

The first perception of beauty ideal is never a cognition, but a *recognition*. No mathematical or geometrical theory of æsthetics will ever interpret the delicious shock that follows upon the boy's first vision of beauty supreme. He himself could not even try to explain why the newly seen form appears to him lovelier than aught upon earth. He only feels the sudden power that the vision exerts upon the mystery of his own life — and that feeling is but dim deep memory — a blood-remembrance.

Many do not remember, and therefore cannot see —

at any period of life. There are myriad minds no more capable of perceiving the higher beauty than the blind wan fish of caves — offspring of generations that swam in total darkness — is capable of feeling the gladness of light. Probably the race producing minds like these had no experience of higher things — never beheld the happier vanished world of immortal art and thought. Or perhaps in such minds the higher knowledge has been effaced or blurred by long dull superimposition of barbarian inheritance.

But he who receives in one sudden vision the revelation of the antique beauty — he who knows the thrill divine that follows after — the unutterable mingling of delight and sadness — he *remembers!* Somewhere, at some time, in the ages of a finer humanity, he must have lived with beauty. Three thousand — four thousand years ago: it matters not; what thrills him now is the shadowing of what has been, the phantom of rapture forgotten. Without inherited sense of the meaning of beauty as power, of the worth of it to life and love, never could the ghost in him perceive, however dimly, the presence of the gods.

Now I think that something of the ghostliness in this present shell of me must have belonged to the vanished world of beauty — must have mingled freely with the best of its youth and grace and force — must have known the worth of long light limbs on the course of glory, and the pride of the winner in contests, and the praise of maidens stately as that young sapling of a palm, which Odysseus beheld, springing by the altar in Delos. . . . All this I am able to believe, because I could feel, while yet a boy, the divine humanity of the ancient gods. . . .

But this new-found delight soon became for me the source of new sorrows. I was placed with all my small belongings under religious tutelage; and then, of course, my reading was subjected to severe examination. One day the beautiful books disappeared; and I was afraid

BOYHOOD

to ask what had become of them. After many weeks they were returned to their former place; and my joy at seeing them again was of brief duration. All of them had been unmercifully revised. My censors had been offended by the nakedness of the gods, and had undertaken to correct that impropriety. Parts of many figures, dryads, naiads, graces, muses had been found too charming and erased with a penknife; — I can still recall one beautiful seated figure, whose breasts had been thus excised. Evidently "the breasts of the nymphs in the brake" had been found too charming: dryads, naiads, graces and muses — all had been rendered breastless. And, in most cases, *drawers* had been put upon the gods — even upon the tiny Loves — large baggy bathing-drawers, woven with cross-strokes of a quill-pen, so designed as to conceal all curves of beauty — especially the lines of the long fine thighs.... However, in my case, this barbarism proved of some educational value. It furnished me with many problems of restoration; and I often tried very hard to reproduce in pencil-drawing the obliterated or the hidden line. In this I was not successful; but, in spite of the amazing thoroughness with which every mutilation or effacement had been accomplished, my patient study of the methods of attack enabled me — long before I knew Winckelmann — to understand how Greek artists had idealized the human figure.... Perhaps that is why, in after years, few modern representations of the nude could interest me for any length of time. However graceful at first sight the image might appear, something commonplace would presently begin to reveal itself in the lines of those very forms against which my early tutors had waged such implacable war.

Is it not almost invariably true that the modern naked figure, as chiselled or painted, shadows something of the modern living model — something, therefore, of individual imperfection? Only the antique work of the grand era is super-individual — reflecting the ideal-supreme in the soul of a race.... Many, I know, deny this; — but do we not remain, to some degree, barbarians still? Even the good and great Ruskin, on the topic of Greek art, spake often like a Goth. Did he not call the Medicean Venus "an uninteresting little person"?

Now after I had learned to know and to love the elder gods, the world again began to glow about me. Glooms that had brooded over it slowly thinned away. The terror was not yet gone; but I now wanted only reasons to disbelieve all that I feared and hated. In the sunshine, in the green of the fields, in the blue of the sky, I found a gladness before unknown. Within myself new thoughts, new imaginings, dim longings for I knew not what were quickening and thrilling. I looked for beauty, and everywhere found it: in passing faces — in attitudes and motions — in the poise of plants and trees — in long white clouds — in faint-blue lines of far-off hills. At moments the simple pleasure of life would quicken to a joy so large, so deep, that it frightened me. But at other times there would come to me a new and strange sadness — a shadowy and inexplicable pain.
I had entered into my Renaissance.

Already must have begun the inevitable fissure between himself and his pious protectress, and one may imagine the emotions of his spiritual pastors and masters aroused by such an incident as this — related in one of his letters of later years:

This again reminds me of something. When I was a boy I had to go to confession, and my confessions were honest ones. One day I told the ghostly father that I had been guilty of desiring that the devil would come to me in the shape of the beautiful women in which he came

BOYHOOD

to the anchorites in the desert, and that I thought I should yield to such temptations. He was a grim man who rarely showed emotion, my confessor, but on that occasion he actually rose to his feet in anger.

"Let me warn you!" he cried, "let me warn you! Of all things never wish that! You might be more sorry for it than you can possibly believe!"

His earnestness filled me with a fearful joy; — for I thought the temptation might actually be realized — so serious he looked . . . but the pretty *succubi* all continued to remain in hell.

From these indications the belief is unavoidable that there was never the slightest foundation for the assertion that an endeavour was made to train him for the priesthood. In a letter to his brother he distinctly denies it. He says:

You were misinformed as to grand-aunt educating your brother for the priesthood. He had the misfortune to pass some years in Catholic colleges, where the educational system chiefly consists in keeping the pupils as ignorant as possible. He was not even a Catholic.

Indeed his bitterness against the Roman Church eventually crystallized into something like an obsession, aroused perhaps by inherited tendencies, by the essential character of his mind, and by those in authority over him in his boyhood driving him, by too great an insistence, to revolt. He was profoundly convinced that the Church, with its persistent memory and far-reaching hand, had never forgotten his apostasy, nor failed to remind him of the fact from time to time. This conviction remained a dim and

LAFCADIO HEARN

threatening shadow in the background of his whole life; to all remonstrance on the subject his only reply was, "You don't know the Church as I do"; and several curious coincidences in crises of his career seemed to him to justify and confirm this belief.

Of the course and character of his education but little is known. He is said to have spent two years in a Jesuit college in the north of France, where he probably acquired his intimate and accurate knowledge of the French tongue. He was also for a time at Ushaw, the Roman Catholic college at Durham,[1]

[1] A cousin writes of him at this period: "I remember him a boy with a great taste for drawing. Very near-sighted, but so tender and careful of me as a little child. He was at a priest's college where I was taken by my grand-aunt (who had adopted him), to see him. I remember his taking me upstairs to look at the school-room, and on the way bidding me bow to an image of the Virgin, which I refused to do. He became very much excited and begged me to tell him the reason of my refusal. He always seemed very much in earnest, and to have a very sensitive nature."

A fellow-pupil at Ushaw says of him:

"My acquaintance with him began at Ushaw College, near Durham. Discovering that we had some tastes in common, we chummed a good deal, discussing our favourite authors, which in Lafcadio's case were chiefly poets, though he also took considerable interest in books of travel and adventure. Even then his style was remarkable for graphic power, combined with graceful expression.... He was of a very speculative turn of mind, and I have a lively recollection of the shock it occasioned to several of us when he one day announced his disbelief in the Bible. I am of opinion, however, that he was then only posing as an *esprit fort*, for a few days afterwards, during a walk with the class in the country, he returned to this subject in discussion with a master, and I inferred from what he said to me that he was quite satisfied with the evidences of the truth of the Scriptures. It is interesting in connection with this to recall his subsequent adoption of Buddhism. I am rather inclined to think that in either 1864 or 1865 Lafcadio devoted more attention to general literature than to his school studies, as (if my memory

BOYHOOD

and here occurred one of the greatest misfortunes of his life. In playing the game known as "The Giant's Stride" he was accidentally blinded in one eye by the knotted end of a rope suddenly released from the hand of one of his companions. In consequence of this the work thrown upon the other eye by the enormous labours of his later years kept him in constant terror of complete loss of sight. In writing and reading he used a glass so large and heavy as to oblige him to have it mounted in a handle and to hold it to his eye like a lorgnette, and for distant observation he carried a small folding telescope.

The slight disfigurement, too — it was never great — was a source of perpetual distress. He imagined that others, more particularly women, found him disgusting and repugnant in consequence of the film that clouded the iris.

This accident seems to have ended his career at Ushaw, for his name appears upon the rolls for 1865, does not play me false) he was 'turned back' on our class moving into 'Grammar.'...

"Longfellow was one of his favourite poets, his beautiful imagery and felicity of expression appealing with peculiar force to a kindred soul. He was fond of repeating scraps of poetry descriptive of heroic combats, feats of arms, or of the prowess of the Baresarks, or Berserkers, as described in Norse sagas.... He used to dwell with peculiar satisfaction on the line:

'Like Thor's hammer, huge and dinted, was his horny hand.'

Lafcadio was proud of his biceps, and on repeating this line he would bend his right arm and grasp the muscle with his left hand. I often addressed him as 'The Man of Gigantic Muscle.' After he went to America I had little communication with him beyond, I think, one letter. We then drifted different ways. He was a very lovable character, extremely sympathetic and sincere."

when he was in his sixteenth year, and in a letter written in Japan to one of his pupils, whom he reproves for discouragement because of an interruption of his studies caused by illness, he says:

A little bodily sickness may come to any one. Many students die, many go mad, many do foolish things and ruin themselves for life. You are good at your studies, and mentally in sound health, and steady in your habits — three conditions which ought to mean success. You have good eyes and a clear brain. How many thousands fail for want of these?

When I was a boy of sixteen, although my blood relations were — some of them — very rich, no one would pay anything to help me finish my education. I had to become what you never have had to become — a servant. I partly lost my sight. I had two years of sickness in bed. I had no one to help me. And I had to educate myself in spite of all difficulties. Yet I was brought up in a rich home, surrounded with every luxury of Western life.

So, my dear boy, do not lie there in your bed and fret, and try to persuade yourself that you are unfortunate.

This is the only light to be found upon those three dark years between his leaving Ushaw and his arrival in America. The rupture with his grand-aunt was complete. Among the fanatic converts were not wanting those to widen the breach made by the pagan fancies of the boy. Her property, which he had been encouraged to look upon as his inheritance, was dribbling away in the hands of those whose only claim to business ability was their religious convictions, and a few years after their separation her death put an end to any efforts at reconciliation and showed what

BOYHOOD

great financial sacrifices she had made in the interests of her faith. Some provision was made for him in her will, but he put forward no claims, and the property was found practically to have vanished.

To what straits the boy was driven at this time in his friendlessness there is no means of knowing. One of his companions at Ushaw says:

In 1866 I left Ushaw, and I am unable to recall now whether he was there at that time. I had several letters from him subsequently, at a time when he was suffering the *peine forte et dure* of direct penury in London. In some evil quarter by the Thames poverty obliged him to take refuge in the workhouse. In a letter received from him while living in that dreadful place, he described the sights and sounds of horror which even then preferred the shade of night — of windows thrown violently open, or shattered to pieces, shrieks of agony, or cries of murder, followed by a heavy plunge in the river.

The reference in the Japanese letter mentioned above is the only one to be found in his correspondence, and in even the most intimate talk with friends he avoided reference to this period as one too painful for confidence. Another fragment of the autobiography — "Stars" — can, however, be guessed to refer to an experience of this cruel time.

I take off my clothes — few and thin — and roll them up into a bundle, to serve me for a pillow: then I creep naked into the hay.... Oh, the delight of my hay-bed — the first bed of any sort for many a long night! — oh, the pleasure of the sense of rest! The sweet scent of the hay! ... Overhead, through a skylight, I see stars — sharply shining: there is frost in the air.

LAFCADIO HEARN

The horses, below, stir heavily at moments, and paw. I hear them breathe; and their breath comes up to me in steam. The warmth of their great bodies fills the building, penetrates the hay, quickens my blood; — their life is my fire.

So contentedly they breathe!... They must be aware that I am here — nestling in their hay. But they do not mind; — and for that I am grateful. Grateful, too, for the warmth of their breath, the warmth of their pure bodies, the warmth of their good hay — grateful even for those stirrings which they make in their rest, filling the dark with assurance of large dumb tolerant companionship.... I wish I could tell them how thankful I am — how much I like them — what pleasure I feel in the power that proceeds from them, in the sense of force and life that they spread through the silence, like a large warm Soul....

It is better that they cannot understand. For they earn their good food and lodging; — they earn the care that keeps them glossy and beautiful; — they are of use in the world. And of what use in the world am I?...

Those sharply shining stars are suns — enormous suns. They must be giving light to multitudes unthinkable of other worlds.... In some of those other worlds there must be cities, and creatures resembling horses, and stables for them, and hay, and small things — somewhat like rats or mice — hiding in the hay.... I know that there are a hundred millions of suns. The horses do not know. But, nevertheless, they are worth, I have been told, fifteen hundred dollars each: they are superior beings! How much am I worth?...

To-morrow, after they have been fed, I also shall be fed — by kindly stealth; — and I shall not have earned the feeding, in spite of the fact that I know there are hundreds of millions of suns!

BOYHOOD

Sometime during the year 1869 — the exact date cannot be ascertained — Lafcadio Hearn, nineteen years old, penniless, delicate, half-blind, and without a friend, found himself in the streets of New York.

CHAPTER II

THE ARTIST'S APPRENTICESHIP

It is more than doubtful if any individual amid the hurrying multitudes swarming in the streets of New York in 1869 and 1870 ever noticed with interest — though many of them must have seen — the shy, shabby boy, Lafcadio Hearn. He was thin to attenuation, for his meals were scant and uncertain; his dress was threadbare, for in all the two years he never possessed enough money to renew the garments he had worn upon landing, and his shabbiness must have been extreme, for he had during the greater part of that period no home other than a carpenter's shop, where a friendly Irish workman allowed him to sleep on the shavings and cook his meals upon the small stove, in return for a little rough book-keeping and running of errands. Yet a few may have turned for a second glance at the dark face and eagle profile of the emaciated, unkempt boy, though unsuspecting that this was one — few in each generation — of those who have dreamed the Dream, and seen the Vision, that here was one of those whom Socrates termed "dæmonic." One who had looked in secret places, face to face, upon the magic countenance of the Muse, and was thereafter vowed to the quest of the Holy Cup wherein glows the essential blood of beauty. One who must follow forever in poverty

THE ARTIST'S APPRENTICESHIP

hard after the Dream, leaving untouched on either hand the goods for which his fellows strove; falling at times into the mire, torn by the thorns that others evade, lost often, and often overtaken by the night of discouragement and despair, but rising again from besmirchments and defacings to follow the vision to the end. It is hard for those who have never laboured wearily after the glimmering feet of the bearer of the Cup, who have never touched even the hem of her garment, to understand the spiritual *possession* of one under the vow. To them in such a career will be visible only the fantastic or squalid episodes of the quest.

What were the boy's thoughts at this period; what his hopes, his aims, or his intentions it is now impossible to know. Merely to keep life in his body taxed his powers, and while much of his time was spent in the refuge of the public libraries he was often so faint from inanition as to be unable to benefit by the books he sought.

The fourth fragment of the autobiography appears to refer to this unhappy period.

INTUITION

I WAS nineteen years old, and a stranger in the great strange world of America, and grievously tormented by grim realities. As I did not know how to face those realities, I tried to forget them as much as possible; and romantic dreams, daily nourished at a public library, helped me to forget. Next to this unpaid luxury of reading, my chief pleasure was to wander about the streets of the town, trying to find in passing faces — faces of girls — some realization of certain ideals. And I found an almost equal pleasure in looking at the photographs placed on display at the doors of photographers' shops — called, in that place and time, "galleries." Picture-galleries they were indeed for me, during many, many penniless months.

One day, in a by-street, I discovered a new photographer's shop; and in a glass case, at the entrance, I beheld a face the first sight of which left me breathless with wonder and delight — a face incomparably surpassing all my dreams. It was the face of a young woman wearing, for head-dress, something that looked like an embroidered scarf; and this extraordinary head-dress might have been devised for the purpose of displaying, to artistic advantage, the singular beauty of the features. The gaze of the large dark eyes was piercing and calm; the aquiline curve of the nose was clear as the curve of a sword; the mouth was fine, but firm; — and, in spite of the sensitive delicacy of this face, there was a something accipitrine about it — something sinister and superb, that made me think of a falcon. . . . For a long, long time I stood looking at it, and the more I looked, the more the splendid wonder of it seemed to grow — like a fascination. I thought that I would suffer much — ever so much! — for the privilege of worshipping the real woman. But who was she? I dared not ask the owner of the "gallery"; and I could not think of any other means of finding out.

I had one friend in those days — the only fellow countryman whom I knew in that American town — a man who had preceded me into exile by nearly forty years — and to him I went. With all of my boyish enthusiasms he used to feel an amused sympathy; and when I told him about my discovery, he at once proposed to go with me to the photograph-shop.

THE ARTIST'S APPRENTICESHIP

For several moments he studied the picture in silence, knitting his grey brows with a puzzled expression. Then he exclaimed emphatically:

"That is not an American."

"What do you think of the face?" I queried, anxiously.

"It is a wonderful face," he answered — " a very wonderful face. But it is not an American, nor an English face."

"Spanish?" I suggested. "Or Italian?"

"No, no," he returned, very positively. "It is not a European face at all."

"Perhaps a Jewess?" — I ventured.

"No; there are very beautiful Jewish faces — but none like that."

"Then what can it be?"

"I do not know; — there is some strange blood there."

"How can you tell?" I protested.

"Why, I feel it; — I am quite sure of it.... But wait here a moment! — I know this photographer, and I shall ask him."

And, to my delight, he went in.... Alas! the riddle was not to be solved so quickly as we had hoped. The owner of the picture said that he did not know whose portrait it was. He had bought it, with a number of other "stock-photographs," from a wholesale dealer in photographic wares. It had been taken in Paris; but the card upon which it was now mounted did not bear the name of the French photographer.

Now my friend was a wanderer whose ties with England had been broken before I was born; — he knew the most surprising things about weird places and strange peoples, but had long ceased to feel any interest in the life of the mother country. For that reason, probably, the picture proved not less of a riddle to him than to me. The photographer was a young man who had never left his native State; and his stock-in-trade had been obtained, of course, through an agency. As for myself, I was hopelessly separated, by iron circumstances, from that ordered society which seeks its pleasures in art and music and drama. Otherwise, how easily might I have learned the name of the marvellous being who had cast that shadow! But many long years went by before I learned it.

I had then forgotten all about the picture. I was in a Southern city, hundreds of miles away; and I happened to be leaning on the counter of a druggist's shop, talking to the druggist, when I suddenly perceived, in a glass case at my elbow, the very same enigmatic photograph. It had been pasted, as a label, on the lid of some box of cosmetic. And again there tingled, through all my blood, the same thrill of wonder and delight that I had felt as a boy, at the door of that photographer....

"Excuse me for interrupting you a moment," I exclaimed; — "please tell me whose face is that."

The druggist glanced at the photograph, and then smiled — as people smile at silly questions.

"Is it possible that you do not know?" he responded.

"I do not," I said. "Years ago I saw that photograph and I could not find out whose picture it was."

"You are joking!"

"Really I am not," I said; — "and I very much want to know."

Then he told me — but I need not repeat the name of the great tragédienne.... At once flashed back to me the memory of my old friend's declaration: "*There is some strange blood there.*" After all, he was right! In the veins of that wonderful woman ran the blood of Indian kings.

What drove him at the end of the two years to endeavour to reach Cincinnati, Ohio, is not clear. The only light to be gathered upon the subject is from the fifth part of the autobiographical fragments, which

THE ARTIST'S APPRENTICESHIP

suggests that he made the journey in an emigrant train and had not money for food upon the way. After thirty years, the clearest memory of that dolorous pilgrimage was of the distress of being misunderstood by the friendly girl who pitied his sufferings. The record of it bears the title of

MY FIRST ROMANCE

THERE has been sent to me, across the world, a little book stamped, on its yellow cover, with names of Scandinavian publishers — names sounding of storm and strand and surge. And the sight of those names, worthy of Frost-Giants, evokes the vision of a face — simply because that face has long been associated, in my imagination, with legends and stories of the North — especially, I think, with the wonderful stories of Björnstjerne Björnson.

It is the face of a Norwegian peasant-girl of nineteen summers — fair and ruddy and strong. She wears her national costume: her eyes are grey like the sea, and her bright braided hair is tied with a blue ribbon. She is tall; and there is an appearance of strong grace about her, for which I can find no word. Her name I never learned, and never shall be able to learn; — and now it does not matter. By this time she may have grandchildren not a few. But for me she will always be the maiden of nineteen summers — fair and fresh from the land of the Hrimthursar — a daughter of gods and Vikings. From the moment of seeing her I wanted to die for her; and I dreamed of Valkyrja and of Vala-maids, of Freyja and of Gerda....

She is seated, facing me, in an American railroad-car — a third-class car, full of people whose forms have become indistinguishably dim in memory. She alone remains

LAFCADIO HEARN

luminous, vivid: the rest have faded into shadow — all except a man, sitting beside me, whose dark Jewish face, homely and kindly, is still visible in profile. Through the window on our right she watches the strange new world through which we are passing: there is a trembling beneath us, and a rhythm of thunder, while the train sways like a ship in a storm.

An emigrant-train it is; and she, and I, and all those dim people are rushing westward, ever westward — through days and nights that seem preternaturally large — over distances that are monstrous. The light is of a summer day; and shadows slant to the east.

The man beside me says:

"She must leave us to-morrow; — she goes to Redwing, Minnesota.... You like her very much? — yes, she's a fine girl. I think you wish that you were also going to Redwing, Minnesota?"

I do not answer. I am angry that he should know what I wish. And it is very rude of him, I think, to let me know that he knows.

Mischievously, he continues:

"If you like her so much, why don't you talk to her? Tell me what you would like to say to her; and I'll interpret for you.... Bah! you must not be afraid of the girls!"

Oh! — the idea of telling *him* what I should like to say to her!... Yet it is not possible to see him smile, and to remain vexed with him.

Anyhow, I do not feel inclined to talk. For thirty-eight hours I have not eaten anything; and my romantic dreams, nourished with tobacco-smoke only, are frequently interrupted by a sudden inner aching that makes me wonder how long I shall be able to remain without food. Three more days of railroad travel — and no money!... My neighbour yesterday asked me why I did not eat; — how quickly he changed the subject when

THE ARTIST'S APPRENTICESHIP

I told him! Certainly I have no right to complain: there is no reason why he should feed me. And I reflect upon the folly of improvidence.

Then my reflection is interrupted by the apparition of a white hand holding out to me a very, very large slice of brown bread, with an inch-thick cut of yellow cheese thereon; and I look up, hesitating, into the face of the Norwegian girl. Smiling, she says to me, in English, with a pretty childish accent:

"Take it, and eat it."

I take it, and devour it. Never before nor since did brown bread and cheese seem to me so good. Only after swallowing the very last crumb do I suddenly become aware that, in my surprise and hunger, I forgot to thank her. Impulsively, and at the wrong moment, I try to say some grateful words.

Instantly, and up to the roots of her hair, she flushes crimson: then, bending forward, she puts some question in a clear sharp tone that fills me with fear and shame. I do not understand the question: I understand only that she is angry; and for one cowering moment my instinct divines the power and the depth of Northern anger. My face burns; and her grey eyes, watching it burn, are grey steel; and her smile is the smile of a daughter of men who laugh when they are angry. And I wish myself under the train — under the earth — utterly out of sight forever. But my dark neighbour makes some low-voiced protest — assures her that I had only tried to thank her. Whereat the level brows relax, and she turns away, without a word, to watch the flying landscape; and the splendid flush fades from her cheek as swiftly as it came. But no one speaks: the train rushes into the dusk of five and thirty years ago... and that is all!

... What *can* she have imagined that I said?... My swarthy comrade would not tell me. Even now my face

LAFCADIO HEARN

burns again at the thought of having caused a moment's anger to the kind heart that pitied me — brought a blush to the cheek of the being for whose sake I would so gladly have given my life.... But the shadow, the golden shadow of her, is always with me; and, because of her, even the name of the land from which she came is very, very dear to me.

In Cincinnati Hearn eventually found work that enabled him to live, though this did not come immediately, as is proved by an anecdote, related by himself, of his early days there. A Syrian peddler employed him to help dispose of some accumulated wares, sending him out with a consignment of small mirrors. Certainly no human being was more unfitted by nature for successful peddling than Lafcadio Hearn and at the end of the day he returned to the Syrian with the consignment intact. Setting down his burden to apologize for his failure he put his foot accidentally upon one of the mirrors, and thrown into a panic by the sound of the splintering glass, he fled incontinently, and never saw the merchant again, nor ever again attempted mercantile pursuits.

The first regular work he obtained was as a type-setter and proof-reader in the Robert Clarke Company, where — as he mentions in one of his letters — he endeavoured to introduce reforms in the American methods of punctuation, and assimilate it more closely to the English standards, but without, as he confesses, any success. It was from some of

THE ARTIST'S APPRENTICESHIP

these struggles for typographical changes, undertaken with hot-headed enthusiasm for perfection, that he derived his nickname of "Old Semicolon," given him in amiable derision by his fellows. Mechanical work of this character could not satisfy him long, though the experience was useful to the young artist in words beginning his laborious self-training in the use of his tools. Punctuation and typographical form remained for him always a matter of profound importance, and in one of his letters he declared that he would rather abandon all the royalties to his publisher than be deprived of the privilege of correcting his own proofs; corrections which in their amplitude often devoured in printer's charges the bulk of his profits.

Later he secured, for a brief period, a position as private secretary to Thomas Vickers, at that time librarian of the public library of Cincinnati, and here again he found food for his desires in a free access to the recondite matters to which already his genius was tending; but again he was driven by poverty and circumstance into broader fields, and early in 1874 he was working as a general reporter on the Cincinnati "Enquirer." His work was of a kind that gave him at first no scope for his talents and must have been peculiarly unsympathetic, consisting of daily market reports, until chance opened the eyes of his employers to his capacity for better things. A peculiarly atrocious crime, still known in Cincinnati annals as the "Tanyard Murder," had been communicated to the office of the "Enquirer" at a moment when all the members of the staff, usually detailed to cover such assignments, were absent. The editor calling upon the indifferent gods for some one instantly to take up the matter, was surprised by a timid request from the shy cub-reporter who turned in daily market "stuff," to be allowed to deal with this tragedy, and after some demur, he consented to accept what appeared an inadequate answer from the adjured deities. The "copy" submitted some hours later caused astonished eyebrows, was considered worthy of "scare-heads," and for the nine succeeding days of the life of the wonder, Cincinnati sought ardently the Hoffmannesque story whose poignantly chosen phrases set before them a grim picture that caused the flesh to crawl upon their bones. It was realized at once that the cub-reporter had unsuspected capacities and his talents were allowed expansion in the direction of descriptive stories. One of the most admired of these was a record of a visit to the top of the spire of Saint Peter's Cathedral, where hauled in ropes by a steeple-jack to the arms of the cross which crowned it, he obtained a lofty view of the city and returned to write an article that enabled all the town to see the great panorama through his myopic eyes, which yet could bear testimony to colour and detail not obvious to clearer vision.

It was in this year that some trusting person was found willing to advance a small sum of money for the publication of an amorphous little Sunday sheet, pro-

THE ARTIST'S APPRENTICESHIP

fessedly comic and satiric, entitled "Ye Giglampz." H. F. Farny contributed the cartoons, and Lafcadio Hearn the bulk of the text. On June 21st of that year the first number appeared, with the announcement that it was to be "published daily, except week days," and was to be "devoted to art, literature, and satire." The first page was adorned with a Dicky Doylish picture of Herr Kladderadatsch presenting Mr. Giglampz to an enthusiastic public, which showed decided talent, but the full page cartoon, though it may have been amusing when published, is satire turned dry and dusty after the lapse of thirty-two years, and it may be only vaguely discerned now to refer in some way to the question of a third term for President Grant.

The pictures are easily preferable to the text, though no doubt it too has suffered from the desiccation of time, but Lafcadio Hearn was at no time, one might infer, better fitted for satire than for peddling; "Ye Giglampz" plainly "jooks wi' deefeculty," and the young journalist's views upon art and politics are such as might be expected from a boy of twenty-four.

The prohibition question, the Chicago fire, a local river disaster, and the Beecher scandal are all dealt with by pen and pencil, much clipping from "Punch" and some translations from the comic journals of Paris fill the columns, and after nine weeks "Ye Giglampz" met an early and well-deserved death. The only copies of the paper now known to be in existence are contained in a bound volume belonging to

LAFCADIO HEARN

Mr. Farny, discovered by him in a second-hand bookshop, with some pencil notes in the margin in Hearn's handwriting. One of these notes records that an advertisement — there were but three in the first number — was never paid for, so presumably this volume, monument of an unfortunate juvenile exploit, was once in Hearn's meagre library, but was discarded when he left Cincinnati.

In the following year Hearn had left the "Enquirer" and was recording the Exposition of 1876 for the "Gazette," and in the latter part of that year he was a regular reporter for the "Commercial."

In 1895 — writing to Professor Basil Hall Chamberlain — Hearn speaks of John Cockerill, then visiting Japan, and draws an astonishingly vivid picture of the editor who was in command of the Cincinnati "Enquirer" in the seventies. These occasional trenchant, accurate sketches from life, to be found here and there in his correspondence, show a shrewdness of judgment and coolness of observation which his companions never suspected. He says:

I began daily newspaper work in 1874, in the city of Cincinnati, on a paper called the "Enquirer" edited by a sort of furious young man named Cockerill. He was a hard master, a tremendous worker, and a born journalist. I think none of us liked him, but we all admired his ability to run things. He used to swear at us, work us half to death (never sparing himself), and he had a rough skill in sarcasm that we were all afraid of. He was fresh from the army, and full of army talk. In a few years he had forced up the circulation of the paper to a very large

THE ARTIST'S APPRENTICESHIP

figure and made a fortune for the proprietor, who got jealous of him and got rid of him. . . . He afterwards took hold of a St. Louis paper — then of a New York daily, the "World.". . . He ran the circulation up to nearly a quarter of a million, and again had the proprietor's jealousy to settle with. . . . He also built up the "Advertiser," but getting tired, sold out, and went travelling. Finally Bennett of the "Herald" sends him to Japan at, I believe, ten thousand dollars a year.

I met him here to-day and talked over old times. He has become much gentler and more pleasant, and seems to be very kindly. He is also a little grey. What I have said about him shows that he is no very common person. The man who can make three or four fortunes for other men, without doing the same thing for himself, seldom is. He is not a literary man, nor a well-read man, nor a scholar — but has immense common sense, and a large experience of life — besides being, in a Mark-Twainish way, much of a humourist.

Those who knew John Cockerill will find in this portrait not one line omitted which would make for truth and sympathy. One of Hearn's associates of this period, Joseph Tunison, says of his work:

In Cincinnati such work was much harder than now, because more and better work was demanded of a man for his weekly stipend than at present. . . . Had he been then on a New York daily his articles would have attracted bidding from rival managements, but in Cincinnati there was little, if any, encouragement for such brilliant powers as his. The "Commercial" took him on at twenty dollars a week. . . . Though he worked hard for a pittance he never slighted anything he had to do. . . . He was never known to shirk hardship or danger in filling an assignment. . . . His employers kept him at the most arduous work of a daily morning paper — the night stations — for in that field developed the most sensational events, and he was strongest in the unusual and the startling.

For two years more this was the routine of his daily life. He formed, in spite of his shyness, some ties of intimacy; especially with Joseph Tunison, a man of unusual classical learning, with H. F. Farny, the artist, and with the now well-known musical critic and lecturer, H. E. Krehbiel. Into these companionships he threw all the ardour of a very young man; an ardour increased beyond even the usual intensity of young friendships, by the natural warmth of his feelings and the loneliness of his life, bereft of all those ties of family common to happier fates. In their company he developed a quality of bonhomie that underlay the natural seriousness of his temperament, and is frequently visible in his letters, breaking through the gravity of his usual trend of thought. Absence and time diminished but little his original enthusiasm, as the letters included in this volume will bear testimony, though in later years one by one his early friendships were chilled and abandoned. One of the charges frequently brought against Lafcadio Hearn by his critics in after years was that he was inconstant in his relations with his friends. Mr. Tunison says of him:

He had a fashion of dropping his friends one by one, or of letting them drop him, which comes to the same thing. Whether indifference or suspicion was at the bottom of

THE ARTIST'S APPRENTICESHIP

this habit would be hard to say, but he never spoke ill of them afterwards. He seemed to forget all about them, though two or three acquaintances of his early years of struggle and privation were always after spoken of with the tenderest regard, and their companionship was eagerly sought whenever this was possible.

The charge of inconstancy is, to those who knew Lafcadio Hearn well, of a sufficiently serious nature to warrant some analysis at this point, while dealing with the subject of his first intimacies, for up to this period he appears to have had no ties other than those, so bitterly ruptured, with the people of his own blood, or the mere passing amities of school-boy life. That many of his closest friendships were either broken abruptly or sank into abeyance is quite true, but the reason for this was explicable in several ways. The first and most comprehensible cause was his inherent shyness of nature and an abnormal sensitiveness, which his early experiences intensified to a point not easily understood by those of a naturally self-confident temperament unqualified by blighting childish impressions. A look, a word, which to the ordinary robust nature would have had no meaning of importance, touched the quivering sensibilities of the man like a searing acid, and stung him to an anguish of resentment and bitterness which nearly always seemed fantastically out of proportion to the offender, and this bitterness was usually misjudged and resented. Only those cursed with similar sensibilities — "as tender as the horns of cockled snails"

LAFCADIO HEARN

— could understand and forgive such an idiosyncrasy. It must be remembered that all qualities have their synchronous defects. The nature which is as reflective as water to the subtlest shades of the colour and form of life must of its essential character be subject to rufflement by the lightest breath of harshness or misconception.

Professor Chamberlain, who himself suffered from this tendency to unwarranted estrangement, has dealt with another phase of the matter with a noble sympathy too rare among Hearn's friends. He says, in a letter to the biographer:

> The second point was his attitude toward his friends — his quondam friends — all of whom he gradually dropped, with but very few exceptions. Some I know who were deeply and permanently irritated by this neglect, or ingratitude, as they termed it. I never could share such a feeling, though of course I lamented the severance of connection with one so gifted, and made two or three attempts at a renewal of intercourse, which were met at first by cold politeness, afterwards with complete silence, causing me to desist from further endeavours. The reason I could not resent this was because Lafcadio's dropping of his friends seemed to me to have its roots in that very quality which made the chief charm of his works. I mean his idealism. Friends, when he first made them, were for him more than mere mortal men, they stood endowed with every perfection. He painted them in the beautiful colours of his own fancy, and worshipped them, pouring out at their feet all the passionate emotionalism of his Greek nature. But Lafcadio was not emotional merely; another side of his mind had the keen insight of a man of science. Thus he soon came to see that his idols had

THE ARTIST'S APPRENTICESHIP

feet of clay, and — being so purely subjective in his judgments — he was indignant with them for having, as he thought, deceived him. Add to this that the rigid character of his philosophical opinions made him perforce despise, as intellectual weaklings, all those who did not share them, or shared them only in a lukewarm manner — and his disillusionment with a series of friends in whom he had once thought to find intellectual sympathy is seen to have been inevitable. For no man living, except himself, idolized Herbert Spencer in his peculiar way; turning Spencer's scientific speculations into a kind of mysticism. This mysticism became a religion to him. The slightest cavil raised against it was resented by him as a sacrilege. Thus it was hardly possible for him to retain old ties of friendship except with a few men whom he met on the plane of every-day life apart from the higher intellectual interests. Lafcadio himself was a greater sufferer from all this than any one else; for he possessed the affectionate disposition of a child, and suffered poignantly when sympathy was withdrawn, or — what amounted to the same — when he himself withdrew it. He was much to be pitied — always wishing to love, and discovering each time that his love had been misplaced.

To put the matter in its simplest form, he loved with a completeness and tenderness extremely rare among human beings. When he discovered — as all who love in this fashion eventually do — that the objects of his affection had no such tenderness to give in return, he felt himself both deceived and betrayed and allowed the relation to pass into the silence of oblivion.

There is still another facet of this subject which is made clear by some of the letters written in the

LAFCADIO HEARN

last years of his life, when he had withdrawn himself almost wholly from intercourse with all save his immediate family. Failing strength warned him that not many more years remained in which to complete his self-imposed task, and like a man who nears his goal with shortening breath and labouring pulse, he let slip one by one every burden, and cast from him his dearest possessions, lest even the weight of one love should hold him back from the final grasp upon the ideal he had so long pursued with avid heart. This matter has been dwelt upon at some length, and somewhat out of due place, but the charge of disloyalty to friendship is a serious one, and a full understanding of the facts upon which it rested is important to a comprehension of the man.

In these early days in Cincinnati, however, no blight had yet come upon his young friendships, and they proved a source of great delight. Krehbiel was already deeply immersed in studies of folk-songs and folk-music — his collection of which has since become famous — and Lafcadio threw himself with enthusiasm into similar studies, his natural love for exotic lore rendering them peculiarly sympathetic to his genius. Together they ransacked the libraries for discoveries, and sought knowledge at first hand from wandering minstrels in Chinese laundries, or from the exiles of many lands who gathered in the polyglot slums along the river-banks. In the dedication of "Some Chinese Ghosts" is recorded an echo of one of these experiences, when Krehbiel opened the heart

THE ARTIST'S APPRENTICESHIP

of a reserved Oriental to give up to them all his knowledge, by proving that he himself could play their strange instruments and sing their century-old songs. The dedication runs thus:

> To My Friend,
> Henry Edward Krehbiel,
> The Musician,
> Who, Speaking the Speech of Melody unto the
> Children of Tien-Hia —
> Unto the Wandering Tsing-Jin, Whose Skins
> Have the Colour of Gold —
> Moved Them to Make Strange Sounds upon the
> Serpent-Bellied San Hien;
> Persuaded Them to Play for Me upon the
> Shrieking Ya-Hien;
> Prevailed on Them to Sing Me a Song of Their
> Native Land —
> The Song of Mohli-Wa,
> The Song of the Jasmine-Flower.

This dedication is of peculiar interest; "Chinese Ghosts" has been long out of print, and of the few copies issued — nearly the whole edition was destroyed — but a handful still exist. It gives a typical example of the musical, rhythmic prose which the young reporter was endeavouring to master. He had fallen under the spell of the French Romantic school and of their passion for *le mot juste*, of their love for exotic words, of their research for the grotesque, the fantastic, the bizarre. Already out of his tiny income he was extracting what others in like case spent upon comforts or pleasures, to buy dictionaries and thesauri, and was denying himself food and clothes to purchase rare books. The works of Théophile Gau-

LAFCADIO HEARN

tier were his daily companions, in which he saturated his mind with fantasies of the Orient, Spain, and Egypt, refreshing himself after the dull routine of the day's work with endeavours to transliterate into English the strange and monstrous tales of his model, those abnormal imaginations whose alien aroma almost defied transference into a less supple tongue.

His friend Tunison, writing of Hearn at this period, says:

> But it was impossible for even this slavery of journalism to crush out of him his determination to advance and excel. In the small hours of the morning, into broad daylight, after the rough work of the police rounds and the writing of columns in his inimitable style, he could be seen, under merely a poor jet of gas, with his one useful eye close to book and manuscript, translating from Gautier.

These translations — including "Clarimonde," "Arria Marcella," and "King Candaule" — with three others were published in 1882 under the title of the initial tale, "One of Cleopatra's Nights," having been gathered from the "Nouvelles," and the "Romans et Contes." The preface concludes thus:

> It is the artist who must judge of Gautier's creations. To the lovers of the loveliness of the antique world, to the lovers of physical beauty and artistic truth — of the charm of youthful dreams and young passion in its blossoming — of poetic ambitions and the sweet pantheism that finds all Nature vitalized by the Spirit of the Beautiful — to such the first English version of these graceful

THE ARTIST'S APPRENTICESHIP

phantasies is offered in the hope that it may not be found wholly unworthy of the original.

Up to this time no translation into English of Gautier's "Contes" had been attempted, and the manuscript sought a publisher in vain for half a dozen years. Later, when the little volume had reached a small but appreciative audience, another English version was attempted by Andrew Lang, but proved an unsuccessful rival, lacking the warmth and fidelity of its predecessor.

Other attempts in the same direction met with no better success, partly, in some cases, because of the reluctance any Anglo-Saxon publisher inevitably feels in issuing works which would encounter no barriers of rigid decorum between themselves and the world of French readers. The youthful artist working in any medium is prone to be impatient of the prejudices of Anglo-Saxon pudency. The beautiful is to him always its own justification for being, and his inexperience makes him unafraid of the nudities of art. The refusal to deal freely with any form of beauty seems to him as bloodlessly pietistic as the priest's excision of "the breasts of the nymphs in the brake." Yet many years after, when the boy had himself become the father of a boy and began to think of his son's future, he said: "What shall I do with him?... send him to grim Puritans that he may be taught the Way of the Lord? — I am beginning to think that really much of the ecclesiastical education (bad and cruel as I used to imagine it) is founded on the best experience of man under civilization; and I understand lots of things I used to think superstitious bosh, and now think solid wisdom."

This unavailing struggle to find an outlet for the expression of something more worthy of his abilities than the sensational side of journalism caused him the deepest discouragement and depression; and his youthful ardour, denied a safe channel for its forces, turned to less healthful instincts. The years in Cincinnati were at times marred by experiments and outbursts, undertaken with bitter enthusiasm for fantastic ethical codes, and finally caused severance of his ties with his employers and the town itself. The tendency of his tastes toward the study of strange peoples and civilizations made him find much that was attractive in "the indolent, sensuous life of the negro race, and led him to steep them in a sense of romance that he alone could extract from the study" — says Joseph Tunison — "things that were common to these people in their every-day life his vivid imagination transformed into romance."

This led him eventually into impossible experiments, and brought upon him the resentment of his friends. Many years after, in Japan, he referred to this matter in a letter to one of his pupils, and the letter is so illuminative of this matter as to make it desirable to insert it here, though rightly it should be included in the volume dealing with his life in Japan.

THE ARTIST'S APPRENTICESHIP

Dear Ochiai, — I was very happy to get your kind letter, and the pleasant news it conveyed....

And now that all your trouble is over, perhaps you will sometimes find it hard not to feel angry with those who ostracized you for so long. It would at least be natural that you should feel angry with them, or with some at least. But I hope you will not allow yourself to feel anger toward them, even in your heart. Because the real truth is that it was not really your schoolmates who were offended: it only appeared so. The real feeling against you was what is called a *national* sentiment — that jealous love of country with which every man is born, and which you, quite unknowingly, turned against you for a little while. So I hope you will love all your schoolmates none the less — even though they treated you distantly for so long.

When I was a young man in my twenties, I had an experience very like yours. I resolved to take the part of some people who were much disliked in the place where I lived. I thought that those who disliked them were morally wrong — so I argued boldly for them and went over to their side. Then all the rest of the people stopped speaking to me, and I hated them for it. But I was too young then to understand. There were other moral questions, much larger than those I had been arguing about, which really caused the whole trouble. The people did not know how to express them very well; they only *felt* them. After some years I discovered that I was quite mistaken — that I was under a delusion. I had been opposing a great national and social principle without knowing it. And if my best friends had not got angry with me, I could not have learned the truth so well — because there are many things that are hard to explain and can only be taught by experience....

Ever very affectionately
Your old teacher
Lafcadio Hearn

Kumamoto, *March* 27, 1894

LAFCADIO HEARN

Sick, unhappy, and unpopular, flight to other scenes naturally suggested itself. Mr. Tunison thus describes the influences determining the move to New Orleans, which occurred in 1877:

As Hearn advanced in his power to write, the sense of the discomforts of his situation in Cincinnati grew upon him. His body and mind longed for Southern air and scenes. One morning, after the usual hard work of an unusually nasty winter night in Cincinnati, in a leisure hour of conversation he heard an associate on the paper describe a scene in the Gulf State. It was something about an old mansion of an ante-bellum cotton prince, with its white columns, its beautiful avenue of trees; the whitewashed negro quarters stretching away in the background; the cypress and live-oaks hung with moss, the odours from the blossoming magnolias, the songs of the mocking-birds in the early sunlight.

Hearn took in every word of this with great keenness of interest, as was shown by the usual dilation of his nostrils when excited, though he had little to say at the time. It was as though he could see, and hear, and smell the delights of the scene. Not long after on leaving for New Orleans he remarked:

I had to go, sooner or later, but it was your description of the sunlight, and melodies, and fragrance, and all the delights with which the South appeals to the senses that determined me. I shall feel better in the South, and I believe I shall do better.

Though nostalgia for Southern warmth had given a purpose to his wanderings, the immediate cause of his leaving the paper on which he was employed in

THE ARTIST'S APPRENTICESHIP

Cincinnati was his assignment to deal with a story of hydrophobia, in which he suspected he had been given some misleading information by his superiors; and though his suspicions were possibly unjust, he announced that he had lost his loyalty to the paper and abruptly quitted it.

It is said that he went first to Memphis on leaving Cincinnati, but no proof of this remains save an anecdote he once related, placing the scene of it in Tennessee.

The question of essential wrong and right being under discussion, his companion advanced the theory that morals varied so much with localities and conditions that it was impossible to decide that there was any act of which one might say that it was essentially wrong or essentially right. After thinking this over in his brooding manner, he said:

"Yes, there is one thing that is always wrong, profoundly wrong under any conditions."

"And that?" he was asked.

"To cause pain to a helpless creature for one's own pleasure," was his answer; and then, in illustration, continued: "Once I was walking along a road in Tennessee, and I saw a man who seemed intoxicated with rage — for what cause I don't know. A kitten was crossing the road at the moment. It got under the man's feet and tripped him. He caught it up and blinded it and flung it from him with a laugh. The act seemed to soothe his rage. I was not near enough to stop him, but I had a pistol in my pocket — I al-

LAFCADIO HEARN

ways carried one then — and I fired four times at him; but, you know my sight is so bad, I missed him." After a few moments he added, "It has always been one of the regrets of my life that I missed."

Sometime in 1877 — the time of the year is uncertain — Hearn arrived in New Orleans, and from this date the work of a biographer becomes almost superfluous, for then was begun the admirable series of letters to H. E. Krehbiel, which record the occupations and interests of his life for the next twelve years, setting forth, as no one less gifted than himself could, the impressions he received, the development of his mind, the trend of his studies, the infinite labour by which he slowly built up his mastery of the English tongue and the methods of work which made him eventually one of the great stylists of the nineteenth century. These letters make clear, as no comment could adequately do, how unflinchingly he pursued his purpose to become an artist, through long discouragement, through poverty and self-sacrifice; make clear how the Dream never failed to lead him, and how broad a foundation of study and discipline he laid during his apprenticeship for the structure he was later to rear for his own monument. They also disclose, as again no comment could do, the modesty of his self-appreciation, and the essentially enthusiastic and affectionate nature of his character.

The first work he secured in New Orleans was on

THE ARTIST'S APPRENTICESHIP

the staff of the "Daily Item," one of the minor journals, where he read proof, clipped exchanges, wrote editorials, and occasionally contributed a translation, or some bit of original work in the shape of what came to be known as his "Fantastics." Meanwhile he was rejoicing in the change of residence, for the old, dusty, unpaved squalid New Orleans of the seventies — the city crushed into inanition by war, poverty, pestilence, and the frenzy of carpet-bagger misrule — was far more sympathetic to his tastes than the prosperous growing town he had abandoned.

The gaunt, melancholy great houses where he lodged in abandoned, crumbling apartments — still decorated with the tattered splendours of a prosperous past — where he was served by timid unhappy gentlewomen, or their ex-servants; the dim flower-hung courts behind the blank, mouldering walls; the street-cries; the night-songs of wanderers — all the colourful, polyglot, half-tropical life of the town was a constant appeal to the romantic side of the young man's nature. Of disease and danger — arising out of the conditions of the unhappy city — he took no thought till after the great epidemic of yellow fever which desolated New Orleans the following summer, during which he suffered severely from dengue, a lighter form of the disease. But even the cruelties of his new home were of value to him. In the grim closing chapter of "Chita" the anguish of a death by yellow fever is set forth with a quivering reality which only a personal knowledge of some phases of the disease could have made possible.

Always pursued by a desire to free himself of the harness of daily journalism, he plunged into experiments in economy, reducing at one time his expenses for food to but two dollars a week; trusting his hardly gathered savings to a sharper who owned a restaurant, and who ran away when the enterprise proved a failure. On another occasion he put by everything beyond his bare necessities in one of the mushroom building-loan societies which sprang up all over the country at that time, and with the collapse of this investment he finally and forever abandoned further financial enterprises, regarding them with an absolutely comic distrust, though for some years he continued to dwell now and then on the possibility of starting second-hand bookshops in hopelessly impossible places — such as the then moribund town of St. Augustine, Florida — and would suggest, with lovably absurd naïveté, that a *shrewd* man could do well there.

Meanwhile his gluttony for rare books on recondite matters kept him constantly poor, but proved a far better investment, as tools of trade, than his other and more speculative expenditures. Eventually he gathered a library of several hundred volumes and of considerable value, together with an interesting series of scrapbooks containing his earlier essays in literary journalism, and other clippings showing his characteristic flair for the exotic and the strange.

THE ARTIST'S APPRENTICESHIP

In 1881 he, by great good fortune, was brought into contact with the newly consolidated "Times-Democrat," a journal whose birth marked one of the earliest impulses toward the regeneration of the long depressed community, and whose staff included men, such as Charles Whitney, Honoré Burthe, and John Augustin, who represented the best impulses toward new growth among both the American and Creole members of the city's population. Of Page M. Baker, the editor-in-chief, he drew in after years this faithful pen-picture:

You say my friend writes nicely. He is about the most lovable man I ever met — an old-time Southerner, very tall and slight, with a singular face. He is so exactly the ideal Mephistopheles that he would never get his photograph taken. The face does not altogether belie the character — but the mockery is very tender play, and queerly original. It never offends. The real Mephistopheles appears only when there are ugly obstacles to overcome. Then the diabolic keenness with which motives are read and disclosed, and the lightning moves by which a plot is checkmated, or a net made for the plotter himself, usually startle people. He is a man of immense force — it takes such a one to rule in that community — but as a gentleman I never saw his superior in grace or consideration. I always loved him — but like all whom I like could never get quite enough of his company for myself.

It was an unusual and delightful coterie of men with whom chance had associated him. Men peculiarly fitted to value his special gifts. Honoré Burthe was the ideal of the "beau sabreur" of romantic

LAFCADIO HEARN

French tradition, personally beautiful, brave to absurdity; a soldier of fortune under many flags; withal the pink of gentle courtesy, and a scholar. John Augustin — with less of the "panache" — inherited also the beauty, courage, and breeding of those picturesque ancestors, who had made the French gentleman-adventurers the most ornamental colonists of North America. Charles Whitney, by contrast, had fallen heir to all the shrewd, humorous, amiable vigour of the rival race which had struggled successfully for possession of the great inheritance of America, and which finally met and fused with the Latins in Louisiana.

Among these four rather uncommon types of journalists Lafcadio Hearn found ready sympathy and appreciation, and a chance to develop in the direction of his talents and desires. He was treated by them with courtesy and an indulgent consideration of his idiosyncrasies new in his experience, and was allowed to expand along the natural line of his tastes and capacities, with the result that he soon began to attract attention, and was finally able to find his outlet in the direction to which his preparatory labours and inherent genius were urging him.

He was astonishingly fortunate to have found such companions and such an opportunity. At that period the new journalism was dominant almost everywhere, and perhaps nowhere in the United States, except in New Orleans — with its large French population and its residuum of the ante-

THE ARTIST'S APPRENTICESHIP

bellum leisurely cultivation of taste, and love of lordly beauties of style — could he have found an audience and a daily newspaper which eagerly sought, and rewarded to the best of its ability, a type of belles-lettres which was caviare to the general. His first work consisted of a weekly translation from some French writer — Théophile Gautier, Guy de Maupassant, or Pierre Loti, whose books he was one of the first to introduce to English readers, and for whose beautiful literary manner he always retained the most enthusiastic admiration. Long years afterward in Japan he spoke of one of the worst afflictions of a recent illness as having been the fear that he should die without having finished Loti's "L'Inde sans les Anglais," which he was reading when seized by the malady. These translations were usually accompanied — in another part of the paper — by an editorial, elucidatory of either the character and method of the author, or the subject of the paper itself, and these editorials were often vehicles of much curious research on a multitude of odd subjects, such as the famous swordsmen of history, Oriental dances and songs, muezzin calls, African music, historic lovers, Talmudic legends, monstrous literary exploits, and the like; echoes of which studies appear frequently in the Krehbiel and O'Connor letters in this volume.

From time to time he added transferences, and adaptations, or original papers, unsigned, which found a small but appreciative audience, some of

LAFCADIO HEARN

whom were sufficiently interested to enquire the identity of the author, and who grew into a local clientèle which always thereafter followed the growth of his fame with warm interest. Among these "Fantastics" and translations was published the whole contents of his three early books — "One of Cleopatra's Nights," "Stray Leaves from Strange Literature," and "Some Chinese Ghosts" — but these books were made only of such selections as an ever-increasing severity of taste considered worthy of reproduction. Much delightful matter which failed quite to reach this standard lapsed into extinction in the files of the journal. Among these was one which has been recovered by chance from his later correspondence. Replying to a criticism by a friend of the use of the phrase "lentor inexpressible" in a manuscript submitted for judgment, he promises to delete it, speaks of it as a "trick phrase" of his, and encloses the old clipping to show where he had first used it, and adds "Please burn or tear up after reading ... this essay belongs to the Period of Gush."

Fortunately his correspondent — as did most of those to whom he wrote — treasured everything in his handwriting, and the fragment which bore — my impression is — the title of "A Dead Love" (the clipping lacks its caption) remains to give an example of some of the work that bears the flaws of his 'prentice hand, before he used his tools with the assured skill of a master:

THE ARTIST'S APPRENTICESHIP

... No rest he knew because of her. Even in the night his heart was ever startled from slumber as by the echo of her footfall; and dreams mocked him with tepid fancies of her lips; and when he sought forgetfulness in strange kisses her memory ever came shadowing between.... So that, weary of his life, he yielded it up at last in the fevered summer of a tropical city — dying with her name upon his lips. And his face was no more seen in the palm-shadowed streets,... but the sun rose and sank even as before.

And that vague Something which lingers a little while within the tomb where the body moulders, lingered and dreamed within the long dark resting-place where they had laid him with the pious hope — *Que en paz descanse!* ...

Yet so weary of his life had the Wanderer been, that the repose of the dead was not for him. And while the body shrank and sank into dust, the phantom man found no rest in the darkness, and thought dimly to himself: "I am even too weary to find peace!"

There was a thin crevice in the ancient wall of the tomb. And through it, and through the meshes of the web that a spider had woven athwart it, the dead looked and beheld the amethystine blaze of the summer sky — and pliant palms bending in the warm wind — and the opaline glow of the horizon — and fair pools bearing images of cypresses inverted — and the birds that flitted from tomb to tomb and sang — and flowers in the shadow of the sepulchres.... And the vast bright world seemed to him not so hateful as before.

Likewise the sounds of life assailed the faint senses of the dead through the thin crevice in the wall of the tomb: — always the far-off drowsy murmur made by the toiling of the city's heart; sometimes sounds of passing converse and steps — echoes of music and of laughter — chanting and chattering of children at play — and the liquid babble of the beautiful brown women.... So that the dead man dreamed of life and strength and joy, and the litheness of limbs to be loved: also of that which had been, and of that which might have been, and of that which now could never be. And he longed at last to live again — seeing that there was no rest in the tomb.

But the gold-born days died in golden fire; and blue nights unnumbered filled the land with indigo shadows; and the perfume of the summer passed like a breath of incense ... and the dead within the sepulchre could not wholly die.

Stars in their courses peered down through the crevices of the tomb, and twinkled, and passed on; winds of the sea shrieked to him through the widening crannies of the tomb; birds sang above him and flew to other lands; the bright lizards that ran noiselessly over his bed of stone, as noiselessly departed; the spider at last ceased to repair her web of silk; years came and went with lentor inexpressible; but for the dead there was no rest!

And after many tropical moons had waxed and waned, and the summer was deepening in the land, filling the golden air with tender drowsiness and passional perfume, it strangely came to pass that *She* whose name had been murmured by his lips when the Shadow of Death fell upon him, came to that city of palms, and even unto the ancient place of sepulture, and unto the tomb that bore his name.

And he knew the whisper of her raiment — knew the sweetness of her presence — and the pallid hearts of the blossoms of a plant whose blind roots had found food within the crevice of the tomb, changed and flushed, and flamed incarnadine....

But she — perceiving it not — passed by; and the sound of her footsteps died away forever.

THE ARTIST'S APPRENTICESHIP

To his own, and perhaps other middle-aged taste "A Dead Love" may seem negligible, but to those still young enough, as he himself then was, to credit passion with a potency, not only to survive "the gradual furnace of the world," but even to blossom in the dust of graves, this stigmatization as "Gush" will seem as unfeeling as always does to the young the dry and sapless wisdom of granddams. To them any version of the Orphic myth is tinglingly credible. Yearningly desirous that the brief flower of life may never fade, such a cry finds an echo in the very roots of their inexperienced hearts. The smouldering ardour of its style, which a chastened judgment rejected, was perhaps less faulty than its author believed it to be in later years.

It was to my juvenile admiration for this particular bit of work that I owed the privilege of meeting Lafcadio Hearn, in the winter of 1882, and of laying the foundation of a close friendship which lasted without a break until the day of his death.

He was at this time a most unusual and memorable person. About five feet three inches in height, with unusually broad and powerful shoulders for such a stature, there was an almost feminine grace and lightness in his step and movements. His feet were small and well-shaped, but he wore invariably the most clumsy and neglected shoes, and his whole dress was peculiar. His favourite coat, both winter and summer, was a heavy double-breasted "reefer," while the size of his wide-brimmed, soft-crowned hat was a standing joke among his friends. The rest of his garments were apparently purchased for the sake of durability rather than beauty, with the exception of his linen, which, even in days of the direst poverty, was always fresh and good. Indeed a peculiar physical cleanliness was characteristic of him — that cleanliness of uncontaminated savages and wild animals, which has the air of being so essential and innate as to make the best-groomed men and domesticated beasts seem almost frowzy by contrast. His hands were very delicate and supple, with quick timid movements that were yet full of charm, and his voice was musical and very soft. He spoke always in short sentences, and the manner of his speech was very modest and deferential. His head was quite remarkably beautiful; the profile both bold and delicate, with admirable modelling of the nose, lips, and chin. The brow was square, and full above the eyes, and the complexion a clear smooth olive. The enormous work which he demanded of his vision had enlarged beyond its natural size the eye upon which he depended for sight, but originally, before the accident — whose disfiguring effect he magnified and was exaggeratedly sensitive about — his eyes must have been handsome, for they were large, of a dark liquid brown, and heavily lashed. In conversation he frequently, almost instinctively, placed his hand over the injured eye to conceal it from his companion.

Though he was abnormally shy, particularly with

THE ARTIST'S APPRENTICESHIP

strangers and women, this was not obvious in any awkwardness of manner; he was composed and dignified, though extremely silent and reserved until his confidence was obtained. With those whom he loved and trusted, his voice and mental attitude were caressing, affectionate, and confiding, though with even these some chance look or tone or gesture would alarm him into sudden and silent flight, after which he might be invisible for days or weeks, appearing again as silently and suddenly, with no explanation of his having so abruptly taken wing. In spite of his limited sight he appeared to have the power to divine by some extra sense the slightest change of expression in the faces of those with whom he talked, and no object or tint escaped his observation. One of his habits while talking was to walk about, touching softly the furnishings of the room, or the flowers of the garden, picking up small objects for study with his pocket-glass, and meantime pouring out a stream of brilliant talk in a soft, half-apologetic tone, with constant deference to the opinions of his companions. Any idea advanced he received with respect, however much he might differ, and if a phrase or suggestion appealed to him his face lit with a most delightful irradiation of pleasure, and he never forgot it.

A more delightful or — at times — more fantastically witty companion it would be impossible to imagine, but it is equally impossible to attempt to convey his astounding sensitiveness. To remain on good terms with him it was necessary to be as patient and wary as one who stalks the hermit thrush to its nest. Any expression of anger or harshness to any one drove him to flight, any story of moral or physical pain sent him quivering away, and a look of ennui or resentment, even if but a passing emotion, and indulged in while his back was turned, was immediately conveyed to his consciousness in some occult fashion and he was off in an instant. Any attempt to detain or explain only increased the length of his absence. A description of his eccentricities of manner would be misleading if the result were to convey an impression of neurotic debility, for with this extreme sensitiveness was combined vigour of mind and body to an unusual degree — the delicacy was only of the spirit.

Mrs. Lylie Harris, of New Orleans, one of his intimate friends at this time, in an article written after his death, speaks of his friendship with the children of her family, with whom he was an affectionate playfellow, and with whom he was entirely confident and at his ease. An equally friendly and confident relation existed between himself and the old negro woman who cared for his rooms (as clean and plain as a soldier's); and indeed all his life he was happiest with the young and the simple, who never perplexed or disturbed him by the complexities of modern civilization, which all his life he distrusted and feared.

Among those attracted by his work in the "Times-

THE ARTIST'S APPRENTICESHIP

Democrat" was W. D. O'Connor, in the marine service of the Government, who wrote to enquire the name of the author of an article on Gustave Doré. From this grew a correspondence extending over several years. Jerome A. Hart, of San Francisco, was another correspondent attracted by his work, to whom he wrote from time to time, even after his residence in Japan had begun. Mr. Hart in contributing his letters says that this correspondence began in 1882, through the following reference in the pages of the "Argonaut" to "One of Cleopatra's Nights":

Mr. Lafcadio Hearn, a talented writer on the staff of the New Orleans "Times-Democrat," has just translated some of Gautier's fantastic romances, under the name of "One of Cleopatra's Nights." The book comprises six fascinating stories — the one which gives the title, "Clarimonde," "Arria Marcella, a Souvenir of Pompeii," "The Mummy's Foot," "Omphale, a Rococo Story," and "King Candaule." Mr. Hearn has few equals in this country as regards translation, and the stories lose nothing of their artistic unity in his hands. But his hobby is literalism. For instance, of the epitaph in "Clarimonde" —

> Ici-gît Clarimonde,
> Qui fut de son vivant
> La plus belle du monde,

he remarks: "The broken beauty of the lines is but inadequately rendered thus:

> Here lies Clarimonde,
> Who was famed in her lifetime
> As the fairest of women."

LAFCADIO HEARN [1]

Very true — it is inadequate. But why not vary it? For example:

> Here lieth Clarimonde,
> Who was, what time she lived,
> The loveliest in the land.

The fleeting archaic flavour of the original is not entirely lost here, and the lines are broken, yet metrical. But this is only a suggestion, and a kindly one.

This book — his first — travelled far before finding a publisher, and then only at the cost of the author bearing half the expense of publication.

Other notices had been less kind. The "Observer," as he quotes in a letter to Mr. Hart, had declared that it was a collection of "stories of unbridled lust without the apology of natural passion," and that "the translation reeked with the miasma of the brothel." The "Critic" had wasted no time upon the translator, confining itself to depreciation of Gautier, and this Hearn resented more than severity to himself, for at this period Gautier and his style were his passionate delight, as witness the following note which accompanied a loan of a volume containing a selection from the Frenchman's poems:

DEAR MISS BISLAND, — I venture to try to give you a little novel pleasure by introducing you to the "Emaux et Camées." As you have told me you never read them, I feel sure you will experience a literary surprise. You will find in Gautier a perfection of melody, a warmth of word-colouring, a voluptuous delicacy which no English poet has ever approached and which reveal, I think, a certain capacity of artistic expression no Northern tongue

THE ARTIST'S APPRENTICESHIP

can boast. What the Latin tongues yield in to Northern languages is strength; but the themes in which the Latin poets excel are usually soft and exquisite. Still you will find in the "Rondalla" some fine specimens of violence. It is the song of the Toreador Juan.

These "Emaux et Camées" constitute Gautier's own pet selection from his works. I have seen nothing in Hugo's works to equal some of them ... I won't presume to offer you this copy: it is too shabby, has travelled about with me in all sorts of places for eight years But if you are charmed by this "parfait magicien des lettres françaises" (as Baudelaire called him) I hope to have the pleasure of offering you a nicer copy....

Mr. John Albee wrote to him in connection with the book, and also the Reverend Wayland D. Ball.

"Stray Leaves from Strange Literature" — published by James R. Osgood and Company of Boston — followed in 1884 and was more kindly treated by the critics, though it brought fewer letters from private admirers, and was not very profitable — save to his reputation. In 1885 a tiny volume was issued under the title of "Gombo Zhêbes," being a collection of three hundred and fifty Creole proverbs which he had made while studying the patois of the Louisiana negro — a patois of which the local name is "Gombo." These laborious studies of the grammar and oral literature of a tongue spoken only by and to negro servants in Louisiana seemed rather a work of supererogation at the time, but later during his life in the West Indies they proved of incalculable value to him in his intercourse with the inhabitants.

LAFCADIO HEARN

There the patois — not having been subjected as in New Orleans to that all-absorbing solvent of the English tongue — continued to hold its own alongside the pure French of the educated Creoles, and his book would have been impossible had he not had command of the universal speech of the common people.

"Some Chinese Ghosts" had set out on its travels in search of a publisher sometime earlier, and after several rejections was finally, in the following year, accepted by Roberts Brothers. In regard to some corrections which they desired made in the text, this reference has been found in a letter to his friend Krehbiel, a letter in which, however, time and the ruthless appetite of bookworms have made havoc with words here and there:

1886

DEAR K., — In Promethean agony I write.

Roberts Brothers, Boston, have written me that they want to publish "Chinese Ghosts"; but want me to cut out a multitude of Japanese, Sanscrit, Chinese, and Buddhist terms.

Thereupon unto them I despatched a colossal document of supplication and prayer — citing Southey, Moore, Flaubert, Edwin Arnold, Gautier, "Hiawatha," and multitudinous singers and multitudinous songs, and the rights of prose poetry, and the supremacy of Form.

And no answer have I yet received.

How shall I sacrifice Orientalism, seeing that this my work was inspired by [fragment of a Greek word] by the Holy Spirit, by the Vast . . . [probably Blue Soul] of the Universe . . . but one of the facets of that million-faceted

THE ARTIST'S APPRENTICESHIP

Rose-diamond which flasheth back the light of the Universal Sun? And even as Apocalyptic John I hold —
"And if any man shall take away from the words of the book of this prophecy, God shall take away his part out of the book of life, and out of the holy city, and from the things which are written in this book."

Thy brother in the Holy Ghost of Art wisheth thee many benisons and victories, and the Grace that cometh as luminous rain and the Wind of Inspiration perfumed with musk and the flowers of Paradise.

LAFCADIO

This suggestion was peculiarly afflicting because of his love of exotic words, not only for their own sake, but for the colour they lent to the general scheme of decoration of his style. It was as if a painter of an Oriental picture had been asked to omit all reproduction of Eastern costumes, all representation of the architecture or utensils germane to his scene. To eliminate these foreign terms was like asking a modern actor to play "Julius Caesar" in a full-bottomed wig.

At about this period a friendship formed with Lieutenant Oscar Crosby exerted a most profound and far-reaching influence upon Hearn — an influence which continued to grow until his whole life and manner of thought were coloured by it.

Lieutenant Crosby was a young Louisianian, educated at West Point, and then stationed in New Orleans, a person of very unusual abilities, and Hearn found him a suggestive and inspiring companion. In a letter written to Ernest Crosby from

LAFCADIO HEARN

Japan in 1904, but a month before his death, he says:

A namesake of yours, a young lieutenant in the United States Army, first taught me, about twenty years ago, how to study Herbert Spencer. To that Crosby I shall always feel a very reverence of gratitude, and I shall always find myself inclined to seek the good opinion of any man bearing the name of Crosby.

To Mr. Krehbiel in the same year that he began the study of "The Principles of Ethics" he wrote:

Talking of change in opinions, I am really astonished at myself. You know what my fantastic metaphysics were. A friend disciplined me to read Herbert Spencer. I suddenly discovered what a waste of time all my Oriental metaphysics had been. I also discovered for the first time how to apply the little general knowledge I possessed. I also found unspeakable comfort in the sudden, and for me eternal reopening of the Great Doubt, which renders pessimism ridiculous, and teaches a new reverence for all forms of faith. In short, from the day when I finished the "First Principles," a totally new intellectual life opened for me; and I hope during the next few years to devour the rest of this oceanic philosophy.

He seems not, in these positive assertions, to have overestimated the great change that had come upon his mental attitude. The strong breath of the great thinker had blown from off his mind the froth and ferment of youth, leaving the wine clear and strong beneath. From this time becomes evident a new seriousness in his manner, and beauty became to him not only the mere grace of form but the meaning and truth which that form was to embody.

THE ARTIST'S APPRENTICESHIP

The next book bearing his name shows the effect of this change, and the immediate success of the book demonstrated that, while his love for the exotic was to remain ingrained, he had learned to bring the exotic into vital touch with the normal.

"Chita: A Story of Last Island" had its origin in a visit paid in the summer of 1884 to Grande Isle, one of the islands lying in the Gulf of Mexico, near the mouth of the Mississippi River in the Bay of Barataria. A letter written to Page Baker while there may be inserted at this point to give some idea of the place.

Gentleman's bathing-houses

DEAR PAGE, — I wish you were here; for I am sure that the enjoyment would do you a great deal of good. I had not been in sea-water for fifteen years, and you can scarcely imagine how I rejoice in it — in fact I don't like to get out of it at all. I suppose you have not been at Grand Isle — or at least not been here for so long that you have forgotten what it looks like. It makes a curious impression on me: the old plantation cabins, standing in rows like village-streets, and neatly remodelled for more cultivated inhabitants, have a delightfully rural aspect under their shadowing trees; and there is a veritable country calm by day and night. Grande Isle has suggestions in it of several old country fishing villages I remember, but it is even still more charmingly provincial. The hotel proper, where the tables are laid — formerly, I fancy, a sugar-house or something of that sort — reminds one of nothing so much as one of those big English or Western barn-buildings prepared for a holiday festival or a wedding-party feast. The only distinctively American feature is the inevitable Southern gallery with white wooden pillars. An absolutely ancient purity of morals appears to prevail here: — no one thinks of bolts or locks or keys, everything is left open and nothing is ever touched. Nobody has ever been robbed on the island. There is no iniquity. It is like a resurrection of the days of good King Alfred, when, if a man were to drop his purse on the highway, he might return six months later to find it untouched. At least that is what I am told. Still I would not *like* to leave one thousand golden dinars on the beach or in the middle of the village. I am still a little suspicious — having been so long a dweller in wicked cities.

I was in hopes that I had made a very important discovery; viz. — a flock of really tame and innocuous cows; but the innocent appearance of the beasts is, I have just learned, a disguise for the most fearful ferocity. So far I have escaped unharmed; and Marion has offered to lend me his large stick, which will, I have no doubt, considerably aid me in preserving my life.

Could n't you manage to let me stay down here until after the Exposition is over, doing no work and nevertheless drawing my salary regularly? ... By the way, one could save money by a residence at Grande Isle. There are no temptations — except the perpetual and delicious temptation of the sea.

THE ARTIST'S APPRENTICESHIP

The insects here are many; but I have seen no frogs — they have probably found that the sea can outroar them and have gone away jealous. But in Marion's room there is a beam, and against that beam there is the nest of a "mud-dauber." Did you ever see a mud-dauber? It is something like this when flying; — but when it isn't flying I can't tell you what it looks like, and it has the peculiar power of flying without noise. I think it is of the wasp-kind, and plasters its mud nest in all sorts of places. It is afraid of nothing — likes to look at itself in the glass, and leaves its young in our charge. There is another sociable creature — hope it isn't a wasp — which has built two nests under the edge of this table on which I write to you. There are no specimens here of the *Cimex lectularius;* and the mosquitoes are not at all annoying. They buzz a little, but seldom give evidence of hunger. Creatures also abound which have the capacity of making noises of the most singular sort. Up in the tree on my right there is a thing which keeps saying all day long, quite plainly, "*Kiss, Kiss, Kiss!*" — referring perhaps to the good young married folks across the way; and on the road to the bath-house, which we travelled late last evening in order to gaze at the phosphorescent sea, there dwells something which exactly imitates the pleasant sound of ice jingling in a cut-glass tumbler.

As for the grub, it is superb — solid, nutritious, and without stint. When I first tasted the butter I was enthusiastic, imagining that those mild-eyed cows had been instrumental in its production; but I have since discovered they were not — and the fact astonishes me not at all now that I have learned more concerning the character of those cows.

At some unearthly hour in the morning the camp-meeting quiet of the place is broken by the tolling of a bell. This means "Jump up, lazy-bones; and take a swim before the sun rises." Then the railroad-car comes for the bathers, passing up the whole line of white cottages. The distance is short to the beach; Marion and I prefer to walk; but the car is a great convenience for the women and children and invalids. It is drawn by a single mule, and always accompanied by a dog which appears to be the intimate friend of the said mule, and who jumps up and barks all the grass-grown way. The ladies' bathing-house is about five minutes' plank-walking from the men's — where I am glad to say drawers and bathing-suits are unnecessary, so that one has the full benefit of sun-bathing as well as salt-water bathing. There is a man here called Margot or Margeaux — perhaps some distant relative of Château-Margeaux — who always goes bathing accompanied by a pet goose. The goose follows him just like a dog; but is a little afraid of getting into deep water. It remains in the surf presenting its stern-end to the breakers:

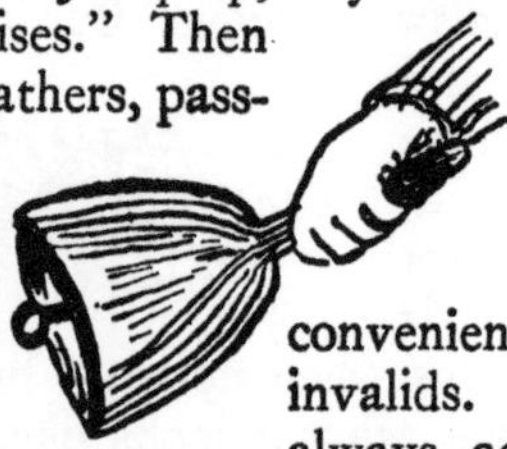

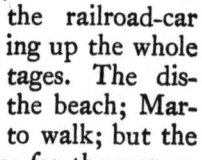

The only trouble about the bathing is the ferocious sun. Few people bathe in the heat of the day, but yester-

THE ARTIST'S APPRENTICESHIP

day we went in four times; and the sun nearly flayed us. This morning we held a council of war and decided upon greater moderation. There are three bars, between which the water is deep. The third bar is, I fear, too "risky" to reach, as it is nearly a mile from the other, and lies beyond a hundred-foot depth of water in which sharks are said to disport themselves. I am almost as afraid of sharks as I am of cows.... Marion made a dash for a drowning man yesterday, in answer to the cry, "Here, you fellows, help! help!" and I followed. We had instantaneous visions of a gold-medal from the Life-Saving Service, and glorious dreams of newspaper fame under the title "Journalistic Heroism" — for my part, I must acknowledge I had also an unpleasant fancy that the drowning man might twine himself about me, and pull me to the bottom — so I looked out carefully to see which way he was heading. But the beatific Gold-Medal fancies were brutally dissipated by the drowning man's success in saving himself before we could reach him, and we remain as obscure as before.

LAFCADIO HEARN
Interlude

Miss B. B. through our lorgnette

Miss Bisland's A No 1. Chaperone

The Agricultural Editor of the T.D. —pursued by his family

THE ARTIST'S APPRENTICESHIP

A N°2
Miss Bisland's Creole Chaperone

A N°3
Miss Bisland: Pickwickian Chaperon

I will now resume the interrupted text of my narration

The proprietor has found what I have vainly been ransacking the world for — a civilized hat, showing the highest evolutional development of the hat as a practically useful article. I am going to make him an offer for it.

Alas! the time flies too fast. Soon all this will be a dream: — the white cottages shadowed with leafy green — the languid rocking-chairs upon the old-fashioned gallery — the cows that look into one's window with the rising sun — the dog and the mule trotting down the flower-edged road — the goose of the ancient Margot — the muttering surf upon the bar beyond which the sharks

87

LAFCADIO HEARN

[Sketch: a man wearing an enormous hat, annotated "Natural Size / the Crown of the hat is not visible"]

are — the bath-bell and the bathing belles — the air that makes one feel like a boy — the pleasure of sleeping with doors and windows open to the sea and its everlasting song — the exhilaration of rising with the rim of the sun.

[Sketches: a view through a window; a shark-like mouth; a hat labeled "Back View reduced 50 diameters" above a pair of legs]

... And then we must return to the dust and the roar of New Orleans, to hear the rumble of wagons instead of the rumble of breakers, and to smell the smell of ancient

THE ARTIST'S APPRENTICESHIP

gutters instead of the sharp sweet scent of pure sea wind. I believe I would rather be old Margot's goose if I could. Blessed goose! thou knowest nothing about the literary side of the New Orleans "Times-Democrat"; but thou dost know that thou canst have a good tumble in the sea every day. If I could live down here I should certainly live to be a hundred years old. One *lives* here. In New Orleans one only exists. . . . And the boat comes — I must post this incongruous epistle.

Good-bye — wish you were here, sincerely.
Very truly
LAFCADIO HEARN

This jesting letter makes but little reference to the beauties of this tropical island, which had, however, made a profound impression upon Hearn, and later they were reproduced with astonishing fidelity in the book. Some distance to the westward of Grande Isle lies L'Isle Dernière, or — as it is now commonly called — Last Island, then a mere sandbank, awash in high tides, but thirty years before that an island of the same character as Grande Isle, and for half a century a popular summer resort for the people of New Orleans and the planters of the coast. On the 10th of August, 1856, a frightful storm swept it bare and annihilated the numerous summer visitors, only a handful among the hundreds escaping. The story of the tragedy remained a vivid tradition along the coast, where hardly a family escaped without the loss of some relation or friend, and on Hearn's return to New Orleans he embodied a brief story of the famous storm, with his impressions of the splendours of the Gulf, under the title of "Torn Letters," purporting to be the fragments of an old correspondence by one of the survivors. This story — published in the "Times-Democrat" — was so favourably received that he was later encouraged to enlarge it into a book, and the Harpers, who had already published some articles from his pen, issued it as a serial in their magazine, where it won instant recognition from a large public that had heretofore been ignorant of, or indifferent to, his work.

Oscar Wilde once declared that life and nature constantly plagiarized from art, and would have been pleased with the confirmation of his suggestion afforded by the fact that nearly twenty years after the publication of "Chita" a storm, similar to the one described in the book, swept away in its turn Grande Isle, and Les Chenières, and a girl child was rescued by Manila fishermen as Hearn had imagined. After living with one of their families for some time she was finally recovered by her father (who had believed her lost in the general catastrophe), under circumstances astoundingly like those invented by the author so many years before.

The book was dedicated to Dr. Rodolfo Matas, a Spanish physician in New Orleans, and an intimate friend — frequently mentioned in the letters to Dr. George M. Gould of Philadelphia, with whom a correspondence was begun at about this time.

It was because of the success of "Chita" that Hearn was enabled to realize his long-nourished

THE ARTIST'S APPRENTICESHIP

dream of penetrating farther into the tropics, and with a vague commission from the Harpers he left New Orleans, in 1887, and sailed for the Windward Islands. The journey took him as far south as British Guiana, the fruit of which was a series of travel-sketches printed in "Harper's Magazine." So infatuated with the Southern world of colour, light, and warmth had he become that — trusting to the possible profits of his books and the further material he hoped to gather — two months after his return from this journey, and without any definite resources, he cast himself back into the arms of the tropics, for which he suffered a lifelong and unappeasable nostalgia.

It was to Saint Pierre in the island of Martinique — the place that had most attracted him on his travels — that he returned. That island of "gigantic undulations," that town of "bright long narrow streets rising toward a far mass of glowing green . . . which looks as if it had slid down the hill behind it, so strangely do the streets come tumbling to the port in a cascade of masonry — with a red billowing of tiled roofs over all, and enormous palms poking up through it." That town with "a population fantastic, astonishing — a population of the Arabian Nights . . . many coloured, with a general dominant tint of yellow, like that of the town itself . . . always relieved by the costume colours of Martinique — brilliant yellow stripings or chequerings which have an indescribable luminosity, a wonderful power of bringing out the fine warm tints of tropical flesh ... the hues of those rich costumes Nature gives to her nearest of kin and her dearest — her honey-lovers — her insects: wasp-colours." Here, under the shadow of Mont Pelée "coiffed with purple and lilac cloud ... a magnificent *Madras*, yellow-banded by the sun," he remained for two years, and from his experiences there created his next book. "Two Years in the French West Indies" made a minute and astonishing record of the town and the population, now as deeply buried and as utterly obliterated as was Pompeii by the lava and ashes of Vesuvius. Eighteen centuries hence, could some archæologist, disinterring the almost forgotten town, find this book, what passionate value would he give to this record of a community of as unique a character as that of the little Græco-Roman city! What price would be set to-day upon parchments which reproduced with such vivid fidelity the world, so long hid in darkness, of that civilization over whose calcined fragments we now yearningly ponder!

One English commentator upon the work of Lafcadio Hearn speaks of "Chita" and "Two Years in the French West Indies" with negligent contempt as of "the orchid and cockatoo type of literature," and passes on to his Japanese work as the first of considerable importance. Other critics have been led into the same error, welcoming the cooler tones of his later pictures as a growth in power and a development of taste. It is safe to say that the makers of

THE ARTIST'S APPRENTICESHIP

such criticisms have not seen the lands and peoples of whom these books attempt to reproduce the charm. Those who have known tropic countries will realize how difficult is the task of reproducing their multi-coloured glories, and that to bring even a faint shadow of their splendours back to eyes accustomed to the pale greys and half tints of Northern lands is a labour not only arduous in itself, but more than apt to be ungratefully received by those for whom it is undertaken. A mole would find a butterfly's description of an August landscape exaggerated to the point of vulgarity, and the average critic is more likely to find satisfaction in "A Grey Day at Annisquam" than in the most subtly handled picture of the blaze of noon at Luxor.

"Chita" is marred occasionally by a phrase that suggests the journalism in which the hand of the writer had been so long submerged, but in "Two Years in the French West Indies" the artist has at last emancipated his talent and finished his long apprenticeship. Though the author himself in later years finds some fault with it, giving as excuse that much of it was done when he was physically exhausted by fever and anxiety, and "with but a half-filled stomach," it remains one of his most admirable achievements.

The risks he had assumed in returning to the tropics proved greater than he had imagined. Publishers' delays and rigid exactions of all their part of the writer's pound of flesh left him at times entirely

LAFCADIO HEARN

without means, and had it not been for the generosity and kindliness of the people of the now vanished city he would not have lived to return. It was some memory of humble friends there that is recorded in the sixth part of the autobiographical fragments, written after the disaster at Saint Pierre.

IN VANISHED LIGHT

... A bright long narrow street rising toward a far mass of glowing green — burning green of lianas: the front of a tropic wood. Not a street of this age, but of the seventeenth century: a street of yellow façades, with yellow garden-walls between the façades. In sharp bursts of blue light the sea appears at intervals — blue light blazing up old, old flights of mossy steps descending to the bay. And through these openings ships are visible, far below, riding in azure.

Walls are lemon-colour; — quaint balconies and lattices are green. Palm-trees rise from courts and gardens into a warm blue sky — indescribably blue — that appears almost to touch the feathery heads of them. And all things, within or without the yellow vista, are steeped in a sunshine electrically white — in a radiance so powerful that it lends even to the pavements of basalt the glitter of silver ore.

Men wearing only white canvas trousers, and immense hats of bamboo-grass — men naked to the waist, and muscled like sculptures — pass noiselessly with barefoot stride. Some are very black; others are of strange and beautiful colours: there are skins of gold, of brown bronze, and of ruddy bronze. And women pass in robes of brilliant hue — women of the colour of fruit: orange-colour, banana-colour — women wearing turbans banded with just such burning yellow as bars the belly of a wasp. The warm thick air is sweet with scents of sugar and of cinna-

THE ARTIST'S APPRENTICESHIP

mon — with odours of mangoes and of custard-apples, of guava-jelly and of fresh cocoanut milk.

Into the amber shadow and cool moist breath of a great archway I plunge, to reach a court filled with flickering emerald and the chirrup of leaping water. There a little boy and a little girl run to meet me, with Creole cries of "Mi y!" Each takes one of my hands; — each holds up a beautiful brown cheek to kiss. In the same moment a voice, the father's voice — deep and vibrant as the tone of a great bell — calls from an inner doorway, "Entrez donc, mon ami!" And with the large caress of that voice there comes to me such joy of sympathy, such sense of perfect peace, as Souls long-tried by fire might feel when passing the Gateway of Pearl....

But all this was — and is not!... Never again will sun or moon shine upon the streets of that city; — never again will its ways be trodden; — never again will its gardens blossom... except in dreams.

He was again in New York in 1889, occupied with the final proofs of "Chita" before its appearance in book form, preparing the West Indian book for the press, but in sore distress for money, and making a translation of Anatole France's "Le Crime de Sylvestre Bonnard" in a few weeks by Herculean labour, in order to exist until he could earn something by his original work. The half-yearly payment of royalties imposed by publishers bears hardly on the author who must pay daily for the means to live. For a time he visited Dr. Gould in Philadelphia, but after his return to New York an arrangement was entered into with Harper and Brothers to go to Japan for the purpose of writing articles from there, after the manner of the West Indian articles, later to be made into a book. An artist was to accompany him to prepare the illustrations, and their route was by way of the Canadian Pacific Railway.

His last evening in New York was spent in the company of his dear friend Mr. Ellwood Hendrick, to whom many of the most valuable letters contained in the second volume were written, and on May 8, 1890, he left for the East — never again to return.

CHAPTER III

A MASTER-WORKMAN

IT was characteristic of the oddity of Hearn's whole life that his way to the Farthest East should have led through the Farthest West, and that his way to a land where one's first impressions are of having strayed into a child's world of faëry — so elfishly frail and fantastically small that one almost fears to move lest a rude gesture might destroy a baby's dear "make-believe" — should have led through plains as gigantic as empires, and mountain gorges vast as dreams.

Something of the contrast and amazement are recorded in "My First Day" — the introductory paper in "Glimpses of Unfamiliar Japan":

The first charm is intangible and volatile as a perfume.... Elfish everything seems; for everything as well as everybody is small and queer and mysterious: the little houses under their blue roofs, the little shop-fronts hung with blue, and the smiling little people in their blue costumes.... Hokusai's own figures walking about in straw rain-coats and straw sandals — bare-limbed peasants; and patient-faced mothers, with smiling bald babies on their backs, toddling by upon their geta.... And suddenly a singular sensation comes upon me as I stand before a weirdly sculptured portal — a sensation of dream and doubt. It seems to me that the steps, and the dragon-swarming gate, and the blue sky arching over the roofs of the town, and the ghostly beauty of Fuji, and the shadow of myself there stretching upon the grey masonry, must all vanish presently... because the forms before me — the curved roofs, the coiling dragons, the Chinese grotesqueries of carving — do not really appear to me as things new, but as things dreamed.... A moment and the delusion vanishes; the romance of reality returns, with freshened consciousness of all that which is truly and deliciously new; the magical transparencies of distance, the wondrous delicacy of tones, the enormous height of the summer blue, and the white soft witchery of the Japanese sun.

That first witchery of Japan never altogether failed to hold him during the fourteen years in which he wrought out the great work of his life, though he exclaims in one of his letters of a later time, "The oscillation of one's thoughts concerning Japan! It is the hardest country to learn — except China — in the world." He grew aware too in time that even he, with his so amazing capacity for entering into the spirit of other races, must forever remain alien to the Oriental. After some years he writes:

The different ways of thinking and the difficulties of the language render it impossible for an educated Japanese to find pleasure in the society of a European. Here is an astounding fact. The Japanese child is as close to you as a European child — perhaps closer and sweeter because infinitely more natural and naturally refined. Cultivate his mind, and the more it is cultivated the farther you push him from you. Why? — Because here the race antipodalism shows itself. As the Oriental thinks naturally to the left where we think to the right, the more you cultivate him the more he will think in the opposite direction from you.

A MASTER-WORKMAN

Though he arrived at a happy moment, his artistic Wanderjahre done, and the tools of his art, after long and bitter apprenticeship, at last obedient to his will and thought in the hand of a master-workman; the material with which he was to labour new and beautiful; yet he never ceased to believe that his true medium was denied to him. In one of his letters he cries:

Pretty to talk of my "pen of fire." I've lost it. Well, the fact is, it is of no use here. There is n't any fire here. It is all soft, dreamy, quiet, pale, faint, gentle, hazy, vapoury, visionary — a land where lotus is a common article of diet — and where there is scarcely any real summer. Even the seasons are feeble ghostly things. Don't please imagine there are any tropics here. Ah! the tropics — they still pull at my heart-strings. Goodness! my real field was there — in the Latin countries, in the West Indies and Spanish America; and my dream was to haunt the old crumbling Portuguese and Spanish cities, and steam up the Amazon and the Orinoco, and get romances nobody else could find. And I could have done it, and made books that would sell for twenty years.

Perhaps he never himself quite realized how much greater in importance was the work chance had set him to do. In place of gathering up in the outlying parts of the new world the dim tattered fragments of Old-World romance — as a collector might seek in Spanish-American cities faded bits of what were once the gold-threaded, glowing tapestries brought to adorn the exile of Conquistadores — he had the good fortune to be chosen to assist at one of the great births of history. Out of "a race as primitive as the Etruscan before Rome was" — as he declared he found them — he was to see a mighty modern nation spring full-armed, with all the sudden miraculous transformation of some great mailed beetle bursting from the grey hidden shell of a feeble-looking pupa. He saw the fourteenth century turn swiftly, amazingly, into the twentieth, and his twelve volumes of studies of the Japanese people were to have that unique and lasting value that would attach to equally painstaking records of Greek life before the Persian wars. Inestimable, immortal, would be such books — could they anywhere be found — setting down the faiths, the traditions, the daily lives, the songs, the dances, the names, the legends, the humble lore of plants, birds, and insects, of that people who suddenly stood up at Thermopylæ, broke the wave from the East, made Europe possible, and set the corner-stone of Occidental thought. This was what Lafcadio Hearn, a little penniless, half-blind, eccentric wanderer had come to do for Japan. To make immortal the story of the childhood of a people as simple as the early Greek, who were to break at Mukden the great wave of conquest from the West and to rejuvenate the most ancient East.

So naturally humble was his estimate of himself that it is safe to assert that not at this time, perhaps at no time, was he aware of the magnitude and importance of the work he had been set to do. For the

A MASTER-WORKMAN

moment he was concerned only with the odylic charm of the new faëry world in which he found himself, but even in faëry-land one may find in time rigidities underlying the charm. No Occidental at that period had as yet divined the iron core underlying the silken courtesy of the Japanese character. Within the first lustrum of his residence there Hearn had grasped the truth, and expressed it in a metaphor. In the volume entitled "Out of the East" he says:

> Under all the amazing self-control and patience there exists an adamantine something very dangerous to reach. ... In the house of any rich family the guest is likely to be shown some of the heirlooms.... A pretty little box, perhaps, will be set before you. Opening it you will see only a beautiful silk bag, closed with a silk running-cord decked with tiny tassels. Very soft and choice the silk is, and elaborately figured. What marvel can be hidden under such a covering? You open the bag and see within another bag, of a different quality of silk, but very fine. Open that, and lo! a third, which contains a fourth, which contains a fifth, which contains a sixth, which contains a seventh bag, which contains the strangest, roughest, hardest vessel of Chinese clay that you ever beheld. Yet it is not only curious but precious; it may be more than a thousand years old.

In time he came to know better than any other Occidental has ever known all those smooth layers of the Japanese nature, and to understand and admire that rough hard clay within — old and wonderful and precious. Again he says:

> For no little time these fairy folk can give you all the

softness of sleep. But sooner or later, if you dwell long with them, your contentment will prove to have much in common with the happiness of dreams. You will never forget the dream — never; but it will lift at last, like those vapours of spring which lend preternatural loveliness to a Japanese landscape in the forenoon of radiant days. Really you are happy because you have entered bodily into Fairyland, into a world that is not, and never could be your own. You have been transported out of your own century, over spaces enormous of perished time, into an era forgotten, into a vanished age, back to something ancient as Egypt or Nineveh. That is the secret of the strangeness and beauty of things, the secret of the thrill they give, the secret of the elfish charm of the people and their ways. Fortunate mortal; the tide of Time has turned for you! But remember that here all is enchantment, that you have fallen under the spell of the dead, that the lights and the colours and the voices must fade away at last into emptiness and silence.

For in time he realized that feudal Japan, with its gentleness and altruism, had attained to its noble ideal of duty by tremendous coercion of the will of the individual by the will of the rest, with a resultant absence of personal freedom that was to the individualism of the Westerner as strangling as the stern socialism of bees and ants.

These, however, were the subtler difficulties arising to confront him as the expatriation stretched into years. The immediate concern was to find means to live. His original purpose of remaining only long enough to prepare a series of illustrated articles for "Harper's Magazine" — to be later collected in

A MASTER-WORKMAN

book form — was almost immediately subverted by a dispute with the publishers. The discovery, during the voyage, that the artist who accompanied him was to receive more than double the pay allowed for the text, angered him beyond measure, and this, added to other matters in which he considered himself unjustly treated, caused him to sever abruptly all his contracts.

It was an example of his incapacity to look at business arrangements from the ordinary point of view that he declined even to receive his royalties from the books already in print, and the publishers could discharge their obligations to him only by turning over the money to a friend, who after some years and by roundabout methods succeeded in inducing him to accept it. That his indignation at what he considered an injustice left him without resources or prospects in remote exile caused him not a moment's hesitation in following this course. Fortunately a letter of introduction carried him within the orbit of Paymaster Mitchell McDonald, a young officer of the American navy stationed in Yokohama. Between these two very dissimilar natures there at once sprang up a warm friendship, from which Hearn derived benefits so delicately and wisely tendered that even his fierce pride and sensitiveness could accept them; and this friendship, which lasted until the close of his life, proved to be a beautiful and helpful legacy for his children. The letters to Paymaster McDonald have a special character of gaiety and good fellowship — with him he forgot in great measure the prepossessions of his life, and became merely the man-of-the-world, delighting in the memories of good dinners, good wine and cigars, enjoyed together; long evenings of gay talk and reminiscences of a naval officer's polyglot experiences; long days of sea and sunshine; but agreeable as were these cheerful experiences — so foreign to his ordinary course of existence — he was continually driving from him, in comic terror, the man who drew him now and again to forget the seriousness of his task.

Professor Basil Hall Chamberlain, already famous for his studies of Japanese life and literature, also became interested in the wanderer — and through his potent influence Hearn received an appointment to the Jinjō-chūgakkō or Ordinary Middle School at Matsue, in the province Izumo, in Shimane Ken, to which he went in August of 1890.

Matsue lies on the northern coast, near that western end of Japan which trails like a streaming feather of land through the Eastern Pacific along the coast of China. It is a town of about thirty-five thousand inhabitants, situated at the junction of Lake Shinji and the Bay of Naka-umi, and was at that time far out of the line of travel or Western influence, the manners of the people remaining almost unchanged, affording a peculiarly favourable opportunity for the study of feudal Japan. The ruins of the castle of the Daimyō, Matsudaira — descendant of the great

A MASTER-WORKMAN

Shōgun Ieyasu — who was overthrown in the wars of the Meiji, still frowned from the wooded hill above the city, and still his love of art, his conservatism of the old customs, his rigid laws of politeness were stamped deeply into the culture of the subjects over whom he had reigned, though ugly modern buildings housed the schools of that Western learning he had so contemned, and which the newcomer had been hired to teach. But this was a teacher of different calibre from those who had preceded him. Here was not a holder of the "little yellow monkey" prepossession. Here was a rare mind capable at the age of forty of receiving new impressions, of comprehending a civilization alien to all its previous knowledge.

Out of this remarkable experience — a stray from the nineteenth century moving about in the unrealized world of the fourteenth — grew that portion of his first Japanese book, "Glimpses of Unfamiliar Japan," which he called "From the Diary of an English Teacher," and "The Chief City of the Province of the Gods." It is interesting to compare the impression made upon the teacher by his pupils with the opinion formed by the pupils of their foreign teacher.

Hearn says:

I have had two years' experience in large Japanese schools; and I have never had personal knowledge of any serious quarrel between students. . . . A teacher is a teacher only: he stands to his pupils in the relation of an

LAFCADIO HEARN

elder brother. He never tries to impose his will upon them ... severity would scarcely be tolerated by the students. ... Strangely pleasant is the first sensation of a Japanese class, as you look over the ranges of young faces. ... Those traits have nothing incisive, nothing forcible: compared with Occidental faces they seem but "half-sketched," so soft their outlines are. ... Some have a childish freshness and frankness indescribable ... all are equally characterized by a singular placidity — expressing neither love nor hate nor anything save perfect repose and gentleness. ... I find among the students a healthy tone of skepticism in regard to certain forms of popular belief. Scientific education is rapidly destroying credulity in old superstitions. ... But the deeper religious sense remains with him; and the Monistic Idea in Buddhism is being strengthened ... by the new education. ... Shintō the students all sincerely are ... what the higher Shintō signifies — loyalty, filial piety, obedience to parents, and respect for ancestors. ... The demeanour of a class during study hours is if anything too faultless. Never a whisper is heard; never is a head raised from the book without permission. ... My favourite students often visit me of afternoons. ... Their conversation and thoughts are of the simplest and frankest. ... Often they bring me gifts of flowers, and sometimes they bring books and pictures to show me — delightfully queer things — family heirlooms. Never by any possible chance are they troublesome, impolite, curious, or even talkative. Courtesy in its utmost possible exquisiteness seems as natural to the Izumo boy as the colour of his hair or the tint of his skin.

Of the teacher one of his pupils, Teizaburō Inomata, now a student at Yale College, says: "We liked him for his appearance and for his gentle man-

A MASTER-WORKMAN

ners. He seemed more pleasing in his looks than most foreigners do to the Japanese."

Masanobu Ōtani, his favourite pupil in Matsue, says: "He was a very kind and industrious teacher, incomparable to the common foreigners engaged in the Middle Schools of those days. No wonder therefore that he won at once the admiration of all the teachers and students of the school." He sends a copy of one of his own compositions corrected and annotated by Hearn, and observes: "How he was kind and earnest in his teaching can well be seen by the above specimen. It seems that themes for our composition were such as he could infer our artless, genuine thoughts and feelings. . . . He attentively listened to our reading, corrected each mispronunciation whenever we did. . . . We Japanese feel much pain to pronounce 'l' and 'th.' He kindly and scrupulously taught the pronunciation of these sounds. He was not tired to correct mispronunciation. . . . He was always exact, but never severe."

Hearn's first residence in Matsue was at an inn in the quarter called Zaimoku-chō, "but," says his wife in the reminiscences which she set down to assist his biographer, "circumstances made him resolve to leave it very soon. The chief cause was as follows: The daughter of the innkeeper was suffering from a disease of the eyes. This aroused his sympathy (as did all such troubles in a special manner); he asked the landlord to send her to a hospital for treatment, but the landlord did not care much about her, and refused, to Hearn's great mortification. 'Unmerciful fellow! without a father's heart,' he said to himself, and removed to a house of his own on the shore of the lake."

This house was near the bridge Ōhashi which crossed the largest of the three outlets from the lake to the bay, and commanded the beautiful scenery described in "The Chief City of the Province of the Gods":

I slide open my little Japanese paper window to look out upon the morning over a soft green cloud of foliage rising from the river-bounded garden below. Before me, tremulously mirroring everything upon its farther side, glimmers the broad glassy mouth of the Ōhashi-gawa, opening into the Shinji Lake, which spreads out broadly to the right in a dim grey frame of peaks. . . . But oh, the charm of the vision — those first ghostly love-colours of a morning steeped in mist soft as sleep itself! . . . Long reaches of faintly tinted vapour cloud the far lake verge. . . . All the bases of the mountains are veiled by them . . . so that the lake appears incomparably larger than it really is, and not an actual lake, but a beautiful spectral sea of the same tint as the dawn-sky and mixing with it, while peak-tips rise like islands from the brume — an exquisite chaos, ever changing aspect as the delicate fogs rise, slowly, very slowly. As the sun's yellow rim comes into sight, fine thin lines of warmer tone — violets and opalines — shoot across the flood, tree-tops take tender fire. . . . Looking sunward, up the long Ōhashi-gawa, beyond the many-pillared wooden bridge, one high-pooped junk, just hoisting sail, seems to me the most fantastically beautiful craft I ever saw — a dream of Orient seas, so idealized by the vapour is it; the ghost of a junk, but a ghost that catches the light as clouds do; a shape of gold

A MASTER-WORKMAN

mist, seemingly semidiaphanous, and suspended in pale blue light.

Here, constantly absorbed when off duty in the study of the sights and sounds of the city — the multitudinous soft clapping of hands that greeted the rising sun, the thin ringing of thousands of wooden geta across the bridge, the fantastic craft of the water traffic, the trades of the street merchants, the plays and songs of the children — he began to register his first impressions, to make his first studies for his first book. Of its two volumes he afterwards spoke slightingly as full of misconceptions and errors, but it at once, upon its appearance in print, attracted the serious consideration of literary critics, and is the work which, with "Japan: an Interpretation," remains most popular with his Japanese friends. It records his many expeditions to the islands and ports of the three provinces included in the Ken of Shimane, and his study of the manners, customs, and religion of the people. Of special value was his visit to the famous temple at Kizuki, to whose shrine he was the first Westerner ever admitted. Lord Senke Takamori, priest of this temple, was a friend of the family of the lady who became Hearn's wife, and prince of a house which had passed its office by direct male line through eighty-two generations; as old a house as that of the Mikado himself. From him Hearn received the unusual courtesy of having ordered for his special benefit a religious dance by the temple attendants.

LAFCADIO HEARN

It was while Lafcadio was living in the house by the Ōhashi bridge that he married, in January, 1891, Setsu Koizumi, a lady of high samurai rank. The revolution in Japan which overthrew the power of the Shōguns and restored the Mikado to temporal power had broken the whole feudal structure of Japanese society, and with the downfall of the daimyōs, whose position was similar to that of the dukes of feudal England, fell the lesser nobility, the samurai, or "two-sworded" men. Many of these sank into as great poverty as that which befel the émigrés after the French Revolution, and among those whose fortunes were entirely ruined were the Koizumis. Sentarō Nishida, who appears to have been a sort of head master of the Jinjō-chūgakkō, in special charge of the English department, was of one of the lesser samurai families, his mother having been an inmate of the Koizumi household before the decline of their fortunes. Because of his fluency in English, as well as because of what seems to have been a peculiar sweetness and dignity of character, he soon became the interpreter and special friend of the new English teacher. It was through his mediation that the marriage was arranged. Under ordinary circumstances a Japanese woman of rank would consider an alliance with a foreigner an inexpugnable disgrace; but the circumstances of the Koizumis were not ordinary, and whatever may have been the secret feelings of the girl of twenty-two, it is certain that she immediately became pas-

Mrs. Hearn at her Writing-Desk

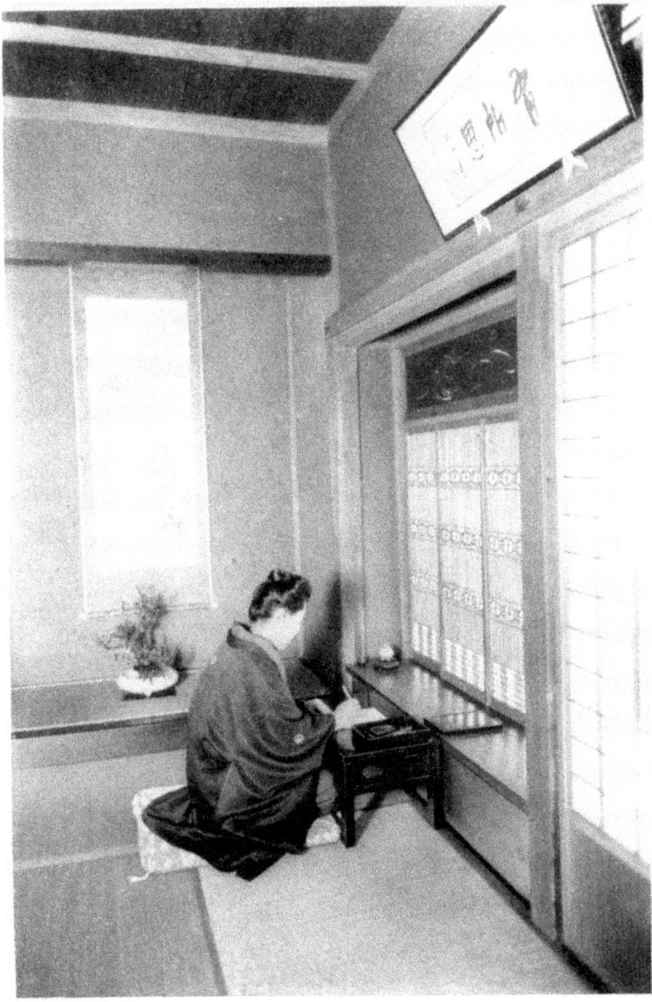

A MASTER-WORKMAN

sionately attached to her husband, and the marriage continued to the end to be a very happy one. It was celebrated by the local rites, as to have married according to English laws, under the then existing treaties, would have deprived her of her Japanese citizenship and obliged them to remove to one of the open ports; but the question of the legality of the marriage and of her future troubled Hearn from the beginning, and finally obliged him to renounce his English allegiance and become a subject of the Mikado in order that she and her children might never suffer from any complications or doubts as to their position. This could be achieved only by his adoption into his wife's family. He took their name, Koizumi, which signifies "Little Spring," and for personal title chose the classical term for Izumo province, Yakumo, meaning "Eight Clouds" — or "the place of the issuing of clouds" — and also being the first word of the oldest known Japanese poem.

Mrs. Hearn says: "We afterwards removed to a samurai house where we could have a home of our own conveniently equipped with numbers of rooms — our household consisting of us two, maids, and a small cat. Now about this cat: while we lived near the lake, when the spring was yet cold, as I was watching from the veranda the evening shadow falling upon the lake one day, I found a group of boys trying to drown a small cat near our house. I asked the boys and took it home. 'O pity! cruel boys!' Hearn said, and took that all-wet, shivering creature into his own bosom (underneath the cloth) and kindly warmed it. This strongly impressed me with his deep sincerity, which I ever after witnessed at various occasions. Such conduct would be very extreme, but he had such an intensity in his character."

This cat seems to have been an important member of the household. Professor Ōtani in referring to it says: "It was a purely black cat. It was given the name of Hinoko (a spark) by him, because of its glaring eyes like live coals. It became his pet. It was often held in his hat."

Later another pet was added to the establishment — an uguisu, sent to him by "the sweetest lady in Japan, daughter of the Governor of Izumo, who, thinking the foreign teacher might feel lonesome during a brief illness, made him the gift of this dainty creature."

"You do not know what an uguisu is?" he says. "An uguisu is a holy little bird that professes Buddhism... very brief indeed is my little feathered Buddhist's confession of faith — only the sacred name of the sutras reiterated over and over again, like a litany — 'Ho-ke-kyō!' — a single word only. But also it is written: 'He who shall joyfully accept but a single word from this sutra, incalculably greater shall be his merit than the merit of one who should supply all the beings in the four hundred thousand worlds with all the necessaries for happiness.'... Always he makes a reverent little pause after uttering it. First the warble; then a pause of

A MASTER-WORKMAN

about five seconds; then a slow, sweet, solemn utterance of the holy name in a tone as of meditative wonder; then another pause; then another wild, rich, passionate warble. Could you see him you would marvel how so powerful and penetrating a soprano could ripple from so minute a throat, yet his chant can be heard a whole chō away . . . a neutral-tinted mite almost lost in his box-cage darkened with paper screens, for he loves the gloom. Delicate he is, and exacting even to tyranny. All his diet must be laboriously triturated and weighed in scales, and measured out to him at precisely the same hour each day."

In this house, surrounded with beautiful gardens, and lying under the very shadow of the ruined daimyō castle, Hearn and his wife passed a very happy year. The rent was about four dollars a month; his salaries from the middle and normal schools, added to what he earned with his pen, made him for the first time in his life easy about money matters. He was extremely popular with all classes, from the governor to the barber; the charm and wonder of the life about him was still unstaled by usage, and he found himself at last able to achieve some of that beauty and force of style for which he had so long laboured. He even found pleasure in the fact that most of his friends were of no greater stature than himself. It seems to have been in every way the happiest portion of his life. Mrs. Hearn's notes concerning it are so delightful as to deserve literal reproduction.

LAFCADIO HEARN

The governor of the prefecture at that time was Viscount Yasusada Koteda, an earnest advocate of preserving old, genuine Japanese essentials, a conservatist. He was very much skilful in fencing; was much respected by the people in general.

Mr. Koteda was also very kind to Lafcadio.

Thus all Izumo proved favourable to him. The place welcomed him and treated him as a member of its family, a guest, a good friend, and not as a stranger or a foreigner. To him all things were full of novel interest; and the hospitality and good-naturedness of the city-people were the great pleasure for him. Matsue was, as it were, a paradise for him; and he became enthusiastically fond of Matsue. The newspapers of the city often published his anecdotes for his praise. The students were very pleased that they had a good teacher. In the meantime, the wonderful thread of marriage happened to unite me with Lafcadio. . . .

When I first saw Lafcadio, his property was a very scanty one — only a table, a chair, a few number of books, a suit of both foreign and Japanese cloth [clothes], etc.

When he came home from school, he put on Japanese cloth and sat on cushion and smoked.

By this time he began to be fond of living in all ways like Japanese. He took Japanese food with chopsticks.

In his Izumo days, he was pleased to be present on all banquets held by the teachers; he also invited some teachers very often and was very glad to listen to the popular songs.

On the New Year's day of 1891, he went round for a formal call with Japanese haori and hakama. . . .

But on those days I had to suffer from the inconvenience of conversation between us. We could not understand each other very well. Nor was Hearn familiar with complicated Japanese customs. He was a man with a rare

A MASTER-WORKMAN

sensibility of feeling; also he had a peculiar taste. Having been teased by the hard world, and being still in the vigour of his life, he often seemed to be indignant with the world. (This turned in his later years into a melancholic temperament.) When we travelled through the province of Hōki, we had to rest for a while at a tea-house of some hot-spring, where many people were making merry. Hearn pulled my dress, saying: "Stop to enter this house! No good to rest here. It is an hell. Even a moment we should not stay here." He was often offended in such a way. I was younger than now I am and unexperienced with the affairs of the world; and it was no easy task for me then to reconcile him with the occasions.

We visited Kūkedo, which is a cave on a rocky shore in the sea of Japan. Hearn went out from the shore and swam for about two miles, showing great dexterity in various feats of swimming. Our boat entered the dark, hollow cave, and it was very fearful to hear the sounds of waves dashing against the wall. There are many fearful legends concerning this cave. To keep our boat from the evil-spirit, we had to continue tapping our boat with a stone. The deep water below was horribly blue. After hearing my story about the cave, Hearn began to put off his clothes. The sailor said that there would be a great danger if any one swam here, on account of the devil's curse. I dissuaded him from swimming. Hearn was very displeased and hardly spoke with me till the next day....

In the summer of 1891 he visited Kizuki with Mr. Nishida. The next day he sent for me to come. When I arrived at his hotel I found the two had gone to sea for swimming, and Hearn's money, packed in his stocking, was left on the floor. He was very indifferent in regard to money until in later years he became anxious for the future of family, as he felt he would not live very long on account of his failing health....

LAFCADIO HEARN

He was extremely fond of freedom, and hated mere forms and restraint. As a middle school teacher and as a professor in the University he was always democratic and simple in his life. He ordered to make flock-coat when he became University professor, and it was after my eager advice. He at first insisted that he would not appear on public ceremony where polite garments are required, according to the promise with Dr. Toyama, and it was after my eager entreaties that at last he consented to have flock-coat made for him. But it was only some four or five times that he put on that during his life. So whenever he puts on that, he felt the task of putting on very troublesome, and said: "Please attend to-day's meeting instead of me. I do not like to wear this troublesome thing; daily cloth is sufficient, etc." He disliked silk-hat. Some day I said in joke: "You have written about Japan very well. His Majesty the Emperor is calling you to praise. So please put on the flock-coat and silk-hat." He answered: "Therefore I will not attend the meeting; flock-coat and silk-hat are the thing I dislike."

Our conversation was through Japanese language. Hearn would not teach me English, saying: "It is far lovelier for the Japanese women that they talk in Japanese. I am glad that you do not know English."

Some time (when at Kumamoto) I told him of various inconveniences on account of my ignorance of English. He said that if I were able to write my name in English it would be sufficient; and instead he wanted me to teach him Japanese alphabet. He made progress in this and were able to write letters in Japanese alphabet with a few Chinese characters intermixed.

Our *mutual* Japanese language made great progress on account of necessity. This special Japanese of mine proved much more intelligible to him than any skilful English of Japanese friend. Hearn was always delighted with my Japanese. By and by he was able to teach

A MASTER-WORKMAN

Kazuo in Japanese. He also taught Japanese stories to other children in Japanese.

But on Matsue days we suffered in regard to conversations. Sometimes we had to refer to the dictionary. Being fond from my girlhood of old tales, I began from these Matsue days telling him long Japanese old stories, which were not easy for him to understand, but to which he listened with much interest and attention. He called our mutual Japanese language "Hearn san Kotoba" (Hearn's language). So in later years when he met some difficult words he would say in joke to explain them in our familiar "Hearn san Kotoba."

Unfortunately this idyllic interval was cut short by ill-health. The cold Siberian winds that pass across Izumo in winter seriously affected his lungs, and the little hibachi, or box of burning charcoal, which was the only means in use of warming Japanese houses, could not protect sufficiently one who had lived so long in warm climates. Oddly too, cold always affected his eyesight injuriously, and very reluctantly, but under the urgent advice of his doctor, he sought employment in a warmer region and was transferred to the Dai Go Kōtō Gakkō, the great Government College, at Kumamoto, situated near the southern end of the Inland Sea. In "Sayonara" — the last chapter of the "Glimpses" — there is a description of his parting:

The quaint old city has become so endeared to me that the thought of never seeing it again is one I do not venture to dwell upon. . . . These days of farewells have been full of charming surprises. To have the revelation of gratitude where you had no right to expect more than plain satisfaction with your performance of duty; to find affection where you supposed only good will to exist: these are assuredly delicious experiences. . . . I cannot but ask myself the question: Could I have lived in the exercise of the same profession for the same length of time in any other country, and have enjoyed a similar unbroken experience of human goodness? From each and all I have received only kindness and courtesy. Not one has addressed to me a single ungenerous word. As a teacher of more than five hundred boys and men I have never even had my patience tried.

There were presents from the teachers, of splendid old porcelains, of an ancient and valuable sword from the students, of mementoes from every one. A banquet was given, addresses made, the Government officials and hundreds of friends came to bid him good-bye at the docks, and thus closed the most beautiful episode of his life.

Matsue was Old Japan. Kumamoto represented the far less pleasing Japan in the stage of transition. Here Hearn remained for three years, and at the expiration of his engagement abandoned the Government service and returned to journalism for a while. Living was far more expensive, the official and social atmosphere of Kumamoto was repugnant to him, and he fell back into the old solitary, retiring habits of earlier days — finding his friends among children and folk of the humbler classes, excepting only the old teacher of Chinese, whose name signified "Moon-of-Autumn," and to whom he makes reference in several of his letters. In "Out of the East"

A MASTER-WORKMAN

— the book written in Kumamoto — he says of this friend:

He was once a samurai of high rank belonging to the great clan of Aizu. He had been a leader of armies, a negotiator between princes, a statesman, a ruler of provinces — all that any knight could be in the feudal era. But in the intervals of military or political duty he seems always to have been a teacher. Yet to see him now you would scarcely believe how much he was once feared — though loved — by the turbulent swordsmen under his rule. Perhaps there is no gentleness so full of charm as that of the man of war noted for sternness in his youth.

Of his childish friends he relates a pretty story. They came upon one occasion to ask for a contribution of money to help in celebrating the festival of Jizō, whose shrine was opposite his house.

I was glad to contribute to the fund, for I love the gentle god of children. Early the next morning I saw that a new bib had been put about Jizō's neck, a Buddhist repast set before him.... After dark I went out into a great glory of lantern-fires to see the children dance; and I found, perched before my gate, an enormous dragon-fly more than three feet long. It was a token of the children's gratitude for the help I had given them. I was startled for a moment by the realism of the thing, but upon close examination I discovered that the body was a pine branch wrapped with coloured paper, the four wings were four fire-shovels, and the gleaming head was a little teapot. The whole was lighted by a candle so placed as to make extraordinary shadows, which formed part of the design. It was a wonderful instance of art-sense working without a speck of artistic material, yet it was all the labour of a poor little child only eight years old!

LAFCADIO HEARN

It was in Kumamoto that Hearn first began to perceive the fierceness and sternness of the Japanese character. "With Kyūshū Students" and "Jiujutsu" contain some surprising foreshadowings of the then unsuspected future. Such characteristics, however he might respect or understand them, were always antipathetic to his nature, and his relations with the members of the school were for the most part formal. He mentions that the students rarely called upon him, and that he saw his fellow teachers only in school hours. Between classes he usually walked under the trees, smoking, or betook himself to an abandoned cemetery on the ridge of the hill behind the college, where an ancient stone Buddha sat upon a lotus — "his meditative gaze slanting down between half-closed eyelids" — and where he wrought out the chapter in "Out of the East" which is called "The Stone Buddha." It became a favourite resort. Mrs. Hearn says: "When at Kumamoto we two often went out for a walk in the night-time. On the first walk at Kumamoto I was led to a graveyard, for on the previous day he said: 'I have found a pleasant place. Let us go there to-morrow night.' Through a dark path I was led on, until we came up a hill, where were many tombs. Dreary place it was! He said: 'Listen and hear the voices of frogs.'"

He was still in Kumamoto when Japan went to war with China, and his record of the emotion of the people is full of interest. The war spirit manifested

Mrs. Hearn, her Oldest Son, Kazuo, and her Daughter, Suzuko
From a Photograph taken in 1922

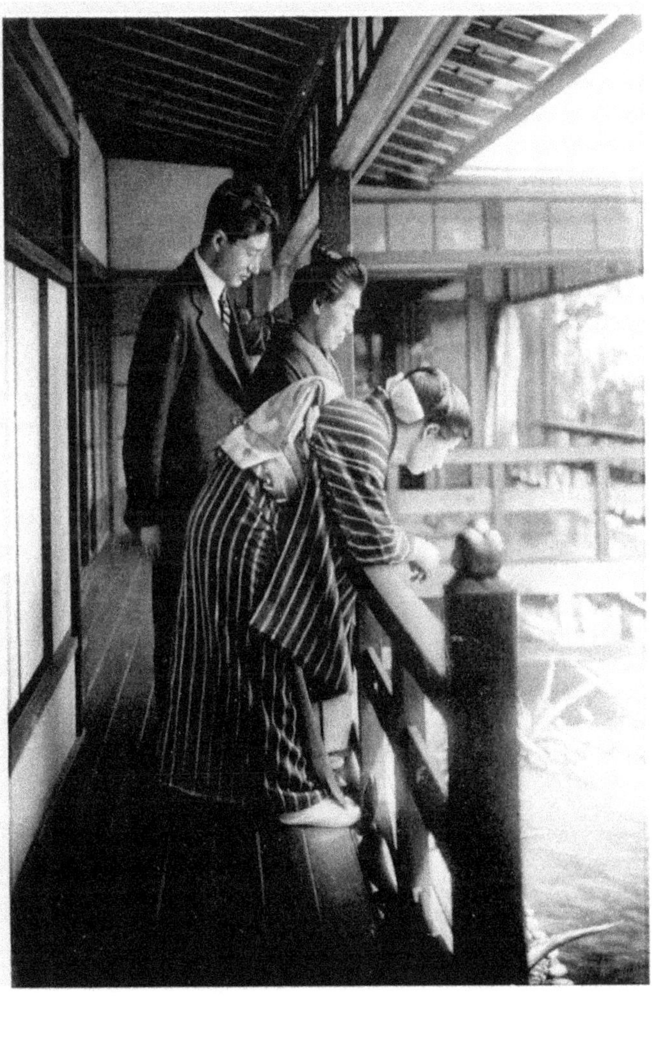

A MASTER-WORKMAN

itself in ways not less painful than extraordinary. Many killed themselves on being refused the chance of military service.

It was here in the previous year, November 17, 1893, that his first child was born, and was named Kazuo, which signifies "the first of the excellent, best of the peerless." The event caused him the profoundest emotion. Indeed, it seemed to work a great change in all his views of life, as perhaps it does in most parents, reconciling them to much against which they may have previously rebelled. Writing to me a few weeks after this event he declared with artless conviction that the boy was "strangely beautiful," and though three other children came in later years, Kazuo always remained his special interest and concern. Up to the time of his death he never allowed his eldest son to be taught by any one but himself, and his most painful preoccupation when his health began to decline was with the future of this child, who appeared to have inherited both his father's looks and disposition.

The constant change in the personnel of the teaching force of the college, and many annoyances to which he was subjected, caused his decision at the end of the three years' term to remove to Kōbe and enter the service of the Kōbe "Chronicle." Explaining to Amenomori he says:

By the way, I am hoping to leave the Gov't service, and begin journalism at Kōbe. I am not sure of success; but Gov't service is uncertain to the degree of terror — a sword of Damocles; and Gov't does n't employ men like you as teachers. If it did, and would give them what they should have, the position of a foreign teacher would be pleasant enough. He would be among thinkers, and find some kindliness — instead of being made to feel that he is only the servant of petty political clerks. And I have been so isolated, that I must acknowledge the weakness of wishing to be among Englishmen again — with all their prejudices and conventions.

Kōbe was at that time, 1895, an open port, that is to say, one of the places in which foreigners were allowed to reside without special Government permission, and under the extra-territorial rule of their own consuls. Of Hearn's external life here there seems to be but scant record. He worked as one of the staff of the "Chronicle" — his editorials frequently bringing upon him the wrath of the missionaries — he contributed some letters to the McClure Syndicate, and there was much talk of a projected expedition, in search of material for such work, to the Philippines or the Loo Choo Islands; a project never realized. The journalistic work seriously affected his eyes, and his health seems to have been poor at times. He made few acquaintances and had almost no companions outside of his own household, where in 1896 another son was born.

Perhaps because of the narrowness of his social life his mental life deepened and expanded, or possibly his indifference to the outer world may have resulted from the change manifesting itself in his mental view.

A MASTER-WORKMAN

"Kokoro" (a Japanese word signifying "The Heart of Things") was written in Kōbe, as was also "Gleanings in Buddha-Fields," and they quite remarkably demonstrate his growing indifference to the externals of life, the deepening of his thought toward the intrinsic and the fundamental. The visible beauty of woman, of nature, of art, grew to absorb him less as he sought for the essential principle of beauty.

In one of the letters written about this time he says:

I have to acknowledge to feeling a sort of resentment against certain things in which I used to take pleasure. I can't look at a number of the "Petit Journal pour Rire" or the "Charivari" without vexation, almost anger. I can't find pleasure in a French novel written for the obvious purpose of appealing to instincts that interfere with perception of higher things than instincts. I should not go to the Paris Opera if it were next door. I should not like to visit the most beautiful lady and be received in evening dress. You see how absurd I have become — and this without any idea of principle about the matter except the knowledge that I ought to avoid everything which does not help me to make the best of myself — small as it may be.

And again:

I might say that I have become indifferent to personal pleasure of any sort . . . what is more significant, I think, is the feeling that the greatest pleasure is to work for others — for those who take it as a matter of course that I should do so, and would be as much amazed to find me selfish about it as if an earthquake had shaken the house down. . . . It now seems to me that time is the most precious of all things conceivable. I can't waste it by going out to hear people talk nonsense. . . . There are rich natures that can afford the waste, but I can't, because the best part of my life has been wasted in the wrong direction and I shall have to work like thunder till I die to make up for it.

The growing gravity and force of his thought was shown not only in his books but in his correspondence. Most of the letters written at this period were addressed to Professor Chamberlain, dealing with matters of heredity and the evolution of the individual under ancestral racial influences. The following extract is typical of the tone of the whole:

Here comes in the consideration of a very terrible possibility. Suppose we use integers instead of quintillions or centillions, and say that an individual represents by inheritance a total of 10 − 5 of impulses favourable to social life, 5 of the reverse. (Such a balance would really occur in many cases.) The child inherits, under favourable conditions, the father's balance plus the maternal balance of 9 — four of the number being favourable. We have then a total which becomes odd, and the single odd number gives preponderance to an accumulation of ancestral impulse incalculable for evil. It would be like a pair of scales, each holding a mass as large as Fuji. If the balance were absolutely perfect the weight of *one* hair would be enough to move a mass of millions of tons. Here is your antique Nemesis awfully magnified. Let the individual descend below a certain level and countless dead suddenly seize and destroy him — like the Furies.

One begins to miss the beautiful landscapes against which he had set his enchantingly realistic

A MASTER-WORKMAN

pictures of beautiful things and people, but in the place of the sensuous charm, the honeyed felicities of phrase, he offered such essays as the "Japanese Civilization" in "Kokoro," with its astounding picture of New York City, and its sublimated insight into the imponderable soul of the Eastern world — such intolerable imaginings as "Dust" in the "Gleanings from Buddha-Fields," and the delicate poignancies of "The Nun of the Temple of Amida" or of "A Street Singer."

I think it was at Kōbe he reached his fullest intellectual stature. None of the work that followed in the next eight years surpassed the results he there achieved, and much was of lesser value, despite its beauty. He had attained to complete mastery of his medium, and had, moreover, learned completely to master his thought before clothing it in words — a far more difficult and more important matter.

Yet the clothing in words was no small task, as witness the accompanying examples of how he laboured for the perfection of his vehicle. These are not the first struggles of a young and clumsy artist, but the efforts at the age of fifty-three of one of the greatest masters of English.

It was done, too, by a man who earned with his pen in a year less than the week's income of one of the facile authors of the "six best sellers."

As has been said of De Quincey, whom Hearn in many ways resembled, "I can grasp a little of his morbid suffering in the eternal struggle for perfection

LAFCADIO HEARN

of utterance; I can share a part of his æsthetic torment over cacophony, redundance, obscurity, and all the thousand minute delicacies and subtleties of resonance and dissonance, accent and cæsura, that only a De Quincey's ear appreciates and seeks to achieve or evade. How many care for these fine things today? How many are concerned if De Quincey uses a word with the long 'a' sound, or spends a sleepless night in his endeavour to find another with the short 'a,' that shall at once answer his purpose and crown his sentence with harmony? Who lovingly examine the great artist's methods now, dip into the secret of his mystery, and weigh verb against adjective, vowel against consonant, that they may a little understand the unique splendour of this prose? And who, when an artist is the matter, attempt to measure his hopes as well as his attainments or praise a noble ambition perhaps shining through faulty attempt? How many even among those who write, have fathomed the toil and suffering, the continence and self-denial of our great artists in words?".

CHAPTER IV
THE LAST STAGE

WITH methods of work such as those of which the foregoing examples give suggestion, with increasing indifference to the external details of life, and growing concentration of esoteric thought, it was plain that literature and journalism would not suffice to sustain a family of thirteen persons. For Hearn in becoming a Japanese subject had accepted the Japanese duty of maintaining the elder members of the family into which he had been adopted, and his household included the ancestors of his son. He referred to the fact occasionally with amused impatience, but seems never to have really resented or rebelled against the filial duties which to the Western point of view might appear excessive. His eyes, too, began to give warnings that could not be ignored, and with reluctance he yielded to the necessity of earning a larger income by reëntering the Government service as a teacher. Professor Chamberlain again came to his aid and secured for him the position of Professor of English in the Imperial University of Tōkyō, where his salary was large compared to anything he had as yet received, and where he was permitted an admirable liberty as to methods of teaching.

Of his lectures an example is given in the Appendix, under the title "Naked Poetry." [1] This, it is interesting to mention, was taken down in long-hand during its delivering by Teizaburō Inomata, who possesses five manuscript volumes of these records, for Hearn transcribed none of his lectures, delivering them without notes, and had it not been for this astonishing feat by a member of one of his classes all written record of his teaching would have been lost. Mr. Inomata is the Ochiai of the letter given on page fifty-nine of the present volume, and was one of the pupils of the Jinjō-chūgakkō of Matsue. Another of these Matsue pupils was Masanobu Ōtani, whom Hearn assisted to pass through the university by employing him to collect data for many of his books. In the elaborately painstaking manuscript volume of information which Mr. Ōtani sent me to assist in the writing of these volumes, he says:

> Here I want not to forget to add that I had received from him twelve yen (six dollars) for my work each month. It was too kind of him that a poor monthly work of mine was paid with the money above mentioned. To speak frankly, however, it was not very easy for me to pass each month with the money through the three years of my university course. I had to pay two yen and a half as the monthly fee to the university; to pay six or seven yen for my lodging and eating every month; to buy some necessary textbooks, and to pay for some meetings inevitable. So I was forced to make some more money beside his favour. Each month I contributed to some newspapers and magazines; I reprinted the four books of Nesfield's

[1] See Volume XVI.

THE LAST STAGE

grammar; I published some pamphlets. Thus I could equal the expense of each month, but I need hardly say that it was by his extraordinary favour that I could finish my study in the university. I shall never forget his extreme kindness forever and ever.

A revelation this, confirmatory of the constant references made by Hearn to the frightful price paid in life and energy by Japan in the endeavour to assimilate a millennium of Western learning in the brief space of half a century.

From these notes by Mr. Ōtani, Mrs. Hearn, and Mr. Inomata it is possible to reconstruct his life in Tōkyō with that minuteness demanded by the professors of the "scientific school" of biography:

When he came to the university he immediately entered the lecture room, and at the recreation hour he was always seen in a lonely part of the college garden, smoking, and walking to and fro. No one dared disturb his meditations. He did not mingle with the other professors. ... Very regular and very diligent in his teaching, he was never absent unless ill. His hours of teaching being twelve in the week. ...

He never used an umbrella. ...

He liked to bathe in tepid water. ...

He feared cold; his study having a large stove and double doors; he never, however, used gloves in the coldest weather. ...

And so on, to the nth power of fatigue. Personally nothing would have been so obnoxious to the man as this piling-up of unimportant detail and banal ana about his private life. He was entirely free of that egotism, frequently afflicting the literary artist, which made the crowing cocks, the black beetles, and the marital infelicities of the Carlyles matters of such import as to deserve being solemnly and meticulously recorded for the benefit of an awestruck world.

At first the change of residence, the necessary interruption of the heavy work of preparing lectures, the teaching, and its attendant official duties seem to have broken the train of his inspiration — for "Gleanings in Buddha-Fields," though published the year after his arrival in Tōkyō, had been completed while in Kōbe, and he complains bitterly in his letters that "the Holy Ghost had departed from him," and was constantly endeavouring to find some means of renewing the fire. In a letter to his friend Amenomori he says:

But somehow working is "against the grain." I get no thrill, no frisson, no sensation. I want new experiences, perhaps; and Tōkyō is no place for them. Perhaps the power to feel thrill dies with the approach of a man's fiftieth year. Perhaps the only land to find the new sensations is in the Past — floats blue-peaked under some beautiful dead sun "in the tropic clime of youth." Must I die and be born again to feel the charm of the Far East; — or will Nobushige Amenomori discover for me some unfamiliar blossom growing beside the Fountain of Immortality? Alas, I don't know!

Indeed, in "Exotics and Retrospectives" he returned for part of his material to old memories of the West Indies, and the next four volumes — "In

THE LAST STAGE

Ghostly Japan" (with its monstrous fantasy of the Mountain of Skulls), "Shadowings," "A Japanese Miscellany," and "Kotto" — show that the altar still waited for the coal, the contents of these being merely studies, masterly as they were, such as an artist might make while waiting for some great idea to form itself, worthy of a broad canvas.

As the letters show, prodigious care and patience were expended upon each of these sketches. In advising a friend he explains his own methods:

> Now with regard to your own sketch or story. If you are quite dissatisfied with it, I think this is probably due *not* to what you suppose — imperfection of expression — but rather to the fact that some *latent* thought or emotion has not yet defined itself in your mind with sufficient sharpness. You feel something and have not been able to express the feeling — only because you do not yet quite know what it is. We feel without understanding feeling; and our most powerful emotions are the most undefinable. This must be so, because they are inherited accumulations of feeling, and the multiplicity of them — superimposed one over another — blurs them, and makes them dim, even though enormously increasing their strength. ... *Unconscious* brain-work is the best to develop such latent feeling or thought. By quietly writing the thing over and over again, I find that the emotion or idea often *develops itself* in the process — unconsciously. Again, it is often worth while to *try* to analyze the feeling that remains dim. The effort of trying to understand exactly what it is that moves us sometimes proves successful. ... If you have any feeling — no matter what — strongly latent in the mind (even only a haunting sadness or a mysterious joy), you may be sure that it is expressible.

LAFCADIO HEARN

Some feelings are, of course, very difficult to develop. I shall show you one of these days, when we see each other, a page that I worked at for *months* before the idea came clearly. . . . When the best result comes, it ought to surprise you, for our best work is out of the Unconscious.

In all these studies the tendency grew constantly more marked to abandon the earlier richness of his style; a pellucid simplicity was plainly the aim of his intention. The transparent, shadowy, "weird stories" of "Kwaidan" were as unlike the splendid floridity of his West Indian studies as a Shintō shrine is unlike a Gothic cathedral. These ghostly sketches might have been made by the brush of a Japanese artist; a grey whirl of water about a phantom fish — a shadow of a pine bough across the face of a spectral moon — an outline of mountains as filmy as dreams: brief, almost childishly simple, and yet suggesting things poignant, things ineffable.

"Ants," the last study in "Kwaidan," was, however, of a very different character. The old Occidental fire and power was visible again; his inspiration was reillumined. Then suddenly the broad canvas was spread for him and he wrote "Japan: an Attempt at Interpretation," one of the most astonishing reviews of the life and soul of a great nation ever attempted.

To understand the generation of this book it is necessary to explain the conditions of the last years of his life in Tōkyō. Of his private existence at this

THE LAST STAGE

time Mrs. Hearn's reminiscences furnish again a delightful and vivid record:

It was on the 27th Aug., 1896, that we arrived at Tōkyō from Kōbe.

Having heard of a house to let in Ushigome district, we went to see it. It was an old house of a pure Japanese style, without an upper story; and having a spacious garden and a lotus-pond in it, the house resembled to a Buddhist temple. Very gloomy house it was and I felt a sense of being haunted. Hearn seemed fond of the house. But we did not borrow it.

We heard afterward that it was reputed to be haunted by the ghost; and though the house-rent was very cheap, no one would dare to borrow the house; and finally it was broken down by its owner. "Why then did we not inhabit that house?" Hearn said, with regret, "It was very interesting house, I thought at that time!"

At last we settled at a house at Tomihisa-chō, Ushigome district, about three miles from the university. The house was situated on a bluff, with a Buddhist temple called Kobu-dera in the neighbourhood. "Kobu-dera" means "Knots Temple," because all the pillars in the building have knots left, the natural wood having been used without carpenter's planes. Formerly it was called Hagi-dera on account of many hagi [1] flowers in the garden.

Being very fond of a temple, he often went for rambling in Kobu-dera, so that he became acquainted with a goodly old priest there, with whom he was pleased to talk on Buddhist subjects, I being always his interpreter in such a case.

Almost every morning and every evening he took walk in Kobu-dera.

[1] Bush clover.

The children always said when he was absent, "Papa is in Kobu-dera."

The following is one of his conversations in one of our ramblings there: "Can I not live in this temple?" "I should be very glad to become a priest — I will make a good priest with large eyes and high nose!" "Then you become a nun! and Kazuo a little boy priest! — how lovely he would be! We shall then every day chant the texts. Oh, a happy life!" "In the next world you shall be born a nun!"

One day we went to the temple for our usual walk. "O, O!" he exclaimed in astonishment. Three large cedars had been lying on the ground. "Why have they cut down these trees? I see the temple people seem to be poor. They are in need of money. Oh, why have they not told me about that? I should be very much pleased to give them some amount. What a long time it must have taken to grow so large from the tiny bud! I have become a little disgusted with that old priest. Pity! he has not money, though. Poor tree!" He was extremely sad and melancholily walked for home. "I feel so sad! I am no more pleasant to-day. Go and ask the people to cut no more trees," he said.

After this he did not go to the temple yard any more.

Sometime after the old priest was removed to another temple; and the younger new priest, the head of temple, began cutting trees.

His desire was to live in a little house, in some lonely suburb, with a spacious garden full of trees. I looked for several places; at Nishi Ōkubo mura I found a house of pure Japanese style and even with no foreign styled house in the neighbourhood, for his desire was to live in the midst of genuine Japan. That the house stood in a lonely suburb and that there was a bamboo bush in the rear of house pleased him much and prompted his immediate decision. Being much afraid of cold winter, he wanted to have one

THE LAST STAGE

room furnished with a stove newly built and that the library should open to the west. His library, with an adjoining room with a stove, and my sitting room were built. He left all else to my choice, saying, "I have only to write; other things I do not care for; you know better, good Mamma San!"

It was on the 19th March, 1902, that we removed on new house at Ōkubo. He used to go to university by a jinrikisha; it took about forty minutes. Our house was all furnished in Japanese fashion, except the stove and the glass-screen on account of the stove, instead of a paper-screen, in regard to that apartment.

On the day we removed I was helping him arrange books in the library. Among the bamboo woods were heard the uguisu or warbler's notes through the stillness of the place. "How happy!" he said, pleased with the new abode. "But my heart is sorry," he added. "Why?" I asked. "To be happy is a cause of anxiousness to me," he said, "I would like to live long in this house. But I do not know whether I can."

He put too much importance to Beauty or Nicety, perhaps. He was too enthusiastic for beauty, for which he wept, and for which he rejoiced, and for which he was angry. This made him shun social intercourse; this made him as if he were an eccentric person. To him meditating and writing were the sole pleasure of life; and for this he disposed of all things else. I often said: "You are too secluded in your room. Please go out when you like and find enjoyment anything you like." "You know my best enjoyment: thinking and writing. When I have things to write upon I am happy. While writing I forget all cares and anxieties. Therefore give me subjects to write. Talk to me more," he said. "I have talked you all things. I have no more story to tell you." "Therefore you go out, and when you come back home, tell me all you have seen and heard. Only reading books is not enough."

LAFCADIO HEARN

I used to tell him ghost-stories in dreary evenings, with the lamp purposely dimly lighted. He seemed always to listen as if he were withholding breath for fear. His manner, so eagerly attentive and looking fearful, made me tell the story with more emphasis. Our house was, as it were, a ghost-house on those times; I began to be haunted with fearful dreams in the night. I told him about that and he said we would stop ghost-stories for some time.

When I tell him stories I always told him at first the mere skeleton of the story. If it is interesting, he puts it down in his notebook and makes me repeat and repeat several times.

And when the story is interesting, he instantly becomes exceedingly serious; the colour of his face changes; his eyes wear the look of fearful enthusiasm.

As I went on as usual the story of Okachinsan [in the beginning of "Kotto"], his face gradually changed pale; his eyes were fixed; I felt a sudden awe. When I finished the narrative he became a little relaxed and said it was very interesting. "O blood!" he repeatedly said; and asked me several questions regarding the situations, actions, etc., involved in the story. "In what manner was 'O blood!' exclaimed? In what manner of voice? What do you think of the sound of 'geta' at that time? How was the night? I think so and so. What do you think? etc." Thus he consulted me about various things besides the original story which I told from the book. If any one happened to see us thus talking from outside, he would surely think that we were mad.

"Papa, come down; supper is ready," three children used to say altogether to him; then "All right, sweet boys," he would say, and come to the table in a cheerful manner. But when he is very much absorbed in writing, he would say, "All right," very quickly. And whenever his answer is quick, he would not come very soon. I then go to him and say: "Papa San! the children are waiting

THE LAST STAGE

for you. Please come soon, or the dishes will lose their good flavour."

"What?" he asks.

"The supper is ready, Papa."

"I do not want supper. Did n't I already take that? Funny!"

"Mercy! please awake from your dream. The little child would weep."

In such occasion, he is very forgetful; and takes bread only to himself. And children ask him to break bread for them. And he would take whiskey for wine or put salt into the cup of coffee. Before meal he took a very little quantity of whiskey. Later when his health was a little hurt he took wine.

But on usual meals we were very pleasant. He tells stories from foreign papers; I from Japanese newspapers. Kiyoshi would peep from the hole of sliding-paper screen. The cat comes; the dog come under the window; and they share some sweets he gives. After meal we used to sing songs innocently and merrily.

Often he danced or laughed heartily when he was very happy.

In one New Year's day it happened that one of the jinrikisha men of our house died suddenly while drinking sake in a narrow room near the portal of our house. The dead man was covered with a bed-covering. A guest came for wishing a happy new year to our home. The guest found that and said: "O, a drunkard sleeping on the New Year's day. A happy fellow!" The rikisha man, who sat near and was watching the dead, said in his vulgar tone: "Not a drunkard, but a Buddha!"[1] The guest was sorely astonished and went out immediately. After some days I told him this fact; he was interested to imagine the manner the guest made in astonishment. And he ordered me to repeat the conversation between the guest and the

[1] "Hotoke-sama" means the dead.

rikisha man. He often imitated the words of "Not a drunkard, but a Buddha," as being a very natural and simple utterance.

Whenever he met with a work of any art suited to his taste, he expressed an intense admiration, even for a very small work. A man with a nice and kind heart he was! We often went to see the exhibition of pictures held occasionally in Tōkyō. If he found any piece of work very interesting to him, he spoke of it as cheap though very high in price. "What do you think of that?" my husband says. "It is too much high price," I say, lest he should immediately buy it quite indifferent of prices. "No, I don't mean about prices. I mean about the picture. Do you think it is very good?" Then I answer: "Yes, a pretty picture, indeed, I think." "We shall then buy that picture," he says, "the price is however very cheap; let us offer more money for that." As to our financial matter, he was entirely trusting to me. Thus, I, the little treasurer, sometimes suffered on such occasions.

In those innocent talks of our boys he was pleased to find interesting things. In fact his utmost pleasure was to be acquainted with a thing of beauty. How he was glad to hear my stories. Alas! he is no more! though I sometimes get amusing stories, they are now no use. Formalities were the things he most disliked. His likes and dislikes were always to the extreme. When he liked something he liked extremely. He used to wear a plain cloth; only he was particular about shirts on account of cold. When he had new suit of cloth made, he wore it after my repeated entreaties. Being fond of Japanese cloth, he always puts off foreign cloth when he comes back from without, and, sitting on the cushion so pleasantly, he smokes. At Aizu in summer, he often wore bathing cloth and Japanese sandals.

He always chose the best and excellent quality of any kind of things, so in purchasing my dress, he often ordered

THE LAST STAGE

according to his taste. Sometimes he was like an innocent child. One summer we went to a store selling cloth for a bathing cloth (yukata) which I wear in summer-time. The man showed us various kinds of designs, all of which he was so very fond and bought. I said that we need not so many kinds. He said: "But think of that. Only one yen and half for a piece. Please put on various kinds of dress, which only to see is pleasant to me." He bought some thirty pieces, to the amazement of the store people.

He resented in his heart that many Japanese people, forgetting of the fact that there exist many beautiful points in things Japanese, and imitating Western style. He regretted that Japan would thus be lost. So he abhorred the foreign style which Japanese assume. He was glad that many Waseda professors wore Japanese haori and hakama. He disliked unharmonized foreign dress of Japanese lady and proud girl speaking English. We one day went to a bazar at Ueno Park. He asked the price of an article in Japanese. The storekeeper, a girl of new school, replied in English. He was displeased and drew my dress and turned away. When he became the professor of Waseda, Dean Takata invited him to his house. It was very rare that he ever accepted an invitation. At the portal, Mrs. Takata welcomed him in Japanese language. This reception greatly pleased him, so he told me when he returned home. In our home, furnitures and even the manner of maids' hair-dressing were all in genuine Japanese style. If I happened to buy some articles of foreign taste, he would say: "Don't you love Japanese arts?" He wanted our boy put on Japanese cloths and wear geta instead of shoes. Sometimes in company with him in usual walks, one of our boys would wear shoes. He say: "Mamma San, look at my toes. Don't you mind that our dear children's toes should become disfigured in such manner as mine?" As Kazuo's appearance is very much like a foreigner, he taught him English. Other boys were taught and brought up in Japanese way. We kept no interpreter since our Matsue days. A Japanese guest would come to our house in Western style and smoke cigarettes, but the host receives him in Japanese cloth and does all in Japanese fashion — a curious contrast. With one glance of his nose-glass which he keeps he catches the whole appearance of any first visitor even to the smallest details of the physiognomy. He is extremely near-sighted; and the minute he takes a glance is the whole time of his observation; still his wonderfully keen observation often astonished me.

One day I read the following story to him from a Japanese paper: "A certain nobleman's old mother is extremely fond of classical Japanese ways, absolutely antagonistic to the modern manners. The maids were to wear obi in old ways. Lamps were not allowed, but paper andō was used instead. Nor soaps were to be used in this household. So maids and servants would not endure long." Hearn was very much delighted to learn that there still existed such a family. "How I like that!" he said. "I would like to visit them." One time I said to him in joke: "You are not like Westerner, except in regard to your nose." Then he said: "What shall I do with this nose? But I am a Japanese. I love Japan better than any born Japanese."

Indeed, he loved Japan with his whole heart, but his sincere love for Japan was not very well understood by Japanese.

When asked anything to him, he would not readily accept that; but everything he did he did it with his sincere and whole heart!

One day he said to me: "Foreign people are very desirous to know of my whereabouts. Some papers have reported that Hearn disappeared from the world. What do you think of this? How funny! — disappeared from the

THE LAST STAGE

world." Thus his chief pleasure was only to write, without being disturbed from without. O, while I thus talk of my dear husband's life, I feel in myself as if I were being scolded by him why I was thus talking of him. "Where is Hearn now? He has disappeared from the world." This was his desire — unknown to the rest of the world. But though he would scold me I wish to tell about him more and more.

When he was engaged in writing he was so enthusiastically that any small noise was a great pain to him. So I always tried to keep the house still in regard to the opening and shutting of doors, the footsteps of family, etc.; and I always chose to enter his room when necessary as I heard the sound of his pipes (tobacco-smoking pipes) and his songs in a high voice. But after removal to Ōkubo, our house was wide enough and his library was very remote from the children's room and the portal. So he could enjoy his enjoyment in the world of calmness.

When writing the story of "Miminashi Hōichi," he was forgetful of the approach of evening. In the darkness of the evening twilight he was sitting on the cushion in deep thought. Outside of the paper-screens of his room, I for a trial called with a low voice, "Hōichi! Hōichi!" "Yes, I am a blind man. Who are you?" he replied from within; he had been imagining as if he himself were Hōichi with a biwa in his hand. Whenever he writes he is entirely absorbed with the subject. On those days I one day went to the city and bought a little doll of blind priest with a biwa. I put it secretly upon his desk. As he found it he was overjoyed with it and seemed as if he met an expecting friend. When a rustling noise of fallen leaves in the garden woods he said seriously: "Listen! the Heike are fallen. They are the sounds of waves at Dan-no-ura." And he listened attentively. Indeed sometimes I thought he was mad, because he seemed too frequently he saw things that were not and heard things that were not.

LAFCADIO HEARN

His life outside of the university and of his own home he narrowed down to a point where the public began to create legends about him, so seldom was he seen. The only person ever able to draw him forth was his friend Mitchell McDonald, whose sympathy and hospitality he constantly fled from and constantly yielded to. To Mrs. Fenollosa he wrote:

My friends are much more dangerous than my enemies. These latter — with infinite subtlety — spin webs to keep me out of places where I hate to go . . . and they help me so much by their unconscious aid that I almost love them. They help me to maintain the isolation absolutely essential to thinking. . . . Blessed be my enemies, and forever honoured all them that hate me!

But my friends! — ah! my friends! They speak so beautifully of my work; they say they want more of it — and yet they would destroy it! They do not know what it costs, and they would break the wings and scatter the feather-dust, even as the child that only wanted to caress the butterfly. And they speak of converse and sympathy. . . . And they say — only a day — just an afternoon — but each of them says this thing. And the sum of the days is a week of work dropped forever into the Abyss. . . . I must not even think about people's kind words and faces, but work, work, work, while the Scythe is sharpening within vision.

Under the strain of constant work his eyesight again began to fail, and in 1902 he wrote to friend in America asking for aid to find work there, desiring to consult a specialist, and to bring for instruction in English his beloved Kazuo — from whom he would never be parted for a day. He was entitled to

THE LAST STAGE

his sabbatical year of vacation from the university, and while he took advantage of it he wished to form other connections, as intrigues among those inimical to him made him fear for the tenure of his position. His family had increased by the birth of another son, and his responsibilities — with weakening lungs and eyesight — began to weigh heavily on his mind. An arrangement was made for him to lecture for a season in Cornell University at a salary of twenty-five hundred dollars, and these lectures he at once began to prepare. When, however, he applied for leave, it was refused him, and an incident occurring at this juncture, of the intrusion of an English traveller into his classroom during one of his lectures — an incident which had its origin in mere curiosity — seemed to his exacerbated imagination to have a significance out of all proportion to its real meaning; and convinced that it was intended as a slight by the authorities in their purpose to be rid of him, he resigned. The students — aware that influences were at work to rob him of his place — made some demonstrations of resentment, but finally abandoned them at his personal request.

He plunged more deeply, at once, into the preparation of his work for the American lectures, but shortly before he was to have sailed for America the authorities at Cornell withdrew from their contract on the plea that the epidemic of typhoid at Ithaca the previous summer had depleted the funds at their command.

LAFCADIO HEARN

Vigorous efforts were at once undertaken by his friends in America to repair this breach of contract by finding him employment elsewhere, with but partial success, but all these efforts were rendered useless by a sudden and violent illness, attended by bleeding from the lungs, and brought on by strain and anxiety. After his recovery the lectures prepared for Cornell were recast to form a book, but the work proved a desperate strain upon already weakened forces.

Mrs. Hearn says this:

Of his works, "Japan: an Interpretation" seemed a great labour to him. So hard a task it was that he said at one occasion: "It is not difficult that this book will kill me." At another time he said: "You can imagine how hard it is to write such a big book in so short a time with no helper." To write was his life; and all care and difficulties he forgot while writing. As he had no work of teaching in the university, he poured forth all his forces in the work of "Japan."

When the manuscripts of "Japan" were completed, he was very glad and had them packed in strong shape and wrote addresses upon the cover for mail. He was eagerly looking forward to see the new volume. A little before his death he still said that he could imagine that he could hear the sound of type-work of "Japan" in America. But he was unable to see the book in his lifetime.

To me he wrote, in that lassitude always following on the completion of creative work:

The "rejected addresses" will shortly appear in book form. I don't like the work of writing a serious treatise on sociology. . . . I ought to keep to the study of birds and

THE LAST STAGE

cats and insects and flowers, and queer small things — and leave the subject of the destiny of empires to men with brains.

Despite which verdict he probably recognized it as the crowning achievement of his long effort to interpret his adopted country to the world.

Shortly after its completion he accepted the offer of the chair of English in the Waseda University, founded by Count Okuma, for he was expecting again to be a father and his pen was unable to meet all the demands upon his income. Meantime the University of London had entered into negotiation with him for a series of lectures, and it was suggested that Oxford also wished to hear him. It had always been the warmest of his desires to win recognition from his own country, and these offers were perhaps the greatest satisfaction he had ever known. But his forces were completely exhausted. The desperate hardships of his youth, the immense labours of his manhood, had burned away the sources of vitality.

On the 26th of September, 1904 — shortly after completing the last letter included in these volumes, to Captain Fujisaki, who was then serving on Marshal Ōyama's staff — while walking on the veranda in the twilight he sank down suddenly as if the whole fabric of life had crumbled within, and after a little space of speechlessness and pain, his long quest was over.

In "Kwaidan" he had written:

LAFCADIO HEARN

I should like, when my time comes, to be laid away in some Buddhist graveyard of the ancient kind, so that my ghostly company should be ancient, caring nothing for the fashions and the changes and the disintegrations of Meiji. That old cemetery behind my garden would be a suitable place. Everything there is beautiful with a beauty of exceeding and startling queerness; each tree and stone has been shaped by some old, old ideal which no longer exists in any living brain; even the shadows are not of this time and sun, but of a world forgotten, that never knew steam or electricity or magnetism. . . . Also in the boom of the big bell there is a quaintness of tone which wakens feelings so strangely far away from all the nineteenth-century part of me that the faint blind stirrings of them make me afraid — deliciously afraid. Never do I hear that billowing peal but I become aware of a striving and a fluttering in the abyssal part of my ghost — a sensation as of memories struggling to reach the light beyond the obscurations of a million million deaths and births. I hope to remain within hearing of that bell.

In so far as was possible this was complied with. Though not a Buddhist he was buried according to Buddhist rites. One who was present at his funeral thus describes it:

The procession left his residence, 266 Nishi Ōkubo, at half past one and proceeded to the Jitō-in Kobu-dera Temple in Ichigaya. . . . First came the bearers of white lanterns and wreaths and great pyramidal bouquets of asters and chrysanthemums; next, men carrying long poles from which hung streamers of paper gohei; after them two boys in 'rickshas carrying little cages containing birds to be released, symbols of the soul released from its earthly prison. . . .

The emblems were all Buddhist. The portable hearse,

THE LAST STAGE

carried by six men in blue, was a beautiful object of unpainted, perfectly fresh, white wood trimmed with blue silk tassels and with gold and silver lotus flowers at the corners.... Priests carrying food for the dead, university professors, and a multitude of students formed the end of the procession.... In the comparative darkness of the temple, against the background of black lacquer and gold, eight priests chanted a dirge. Their heads were cleanshaven and they were clothed in white, with several brilliantly tinted gauze robes imposed. After a period of chanting punctuated by the tinkling of a bell, the chief Japanese mourner arose from the other side and led forward the son. Together they knelt before the hearse, touching their foreheads to the floor, and placing some grains of incense upon the little brazier burning between the candles. A delicate perfume filled the air.... The wife next stepped forward with expressionless face — her hair done in stiff loops like carved ebony, her only ornament the magnificent white obi, reserved for weddings and funerals. She and the younger sons also burned incense. The chief mourner and the eldest son again bowed to the ground, and the ceremony was ended.

The students presented a laurel wreath with the inscription "In memory of Lafcadio Hearn, whose pen was mightier than the sword of the victorious nation which he loved and lived among, and whose highest honour it is to have given him citizenship and, alas, a grave!" The body was then removed to a crematory, the ashes being interred at the cemetery of Zōshigaya, his tombstone bearing the inscription "Shōgaku In-den Jō-ge Hachi-un Koji," which literally translated means: "Believing Man Similar to Undefiled Flower Blooming like Eight

LAFCADIO HEARN

Rising Clouds, who dwells in Mansion of Right Enlightenment."

Amenomori — whom he called "the finest type of the Japanese man" — writing of him after his death, said:

Like a lotus the man was in his heart . . . a poet, a thinker, loving husband and father, and sincere friend. . . . Within that man there burned something pure as the vestal fire, and in that flame dwelt a mind that called forth life and poetry out of the dust, and grasped the highest themes of human thought.

Yone Noguchi wrote:

Surely we could lose two or three battleships at Port Arthur rather than Lafcadio Hearn.

After his death were issued a few of his last studies of Japan under the title of "A Romance of the Milky Way," and these, with his autobiographical fragments included in this volume, conclude his work. The last of these fragments, three small pages, is named "Illusion":

An old, old sea-wall, stretching between two boundless levels, green and blue; — on the right only rice-fields, reaching to the sky-line; — on the left only summer-silent sea, where fishing-craft of curious shapes are riding. Everything is steeped in white sun; and I am standing on the wall. Along its broad and grass-grown top a boy is running toward me — running in sandals of wood — the sea-breeze blowing aside the long sleeves of his robe as he runs, and baring his slender legs to the knee. Very fast he runs, springing upon his sandals; — and he has in his hands something to show me: a black dragon-fly, which

Iwao and Kyoshi, the Second and Third Sons of Hearn

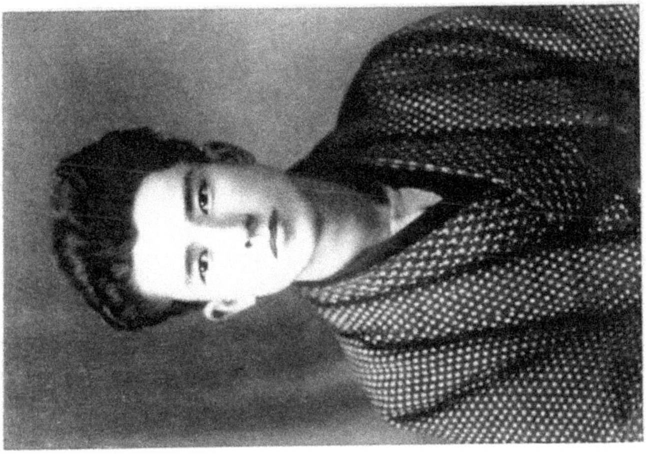

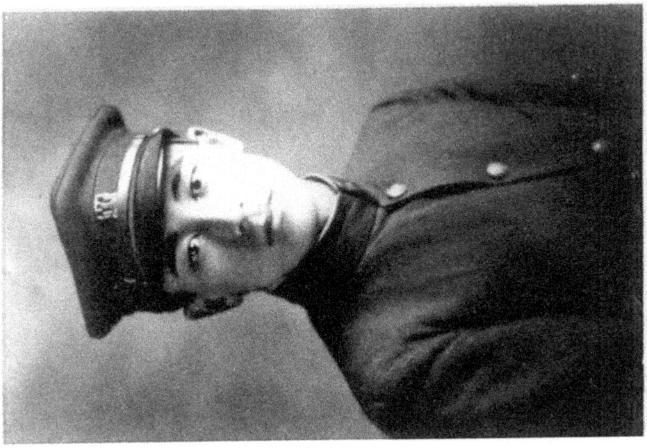

THE LAST STAGE

he is holding carefully by the wings, lest it should hurt itself struggling. ... With what sudden incommunicable pang do I watch the gracious little figure leaping in the light — between those summer silences of field and sea! ... A delicate boy, with the blended charm of two races. ... And how softly vivid all things under this milky radiance — the smiling child-face with lips apart — the twinkle of the light quick feet — the shadows of grasses and of little stones! ...

But, quickly as he runs, the child will come no nearer to me — the slim brown hand will never cling to mine. For this light is the light of a Japanese sun that set long years ago. ... Never, dearest! — never shall we meet — not even when the stars are dead!

And yet — can it be possible that I shall not remember? — that I shall not still see, in other million summers, the same sea-wall under the same white moon — the same shadows of grasses and of little stones — the running of the same little sandalled feet that will never, never reach my side?

The compression found necessary in order to yield room for the letters, which I think will bear comparison with the most famous letters in literature, has forced me to content myself with depicting the man merely in profile and giving a bare outline of his work as an artist. It has obliged me to abandon all temptation to dwell upon his more human side, his humour, tenderness, sympathy, eccentricity, and the thousand queer, charming qualities that made up his many-faceted nature. These omissions are in great part supplied by the letters themselves, where he turns different sides of his mind to each correspondent, and where one sees in consequence a shadow of the writers themselves reflected in his own mental attitude.

In the turbid, shallow flood of the ephemeral books of our time, Lafcadio Hearn's contribution to English letters has been partially obscured. But day by day, as these sink unfruitfully into the sands of time, more clearly emerge the stern and exquisite outlines of his patient work. While still a boy he said playfully, in answer to an appeal to concede something to the vulgarer taste for the sake of popularity: "I shall stick to my pedestal of faith in literary possibilities like an Egyptian Colossus with a broken nose, seated solemnly in the gloom of my own originality."

To that creed he held through all the bitter permutations of life, and at the end it may be fitly said of him that, "despite perishing principles and decaying conventions, despite false teaching, false triumphs, and false taste, there were yet those who strove for the immemorial grandeur of their calling, who pandered to no temptation from without or from within, who followed none of the great world-voices, were dazzled by none of the great world-lights, and used their gift as stepping-stone to no meaner life; but clear-eyed and patient, neither elated nor cast down, still lifted the lamp as high as their powers allowed, still pursued art singly for her own immortal sake."

LETTERS OF LAFCADIO HEARN
1877-1886

LETTERS
1877-1886
. .

TO H. E. KREHBIEL

NEW ORLEANS, 1877 [1]

DEAR KREHBIEL, — I have just received your second pleasant letter, enclosing a most interesting article on music. The illustrations interested me greatly. You could write a far more entertaining series of essays on the history of musical instruments than that centennial humbug who, as you say, did little more than merely to describe what he saw.

I have been reading in "Curiosités des Arts" — a curious book now out of print — an article on the musical instruments of the Middle Ages, which is of deep interest even to such an ignoramus as myself. I would have translated it for your amusement, but that my eyes have been so bad as to cripple me. Let me just give you an extract, and as soon as I feel better I will send the whole thing if you deem it worth while:

The Romans, at the termination of their conquests, had brought to this country and adopted nearly all the musical instruments they had discovered among the peo-

[1] Hearn rarely dated his letters, but in most cases internal evidence makes possible the assignment of a fairly definite date.

ples they had conquered. Thus Greece furnished Rome with nearly all the soft instruments of the family of flutes and of lyres; Germany and the provinces of the North, inhabited by warlike races, taught their conquerors to acquire a taste for terrible instruments, of the family of trumpets and of drums; Asia, and in particular Judæa, which had greatly multiplied the number of metallic instruments for use in ceremonies of religion, naturalized among the Romans clashing instruments of the family of bells and tam-tams; Egypt introduced the sistrum into Italy together with the worship of Isis; and no sooner had Byzantium invented the first wind organs than the new religion of Christ adopted them, that she might consecrate them exclusively to the solemnities of her worship, West and East.

All the varieties of instruments in the known world had thus, in some sort, taken refuge in the capital of the Empire; first at Rome, then at Byzantium; when the Roman decline marked the last hour of this vast concert, then, at once ceased the orations of the Emperors in the Capitol and the festivals of the pagan gods in the temples; then were silenced and scattered those musical instruments which had taken part in the pomps of trumphs or of religious celebrations; then disappeared and became forgotten a vast number of those instruments which pagan civilization had made use of, but which became useless amidst the ruins of the antique social system.

Following is the description of an organ — a wonderful organ — in a letter from Saint Jerome to Dardanas — made of fifteen pipes of brass, two air-reservoirs of elephant's skin, and two forge bellows for the imitation of the sound of thunder. The writer compiled his essay from eighteen ancient Latin authors, eight early Italian, about ten early

Lafcadio Hearn, from a Photograph taken about 1873

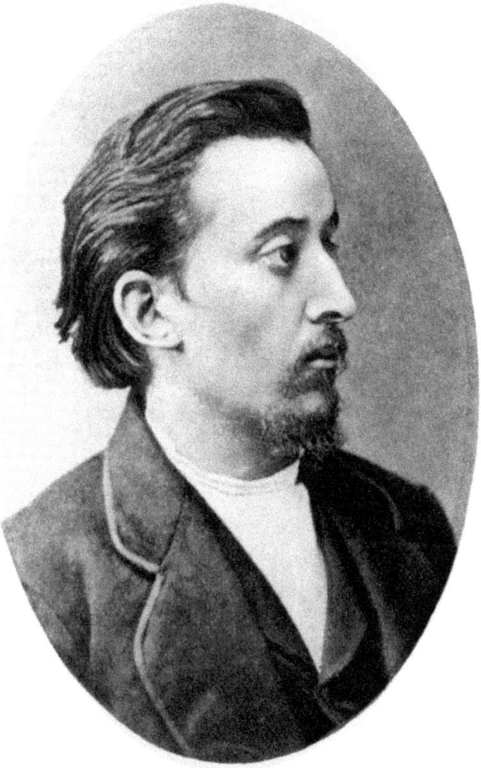

TO H. E. KREHBIEL

French, and some Spanish authors — all antiquated and unfamiliar.

As you are kindly interested in what I am doing I shall talk about EGO — I shall talk about ME.

I am (this is not for public information) barely making a living here by my letters to the paper. I think I can make about forty dollars per month. This will keep me alive and comfortable. I am determined never to resume local work on a newspaper. I could not stand the gaslight; and then you know what a horrid life it is.

While acting as correspondent I shall have time to study, study, study; and to write something better than police news. I have a lot of work mapped out for magazine essays; and though I never expect to make much money, I think I shall be able to make a living. So far I have had a real hard time; but I hope to do better now, as they send me money more regularly.

I do not intend to leave New Orleans, except for farther South — the West Indies, or South America. I am studying Spanish hard and will get along well with it soon.

I think I can redeem myself socially here. I have got into good society; and as everybody is poor in the South, my poverty is no drawback.

        Yours truly

                        Λαϝκαδιη

LAFCADIO HEARN

TO H. E. KREHBIEL

NEW ORLEANS, 1877

MY DEAR KREHBIEL, — I am charmed with your letter — your paper, and your exquisite little jocose programme. The "Fantaisie Chinoise" was to me something that really smacked of a certain famous European art-cenacle where delightful little parties of this kind were given. That cenacle was established by the disciples of Victor Hugo — les Hugolâtres, as they were mockingly but perhaps also nobly named; and the records of its performances are some of the most delicate things in French literature. Hector Berlioz was one of the merry crowd — and Berlioz, by the way, had written some fine romances as well as fine musical compositions.

There is a touch, a brilliant touch, of real art in all these little undertakings of yours, which gives me more enjoyment than I could tell you. Remember I am speaking of the tout-ensemble. Were I to make any musical observations you might rightly think I was talking about something of which I am disgracefully ignorant. Do you know, however, that I have never forgotten that pretty Chinese melody I heard at the club that day; and I sometimes find myself whistling it involuntarily.

I am indeed delighted to know that you have got Char Lee's instruments, and are soon to receive others. Were there any Indian instruments in use among the Choctaws here, I could get you some, but

TO H. E. KREHBIEL

they are no longer a musical people. The sadness that seems peculiar to dying races could not be more evident than in them. Le Père Rouquette, their missionary, tells me he has seen them laugh; but that might have been half a century ago. He is going to take me out to one of their camps on Lake Pontchartrain soon, and I shall try to pick you up something queer.

As yet I have not received the Chinese Play, etc., but will write when I do, and return it as promptly as possible.

I am just recovering from a week's sickness — fever and bloody flux — and I don't believe I weigh ninety pounds. You never saw such a sight as I am. I have been turned nearly black; and my face is so thin that I can see every bone as if it had only a piece of parchment drawn over it. And then all my hair is cut close to the skin. I have had hard work to crawl out of bed the last few days, but am getting better now. If I were to get regular yellow fever now I would certainly go to the cemetery; for I am only a skeleton as it is.

The newspaper generally gives only wages to its employees, and small wages — and literary reputation to its capitalists; although in France the opposite condition exists. There are exceptions, of course, when a man has exceedingly superior talent; and his employer, knowing its value, allows its free exercise. That has been your case to a certain degree; you have not only won a reputation for yourself, but have given a tone and a standing to the paper which in my opinion has been of immense value to it.

I have got everything here down to a fine point — three hours' work a day!

There is but one thing here to compensate for the abominable heat — Figs. They are remarkably cool, sweet, juicy, and tender. Unfortunately they are too delicate to bear shipment. The climate is so debilitating that even energetic *thought* is out of the question; and unfortunately the only inspiring hour, the cool night, I cannot utilize on account of gaslight. When the night comes on here, it is not the night of Northern summers, but that night of which the divine Greek poet wrote — "O holy night, how well dost thou harmonize with me; for to me thou art all eye — thou art all ear — thou art all fragrance!"

The infinite gulf of blue above seems a shoreless sea, whose foam is stars, a myriad million lights are throbbing and flickering and palpitating, a vast stillness filled with perfume prevails over the land — made only more impressive by the voices of the night-birds and crickets; and all the busy voices of business are dead. The boats are laid up, cotton presses closed, and the city is half empty. So that the time is really inspiring. But I must wait to record the inspiration in some more energetic climate.

Do you get "Mélusine" yet? You are missing a great deal if you are not. "Mélusine" is preserving all those curious peasant songs with their music —

TO H. E. KREHBIEL

some of which date back hundreds of years. They would be a delightful relish to you.

   Yours à jamais

       L. Hearn

TO H. E. KREHBIEL

NEW ORLEANS, 1877

"O-ME-TAW-BOODH!" — Have I not indeed been much bewitched by thine exotic comedy, which hath the mild perfume and yellow beauty of a Chinese rose? Assuredly I have been enchanted by the Eastern fragrance of thy many-coloured brochure; for mine head "is not as yellow as mud." In thy next epistle, however, please to enlighten my soul in regard to the mystic title-phrase — "Remodelled from the original English"; for I have been wearing out the iron shoes of patience in my vain endeavour to comprehend it. What I most desired, while perusing the play, was that I might have been able to hear the musical interludes — the barbaric beauty of the melodies — and the plaintive sadness of thy serpent-skinned instruments. I shall soon return the MSS. to thy hands.

By the bye, did you ever hear a *real* Chinese gong? I don't mean a d——d hotel gong, but one of those great moon-disks of yellow metal which have so terrible a power of utterance. A gentleman in Bangor, North Wales, who had a private museum of South Pacific and Chinese curiosities, exhibited one to me. It was hanging amidst Fiji spears beautifully barbed

LAFCADIO HEARN

with shark's teeth, which, together with grotesque New Zealand clubs of green stone and Sandwich Island paddles wrought with the baroque visages of the Shark-God, were depending from the walls. Also there were Indian elephants in ivory, carrying balls in their carven bellies, each ball containing many other balls inside it. The gong glimmered pale and huge and yellow, like the moon rising over a Southern swamp. My friend tapped its ancient face with a muffled drumstick, and it commenced to sob, like waves upon a low beach. He tapped it again, and it moaned like the wind in a mighty forest of pines. Again, and it commenced to roar, and with each tap the roar grew deeper and deeper, till it seemed like thunder rolling over an abyss in the Cordilleras, or the crashing of Thor's chariot wheels. It was awful, and astonishing as awful. I assure you I did not laugh at it at all. It impressed me as something terrible and mysterious. I vainly sought to understand how that thin, thin disk of trembling metal could produce so frightful a vibration. He informed me that it was very expensive, being chiefly made of the most precious metals — silver and gold.

Let me give you a description of my new residence. I never knew what the beauty of an old Creole home was until now. I do not believe one could find anything more picturesque outside of Venice or Florence. For six months I had been trying to get a room in one of these curious buildings; but the rents seemed to me maliciously enormous. However, I at last ob-

TO H. E. KREHBIEL

tained one for three dollars per week. Yet it is on the third floor, rear building; — these old princes of the South built always double edifices, covering an enormous space of ground, with broad wings, courtyards, and slave quarters.

The building is on Saint Louis Street, a street several hundred years old. I enter by a huge archway about a hundred feet long — full of rolling echoes, and commencing to become verdant with a thin growth of bright moss. At the end, the archway opens into a court. There are a few graceful bananas here with their giant leaves splitting in ribbons in the summer sun, so that they look like young palms. Lord! How the carriages must have thundered under that archway and through the broad paved court in the old days. The stables are here still; but the blooded horses are gone, and the family carriage, with its French coat of arms, has disappeared. There is only a huge wagon left to crumble to pieces. A hoary dog sleeps like a stone sphinx at a corner of the broad stairway; and I fancy that in his still slumbers he might be dreaming of a Creole master who went out with Beauregard or Lee and never came back again. Wonder if the great greyhound is waiting for him.

The dog never notices me. I am not of his generation, and I creep quietly by lest I might disturb his dreams of the dead South. I go up the huge stairway. At every landing a vista of broad archways reëchoes my steps — archways that once led to rooms worthy of a prince. But the rooms are now cold and cheerless and vast with emptiness. Tinted in pale green or yellow, with a ceiling moulded with Renaissance figures in plaster, the ghost of luxury and wealth seems trying to linger in them. I pass them by, and taking my way through an archway on the right, find myself on a broad piazza, at the end of which is my room.

It is vast enough for a Carnival ball. Five windows and glass doors open flush with the floor and rise to the ceilings. They open on two sides upon the piazza, whence I have a far view of tropical gardens and masses of building, half-ruined but still magnificent. The walls are tinted pale orange colour; green curtains drape the doors and windows; and the mantelpiece, surmounted by a long oval mirror of Venetian pattern, is of white marble veined like the bosom of a Naiad. In the centre of the huge apartment rises a bed as massive as a fortress, with tremendous columns of carved mahogany supporting a curtained canopy at the height of sixteen feet. It seems to touch the ceiling, yet it does not. There is no carpet on the floor, no pictures on the wall — a sense of something dead and lost fills the place with a gentle melancholy; — the breezes play fantastically with the pallid curtains, and the breath of flowers ascends into the chamber from the verdant gardens below. Oh, the silence of this house, the perfume, and the romance of it. A beautiful young Frenchwoman appears once a day in my neighbourhood to ar-

TO H. E. KREHBIEL

range the room; but she comes like a ghost and disappears too soon in the recesses of the awful house. I would like to speak with her, for her lips drop honey, and her voice is richly sweet like the cooing of a dove. "O my dove, that art in the clefts of the rock, in the secret hiding-places of the stairs, let me see thy face, let me hear thy voice, for thy voice is sweet and thy countenance is comely!"

Let me tell thee, O Bard of the Harp of a Thousand Strings, concerning a Romance of Georgia. I heard of it among the flickering shadow of steamboat smoke and the flapping of sluggish sails. It has a hero greater, I think, than Bludso; but his name is lost. At least it is lost in Southern history; yet perhaps it may be recorded on the pages of a great book whose leaves never turn yellow with Time, and whose letters are eternal as the stars. But the reason his name is not known is because he was a "d——d nigger."

TO H. E. KREHBIEL

NEW ORLEANS, 1878

MY DEAR MUSICIAN, — I wrote you such a shabby, disjointed letter last week that I feel I ought to make up for it — especially after your newsy, fresh, pleasant letter to me, which came like a cool Northern breeze speaking of life, energy, success, and strong hopes.

I am very much ashamed that I have not yet been able to keep all my promises to you. There is that

Creole music I had hoped to get copied by Saturday, and could not succeed in obtaining. But it is only delayed, I assure you; and New Orleans is going to produce a treat for you soon. George Cable, a charming writer, some of whose dainty New Orleans stories you may have read in "Scribner's Monthly," is writing a work containing a study of Creole music, in which the songs are given, with the musical text in footnotes. I have helped Cable a little in collecting the songs; but he has the advantage of me in being able to write music by ear. Scribner will publish the volume. This is not, of course, for publicity.

My new journalistic life may interest you — it is so different from anything in the North. I have at last succeeded in getting right into the fantastic heart of the French quarter, where I hear the antiquated dialect all day long. Early in the morning I visit a restaurant, where I devour a plate of figs, a cup of black coffee, a dish of cream-cheese — not the Northern stuff, but a delightful cake of pressed milk floating in cream — a couple of corn muffins, and an egg. This is a heavy breakfast here, but costs only about twenty-five cents. Then I slip down to the office, and rattle off a couple of leaders on literary or European matters and a few paragraphs based on telegraphic news. This occupies about an hour. Then the country papers — half French, half English — altogether barbarous, come in from all the wild, untamed parishes of Louisiana. Madly I seize

TO H. E. KREHBIEL

the scissors and the paste-pot and construct a column of crop-notes. This occupies about half an hour. Then the New York dailies make their appearance. I devour their substance and take notes for the ensuing day's expression of opinion. And then the work is over, and the long golden afternoon welcomes me forth to enjoy its perfume and its laziness. It would be a delightful existence for one without ambition or hope of better things. On Sunday the brackish Lake Pontchartrain offers the attraction of a long swim, and I like to avail myself of it. Swimming in the Mississippi is dangerous on account of great fierce fish, the alligator-gars, which attack a swimmer with ferocity. An English swimmer was bitten by one only the other day in the river, and, losing his presence of mind, was swept under a barge and drowned.

 Folks here tell me now that I have been sick I have nothing more to fear, and will soon be acclimatized. If acclimatization signifies becoming a bundle of sharp bones and saddle-coloured parchment, I have no doubt of it at all. It is considered dangerous here to drink much water in summer. For five cents one can get half a bottle of strong claret, and this you mix with your drinking-water, squeezing a lemon into it. Limes are better, but harder to get — you can only buy them when schooners come in from the Gulf Islands. But no one knows how delicious lemonade can be made until he has tasted lemonade made of limes.

LAFCADIO HEARN

I saw a really pleasing study for an artist this morning. A friend accompanied me to the French market, and we bought an enormous quantity of figs for about fifteen cents. We could not half finish them; and we sought rest under the cool, waving shadow of a eunuch banana-tree in the Square. As I munched and munched a half-naked boy ran by — a fellow that would have charmed Murillo, with a skin like a new cent in colour, and heavy masses of hair massed as tastefully as if sculptured in ebony. I threw a fig at him and hit him in the back. He ate it, and coolly walked toward us with his little bronze hands turned upward and opened to their fullest capacity, and a pair of great black eyes flashed a request for more. You never saw such a pair of eyes — deep and dark — a night without a moon. Spoke to him in English — no answer; in French — no response. My friend bounced him with "Spak-ne Italiano," or something of that kind, but it was no good. We asked him by signs where he came from, and he pointed to a rakish lugger rocking at the Picayune pier. I filled his little brown hands with figs, but he did not smile. He gravely thanked us with a flash of the eye like a gleam of a black opal, and murmured, "Ah, mille gratias, Señor." Why, that boy *was* Murillo's boy after all, propria persona. He departed to the rakish lugger, and we dreamed of Moors and gipsies under the emasculated banana.

L. HEARN

TO H. E. KREHBIEL

TO H. E. KREHBIEL

NEW ORLEANS, 1878

MY DEAR KREHBIEL, — Your letter took a long week to reach me; perhaps by reason of the quarantine regulations which interpose some extraordinary barriers, little Chinese walls, across the country below Memphis. Thus am I somewhat tardy in responding.

The same sentiment which caused me so much pleasure on reading your ideas on the future of musical philosophy occasioned something of sincere regret on reading your words — "I am not a thoroughly educated musician," etc. I had hoped (and still hope, and believe with all my heart, dear Krehbiel) that the Max Müller of Music would be none other than yourself. Perhaps you will therefore pardon some little observations from one who knows nothing about music.

I fancy that you have penetrated just so far into the Temple of your Art that, like one of the initiates of Eleusis, you commence to experience such awe and reverence for its solemn vastness and its whispers of mystery as tempt you to forego further research. You suddenly forget how much farther you have advanced into the holy precincts than most mortals, who seldom cross the vestibule; — the more you advance the more seemingly infinite becomes the vastness of the place, the more interminable its vistas of arches, and the more mysterious its endless successions of aisles. The Vatican with its sixty thousand rooms is but a child's toy house compared with but one of the countless wings of Art's infinite temples; and the outer world, viewing only the entrance, narrow and low as that of a pyramid, can no more comprehend the Illimitable that lies beyond it than they can measure the deeps of the Eternities beyond the fixed stars. I cannot help believing that the little shadow of despondency visible in your last letter is an evidence of how thoroughly you have devoted yourself to Music, and a partial contradiction of your own words. It would be irrational in you to expect that you could achieve your purposes in the very blush of manhood, as it were; but you ought not to forget altogether that you already stand in knowledge on a footing with many grey-haired disciples and apostles of the art, whose names are familiar in musical literature. I believe you can become anything musical you desire to become; but in art-study one must devote one's whole life to self-culture, and can only hope at last to have climbed a little higher and advanced a little farther than anybody else. You should feel the determination of those neophytes of Egypt who were led into subterranean vaults and suddenly abandoned in darkness and rising water, whence there was no escape save by an iron ladder. As the fugitive mounted through heights of darkness, each rung of the quivering stairway gave way immediately he had quitted it, and fell back into the abyss, echoing; but the

TO H. E. KREHBIEL

least exhibition of fear or weariness was fatal to the climber.

It seems to me that want of confidence in one's self is not less a curse than it appears to be a consequence of knowledge. You hesitate to accept a position on the ground of your own feeling of inadequacy; and the one who fills it is somebody who does not know the rudiments of his duty. "Fools rush in," etc., and were you to decline the situation proffered by Mr. Thomas, merely because you don't think yourself qualified to fill it, I hope you do not imagine that any better scholar will fill the bill. On the contrary, I believe that some d——d quack would take the position, even at a starvation salary, and actually make himself a reputation on the mere strength of cheek and ignorance. However, you tell me of many other reasons. Of course, —— is a vast and varied ass — a piebald quack of the sort who makes respectability an apology for lack of brains; but I fancy that you would be sure to find some asses at the head of any institution of the sort in this country. The demand for art of any kind is new, and so long as people cannot tell the difference between a quack and a scholar the former, having the cheek of a mule and a pompous deportment, is bound to get his work in. I don't think I should care much about the plans and actions of such people, but content myself, were I in your place, by showing myself superior to them. There is one thing in regard to a position like that you speak of — it would afford you large opportunity for study, and in fact compel study upon you as a public instructor. At least it seems so to me. Then, again, remember that your connection with the "Gazette" leaves you in the position of the Arabian prince who was marbleized from his loins down. As an artist you are but half alive there; one half of your existence is paralyzed; you waste your energies in the creation of works which are coffined within twelve hours after their birth; your power of usefulness is absorbed in a direction which can give you no adequate reward hereafter; and the little time you can devote to your studies and your really valuable work is too often borrowed from sleep. From the daily press I think you have obtained about all you will get from it in the regard of reputation, etc.; and there is no future really worth seeking in it. Even the most successful editors live a sort of existence which I certainly do not envy, and I am sure you would soon sicken of. Do you not think, too, that any situation like that now offered you might lead to a far better one under far better conditions? It would certainly introduce you to many whose friendship and appreciation would be invaluable. I do not believe that Cincinnati is your true field for future work, and I cannot persuade myself that the city will ever become a *permanent* artistic centre; but I am satisfied that you will drift out of the newspaper drudgery before long, and if you have an opportunity to obtain a good footing in the East, I would take it. Thomas ought to be capable of making an Eastern pedestal for you to light on; for,

TO H. E. KREHBIEL

judging by the admiration expressed for him by the "Times," "Tribune," "World," "Herald," "Sun," etc., he must have some influence with musical centres. Then Europe would be open to you in a short time with its extraordinary opportunities of art-study, and its treasures of musical literature, to be devoured free of cost. Your researches into the archæology of music, I need hardly say, must be made in Europe rather than here; and I hope you will before many twelvemonths be devouring the Musical Department of the British Museum, and the libraries of Paris and the Eternal City.

However, I do not pretend to be an adviser — only a *suggester*. I think your good little wife would be a good adviser; for women seem blessed with a kind of divine intuition, and I sometimes believe they can see much farther into the future than men. You must not get disgusted with my long letter. I could not help telling you what interest your last excited in me regarding your own prospects.

Let me tell you something that I have been thinking about the bagpipe. Somewhere or other I have read that the bagpipe was a Roman military instrument, and was introduced into Scotland by the Roman troops, together with the "kilt." It must have occurred to you that the Highland dress bears a ghostly resemblance to that of the Roman private as exhibited on the Column of Trajan. I cannot remember where I have read this, but you can doubtless inform me.

LAFCADIO HEARN

I am still well, although I have even had the experience of nursing a friend sick of yellow fever. The gods are sparing me for some fantastic reason. I enclose some specimens of the death notices which sprinkle our town, and send a copy of the last "Item."

My eyes are eternally played out, and I shall have to abandon newspaper work altogether before long. Perhaps I shall do better in some little business. What is eternally rising up before me now like a spectre is the? — "Where shall I go? — what shall I do?" Sometimes I think of Europe, sometimes of the West Indies — of Florida, France, or the wilderness of London. The time is not far off when I must go somewhere — if it is not to join the "Innumerable Caravan." Whenever I go down to the wharves, I look at the white-winged ships. O ye messengers, swift Hermæ of Traffic, ghosts of the infinite ocean, whither will ye bear me? — what destiny will ye bring me — what hopes, what despairs?

Your sincere friend and admirer

L. Hearn

TO H. E. KREHBIEL

New Orleans, 1878

My dear Krehbiel, — I received your admirable little sketch. It pleased me more that the others — perhaps because, having to deal with a simpler subject, you were less hampered by mechanical details and could maintain your light, gossipy, fresh method of instruction in all its simple force.

TO H. E. KREHBIEL

I recognized several of the cuts. That of the uppermost figure at the right-hand corner was of the god Terminus, a most ancient deity, and his instrument is of corresponding antiquity perhaps, although in country districts the Termina were generally characterized by a certain sylvan rudeness. The earliest Termina were mere blocks of wood or stone. Among the ancients a circle of ground, or square border — it was set by law in Rome at two feet wide — surrounded every homestead. This was inviolate to the gods, and the Termina were placed at intervals along its borders, or at the corners. At certain days in the year the proprietor made the circuit, pushing victims before him, and chanting hymns to the god of boundaries. The same gods existed among the ancient Hindoos, with whom the Greeks and Romans must have had a close relationship in remote antiquity. The Greeks called these deities the θεοὶ ὅριοι. I do not know whence you got the figure; but I know it is a common one of Terminus; and such eau-forte engravers as Gessner, who excelled in antique subjects, delighted to introduce it in sylvan scenes. I have an engraving by Leopold Flameng — called "La Satyresse" — a female satyr playing on the double flute (charming figure) and old Terminus with his single flute accompanies her in the background — smiling from his pedestal of stone.

The first flute-player on the left-hand side, at the lower corner, is evidently from a vase, as the treatment of the hair denotes — I should say a Greek vase; and the second one, with the mouth-bandage, in spite of the half-Egyptian face, appears to be an Etruscan figure. The treatment of the eyes and profile looks Etruscan. Some of the flutes in the upper part of the drawing are much more complicated than I had supposed any of the antique flutes were.

You will find a charming version of the Medusa story in Kingsley's "Heroes" — for little ones. Of course he does not tell why Medusa's hair was turned into snakes. There are several other versions of the legend. I prefer that in which the sword is substituted for the sickle — a most unwarlike weapon, and a utensil, moreover, sacred to the Goddess of Harvests. The sword given by Hermes to Perseus is said to have been that wherewith he slew the monster Argus — a diamond blade. Like the Runic swords forged by the gnomes under the roots of the hills of Scandinavia, this weapon slew whenever brandished.

Fever is bad still. I had another attack of dengue, but have got nearly over it. I find lemon-juice the best remedy. All over town there are little white notices pasted on the lamp-posts or the pillars of piazzas, bearing the dismal words:

Décédé
Ce matin, à 3½ heures
Julien
Natif de ——

and so on. The death notices are usually surmounted

TO H. E. KREHBIEL

by an atrocious cut of a weeping widow sitting beneath a weeping willow — with a huge mausoleum in the background. Yellow fever deaths occur every day close by. Somebody is advocating firing off cannon as a preventive. This plan of shooting Yellow Jack was tried in '53 without success. It brings on rain; but a rainy day always heralds an increase of the plague. You will see by the "Item's" tabulated record that there is a curious periodicity in the increase. It might be described by a line like this —

[wavy line drawing showing graduated pulsations]

You have doubtless seen the records of pulsations made by a certain instrument, for detecting the rapidity of blood-circulation. The fever actually appears to have a pulsation of graduated increase like that of a feverish vein. I think this demonstrates a regularity in the periods of germ incubation — affected, of course, more or less by atmospheric changes.

Hope you will have your musical talks republished in book form. Send us "Golden Hours" once in a while. It will always have a warm notice in the "Item." Yours in much hurry, with promise of another epistle soon.

L. HEARN

Regards to all the boys.

LAFCADIO HEARN

TO H. E. KREHBIEL

NEW ORLEANS, 1878

MY DEAR KREHBIEL, — I received yours, with the kind wishes of Mrs. Krehbiel, which afforded me more pleasure than I can tell you — also the "Golden Hours" with your instructive article on the history of the piano. It occurs to me that when completed your musical essays would form a delightful little volume, and ought certainly to find a first-class publisher. I hope you will entertain the suggestion, if it has not already occurred to you. I do not know very much about musical literature; but I fancy that no work in the English tongue has been published of a character so admirably suited to give young people a sound knowledge of the romantic history of music intruments as your essays would constitute, if shaped into a volume. The closing observations of your essay, markedly original and somewhat startling, were very entertaining. I have not yet returned your manuscript, because Robinson is devouring and digesting that Chinese play. He takes a great interest in what you write.

I send you, not without some qualms of conscience, a copy of our little journal containing a few personal remarks, written with the idea of making you known here in musical circles. I have several apologies to make in regard to the same. Firstly, the "Item" is only a poor little sheet, in which I am not able to obtain space sufficient to do you or your

TO H. E. KREHBIEL

art labour justice; secondly, I beg of you to remember that if I have spoken too extravagantly from a strictly newspaper standpoint, it will not be taken malicious advantage of by anybody, as the modest "Item" goes no farther north than Saint Louis.

The Creole rhymes I sent you were unintelligible chiefly because they were written phonetically after a fashion which I hold to be an abomination. The author, Adrien Rouquette, is the last living Indian missionary of the South — the last of the Blackrobe Fathers, and is known to the Choctaws by the name of Charitah-Ima. You may find him mentioned in the American Encyclopædia published by the firm of Lippincott & Co. There is nothing very remarkable about his poetry, except its eccentricity. The "Chant d'un jeune Créole" was simply a personal compliment — the author gives something of a sketch of his own life in it. It was published in "Le Propagateur," a French Catholic paper, for the purpose of attracting my attention, as the old man wanted to see me, and thought the paper might fall under my observation. The other, the "Moqueur-Chanteur" — as it ought to have been spelled — or "Mocking Singer," otherwise the mocking-bird, has some pretty bits of onomatopœia. (This dreamy, sunny State, with its mighty forests of cedar and pine, and its groves of giant cypress, is the natural home of the mocking-bird.) These bits of Creole rhyming were adapted to the airs of some old Creole songs, and the music will, perhaps, be the most interesting part of them.

I am writing you a detailed account of the Creoles of Louisiana, and their blending with Creole emigrants from the Canaries, Martinique, and San Domingo; but it is a subject of great latitude, and I can only outline it for you. Their characteristics offer an interesting topic, and the bastard offspring of the miscegenated French and African, or Spanish and African, dialects called Creole offer pretty peculiarities worth a volume. I will try to give you an entertaining sketch of the subject. I must tell you, however, that Creole music is mostly negro music, although often remodelled by French composers. There could neither have been Creole patois nor Creole melodies but for the French and Spanish blooded slaves of Louisiana and the Antilles. The melancholy, quavering beauty and weirdness of the negro chant are lightened by the French influence, or subdued and deepened by the Spanish.

Yes, I *did* send you that song as something queer. I had only hoped that the music would own the charming naïveté of the words; but I have been disappointed. But you must grant the song is pretty and has a queer simplicity of sentiment. Save it for the words. (Alas! "Mélusine" — according to information I have just received from Christern of New York — is dead. Poor, dear, darling "Mélusine"! I sincerely mourn for her with archæological and philological lament.) L'Orient is in Brit-

TO H. E. KREHBIEL

tany, and the chant is that of a Breton fisher village. That it should be melancholy is not surprising; but that it should be melancholy without weirdness or sweetness is lamentable. "Mélusine" for 1877 had a large collection of Breton songs, with music; and I think I shall avail myself of Christern's offer to get it. I want it for the legends; you will want, I am sure, to peep at the music. Your criticism about the resemblance of the melody to the Irish keening wail does not surprise me, although it disappointed me; for I believe the Breton peasantry are of Celtic origin. Your last letter strengthened a strange fancy that has come to me at intervals since my familiarity with the Chinese physiognomy — namely, that there are such strong similarities between the Mongolian and certain types of the Irish face that one is inclined to suspect a far-distant origin of the Celts in the East. The Erse and the Gaelic tongues, you know, are very similar in construction, also the modern Welsh. I have heard them all, and met Irish people able to comprehend both Welsh and Gaelic from the resemblance to the Erse. I suppose you have lots of Welsh music, the music of the Bards, some of which is said to have had a Druidic origin. Tell me if you have ever come across any Scandinavian music — the terrible melody of the Berserker songs, and the Runic chants, so awfully potent to charm; the Raven song of the Sweyn maidens to which they wove the magic banner; the death-song of Ragnar Lodbrok, or the songs of the warlocks and Norse priests; the many sword-songs sung by the Vikings, etc. I suppose you remember Longfellow's adaptation of the Heimskringla legend:

> Then the Scald took his harp and sang,
> And loud through the music rang
> The sound of that shining word;
> And the harp-strings a clangor made,
> As if they were struck with the blade
> Of a sword.

I am delighted to hear that you have got some Finnish music. Nothing in the world can compare in queerness and all manner of grotesqueness to Finnish tradition and characteristic superstition. I see an advertisement of "Le Chant de Roland," price one hundred dollars, splendidly illustrated. Wonder if the original music of the Song of Roland has been preserved. You know the giant Taillefer sang that mighty chant as he hewed down the Saxons at the battle of Hastings.

With grateful regards to Mrs. Krehbiel, I remain
Yours à jamais

L. H.

TO H. E. KREHBIEL

NEW ORLEANS, 1878

MY DEAR KREHBIEL, — That I should have been able even by a suggestion to have been of any use to you is a great pleasure. Your information in regard to Père Rouquette interested me. The father — the last of the Blackrobe Fathers — is at present

TO H. E. KREHBIEL

with his beloved Indians at Ravine-les-Cannes; but I will see him on his return and read your letter to the good old soul. If the columns of a good periodical were open to me, I should write the romance of his life — such a wild strange life — inspired by the magical writings of Châteaubriand in the commencement; and latterly devoted to a strangely beautiful religion of his own — not only the poetic religion of "Atala" and "Les Natchez," but that religion of the wilderness which flies to solitude, and hath no other temple than the vault of Heaven itself, painted with the frescoes of the clouds, and illuminated by the trembling tapers of God's everlasting altar, the stars of the firmament.

I have received circular and organ-talk. You are right, I am convinced, in your quotation of Saint Jerome. To-day I send you the book — an old copy I had considerable difficulty in coaxing from the owner. It will be of use to you chiefly by reason of the curious list of writers on mediæval and antique music quoted at the end of the volume.

If you do not make a successful volume of your instructive "Talks," something dreadful ought to happen to you — *especially as Cincinnati has now a musical school in which children will have to learn something about music.* You are the professor of musical history at that college. Your work is a work of instruction for the young. As the professor of that college, you should be able to make it a success. This is a suggestion. I know you are not a wirepuller — could n't be if you tried; but I want to see those talks put to good use, and made profitable to the writer, and you have friends who should be able to do what I think.

Your friend is right, no doubt, about the

> Tig, tig, malaboin
> La chelema che tango
> Redjoum!

I asked my black nurse what it meant. She only laughed and shook her head — "Mais c'est Voudoo, ça; je n'en sais rien!" "Well," said I, "don't you know anything about Voudoo songs?" "Yes," she answered, "*I know Voudoo songs; but I can't tell you what they mean.*" And she broke out into the wildest, weirdest ditty I ever heard. I tried to write down the words; but as I did not know what they meant I had to write by sound alone, spelling the words according to the French pronunciation:

> Yo so dan godo
> Héru mandé
> Yo so dan godo
> Héru mandé
> Héru mandé
> Tigà la papa,
> No Tingodisé
> Tigà la papa
> Ha Tinguoaiée
> Ha Tinguoaiée
> Ha Tinguoaiée.

I have undertaken a project which I hardly hope to succeed in, but which I feel some zeal regarding, viz., to collect the Creole legends, traditions, and

TO H. E. KREHBIEL

songs of Louisiana. Unfortunately I shall never be able to do this thoroughly without money — plenty of money — but I can do a good deal, perhaps.

I must also tell you that I find Spanish remarkably easy to acquire; and believe that at the end of another year I shall be able to master it — write it and speak it well. To do the latter, however, I shall be obliged to spend some time in some part of the Spanish-American colonies — whither my thoughts have been turned for some time. With a good knowledge of three languages, I can prosecute my wanderings over the face of the earth without timidity — without fear of starving to death after each migration.

After all, it has been lucky for me that I was obliged to quit hard newspaper work; for it has afforded me opportunities for self-improvement which I could not otherwise have acquired. I should like, indeed, to make more money; but one must sacrifice something in order to study, and I must not grumble, as long as I can live while learning.

I have really given up all hope of creating anything while I remain here, or, indeed, until my condition shall have altered and my occupation changed.

What material I can glean here, from this beautiful and legendary land — this land of perfume and of dreams — must be chiselled into shape elsewhere.

One cannot write of these beautiful things while surrounded by them; and by an atmosphere, heavy and drowsy as that of a conservatory. It must be afterward, in times to come, when I shall find myself in some cold, bleak land where I shall dream regretfully of the graceful palms; the swamp groves, weird in their ragged robes of moss; the golden ripples of the cane-fields under the summer wind, and this divine sky — deep and vast and cloudless as Eternity, with its far-off horizon tint of tender green.

I do not wonder the South has produced nothing of literary art. Its beautiful realities fill the imagination to repletion. It is regret and desire and the Spirit of Unrest that provoketh poetry and romance. It is the North, with its mists and fogs, and its gloomy sky haunted by a fantastic and ever-changing panorama of clouds, which is the land of imagination and poetry.

The fever is dying. A mighty wind, boisterous and cool, lifted the poisonous air from the city at last.

I cannot describe to you the peculiar effect of the summer upon one unacclimated. You feel as though you were breathing a drugged atmosphere. You find the very whites of your eyes turning yellow with biliousness. The least over-indulgence in eating or drinking prostrates you. My feeling all through the time of the epidemic was about this: I have the fever-principle in my blood — it shows its presence in a hundred ways — if the machinery of the body gets the least out of order, the fever will get me

TO H. E. KREHBIEL

down. I was not afraid of serious consequences, but I felt conscious that nothing but strict attention to the laws of health would pull me through. The experience has been valuable. I believe I could now live in Havana or Vera Cruz without fear of the terrible fevers which prevail there. Do you know that even here we have no less than eleven different kinds of fever — most of which know the power of killing?

I am very glad winter is coming, to lift the languors of the air and restore some energy to us. The summer is not like that North. At the North you have a clear, dry, burning air; here it is clear also, but dense, heavy, and so moist that it is never so hot as you have it. But no one dares expose himself to the vertical sun. I have noticed that even the chickens and the domestic animals, dogs, cats, etc., always seek shady places. They fear the sun. People with valuable horses will not work them much in summer. They die very rapidly of sunstroke.

In winter, too, one feels content. There is no nostalgia. But the summer always brings with it to me — always has, and I suppose always will — a curious and vague species of homesickness, as if I had friends in some country far off, where I had not been for so long that I have forgotten even their names and the appellation of the place where they live. I hope it will be so next summer that I can go whither the humour leads me — the propensity

LAFCADIO HEARN

which the author of "The Howadji in Syria" calleth the Spirit of the Camel.

But this is a land where one can really enjoy the Inner Life. Every one has an inner life of his own — which no other eye can see, and the great secrets of which are never revealed, although occasionally when we create something beautiful, we betray a faint glimpse of it — sudden and brief, as of a door opening and shutting in the night. I suppose you live such a life, too — a double existence — a dual entity. Are we not all doppelgängers? — and is not the invisible the only life we really enjoy?

You may remember I described this house to you as haunted-looking. It is delicious, therefore, to find out that it is actually a haunted house. But the ghosts do not trouble me; I have become so much like one of themselves in my habits. There is one room, however, where no one likes to be alone; for phantom hands clap, and phantom feet stamp behind them. "And what does that signify?" I asked a servant. "Ça veut dire, Foulez-moi le camp" — a vulgar expression for "Git!"

There is to be a *literary* (God save the mark!) newspaper here. I have been asked to help edit it. As I find that I can easily attend to both papers I shall scribble and scrawl and sell 'em translations which I could not otherwise dispose of. Thus I shall soon be making, instead of forty dollars, about one

TO H. E. KREHBIEL

hundred dollars per month. This will enable me to accumulate the means of flying from American civilization to other horrors which I know not of — some place where one has to be a good Catholic (in outward appearance) for fear of having a navaja stuck into you, and where the whole population is so mixed up that no human being can tell what nation anybody belongs to. So in the meantime I must study such phrases as:

¿Tiene V. un leoncito? Have you a small lion?
No señor, pero tengo un fero perro. No: but I've an ugly dog.
¿Tiene V. un muchachona? Have you a big strapping girl?
No: pero tengo un hombrecillo. No: but I've a miserable little man.

May the Gods of the faiths, living and dead, watch over thee, and thy dreams be made resonant with the sound of mystic and ancient music, which on waking thou shalt vainly endeavour to recall, and forever regret with a vague and yet pleasant sorrow; knowing that the gods permit not mortals to learn their sacred hymns.

L. Hearn

By the way, let me send you a short translation from Baudelaire. It is so mystic and sad and beautiful.

LAFCADIO HEARN

TO H. E. KREHBIEL

New Orleans, 1879

Querido Amigo, — Your words in regard to my former letter flatter me considerably, for I feel rather elated at being able to be of the smallest service to you; and as to your unavoidable delays in writing, never allow them to trouble you, or permit your correspondence to encroach upon your study hours for my sake. Indeed, it is a matter of surprise to me how you are able to spare any time at present in view of your manifold work.

So *your* literary career — at least the brilliant portion of it — commences in January; and mine ends at the same time, without a single flash of brightness or a solitary result worthy of preservation. My salary has been raised three times since I heard from you — encouraging, perhaps, but I do not suffer myself to indulge in any literary speculations. Since the close of the sickly season my only thought has been to free myself from the yoke of dependence on the whims of employers — from the harness of journalism. I hired myself a room in the northern end of the French Quarter (near the Spanish), bought myself a complete set of cooking utensils and kitchen-ware, and kept house for myself. I got my expenses down to two dollars per week, and kept them at that (exclusive of rent, of course) although my salary rose to twenty dollars. Thus I learned to cook pretty well; also to save money, and will start a little business for

TO H. E. KREHBIEL

myself next week. I have an excellent partner — a Northern man — and we expect by spring to clear enough ready money to start for South America. By that time I shall have finished my Spanish studies — all that are necessary and possible in an American city, and shall — please (not God but) the good old gods — play gipsy for a while in strange lands. Many unpleasant things may happen; but with good health I have no fear of failure, and the new life will enable me to recruit my eyes, fill my pockets, and improve my imagination by many strange adventures and divers extraordinary archæological pursuits.

How is that for Bohemianism? But I wish I could spend a day with you in order to recount the many wonderful and mystic adventures I have had in this quaint and ruinous city. To recount them in a letter is impossible. But I came here to enjoy romance, and I have had my fill.

Business — ye Antiquities! — hard, practical, unideal, realistic business! But what business? Ah, mi corazon, I would never dare to tell you. Not that it is not honourable, respectable, etc., but that it is so devoid of dreamful illusions. Yet hast thou not said — "This is no world for dreaming" — and divers other horrible things which I shall not repeat?

Tell me all about your exotic musical instruments, when you have time — you know they will interest me; and may not I, too, some day be able to forward to you various barbaric symbols and sackfuls from outlandish places? — from the pampas or the llanos

— from some palm-fringed islands of the Eastern sea, where even Nature dreams opiated dreams? How knowest thou but that I shall make the Guacho and llanero, the Peruvian and the Chilian, to contribute right generously to thy store of musical wealth?

I have not made much progress in the literature most dear to you; inasmuch as my time has been rather curtailed, and the days have become provokingly short. But I have been devouring Hoffmann (Emile de la Bédollière's translation in French — could not get a complete English one); and I really believe he has no rival as a creator of musical fantasticalities. "The Organ-Stop," "The Sanatus," "Lawyer Krespel" (a story of a violin, replete with delightful German mysticism), "A Pupil of the Great Tartini," "Don Juan" — and a dozen other stories evidence an enthusiasm for music and an extraordinary sensitiveness to musical impressions on the author's part. You probably read these in German — if not, I am sure many of them would delight you. The romance of music must, I fancy, be a vast aid to the study of the art — it seems to me like the setting of a jewel, or the frame of a painting. I also have observed in the "New York Times" a warm notice of a lady who is an enthusiast upon the subject of Finnish music, and who has collected a valuable mass of the quaint music and weird ditties of the North. As you speak of having a quantity of Finnish music, however, I have no doubt that you know much more about the young lady than I could tell you.

TO H. E. KREHBIEL

Prosper Mérimée's "Carmen" has fairly enthralled me — I am in love with it. The colour and passion and rapid tragedy of the story is marvellous. I think I was pretty well prepared to enjoy it, however. I had read Simpson's "History of the Gipsies," Borro's [1] "Gypsies of Spain," a volume of Spanish gipsy ballads — I forget the name of the translator — and everything in the way of gipsy romance I could get my hands on — by Sheridan Le Fanu, Victor Hugo, Reade, Longfellow, George Eliot, Balzac, and a brilliant novelist also whose works generally appear in the "Cornhill Magazine." Balzac's "Le Succube" gives a curious picture of the persecution of the Bohemians in mediæval France, founded upon authentic records. Le Fanu wrote a sweet little story called "The Bird of Passage," which contained a remarkable variety of information in regard to gipsy secrets; but it is only within very recent years that a really good novel on a gipsy theme has been written in English; and I am sorry that I cannot remember the author's name. I found more romance as well as information in Borro and Simpson than in all the novels and poems put together; and I obtained a fair idea of the artistic side of Spanish gipsy life from Doré's "Spain." Doré is something of a musician as well as a limner; and his knowledge of the violin enabled him to make himself at home in the camps of that music-loving people. He played wild airs to them, and studied their poses and gestures

[1] See page 195.

with such success that his gipsies seem actually to dance in the engravings. I read that Miss Minnie Hauck plays Carmen in gorgeous costume, which is certainly out of place, except in one act of the opera. Otherwise from the first scene of the novel in which she advances "poising herself on her hips, like a filly from the Cordovan Stud," to the ludicrous episode at Gibraltar, her attire is described as more nearly resembling that picturesque rag-blending of colour Doré describes and depicts. If you see the opera — please send me your criticism in the "Gazette."

You may remember some observations I made — based especially on De Coulanges — as to the derivation of the Roman and Greek tongues from the Sanscrit. Talking of Borro reminds me that Borro traces the gipsy dialects to the mother of languages; and Simpson naturally finds the Romany akin to modern Hindostanee, which succeeded the Sanscrit. Now here is a curious fact. Rommain is simply Sanscrit for "The Husbands" — a domestic appellation applicable to the gipsy races above all others, when the ties of blood are stronger than even among the Jewish people; and Borro asks timidly what is then the original meaning of those mighty words, "Rome" and the "Romans," of which no scholar (he claims) has yet ventured to give the definition. Surely all mysteries seem to issue from the womb of nations — from the heart of Asia.

I see that the musical critic of the "New York Times" speaks of certain airs in the opera of "Car-

TO H. E. KREHBIEL

men" as Havanese airs — "Avaneras." If there be a music peculiar to Havana, I expect that I shall hear some of it next summer. If I could only write music, I could collect much interesting matter for you.

There is a New Orleans story in the last issue of "Scribner's Monthly" — "Ninon" — which I must tell you is a fair exemplification of how mean French Creoles can be. The great cruelties of the old slave régime were perpetuated by French planters. Anglo-Saxon blood is not cruel. If you want to find cruelty, either in ancient or modern history, it must be sought for among the Latin races of Europe. The Scandinavian and Teutonic blood was too virile and noble to be cruel; and the science of torture was never developed among them.

Before I commenced to keep house for myself, I must tell you about a Chinese restaurant which I used to patronize. No one in the American part of the city — or at least very few — know even of its existence. The owner will not advertise, will not hang out a sign, and seems to try to keep his business a secret. The restaurant is situated in the rear part of an old Creole house on Dumaine Street — about the middle of the French Quarter; and one must pass through a dark alley to get in. I had heard so much of the filthiness of the Chinese, that I would have been afraid to enter it, but for the strong recommendations of a Spanish friend of mine — now a journalist and a romantic fellow. (By the way, he killed a stranger here in 1865 one night, and had to fly the country. A few hot words in a saloon; and the Spanish blood was up. The stranger fell so quickly and the stab was given so swiftly — "according to the *rules*" — that my friend had left the house before anybody knew what had happened. Then the killer was stowed away upon a Spanish schooner, and shipped to Cuba, where he remained for four years. And when he came back, *there were no witnesses*.)

But about the restaurant. I was surprised to find the bills printed half in Spanish and half in English; and the room nearly full of Spaniards. It turned out that my Chinaman was a Manilan — handsome, swarthy, with a great shock of black hair, wavy as that of a Malabaress. His movements were supple, noiseless, leopardine; and the Mongolian blood was scarcely visible. But his wife was positively attractive; — hair like his own, a splendid figure, sharp, strongly marked features, and eyes whose very obliqueness only rendered the face piquant — as in those agreeable yet half-sinister faces painted on Japanese lacquerware. The charge for a meal was only twenty-five cents — four dishes allowed, with dessert and coffee, and only five cents for every extra dish one might choose to order. I generally ordered a nice steak, stewed beef with potatoes, stewed tongue, a couple of fried eggs, etc. Everything is cooked before your eyes, the whole interior of the kitchen being visible from the dining-table; and nothing could be cleaner or nicer. I asked him

TO H. E. KREHBIEL

how long he had kept the place; he answered, "Seven years"; and I am told he has been making a fortune even at these prices of five cents per dish. The cooking is perfection.

There is nothing here which would interest you particularly in the newspaper line. We have a new French daily, "Le Courrier de la Louisiane"; but the ablest French editor in Louisiana — Dumez of Le Meschacébé — was killed by what our local poets are pleased to term "The March of the Saffron Steed!" The "Item," beginning on nothing, now represents a capital, and I would have a fine prospect should I be able to content my restless soul in this town. The "Democrat" is in a death struggle with the gigantic lottery monopoly; and cannot live long. Howard is king of New Orleans, and can crush every paper or clique that opposes him. He was once blackballed by the Old Jockey Club, who had a splendid race-course at Métairie. "By God," said Howard, "I'll make a graveyard of their d——d race-course." He did it. The Métairie cemetery now occupies the site of the old race-course; and the new Jockey Club is Howard's own organization.

It just occurs to me that the name of the gypsy novel written by the Cornhill writer is "Zelda's Fortune," and that I spelled the name Borrow wrong. It has a "w." Mérimée refers to B*a*rrow, which is also wrong. Longfellow borrowed (excuse the involuntary pun) nearly all the gypsy songs in his "Spanish Student" from Borrow. I remember, for instance, the songs commencing;

> Upon a mountain's tip I stand,
> With a crown of red gold in my hand;

> Loud sang the Spanish cavalier
> And thus his ditty ran:
> God send the gypsy lassie here,
> And not the gipsy man.

(I have been spelling "gipsy" and "gypsy" — don't know which I like best.) I wonder why Longfellow did not borrow the forge-song, quoted by Borrow — "Las Muchis," "The Sparks":

> More than a hundred lovely daughters I see produced at one time, fiery as roses, in one moment they expire, gracefully circumvolving.

Is it not beautiful, this gipsy poetry? The sparks are compared to daughters, but they are *gitanas* "*fiery* as roses"; and in the words, "I see them expire, gracefully *circumvolving*," we have the figure of the gypsy dance — the Romalis, with its wild bounds and pirouettes.

My letter is too long. I fear it will try your patience; but I cannot say half I should wish to say. You will soon hear from me again; for le père Rouquette hath returned; I must see him, and show him your letter. A villainous wind from your boreal region has overcast the sky with a cope of lead, and filled the sunny city with gloom. From my dovecot-

TO H. E. KREHBIEL

shaped windows I can see only wet roofs and dripping gable-ends. The nights are now starless, and haunted by fogs. Sometimes, in the day there is no more than a suggestion of daylight — a gloaming. Sometimes in the darkness I hear hideous cries of murder from beyond the boundary of sharp gables and fantastic dormers. But murders are so common here that nobody troubles himself about them. So I draw my chair closer to the fire, light up my pipe de terre Gambièse, and in the flickering glow weave fancies of palm-trees and ghostly reefs and tepid winds, and a Voice from the far tropics calls to me across the darkness.

Adios, hermano mio
Forever yours
LAFCADIO HEARN

TO H. E. KREHBIEL

NEW ORLEANS, 1879

MY DEAR KREHBIEL, — I regret very much that I could not reply until now; overstudy obliged me to quit reading and writing for several days; I am just in that peculiar condition of convalescence when one cannot tell how to regulate the strain upon his eyes.

It pleased me very much to hear from you just before you entered upon your duties as a professor of the beautiful art you have devoted yourself to; — that letter informed me of many things more than its written words directly expressed — especially

LAFCADIO HEARN

that you felt I was really and deeply interested in every step you were taking, and that I would on receiving your letter experience that very thrill of indescribable anxiety and hope, timidity and confidence, and a thousand intermingled sensations — which ever besets one standing on the verge of uncertainty ere taking the first plunge into a new life.

I read your lecture with intense interest, and felt happy in observing that your paper did you the justice to publish the essay entire. Still, I fancy that you may have interpolated its delivery with a variety of unpublished comments and verbal notes — such as I have heard you often deliver when reading from print or MSS. These I should much have wished to hear — if they were uttered.

Your lecture was in its entirety a vast mass of knowledge wonderfully condensed into a very small compass. That condensation, which I would regret if applied to certain phases of your whole plan, could not have been avoided in its inception; and only gave to the whole an encyclopædic character which must have astonished many of your hearers. To present so infinite a subject in so small a frame was a gigantic task of itself; and nevertheless it was accomplished symmetrically and harmoniously — the thread of one instructive idea never being broken. I certainly think you need harbour no further fears as to success in the lecture-room, and far beyond it.

The idea of religion as the conservator of Romanticism, as the promoter of musical development,

TO H. E. KREHBIEL

seemed to me very novel and peculiar. I cannot doubt its correctness, although I believe some might take issue with you in regard to the Romantic idea — because the discussions in regard to romantic truth are interminable and will never cease. Religion is beyond any question the mother of all civilizations, arts, and laws; and no archæologic research has given us any record of any social system, any art, any law, antique or modern, which was not begotten and nurtured by an ethical idea. You know that I have no faith in any "faiths" or dogmas; I regard thought as a mechanical process, and individual life as a particle of that eternal force of which we know so little: but the true philosophers who *hold* these doctrines to-day (I cannot say originated them, for they are old as Buddhism) are also those who best comprehend the necessity of the religious idea for the maintenance of the social system which it cemented together and developed. The name of a religion has little to do with this truth; the law of progress has been everywhere the same. The art of the Egyptian, the culture of the Greeks, the successful policy of Rome, the fantastic beauty of Arabic architecture, were the creations of various religious ideas; and passed away only when the faiths which nourished them weakened or were forgotten. So I believe with you that the musical art of antiquity was born of the antique religions, and varied according to the character of that religion. But I have also an inclination to believe that Romanticism itself

LAFCADIO HEARN

was engendered by religious conservation. The amorous Provençal ditties which excited the horror of the mediæval church were certainly engendered by the mental reactions against religious conservatism in Provence; and I fancy that the same reaction everywhere produced similar results, whether in ancient or modern history. This is your idea, is it not; or is it your idea carried perhaps to the extreme of attributing the birth of Romanticism to conservatism, Pallas-Athene springing in white beauty from the head of Zeus?

There is one thing which I will venture to criticize in the lecture — not positively, however. I cannot help believing that the deity whose name you spell Schiva (probably after a German writer) is the same spelled Seeva, Siva, or Shiva, according to various English and French authors. If I am right, then I fear you were wrong in calling Schiva the *goddess* of fire and destruction. The god, yes; but although many of these Hindoo deities, including Siva, are bi-sexual and self-engendering, as the embodiment of any force, they are masculine. Now Siva is the third person of the Hindoo trinity — Brahma, the Creator; Vishnu, the Preserver; Siva, the Destroyer. Siva signifies the wrath of God. Fire is sacred to him, as it is an emblem of the Christian Siva, the *Holy Ghost*. Siva is the Holy Ghost of the Hindoo trinity; and as sins against the Holy Ghost are unforgiven, so are sins against Siva unforgiven. There is an awful legend that Brahma and Vishnu were once

TO H. E. KREHBIEL

disputing as to greatness, when Siva suddenly towered between them as a pillar of fire. Brahma flew upward for ten myriads of years vainly striving to reach the flaming capital of that fiery column; Vishnu flew downward for ten thousand years without being able to reach its base. And the gods trembled. But this legend, symbolic and awful, signifies only that the height and depth of the vengeance of God is immeasurable even by himself. I think the *wife* of Siva is Parvati. See if I am right. I have no works here to which I can refer on the subject.

There is to my mind a most fearful symbolism in the origin of five tones from the head of Siva. I cannot explain the idea; but it is a terrible one, and may symbolize a strange truth. All this Brahminism is half true; it conflicts not with any doctrine of science; its symbolism is only a monstrously figured veil wrought to hide from the ignorant truths they cannot understand; and those elephant-headed or hundred-armed gods do but represent tremendous facts.

On the subject of Romanticism, I send you a translation from an article by Baudelaire. The last part of the chapter, applying wholly to romanticism in form and colour, hardly touches the subject in which you are most interested. His criticism of Raphael is very severe; that of Rembrandt enthusiastic. "The South," he says, is "brutal and positive in its conception of beauty, like a sculptor"; and he remarks that sculpture in the North is always rather picturesque than realistic. Winckelmann and Lessing long since pointed out, however, that antique art was never realistic; it was only a dream of human beauty deified and immortalized, and the ancients were true Romanticists in their day. I wonder what Baudelaire would have thought of our modern Pre-Raphaelites — Rossetti, et als. Surely they are true Romanticists also; but I must not tire you with Romanticism.

Do you not think that outside of the religio-musical system of Egyptian worship, there may have been a considerable development of the art in certain directions — judging from the wonderful variety of instruments — harps, flutes, tamborines, sistrums, drums, cymbals, etc., discovered in the tombs or pictured forth upon the walls? Your remarks on the subject were exceedingly interesting.

I fear my letters will bore you — however, they are long only because I must write as I would talk to you were it possible. I am disappointed in regard to several musical researches I have been undertaking; and can tell you little of interest. The work of Cable is not yet in press — yellow fever killed half his family. Rouquette has been doing nothing but writing mad essays on the beauties of chastity, so that I can get nothing from him in the way of music until his crazy fit is over. Several persons to whom I applied for information became suspicious and refused point-blank to do anything. I traced one source of musical lore to its beginning, and discovered that

TO H. E. KREHBIEL

the individual had been subsidized by another collector to say nothing. Speaking of Pacific Island music, you have probably seen Wilkins' "Voyages," 5 vols., with strange music therein. I have many ditties in my head, but I cannot write them down. ...

    Thine, O Minnesinger

        L. HEARN

TO H. E. KREHBIEL

NEW ORLEANS, 1880

DEAR KREHBIEL, — I was so glad to hear from you. Your letter gave me much amusement. I wish I could have been present at that Chinese concert. It must have been the funniest thing of the kind ever heard of in Cincinnati.

It gives me malicious pleasure to inform you that my vile and improper book will probably be published in a few months. Also that the wickedest story of the lot — "King Candaule" — is being published as a serial in one of the New Orleans papers, with delightful results of shocking people. I will send you copies of them when complete.

I am interested in your study of Assyrian archæology. It is a pity there are so few good works on the subject. Layard's *unabridged* works are very extensive; but I do not remember seeing them in the Cincinnati library. Rawlinson, I think, is more interesting in style and more thorough in research. The French are making fine explorations in this direction.

LAFCADIO HEARN

I find frequent reference made to Overbeck's "Pompeii," a German work, as containing valuable information on antique music, drawn from discoveries at Herculaneum and Pompeii, also to Mazois, a great French writer upon the same subject. I have not seen them; but I fancy you would find some valuable information in them regarding musical instruments. I suppose you have read Sir William Gell's "Pompeiana" — at least the abridged form of it. You know the double flutes, etc., of the ancients are preserved in the museum of Naples. In the Cincinnati library is a splendid copy of the work on Egyptian antiquities prepared under Napoleon I, wherein you will find coloured prints — from photographs — of the musical instruments found in the catacombs and hypogæa. But I do not think there are many good books on the subject of Assyrian antiquities there. Vickers could put you in the way of getting better works on the subject than any one in the library, I believe.

You will master these things much more thoroughly than ever I shall — although I love them. I have only attempted, however, to photograph the rapports of the antiquities in my mind, like memories of a panoramic procession; while to you, the procession will not be one of shadows, but of splendid facts, with the sound of strangely ancient music and the harmonious tread of sacrificial bands — all preserved for you through the night of ages. And the life of vanished cities and the pageantry of dead

TO H. E. KREHBIEL

faiths will have a far more charming reality for you — the Musician — than ever for me — the Dreamer. I can't see well enough yet to do much work. I have written an essay upon luxury and art in the time of Elagabalus; but now that I read it over again, I am not satisfied with it, and fear it will not be published. And by the way — I request, and beg, and entreat, and supplicate, and petition, and pray that you will not forget about Mephistopheles. Here, in the sweet perfume-laden air, and summer of undying flowers, I feel myself moved to write the musical romance whereof I spake unto you in the days that were.

I can't say that things look very bright here otherwise. The prospect is dark as that of stormy summer night, with feverish pulses of lightning in the far sky-border — the lightning signifying hopes and fantasies. But I shall stick to my pedestal of faith in literary possibilities like an Egyptian colossus with a broken nose, seated solemnly in the gloom of its own originality.

Times are not good here. The city is crumbling into ashes. It has been buried under a lava-flood of taxes and frauds and maladministrations so that it has become only a study for archæologists. Its condition is so bad that when I write about it, as I intend to do soon, nobody will believe I am telling the truth. But it is better to live here in sackcloth and ashes, than to own the whole State of Ohio.

Once in a while I feel the spirit of restlessness upon

me, when the Spanish ships come in from Costa Rica and the islands of the West Indies. I fancy that some day, I shall wander down to the levee, and creep on board, and sail away to God knows where. I am so hungry to see those quaint cities of the Conquistadores and to hear the sandalled sentinels crying through the night — Sereño alerto! — sereño alerto! — just as they did two hundred years ago.

I send you a little bit of prettiness I cut out of a paper. Ah! — *that* is style, is it not? — and fancy and strength and height and depth. It is just in the style of Richter's "Titan."

Major sends his compliments. I must go to see the Carnival nuisance. Remember me to anybody who cares about it, and believe me always

Faithfully yours

L. Hearn

TO H. E. KREHBIEL

New Orleans, 1880

My dear Krehbiel, — Pray remember that your ancestors were the very Goths and Vandals who destroyed the marvels of Greek art which even Roman ignorance and ferocity had spared; and I perceive by your last letter that you possess still traces of that Gothic spirit which detests all beauty that is not beautiful with the fantastic and unearthly beauty that is Gothic.

You cannot make a Goth out of a Greek, nor can you change the blood in my veins by speaking to me

TO H. E. KREHBIEL

of a something vague and gnostic and mystic which you deem superior to all that any Latin mind could conceive.

I grant the existence and the weird charm of the beauty that Gothic minds conceived; but I do not see less beauty in what was conceived by the passion and poetry of other races of mankind. This is a cosmopolitan art era: and you must not judge everything which claims art-merit by a Gothic standard.

Let me also tell you that you do not as yet know anything of the Spirit of Greek Art — or the sources which inspired its miraculous compositions; and that to do so you would have to study the climate, the history, the ethnological record, the religion, the society of the country which produced it. My own knowledge is, I regret to say, very imperfect — but it is sufficient to give me the right to tell you that you were wrong to accuse me of abandoning Greek ideals, or to lecture me upon what is and what is not art in matters of form and colour and literature. I might say the same thing in regard to your judgment of French writers: you confound Naturalism with Romanticism, and vice versa.

Again, do not suppose that I am insensible to other forms of beauty. You judge all art, I fear, by inductions from that in which you are a master; but the process in your case is false; — nor will you be able to judge the artistic soul of a people adequately by its musical productions, until you have passed another quarter of a century in the study of the music of different races and ages and civilizations. Then it is possible that you may find that secret key; but you cannot possibly do it now, learned as you are, nor do I believe there are a dozen men in the world who could do it.

Now I am with the Latin; I live in a Latin city; — I seldom hear the English tongue except when I enter the office for a few brief hours. I eat and drink and converse with members of the races you detest like the son of Odin that you are. I see beauty here all around me — a strange, tropical, intoxicating beauty. I consider it my artistic duty to let myself be absorbed into this new life, and study its form and colour and passion. And my impressions I occasionally put into the form of the little fantastics which disgust you so much, because they are not of the Æsir and Jötunheim. Were I able to live in Norway, I should try also to intoxicate myself with the Spirit of the Land, and I might write of the Saga singers —

> From whose lips in music rolled
> The Hamavel of Odin old,
> With sounds mysterious as the roar
> Of ocean on a storm-beat shore.

The law of true art, even according to the Greek idea, is to seek beauty wherever it is to be found, and separate it from the dross of life as gold from ore. You do not see beauty in animal passion; — yet passion was the inspiring breath of Greek art and the mother of language; and its gratification is the

TO H. E. KREHBIEL

act of a creator, and the divinest rite of Nature's temple.

... And writing to you as a friend, I write of my thoughts and fancies, of my wishes and disappointments, of my frailties and follies and failures and successes — even as I would write to a brother. So that sometimes what might not seem strange in words, appears very strange upon paper. And it may come to pass that I shall have stranger things to tell you; for this is a land of magical moons and of witches and of warlocks; and were I to tell you all that I have seen and heard in these years in this enchanted City of Dreams you would verily deem me mad rather than morbid.
    Affectionately yours
        L. HEARN

TO H. E. KREHBIEL
       NEW ORLEANS, 1880

MY DEAR KREHBIEL, — Your letter delighted me. I always felt sure that you would unshackle yourself — sooner or later; but I hardly expected it would come so soon.

 The great advantage of your new position, I think, will be the leisure it will afford you to study, and that, too, while you are still in the flush of youth and ambition, and before your energies are impaired by excess of newspaper drudgery. I think your future is secure now beyond any doubt; — for any man with such talent and knowledge, such real love for art, and such a total absence of vices should find the road before an easy one. It is true that you have a prodigious work to achieve; but the path is well oiled, like those level highways along which the Egyptians moved their colossi of granite. I congratulate you; I rejoice with you; and I envy you with the purest envy possible. Still more, however, I envy your youth, your strength, and that something which is partly hope and partly force and love for the beautiful which I have lost, and which, having passed away with the summer of life, can never be recalled. When a man commences to feel what it is to be young, he is beginning to grow old. You have not felt that yet. I hope you will not for many years. But I do; and my hair is turning grey at thirty!

I liked your letter very much also in regard to our discussion. It is just and pleasant to read. I thought your first reproaches much too violent. But I am still sure you are not correct in speaking of the Greeks as chaste. You will not learn what the Greeks were in the time of the glory of their republics either from Homer or Plato or Gladstone or Mahaffy. Perhaps the best English writer I could refer you to — without mentioning historians proper — is John Addington Symonds, author of "Studies of the Greek Poets," and "Studies and Sketches in Southern Europe." His works would charm you. The Greeks were brave, intelligent, men of genius,

TO H. E. KREHBIEL

men who wrote miracles — un peuple des demi-dieux, as a French poet terms them; but the character of their thought, as reflected in their mythology, their literature, their art, and their history certainly does not indicate the least conception of chastity in the modern signification of the word. No: you will not go down to your grave with the conception you have made of them — unless you should be determined not to investigate the contrary.

I would like to discuss the other affair, also; but I have so little time that I must forego the pleasure.

As to the Fantastics, you greatly overestimate me if you think me capable of doing something much more "worthy of my talents," as you express it. I am conscious they are only trivial; but I am condemned to move around in a sphere of triviality until the end. I am no longer able to study as I wish to, and, being able to work only a few hours a day, cannot do anything outside of my regular occupation. My hope is to perfect myself in Spanish and French; and, if possible, to study Italian next summer. With a knowledge of the Latin tongues, I may have a better chance hereafter. But I fancy the idea of the Fantastics is artistic. They are my impressions of the strange life of New Orleans. They are dreams of a tropical city. There is one twin-idea running through them all — Love and Death. And these figures embody the story of life here, as it impresses me. I hope to be able to take a trip to

LAFCADIO HEARN

Mexico in the summer just to obtain literary material, sun-paint, tropical colour, etc. There are tropical lilies which are venomous, but they are more beautiful than the frail and icy-white lilies of the North. Tell me if you received a Fantastic founded upon the story of Ponce de Leon. I think I sent it since my last letter. I have not written any Fantastics since except one — inspired by Tennyson's fancy:

> My heart would hear her and beat
> Had it lain for a century dead —
> Would start and tremble under her feet —
> And blossom in purple and red.

Jerry, Krehbiel, Ed Miller, Feldwisch! All gone! It is a little strange. But it will always be so. Looking around the table at home at which are gathered wanderers from all nations and all skies, the certainty of separation for all societes and coteries is very impressive. We are all friends. In six months probably there will not be one left. Dissolution of little societies in this city is more rapid than with you. In the tropics all things decay more speedily, or mummify. And I think that in such cities there is no real friendship. There is no time for it. Only passion for women, a brief acquaintance for men. And it is only when I meet some fair-haired Northern stranger here, rough and open like a wind from the great lakes, that I begin to realize I once lived in a city whose heart was not a cemetery two centuries old, and where people who hated did not kiss each other, and

TO H. E. KREHBIEL

where men did not mock at all that youth and faith hold to be sacred.
  Your sincere friend
      L. HEARN

Read Bergerat's article on Offenbach — the long one. I think you will like it.

TO H. E. KREHBIEL
    NEW ORLEANS, *February*, 1881

MY DEAR KREHBIEL, — A pleasant manner, indeed, of breaking thy silence, vast and vague, illuminating my darkness of doubt! — the vision of a sunny-haired baby-girl, inheriting, I hope, those great soft grey eyes of yours, and the artist dream of her artist father. I should think you would feel a sweet and terrible responsibility — like one of those traditional guardian-angels entrusted for the first time with the care of a new life. . . .

I have not much to tell you about myself. I am living in a ruined Creole house; damp brick walls green with age, zigzag cracks running down the façade, a great yard with plants and cacti in it; a quixotic horse, four cats, two rabbits, three dogs, five geese, and a seraglio of hens — all living together in harmony. A fortune-teller occupies the lower floor. She has a fantastic apartment kept dark all day, except for the light of two little tapers burning before two human skulls in one corner of the room. It is a very mysterious house indeed. . . . But I am growing

very weary of the Creole quarter, and think I shall pull up stakes and fly to the garden district where the orange-trees are, but where Latin tongues are not spoken. It is very hard to accustom one's self to live with Americans, however, after one has lived for three years among these strange types. I am swindled all the time and I know it, and still I find it hard to summon up resolution to forsake these antiquated streets for the commonplace and practical American districts. . . .
    Very affectionately
            L. Hearn

TO H. E. KREHBIEL
      New Orleans, *February*, 1881
My dear Krehbiel, — Your letter rises before me as I write like a tablet of white stone bearing a dead name. I see you standing beside me. I look into your eyes and press your hand and say nothing. . . .

Remember me kindly to Mrs. Krehbiel. I am sure you will soon have made a cosy little home in the metropolis. In my last letter I forgot to acknowledge receipt of the musical articles, which do you the greatest credit, and which interested me much, although I know nothing about music further than a narrow theatrical experience and a natural sensibility to its simpler forms of beauty enable me to do. I see your name also in the programme of "The Studio," and hope to see the first number of that periodical containing your opening article. I should like one of

TO H. E. KREHBIEL

these days to talk with you about the possibility of contributing a romantic — not musical — series of little sketches upon the Creole songs and coloured Creoles of New Orleans to some New York periodical. Until the summer comes, however, it will be difficult for me to undertake such a thing; the days here are much shorter than they are in your northern latitudes, the weather has been gloomy as Tartarus, and my poor imagination cannot rise on dampened wings in this heavy and murky atmosphere. This has been a hideous winter — incessant rain, sickening weight of foul air, and a sky grey as the face of Melancholy. The city is half under water. The lake and the bayous have burst their bonds, and the streets are Venetian canals. Boats are moving over the sidewalks, and moccasin snakes swarm in the old stonework of the gutters. Several children have been bitten.

I am very weary of New Orleans. The first delightful impression it produced has vanished. The city of my dreams, bathed in the gold of eternal summer, and perfumed with the amorous odours of orange flowers, has vanished like one of those phantom cities of Spanish America, swallowed up centuries ago by earthquakes, but reappearing at long intervals to deluded travellers. What remains is something horrible like the tombs here — material and moral rottenness which no pen can do justice to. You must have read some of those mediæval legends in which an amorous youth finds the beautiful witch he has embraced all through the night crumble into a mass of calcined bones and ashes in the morning. Well, I feel like such a one, and almost regret that, unlike the victims of these diabolical illusions, I do not find my hair whitened and my limbs withered by sudden age; for I enjoy exuberant vitality and still seem to myself like one buried alive or left alone in some city cursed with desolation like that described by Sinbad the Sailor. No literary circle here; no jovial coterie of journalists; no associates save those vampire ones of which the less said the better. And the thought — Where must all this end? — may be laughed off in the daytime, but always returns to haunt me like a ghost in the night.

Your friend

L. HEARN

TO H. E. KREHBIEL

NEW ORLEANS, 1881

MY DEAR KREHBIEL, — To what could I now devote myself? To nothing! To study art in any one of its branches with any hope of success requires years of patient study, vast reading, and a very considerable outlay of money. This I know. I also know that I could not write one little story of antique life really worthy of the subject without such hard study as I am no longer able to undertake, and a purchase of many costly works above my means. The world of Imagination is alone left open to me. It allows of a vagueness of expression which hides the absence of

TO H. E. KREHBIEL

real knowledge and dispenses with the necessity of technical precision of detail. Again, let me tell you that to produce a really artistic work, after all the years of study required for such a task, one cannot possibly obtain any appreciation of the work for years after its publication. Such works as Flaubert's "Salammbô" or Gautier's "Roman de la Momie" were literary failures until recently. They were too learned to be appreciated. Yet to write on a really noble subject, how learned one must be! There is no purpose, as you justly observe, in my Fantastics — beyond the gratification of expressing a Thought which cries out within one's heart for utterance, and the pleasant fancy that a few kindred minds will dream over them, as upon pellets of green hascheesch — at least should they ever assume the shape I hope for. And do not talk to me of work, dear fellow, in this voluptuous climate. It is impossible! The people here are so languidly lazy that they do not even dream of chasing away the bats which haunt these crumbling buildings.

Is it possible you like Dr. Ebers? I hope not! He has no artistic sentiment whatever — no feeling, no colour. He is dry and dusty as a mummy preserved with bitumen. He gropes in the hypogæa like some Yankee speculator looking for antiquities to sell. You must be Egyptian to write of Egypt; — you must feel all the weird solemnity and mighty ponderosity of the antique life; — you must comprehend the whole force of those ideas which expressed themselves in miracles of granite and mysteries of black marble. Ebers knows nothing of this. Turning from the French writers to his lifeless pages is like leaving the warm and perfumed bed of a beloved mistress for the slimy coldness of a sepulchre.

The Venus of Milo! — the Venus who is not a Venus! Perhaps you have read Victor Rydberg's beautiful essay about that glorious figure! If not, read it; it is worth while. And let me say, my dear friend, no one dare write the whole truth about Greek sculpture. None would publish it. Few would understand it. Winckelmann, although impressed by it, hardly realized it. Symonds, in his exquisite studies, acknowledges that the spirit of the antique life remains, and will always remain to the greater number, an inexplicable although enchanting mystery. But if one dared! . . .

And you speak of the Song of Solomon. I love it more than ever. But Michelet, the passionate freethinker, the divine prose-poet, the bravest lover of the beautiful, has written a terrible chapter upon it. No lesser mind dare touch the subject now with sacrilegious hand.

I doubt if you are quite just to Gautier. I had hoped his fancy might please you. But Gautier did not write those lines I sent you. They are found in the report of conversations held with him by Emile Bergerat; — they are mere memories of a dead voice. Probably had he ever known that these

TO H. E. KREHBIEL

romantic opinions would one day be published to the world, he would never have uttered them.

Your Hindoo legends charmed me; but I do not like them as I love the Greek legends. The fantasies created in India are superhumanly vast, wild, and terrible; — they are typhoons of the tropical imagination; — they seem pictures printed by madness — they terrify and impress, but do not charm. I love better the sweet human story of Orpheus. It is a dream of human love — the love that is not only strong, but stronger than death — the love that breaks down the dim gates of the world of Shadows and bursts open the marble heart of the tomb to return at the outcry of passion. Yet I hold that the Greek mind was infantine in comparison to the Indian thought of the same era; nor could any Greek imagination have created the visions of the visionary East. The Greek was a pure naturalist, a lover of "the bloom of young flesh"; — the Hindoo had fathomed the deepest deeps of human thought before the Greek was born.

Zola is capable of some beautiful things. His "Le Bain" is pure Romanticism, delicate, sweet, coquettish. His contribution to "Les Soirées de Médan" is magnificent. His "Faute de l'Abbé Mouret" does not lack real touches of poetry. But as the copy of Nature is not true art according to the Greek law of beauty, so I believe that the school of Naturalism belongs to the low order of literary creation. It is a sharp photograph, coloured by hand with the minute lines of vein and shading of down. Zola's pupils, however — those who wrote the "Soirées de Médan" — have improved upon his style, and have mingled Naturalism with Romanticism in a very charming way.

I was a little disappointed, although I was also much delighted, with parts of Cable's "Grandissimes." He did not follow out his first plan — as he told me he was going to do — viz., to scatter about fifty Creole songs through the work, with the music in the shape of notes at the end. There are only a few ditties published; and as the Creole music deals in fractions of tones, Mr. Cable failed to write it properly. He is not enough of a musician, I fancy, for that.

By the time you have read this I think you will also have read my articles on Gottschalk and translations. I sent for his life to Havana; and received it with a quaint Spanish letter from Enrique Barrera, begging me to find an agent for him. I found him one here. His West Indian volume is one of the most extraordinary books I have ever seen. It is the wildest of possible romances.

L. H.

TO H. E. KREHBIEL

NEW ORLEANS, 1881

MY DEAR KREHBIEL, — How could you ever think you had offended me? I was so sick — expecting to go blind and "lift the cover of my brains" as

TO H. E. KREHBIEL

the Spaniards say, and also ill-treated — that I had no spirit left to write. You will be glad to know that I have now got so fat that they call me "The Fat Boy" at the office.

Your letter gave me great pleasure. I think your plan — vague as it appears to be — will crystallize into a very happy reality. You have the sacred fire — le vrai feu sacré — and with health and strength must succeed. What you want, and what we all want, who possess devotion to any noble idea, who hide any artistic idol in a niche of the heart, is that independence which gives us at least the time to worship the holiness of beauty — be it in harmonies of sound, of form, or of colour. You have strength, youth — not in years only but in the vital resources of your being — the true parfum de la jeunesse is perceptible in your thoughts and hopes and abilities to create; and you have other advantages I will not mention lest my observations might be "embarrassing." I should be surprised, indeed, to hear in a few years from now that you had not been able to emancipate yourself from the fetters of that intensely vulgar and detestably commonplace thing, called American journalism — of which I, alas! must long remain a slave. A prize in the Havana lottery might alone deliver me speedily; but I mostly rely on the hope of being able next year to open a little French bookstore in one of the tense quaint old streets. I had hoped to leave New Orleans; but with my eyes in their present condition, it would be folly

LAFCADIO HEARN

to fight for life over again in some foreign country. You say you hope to see some day a product of my pen more durable than a newspaper article. But I very much doubt if you ever will. My visual misfortune has reduced my hours of work to one third. I only work from 10 A.M. to 2 P.M. You will see, therefore, that my work must be rapid. At 2 P.M. my eyes are usually worn out. But as you seem to have been interested in some of my little fantasies, I take the liberty of sending you several now. They are too flimsy, however, to be ever collected for publication, unless in the course of a few years I could write a hundred or so, and select one out of three afterward.

Your observations about Amphion and Orpheus prompted me to send you an old issue of the "Item," in which you will find some very extraordinary observations on the subject of Greek music, translated from a charming work in my possession. But you will be disgusted, perhaps, to know that with all his erudition upon musical legends and musical history, Gautier had no ear for music. I almost feel like asking you not to tell that to anybody.

If you could pay a visit this winter I think you would have a pleasant time. I would like to aid you to get some of the Creole music I vainly promised you. I found it impossible so far to obtain any; yet had I the ability to write music down I could have obtained you some. If you were here I could introduce you to the President of the Athénée Louisi-

TO H. E. KREHBIEL

anaise, who would certainly put you in the way of doing so yourself.

What I do hope to obtain for you — if you care about it — is Mexican music. Mexicans are common visitors here; and every educated Mexican can sing and play some instrument. They have sung here for us — guitar accompaniment. Did you ever hear "El Aguardiente"? It is a very queer air — boisterous, merry with a merriment that seems all the time on the point of breaking into a laugh — yet withal half-savage like some Spanish ditties. When they sang it here, it was with a chorus accompaniment of glasses held upside down and tapped with spoons.

Did you ever hear negroes play the piano by ear? There are several curiosities here, Creole negroes. Sometimes we pay them a bottle of wine to come here and play for us. They use the piano exactly like a banjo. It is good banjo-playing, but no piano-playing.

One difficulty in the way of obtaining Creole music or ditties is the fact that the French coloured population are ashamed to speak their patois before whites. They will address you in French and sing French songs; but there must be extraordinary inducements to make them sing or talk in Creole. I have done it, but it is no easy work.

Nearly all the Creoles here — white — know English, French, and Spanish, more or less well, in addition to the patois employed only in speaking to children or servants. When a child becomes about ten years old, it is usually forbidden to speak Creole under any other circumstances.

But I do not suppose this will much interest you. I shall endeavour — this time I'm afraid to promise — to secure you some Mexican or Havanese music; and will postpone further remarks to a future occasion.

I am sorry Feldwisch is ill; and I doubt if the Colorado air will do him good. When he was here I had a vague suspicion I should never see him again.

Remember me to those whom you know I like, and don't think me dilatory if I don't write immediately on receipt of a letter. I have explained the condition of affairs as well as I could.

I remain, dear fellow, yours

L. HEARN

TO H. E. KREHBIEL

NEW ORLEANS, 1882

How are you on Russian music?

You could make a terrible and taking operatic tragedy on Sacher-Masoch's "Mother of God." Get it, if you can, and read it. I send you specimen translation. It was written, I believe, in German.

Have you read in the "Kalewala" of the "Bride of Gold" — of the "Betrothed of Silver"?

Have you read how the mother of Kullevo arose from her tomb, and cried unto him from the deeps of the dust?

TO H. E. KREHBIEL

TO H. E. KREHBIEL
NEW ORLEANS, 1882

DEAR K., — It got dark yesterday before I could finish some extracts from "Kalewala" I wanted to send. They are just suggestion. I must also tell you I have only a very confused idea of the "Kalewala" myself, having read it through simply as a romance, and never having had time to study out all its mythological bearings and meanings. In fact my edition is too incomplete and confusedly arranged in any case: notes are piled in a heap at the end of each volume, causing terrible trouble in making references. See if you can get Castrén.

I want also to tell you that the Pre-Islamic legends I spoke of to you are admirably arranged for musical suggestion. The original narrator breaks into verse here and there, as into song: Rabiah, for instance, recites his own death-song, his mother answers him in verse. All Arabian heroic stories are arranged in the same way; and even in so serious a work as Ibn Khallikan's great biographical dictionary, almost every incident is emphasized by a poetical citation.

Your idea about your style being heavy is really incorrect. Your art has trained you so thoroughly in choosing words that hit the exact meaning desired with the full strength of technical or picturesque expression, that the continual use of certain beauties has dulled your perception of their native force, perhaps. You do not feel, I mean, the full strength of what you write — in a style of immense compressed force. I would not wish you to think you had done your best, though; better to feel dissatisfied, but not good to *underestimate* yourself. I am now, you see, claiming the privilege of criticizing what I could not begin to do myself; but I believe I can see beauty where it exists in style, and I don't want you to be underestimating your own worth.

Are your letters of a character suitable for bookform? Hoppin — I think, is the name — the author of "Old England," a Yale professor, who made an English tour, formed one of the most charming volumes in such a way. Think it over.

Affectionately
LAFCADIO

Please never even suspect that my suggestions to you are made in any spirit of false conceit: a friend of the most limited artistic ability can often suggest things to a real artist, and even give him confidence.

TO H. E. KREHBIEL
NEW ORLEANS, 1882
KALEWALA

DEAR K., — The Society of Finnish Literature celebrated, in 1885, I think, the first centennial of the publication of the "Kalewala."

There are two epics of Finland — just as most peoples have two epics — most people at least of

TO H. E. KREHBIEL

Aryan origin; and the existence of such tremendous poems as the "Kalewala" and "Kanteletar" affords, in the opinion of M. Quatrefages, a strong proof that the Finns are of Aryan origin. Loennrot was the Homer of Finland, the one who collected and edited the oral epic poetry now published under the head of the "Kalewala." But Léouzon Le Duc in 1845 published the first translation. (This I have.) Loennrot followed him three years later. Le Duc's version contained only 12,100 verses. Loennrot's contained 22,800. A second French version was subsequently made (which I have sent for). In 1853 appeared Castrén's magnificent work on Finnish mythology, without which a thorough comprehension of the "Kalewala" is almost impossible.

You will be glad to know that the *definitive* edition of the "Kalewala," as well as the work of Castrén, have both been translated into German by Herr Schiefner (1852-54, I believe is the date). Since then a whole ocean of Finnish poetry and folk-lore and legends has been collected, edited, published, and translated. (I get some of these facts from "Mélusine," some from the work of the anthropologist Quatrefages.)

In order to get a correct idea of what you might do with the "Kalewala," *you must get it and read it.* Try to get it in the German! I can give you some idea of its beauties; but to give you its movement, and plot, or to show you precisely how much operatic value it possesses, would be a task beyond my power. It would be like attempting to make one familiar with Homer in a week.

Once you have digested it, I can then be of real service, perhaps. You would need the work of Castrén also — which I cannot read. To determine the precise mythological value, rank, power, aspect, etc., of gods and demons, and their relation to natural forces, one must read up a little on the Finns. I have Le Duc, but he is deficient.

I don't think that any epic surpasses that weirdest and strangest of runes. It is not so well known as it deserves. It gives you the impression of a work written by wizards, who spoke little to men, and much to nature — but the sinister and misty nature of the eternally frozen North.

You have in the "Kalewala" all the elements of a magnificent operatic episode — weirdness, the passion of love, and the eternal struggle between evil and good, between darkness and light. You have any possible amount of melody — a universe of inspiration for startling and totally novel musical themes. The scenery of such a thing might be made wilder and grander than anything imagined even by the Talmudically vast conceptions of Wagner.

An opera founded on the "Kalewala" might be made a work worthy of the grandest musician who ever lived: think of the possibilities suggested by the picture of Nature's mightiest forces in contention — wind and sea, frost and sun, darkness and luminosity.

TO H. E. KREHBIEL

I don't like the antique theme you suggest, because it has been worn so threadbare that only a miracle could give it a fresh surface. Better search the "Kathā-sarit-Sāgara," or some other Indian collection — or borrow from the sublimely rough and rugged poetry of Pre-Islamic Arabia. You will never regret an acquaintance with these books — even at some cost. They epitomize all the thought, passion, and poetry of a nation and of a period.

I prefer the "Kalewala" to any other theme you suggest. I might suggest many others, but none so vast, so grand, so multiform. Nothing in the Talmud like that. The Talmud is a *Semitic* work; but nothing Jewish rises to the grandeur of Arabic poetry, which expresses the supreme possibilities of the Semitic mind — except, perhaps, the Book of Job, which is thought by some to have had an Arabian creator.

What you say about the disinclination to work for years upon a theme for pure love's sake, without hope of reward, touches me — because I have felt that despair so long and so often. And yet I believe that all the world's art-work — all that which is eternal — was thus wrought. And I also believe that no work made perfect for the pure love of art, can perish, save by strange and rare accident. Despite the rage of religion and of time, we know Sappho found no rival, no equal. Rivers changed their courses and dried up — seas became deserts, since some Egyptian romanticist wrote the story of

Latin-Khamois. Do you suppose he ever received $００ for it?

Yet the hardest of all sacrifices for the artist is this sacrifice to art — this trampling of self under foot! It is the supreme test for admittance into the ranks of the eternal priests. It is the bitter and fruitless sacrifice which the artist's soul is bound to make — as in certain antique cities maidens were compelled to give their virginity to a god of stone! But without the sacrifice can we hope for the grace of heaven?

What is the reward? The consciousness of inspiration only! I think art gives a new faith. I think — all jesting aside — that could I create something I felt to be sublime, I should feel also that the Unknowable had selected me for a mouthpiece, for a medium of utterance, in the holy cycling of its eternal purpose; and I should know the pride of the prophet that had seen God face to face.

All this might seem absurd, perhaps, to a purely practical mind (yours is not *too* practical); but there is a practical side also. In this age of lightning, thought and recognition have become quadruple-winged, like the angels of Isaiah. Do your very best — your very, very best: the century must recognize the artist if he is there. If he is not recognized, it is because he is not great. Have you faith in yourself? I know you are a great natural artist; I have absolute faith in you. You *must* succeed if you make the sacrifice of working for art's sake alone.

Comparing yourself to me won't do! — dear old

TO H. E. KREHBIEL

fellow. I am in most things a botch! You say you envy me certain qualities; but you forget how those qualities are at variance with an art whose beauty is geometrical and whose perfection is mathematical. You also say you envy me my power of application! — If you only knew the pain and labour I have to create a little good work. And there are months when I cannot write. It is not hard to write when the thought is there; but the thought will not always come — there are weeks when I cannot even think.

The only application I have is that of persistence in a small way. I write a rough sketch and labour it over and over again for half a year, at intervals of ten minutes' leisure — sometimes I get a day or two. The work done each time is small. But with the passing of the seasons the mass becomes noticeable — perhaps creditable. This is merely the result of system.

You may laugh at this letter if you please— this friendly protest to one whom I have always recognized as my superior — but there is truth in it. Think over the "Kalewala," and write to
    Your friend and admirer
              LAFCADIO HEARN

TO H. E. KREHBIEL
NEW ORLEANS, 1882

MY DEAR KREHBIEL, — When I got your letter I felt as if a great load was lifted off me — the sky looked brighter and the world seemed a little sweeter than usual. As for me, you could have paid me no higher compliment. Glad you did not disapprove of the article.

Your clippings are superb. I think your style constantly gains in force and terseness. It is admirably crystallized; and I have not yet been able to form a permanent style of my own. I trust I will succeed in time; but in purity and conciseness you will always be my master, for your art has taught you style better than a thousand university professors could do. I suppose, however, you will always be slightly Gothic — not harshly Gothic, but Middle Period — making ornament always subordinate to the general plan. I shall always be more or less Arabesque — covering my whole edifice with intricate designs, serrating my arches, and engraving mysticisms above the portals. You will be grand and lofty; I shall try to be at once voluptuous and elegant, like a colonnade in the mosque of Cordova.

I send you something your article on the Jubilee Singers makes me think of. It is from the pen of a marvellous writer, who long lived at Senegal. If you do not find anything new in it, return it; but if it can be of use to you, keep it. I hope to translate the whole work some day.

       Your friend L. H.

Have heard Patti; but did not understand her power until you explained it me.

TO H. E. KREHBIEL

TO H. E. KREHBIEL

New Orleans, 1882

My dear Krehbiel, — Much as it pleased me to hear from you, I assure you that your letter is shocking. It is shocking to hear of anybody being compelled to work for seventeen hours a day. You have neither time to think, to study, to read, to do your best work, or to make any artistic progress — not even to hint of pleasure — while working seventeen hours a day. Nor is that all; I believe it injures a man's health and capacity for endurance, as well as his style and peace of mind. You have a fine constitution; but if once broken down by overstraining the nervous system you will never get fully over the shock. It is very hard for me to believe that it is really necessary for you to do reportorial work and to write correspondence, unless you have a special financial object to accomplish within a very short space of time. The editorial work touching upon art matters which you are capable of doing for the "Tribune" might be done in the daytime; but what do you want to waste your brain and time upon reportorial work for? D——n reportorial work and correspondence, and the American disposition to work people to death, and the American delight in getting worked to death! Well, I have nothing more to say except to protest my hope that the seventeen-hours-a-day business is going to stop before long; for the longer it lasts the more difficult it will be for you to accomplish your ultimate purpose. The devil of overworking one's self is that it renders it impossible to get fair and just remuneration for value given — impossible also to create those opportunities for self-advancements which form the steps of the stairway to the artistic heaven — impossible to maintain that self-pride and confident sense of worth without which no man, however gifted, can make others fully conscious of it. When you voluntarily convert yourself into a part of the machinery of a great daily newspaper, you must revolve and keep revolving with the wheels; you play the man in the treadmill. The more you involve yourself the more difficult it will be for you to escape. I said I had nothing further to observe; but I find I must say something more — not that I imagine for a moment I am telling you anything new, but because I wish to try to impress anew upon you some facts which do not seem to have influenced you as I believe they ought to do.

Under all the levity of Henri Murger's picturesque Bohemianism, there is a serious philosophy apparent which elevates the characters of his romance to heroism. They followed one principle faithfully — so faithfully that only the strong survived the ordeal — never to abandon the pursuit of an artistic vocation for any other occupation however lucrative — not even when she remained apparently deaf and blind to her worshippers. The conditions pictured by Murger have passed away in Paris as elsewhere: the

TO H. E. KREHBIEL

old barriers to ambition have been greatly broken down. But I think the moral remains. So long as one can live and pursue his natural vocation in art, it is a duty with him never to abandon it if he believes that he has within him the elements of final success. Every time he labours at aught that is not of art, he robs the divinity of what belongs to her.

Do you never reflect that within a few years you will no longer be the YOUNG MAN— and that, like Vesta's fires, the enthusiasm of youth for an art-idea must be well fed with the sacred branches to keep it from dying out? I think you ought really to devote all your time and energies and ability to the cultivation of one subject, so as to make that subject alone repay you for all your pains. And I do not believe that Art is altogether ungrateful in these days: she will repay fidelity to her, and recompense sacrifices. I don't think you have any more right to play reporter than a great sculptor to model fifty-cent plaster figures of idiotic saints for Catholic processions, or certain painters to letter steamboats at so much a letter. In one sense, too, Art is exacting. To acquire real eminence in any one branch of any art, one must study nothing else for a life-time. A very wide general knowledge may be acquired only at the expense of depth. But you are certainly right in thinking of the present for other reasons. Still, there is nothing so important, not only to success but to confidence, hope, and happiness, as good health and a strong constitution; and these you must lose if you choose to keep working seventeen hours a day! It is well to be able to do such a thing on a brief stretch, but it is suicide, moral and physical, to keep it up regularly. The rolling-mill hand, or the puddler, or the moulder, or the common brakeman on a railroad cannot keep up at such hours for a great length of time; and you must know that even hard labour is not so exhausting as brain-work. Don't work yourself sick, old friend — you are in a fair way to do it now.

Your friend
L. H.

TO JEROME A. HART

NEW ORLEANS, *May*, 1882

DEAR SIR, — Thanks for your kindly little article. I suppose it emanated from the same source as the charming translation of Gautier's "Spectre de la Rose" — which we reproduced here, comparing it with the inferior translation — or rather mutilation — of the same poem which appeared in the ⸺.

Your translation of the epitaph seems to me superb as far as the first two lines go; but I can hardly agree with you as to the last. "La plus belle du monde" cannot be perfectly rendered by "the loveliest in the land" — which is a far weaker expression, by reason of the circumscribed idea it involves. "La plus belle du monde" is an expression of paramount force, simple as it is; it conveys the idea of beauty without an equal, not in any one country,

TO JEROME A. HART

but in the whole world. But I think your second line is a masterpiece of faithfulness; and, as you justly remark, my hobby is literalism.
Very sincerely yours
LAFCADIO HEARN

TO JEROME A. HART
NEW ORLEANS, *May*, 1882

DEAR SIR, — I am very grateful for your kind letter and the pleasure of making your acquaintance even through an epistolary medium.

We have the same terrible proverb in Spanish that you cite in Italian; but it certainly can never apply to the "Argonaut's" exquisite translations — preserving metre, colour, and warmth so far as seems to be possible. Still, I must say that I do not believe the poetry of one country can be perfectly reproduced in corresponding metre in the poetry of another: much that is even marvellous may be done — yet a little of the original perfume evaporates in the process. Therefore the French gave *prose* translations of Heine and Byron: especially in regard to the German poet they considered translation in metrical form impossible. Nevertheless it is impossible also to refrain from attempting such things at times — when the beauty of exotic verse seems to take us by the throat with the strangulation of pleasure. I have felt impelled occasionally to make an essay in poetical translation; the result has generally been a dismal failure, but I venture to send you a specimen which appears to be less condemnable than most of my efforts. I cannot presume to call it a translation — it is only an adaptation.

As for the lines in "Clarimonde," if the book ever reaches a second edition, I think I will be able to remedy some of their imperfections. Skaldic verse, I suppose, would be anachronistically vile; but something corresponding to the metre of "La Chanson de Roland," unrhymed, what the French call "vers assonances." This corresponds exactly with your lines in breadth; also in tone, as the accent of the assonance is thrown upon the last syllable of each line.

Very gratefully yours L. H.

P.S. Just received another note from you. Have seen the reproduction; I am exceedingly thankful for the compliment; and you know that so far as the copyright business is concerned, the credit must do the book too much good for Worthington to find any fault. I suppose you receive the "Times-Democrat" of New Orleans. I forward last Sunday's issue, containing a little compliment to the "Argonaut."

Very sincerely yours
LAFCADIO HEARN

TO JEROME A. HART

NEW ORLEANS, *December*, 1882

DEAR SIR, — I venture to intrude upon you to ask a little advice, which as a brother-student of foreign

TO JEROME A. HART

literature you could probably give me better than any other person to whom I could apply. I am informed that in San Francisco there are enterprising and liberal-minded publishers, with whom unknown authors have a better chance than with the austere and pious publishers of the East. It would be a very great favour indeed, if you could give me some positive indication in this matter. I desire to find a publisher for that excessively curious but somewhat audacious book, "La Tentation de Saint Antoine," of Flaubert, of which I have completed and corrected the MS. translation. You who know the original will probably agree with me that it would be little less than a literary crime to emasculate such a masterpiece in the translation. I have translated almost every word of the Heresiarch dispute, and the soliloquy of the god Crepitus, etc.

Consequently I have very little hopes of obtaining a publisher in New York or Boston. Do you think I could obtain one in San Francisco? I would be willing to advance something toward the cost of publishing — if necessary.

Trust you will pardon my intrusion. I think the mutual interest we both feel in one branch of foreign literature is a fair excuse for my letter.

With thanks for previous many kindnesses,
I remain, truly yours
LAFCADIO HEARN

LAFCADIO HEARN

TO JEROME A. HART

New Orleans, *January*, 1883

Dear Sir, — Writing to San Francisco seems, after a sort, like writing to Japan or Malabar, so great is the lapse of time consumed in the transit of mail-matter, especially when one is anxious. I was quite so, fearing you might have considered my letter intrusive; but your exceedingly pleasant reply has dispelled all apprehension.

I am not surprised at the information; for the difficulty of finding publishers in the United States is something colossal, and my hopes burned with a very dim flame. I do not know about Worthington — as he is absent in Europe, perhaps he will undertake the publication; but I fear, inasmuch as he is a Methodist of the antique type, that he will not. Now the holy "Observer" declared that the "Cleopatra" was a collection of "stories of unbridled lust without the apology of natural passion"; that "the translation reeked with the miasma of the brothel," etc., etc. — and Worthington was much exercised thereat. Otherwise I should have suggested the publication in English of "Mademoiselle de Maupin."

I regret that I cannot tell you anything about the fate of "Cleopatra's Nights," but the publisher preserves a peculiar and sinister silence in regard to it. Perhaps he is sitting upon the stool of orthodox repentance. Perhaps he is preparing to be generous. But this I much doubt; and as the translations were

TO JEROME A. HART

published partly at my own expense, I am anxious only regarding the fate of my original capital.

Yes, I read the "Critic" — and considered that the observation on Gautier stultified the paper. If the translator had been dissected by the same hand, I should not have felt very unhappy. But I received some very nice private letters from Eastern readers, which encouraged me very much, and among them several requesting for other translations from Gautier.

"Salammbô" is the greatest, by far, of Flaubert's creations, because harmonious in all its plan and purpose, and because it introduces the reader into an unfamiliar field of history, cultivated with astonishing skill and verisimilitude. It was twice written, like "La Tentation." I translated the prayer to the Moon for the preface to "La Tentation." I sincerely trust you will translate it. As for time, it is astonishing what system will accomplish. If a man cannot spare an hour a day, he can certainly spare a half-hour. I translated "La Tentation" by this method — never allowing a day to pass without an attempt to translate a page or two. The work is audacious in parts; but I think nothing ought to be suppressed. That serpent-scene, the crucified lions, the breaking of the chair of gold, the hideous battles about Carthage — these pages contain pictures that ought not to remain entombed in a foreign museum. I pray you may translate "Salammbô" — a most difficult task, I fancy — but one that you would certainly succeed admirably with. In my preface I spoke of "Salammbô" as the most wonderful of Flaubert's productions.

"Herodias" is another story which ought to be translated. But I would write too long a letter if I dilate upon the French masterpieces.

I will only say that, in regard to recent publications, I have noticed some extraordinary novels which have not earned the attention they deserve. "Le Roman d'un Spahi" seems to me a miracle of art — and "Le Mariage de Loti" contains passages of wonderful and weird beauty. These, with "Aziyadé," are the productions of a French naval officer who signs himself Loti. Think I shall try to translate the first-named next year.

Verily the path of the translator is hard. The Petersons and Estes & Lauriat are deluging the country with bogus translations or translations so unfaithful to the original that they must be characterized as fraudulent. And the great American public like the stuff. One who translates for the love of the original will probably have no reward save the satisfaction of creating something beautiful, and perhaps of saving a masterpiece from desecration by less reverent bards. But this is worth working for.

With grateful thanks, and sincere hopes that you will not be deterred from translating "Salammbô" before some incompetent hand attempts it, I remain,
Sincerely
LAFCADIO HEARN

TO REV. WAYLAND D. BALL

TO REV. WAYLAND D. BALL
                               NEW ORLEANS, 1882

DEAR SIR, — I am very grateful for the warm and kindly sympathy your letter evidences; and as I have already received about a half-dozen communications of similar tenor from unknown friends, I am beginning to feel considerably encouraged. The "lovers of the antique loveliness" are proving to me the future possibilities of a long cherished dream — the English realization of a Latin style, modelled upon foreign masters, and rendered even more forcible by that element of *strength* which is the characteristic of Northern tongues. This no man can hope to accomplish; but even a translator may carry his stone to the master-masons of a new architecture of language.

You ask me about translations. I am sorry that I am not able to answer you hopefully. I have a curious work by Flaubert in the hands of R. Worthington (under consideration); and I have various MSS. filed away in the Cemetery of the Rejected. I tried for six years to obtain a publisher for the little collection you so much like, and was obliged at last to have them published partly at my own expense — a difficult matter for one who is obliged to work upon a salary.

As for "Mademoiselle de Maupin," much as I should desire the honour of translating it, I would dread to work in vain, or at best to work for the profit of some publisher who would have the translator at his mercy. If I could find a publisher willing to publish the work precisely as I would render it, I would be glad to surrender all profits to him; but I fancy that any American publisher would wish to emasculate the manuscript.

I am told that an English translation was in existence in London some years ago, but I could not learn the publisher's name. Chatto & Windus, the printers of the admirable English version of the "Contes Drolatiques," might be able to inform you further. But I am afraid that the English version was scarcely worthy of the original, owing to the profound silence of the press in regard to the matter. An American translation was being offered to New York publishers a few years ago. It was not accepted.

Although my own work is far from being perfect, I think I am capable of judging other translations of Gautier. The American translations are very poor ("Spirite," "Captain Fracasse," "Romance of the Mummy"), in fact they are hardly deserving the name. The English translations of Gautier's works of travel are generally good. Henry Holt has reprinted some of them, I think.

But out of perhaps sixty volumes, Gautier's works include very few romances or stories. I have never seen a translation of "Fortunio" or "Militona" — perhaps because the sexual idea — the Eternal Feminine — prevails too much therein. "Avatar"

TO REV. WAYLAND D. BALL

has been translated in the New York "Evening Post," I cannot say how well; but I have the manuscript translation of it myself, which I could never get a publisher to accept. Then there are the "Contes Humoristiques" (1 vol.) and about a dozen short tales not translated. Besides these, and the four translated already ("Fracasse," "Spirite," "The Mummy," and possibly "Mademoiselle de Maupin"), Gautier's works consist chiefly of critiques, sketches of travel, dramas, comedies — including the charmingly wicked piece, "A Devil's Tear" — and three volumes of poems.

My purpose now is to translate a series of works by the most striking French authors, each embodying a style of a school. I tried in the first collection to offer the best novelettes of Gautier in English, relying upon my own judgment so far as I could. Hereafter with leisure and health I shall attempt to do the same for about five others. I can understand your desire to see more of Gautier, and I trust you will some day; but when you have read "Mademoiselle de Maupin" and the two volumes of short stories, you have read his masterpieces of prose, and will care less for the remainder. His greatest art is of course in his magical poems; except the exotic poetry of the Hindoos, and of Persia, there is nothing in verse to equal them.

I must have fatigued your patience, however, by this time. With many thanks for your kind letter, which I took the liberty to send to Worthington, and

hoping that you will soon be able to see another curious attempt of mine in print, I remain,
Sincerely
LAFCADIO HEARN

I forgot to say that in point of archæologic art the "Roman de la Momie" is Gautier's greatest work. It towers like an obelisk among the rest. But the American translation would disappoint you very much; it is a poor concern all the way through. It would not be a bad idea to drop a line to Chatto & Windus, Publishers, London, and enquire about English versions of Gautier. You know that Austin Dobson translated some of his poems very successfully indeed.
In haste
L. H.

TO REV. WAYLAND D. BALL
NEW ORLEANS, *November*, 1882

DEAR SIR, — I translate hurriedly for you a few extracts from "Mademoiselle de Maupin," some of which have been used or translated by Mallock, who has said many very clever things, but whose final conclusions appear to me to smack of Jesuitic casuistry.

Gautier was not the founder of a philosophic school, but the founder of a system of artistic thought and expression. His "Mademoiselle de Maupin" is an idyl, nothing more, an idyl in which all the vague longings of youth in the blossoming of

TO REV. WAYLAND D. BALL

puberty, the reveries of amorous youth, the wild dreams of two passionate minds, male and female, both highly cultivated, are depicted with a daring excused only by their beauty. I think Mallock wrong in his taking Gautier for a type of Antichrist. There are few who have beheld the witchery of an antique statue, the supple interlacing of nude limbs in frieze or cameo, who have not for the moment regretted the antique. Freethinkers as were Gautier, Hugo, Baudelaire, De Musset, De Nerval, none of them were insensible to the mighty religious art of mediævalism which created those fantastic and enormous fabrics in which the visitor feels like an ant crawling in the skeleton of a mastodon. With the growth of æstheticism there is a tendency to return to antique ideas of beauty, and the last few years has given evidence of a resurrection of Greek influence in several departments of art. But when the first revolution against prudery and prejudice had to be made in France, violent and extreme opinions were necessary — the Gautiers and De Mussets were the Red Republicans of the Romantic Renaissance. Gautier's poems utter the same plaints as his prose; mourning for the death of Pan, crying that the modern world is draped with funeral hangings of black, against which the white skeleton appears in relief. But the dreams of an artist may influence art and literature only; they cannot affect the crystallization of social systems or the philosophy of the eye.

LAFCADIO HEARN

They were all pantheists, these characters of Romanticism, some vaguely like old Greek dreamers, others deeply and studiously, like De Nerval, a lover of German mysticism: nature, whom they loved, must have whispered to them in wind-rustling and wave-lapping some word of the mighty truths she had long before taught to Brahmins and to Bodhisatvas under a more luxuriant sky. They saw the evil beneath their feet as a vast "paste" for which the great Statuary eternally moulded new forms in his infinite crucible, and into which old forms were remelted to reappear in varied shapes; — the lips of loveliness might blossom again in pouting roses, the light of eyes rekindle in amethyst and emerald, the white breast with its delicate network of veins be re-created in fairest marble. The worship within sombre churches, and chapels, seemed to them unworthy of the spirit of Universal Love; — to adore him they deemed no temple worthy save that from whose roof of eternal azure hang the everlasting lamps of the stars; no music, save that never-ending ocean hymn, ancient as the moon, whose words no human musician may learn.

I do not know whether Mallock translated Gautier himself, or made extracts; but Gautier's madrigal pantheistic alone contains the germ of a faith sweeter and purer and nobler than the author of "Is Life Worth Living?" ever dreamed of, or at least comprehended. The poem is a microcosm of artistic pantheism; it contains the whole soul of Gautier,

TO REV. WAYLAND D. BALL

like one of the legendary jewels in which spirits were imprisoned.

Speaking of the "Decameron," Petronius, Angelinus, and so forth, I must say that I think it the duty of every scholar to read them. It is only thus that we can really obtain a correct idea of the thought and lives of those who read them when first related or written. They are historical paintings, they are shadows of the past and echoes of dead voices. Brantôme or De Châteauneuf teach one more about the life of the fifteenth or sixteenth centuries than a dozen ordinary historians could do. The influence of sex and sexual ideas has moulded the history of nations and formed national character; yet, except Michelet, there is perhaps no historian who has read history fairly in this connection. Without such influence there can be no real greatness; the mind remains arid and desolate. Every noble mind is made fruitful by its virility; we all have a secret museum in some corner of the brain, although our Pompeian or Etruscan curiosities are only shown to appreciative friends.

I have read your enclosed slip and am quite pleased with the creditable notice given you by way of introduction, and quite astonished that you should be so young. You have fine prospects before you, I fancy, if so successful already. Of course *Congregational* is so vague a word that I cannot tell how latitudinarian your present ideas are (for people in general), nor how broadly you may extend your studies of philosophy. Your correspondence with a freethinker of an extreme type would incline me to believe you were very liberally inclined, but I have often noticed that clergymen belonging even to the old cast-iron type may be classed among warm admirers of the beautiful and the true for their own sakes.

Very sincerely yours
LAFCADIO HEARN

P.S. Have just been looking at Mallock, and am satisfied that he made the translation himself because he translated the "virginity" by "purity." No one but a Catholic or Jesuit would do that; only Catholics, I believe, consider the consummation of love intrinsically impure, or attempt to identify purity with virginity. Gautier would never have used the word — a word in itself impure and testifying to uncleanliness of fancy. I have translated it properly by the English equivalent. I suppose you know that Mallock's aim is to prove that everybody not a Catholic is a fool.

ENCLOSURE

"Mademoiselle de Maupin," petite édition, Charpentier, 2 vols.; vol. ii, page 12:

I am a man of the Homeric ages; — the world in which I live is not mine, and I comprehend nothing of the social system by which I am surrounded. Never did Christ come into the world for me; I am as pagan as Alcibiades

TO REV. WAYLAND D. BALL

or Phidias. Never have I been to Golgotha to gather passion-flowers; and the deep river flowing from the side of the crucified, and making a crimson girdle about the world, has never bathed me with its waves.

Page 21:

Venus may be seen; she hides nothing; for modesty is created for the ugly alone; and is a modern invention, daughter of the Christian disdain of form and matter.

O ancient worlds! all thou didst revere is now despised; thine idols are overthrown in dust; gaunt anchorites clad in tattered rags, gory martyrs with shoulders lacerated by the tigers of the circuses, lie heaped upon the pedestals of thy gods so comely and so charming; — the Christ has enveloped the world in his winding sheet. Beauty must blush for herself, must wear a shroud.

Pages 22, 23:

Virginity, thou bitter plant, born upon a soil blood-moistened, whose wan and sickly flower opes painfully within the damp shadows of the cloister, under cold lustral rains; — rose without perfume, and bristling with thorns — thou hast replaced for us those fair and joyous roses, besprinkled with nard and Falernian, worn by the dancing girls of Sybaris.

The antique world knew thee not, O fruitless flower! — never wert thou entwined within their garlands, replete with intoxicating perfume; — in that vigorous and healthy life, thou wouldst have been disdainfully trampled under foot! Virginity, mysticism, melancholy — three unknown words, three new maladies brought among us by the Christ. Pale spectres who deluge the world with icy tears and who, etc., etc.

LAFCADIO HEARN

TO REV. WAYLAND D. BALL

NEW ORLEANS, 1883

SECRET AFFINITIES

(A PANTHEISTIC MADRIGAL)

Emaux et Camées — Enamels and Cameos

FOR three thousand years two blocks of marble in the pediment of an antique temple have juxtaposed their white dreams against the background of the Attic heaven.

Congealed in the same nacre, tears of those waves which weep for Venus — two pearls deep-plunged in ocean's gulf, have uttered secret words unto each other; —

Blooming in the cool Generalife, beneath the spray of the ever-weeping fountain, two roses in Boabdil's time spake to each other with whisper of leaves; —

Upon the cupolas of Venice, two white doves, rosy-footed, perched one May-time evening on the nest where love makes itself eternal.

Marble, pearl, rose, and dove — all dissolve, all pass away; — the pearl melts, the marble falls, the rose fades, the bird takes flight.

Leaving each other, all atoms seek the deep Crucible to thicken that universal paste formed of the forms that are melted by God.

By slow metamorphoses, the white marble changes to white flesh, the rosy flowers into rosy lips — remoulding themselves into many fair bodies.

Again do the white doves coo within the hearts of young lovers; and the rare pearls re-form into teeth for the jewel-casket of woman's smile.

And hence those sympathies, imperiously sweet, whereby in all places souls are gently warmed to know each other for sisters.

TO REV. WAYLAND D. BALL

Thus, docile to the summons of an aroma, a sunbeam, a colour, the atom flies to the atom as to the flower the bee.

Then dream-memories return of long reveries in white temple pediments, of reveries in the deeps of the sea — of blossom talk beside the clear-watered fountain —

Of kisses and quivering of wings upon the domes that are tipped with balls of gold; and the faithful molecules seek one another and know the clinging of love once more.

Again love awakens from its slumber of oblivion; — vaguely the Past is re-born; the perfume of the flower inhales and knows itself again in the sweetness of the pink mouth.

In that mother-of-pearl which glimmers in a laugh, the pearl recognizes its own whiteness; — upon the smooth skin of a young girl the marble with emotion recognizes its own coolness.

The dove finds in a sweet voice the echo of its own plaint — resistance becomes blunted, and the stranger becomes the lover.

And thou before whom I tremble and burn — what ocean-billow, what temple-font, what rose-tree, what dome of old knew us together? What pearl or marble, what flower or dove?

L. Hearn

Dear Ball, — Hope you will like the above rough prose version — of course all the unison is gone, all the soul of it has exhaled like a perfume; — this is a faded flower, pressed between the leaves of a book — not the exquisite blossom which grew from the heart of Théophile Gautier.

L. H.

LAFCADIO HEARN

TO REV. WAYLAND D. BALL

NEW ORLEANS, 1883

DEAR BALL, — So far from your last being a "poor letter," as you call it, I derived uncommon pleasure therefrom; and you must not annoy yourself by writing me long letters when you have much more important matters to occupy yourself. To write a letter of twelve pages or more is the labour equivalent to the production of a column article for a newspaper; and it would be unreasonable to expect any correspondent to devote so much time and labour to letter-writing more than once in several months. I have always found the friends who write me short letters write me regularly, and all who write long letters become finally weary and cease corresponding altogether at last. Nevertheless a great deal may be said in a few words, and much pleasure extracted from a letter one page long.

I should much like to hear of your being called to a strong church, but I suppose, as you say, that your youth is for the time being a drawback. But I certainly would not feel in the least annoyed upon that score. You have all your future before you in a very bright glow, and I do not believe that any one can expect to obtain real success before he is thirty-five or forty. You cannot even forge yourself a good literary style before thirty; and even then it will not be perfectly tempered for some years. But from what I have seen of your ability, I should anticipate

TO REV. WAYLAND D. BALL

a more than common success for you, and I believe you will create yourself a very wide and strong weapon of speech. And your position is very enviable. There is no calling which allows of so much leisure for study and so many opportunities for self-cultivation. Just fancy the vast amount of reading you will be able to accomplish within five years, and the immense value of such literary absorption. I have the misfortune to be a journalist, and it is hard work to study at all, and attend to one's diurnal duty. Another misfortune here is the want of a good library. You have in Boston one of the finest in the world, and I believe you will be apt to regret it if you leave. Speaking of study — you know that science has broadened and deepened so enormously of late years, that no man can thoroughly master any one branch of any one science, without devoting his whole life thereunto. The scholars of the twentieth century will have to be specialists or nothing. In matters of literary study, pure and simple, a fixed purpose and plan must be adopted. I will tell you what mine is, for I am quite young too, comparatively speaking, and have my "future" before me, so to speak. I never read a book which does not powerfully impress the imagination; but whatever contains novel, curious, potent imagery I always read, no matter what the subject. When the soil of fancy is really well enriched with innumerable fallen leaves, the flowers of language grow spontaneously. There are four things especially which enrich fancy

LAFCADIO HEARN

— mythology, history, romance, poetry — the last being really the crystallization of all human desire after the impossible, the diamonds created by prodigious pressure of suffering. Now there is very little really good poetry, so it is easy to choose. In history I think one should only seek the extraordinary, the monstrous, the terrible; in mythology the most fantastic and sensuous, just as in romance. But there is one more absolutely essential study in the formation of a strong style — science. No romance equals it. If one can store up in his brain the most extraordinary facts of astronomy, geology, ethnology, etc., they furnish him with a wonderful and startling variety of images, symbols, and illustrations. With these studies I should think one could not help forging a good style at least — an impressive one certainly. I give myself five years more study; then I think I may be able to do something. But with your opportunities I could hope to do much better than I am doing now. Opportunity to study is supreme happiness; for colleges and universities only give us the keys with which to unlock libraries of knowledge hereafter. Is n't it horrible to hold the keys in one's hands and never have time to use them?

Very truly yours
L. Hearn

Don't write again until you have plenty of time; — I know you must be busy. But whenever you

TO REV. WAYLAND D. BALL

would like to hear anything about anything in my special line of study, let me have a line from you, as I might be able to be of some use in matters of reference.

TO REV. WAYLAND D. BALL

NEW ORLEANS, 1883

MY DEAR BALL, — I suppose you are quite disgusted with my silence; but you would excuse it were you to see how busy I have been, especially since our managing editor has gone on a vacation of some months.

I was amused at your ideal description of me. As you supposed, I am swarthy — more than the picture indicates; but by no means interesting to look at, and the profile view conceals the loss of an eye. I am also very short, a small square-set fellow of about one hundred and forty pounds when in good health.

I read with extreme pleasure your essay, and while I do not hold the same views, I believe yours will do good. Furthermore, if you familiarize the public with Buddhism, you are bound to aid in bringing about the very state of things I hope for. Buddhism only needs to be known to make its influence felt in America. I don't think that works like those of Sinnett, or Olcott's curious "Buddhist Catechism," published by Estes & Lauriat, will do any good; — they are too metaphysical, representing a sort of neo-gnosticism which repels by its resemblance to Spiritualistic humbug. But the higher Buddhism — that suggested by men like Emerson, John Weiss, etc. — will yet have an apostle. We shall live, I think, to see some strange things.

I am sorry I cannot gratify you by my reply about your projected literary sketches. The policy of the paper has been to give the preference to lady writers on such subjects, with a few exceptions to which some literary reputation has been attached. You would have a much better chance with theosophic essays; but you would be greatly restricted as to space. You did not write, it appears, to Page; and he is now at Saratoga, where he will remain about two months. Anyhow, I would personally advise you — if you think my advice worth anything — to devote your literary impulse altogether to religious subjects. By a certain class of sermons and addresses you can achieve in a few years much more success than the slow uphill work of professional journalism or literature would bring you in a whole decade. With leisure and popularity you could then achieve such literary work as you could not think of attempting now. As for me, if I succeed in becoming independent of journalism in another ten years, I shall be luckier than men of much greater talent — such as Bayard Taylor.

Believe me, as ever, yours
L. HEARN

TO REV. WAYLAND D. BALL

TO REV. WAYLAND D. BALL

NEW ORLEANS, *June*, 1883

MY DEAR FRIEND, — You have been very kind indeed to give me so pleasant an introduction to your personality; — I already feel as if we were more intimate, as if I knew you better and liked you more. A photograph is generally a surprise; — in your case it was not; — you are very much as I fancied you were — only more so.

I read with pleasure your article. The introduction was especially powerful. I must now, however, tell you frankly what I think would be most to your interest. When I wrote before I had no definite idea as to the scope or plan of your essay, nor did I know the "Inter-Ocean" desired it. Now I think it your duty to give the next article to that paper — as the first is incomplete without it. It does not contain more than the parallel. However, the publication of your writing in the "Inter-Ocean," even though unremunerative, will do you vastly more good than would the publication in our paper at a small price. The "Inter-Ocean" circulation is very large; and you must be advertised. It is not necessary to seek it, but it would be unwise to refuse it. In the mean time I shall call attention to you in our columns occasionally — briefly of course. I only proposed "Times-Democrat" with the idea you might have need of a medium to publish your opinions and ideas. But so long as the "Inter-

Ocean" takes an interest in you — even without compensating you — you have a right to congratulate yourself, as you are only beginning to make your voice heard in the wilderness. I shall bring your paper to Page Baker to-night — who has just returned to town. Will send photo when I write again.

I would scarcely advise you to quote from my book. I am still too small a figure to attract any attention; and I think it would be best for you only to cite generally recognized authorities. Needless to say that I should feel greatly honoured and very grateful; but I think it would not be strictly to your interest to notice me until such time as I am recognized as a thinker, if such time shall ever arrive. With you it is very different; — your *cloth* — as we say in England — gives every gamin the right to review and praise you as a public teacher.

Yours very affectionately
LAFCADIO HEARN

TO W. D. O'CONNOR
NEW ORLEANS, *February*, 1883

DEAR SIR, — Mr. Page M. Baker, managing editor of the "Times-Democrat," to whose staff I belong, handed me your letter relative to the article on Gustave Doré — stating at the same time that it seemed to him the handsomest compliment ever paid to my work. I hasten to confirm the statement, and to thank you very sincerely for that delicate and

TO W. D. O'CONNOR

nevertheless magistral criticism; for no one could have uttered a more forcible compliment in fewer words. As the author of a little volume of translations from Théophile Gautier I received a number of very encouraging and gratifying letters from Eastern literary men; but I must say that your letter upon my editorial gave me more pleasure than all of them, especially, perhaps, as manifesting an artistic sympathy with me in my admiration for the man whom I believe to have been the mightiest of modern artists.

Very gratefully and sincerely yours
LAFCADIO HEARN

TO W. D. O'CONNOR

NEW ORLEANS, *March*, 1883

MY DEAR MR. O'CONNOR, — My delay in answering your charming letter was unavoidable, as I have been a week absent from the city upon an excursion to the swampy region of southern Louisiana, in company with Harpers' artist, for whom I am writing a series of Southern sketches. As I am already on good terms with the Harpers, your delicate letter to them cannot have failed to do me far more good than would have been the case had I been altogether unknown. I don't know how to thank you, but trust that I may yet have the pleasure of trying to do so verbally, if you ever visit New Orleans.

Your books came to hand; and do great credit to your skill — I am myself a compositor and have held the office of proof-reader in a large publishing house, where I tried to establish an English system of punctuation with indifferent success. Thus I can appreciate the work. As yet I have not had time to read much of the report, but as the Life-Saving Service has a peculiar intrinsic interest I will expect to find much to enjoy in the report before long.

You are partly right about Gautier, and, I think, partly wrong. His idea of work was to illustrate with a mosaic of rare and richly coloured words. But there is a wonderful tenderness, a nervous sensibility of feeling, an Oriental sensuousness of warmth in his creations which I like better than Victor Hugo's marvellous style. Hugo, like the grand Goth that he is, liked the horrible, the grotesqueness of tragic mediævalism. Gautier followed the Greek ideal so potently presented in Lessing's "Laocoön," and sought the beautiful only. His poetry is, I believe, matchless in French literature — an engraved gem-work of words. Well, you can judge for yourself a little, by reading his two remarkable prose-fantasies — "Arria Marcella" and "Clarimonde" — in my translations of him, which you will receive from New York in a few days. Something evaporates in translation, of course, and as the book was my first effort, there will be found divers inaccuracies and errors therein; but enough remains to give some idea of Gautier's imaginative powers and descriptive skill. Will also forward you paper you ask for.

I regret having to write very hurriedly, as I have

TO W. D. O'CONNOR

a great press of work upon my hands. You will hear from me again, however, more fully. A letter to my address as above given will reach me sooner than if sent to the "Times-Democrat" office.
Very gratefully your friend

L. HEARN

TO W. D. O'CONNOR

NEW ORLEANS, *August*, 1883

MY DEAR MR. O'CONNOR, — I had feared that I had lost a rare literary friend. Your charming letter undeceived me, and your equally charming present revealed you to me in a totally new light. I had imagined you as a delicate amateur only: I did not recognize in you a Master. And after I had read your two articles — articles written in a fashion realizing my long-cherished dream of English in splendid Latin attire — I felt quite ashamed of my own work. You have a knowledge, too, of languages unfamiliar to me, which I honestly envy, and which is becoming indispensable in the higher spheres of literary criticism — I mean a knowledge of Italian and German. As for your long silence, it only remains for me to say that your letter filled me with that sympathy which, in certain sad moments, expresses itself only by a silent and earnest pressure of the hand — because any utterance would sound strangely hollow, like an echo in some vast dim emptiness.

Your beautiful little book came like a valued supplement to an edition of "Leaves of Grass" in my library. I have always *secretly* admired Whitman, and would have liked on more than one occasion to express my opinion in public print. But in journalism this is not easy to do. There is no possibility of praising Whitman unreservedly in the ordinary newspaper, whose proprietors always tell you to remember that their paper "goes into respectable families," or accuse you of loving obscene literature if you attempt controversy. Journalism is not really a literary profession. The journalist of to-day is obliged to hold himself ready to serve any cause — like the condottieri of feudal Italy, or the free captains of other countries. If he can enrich himself sufficiently to acquire comparative independence in this really *nefarious* profession, then, indeed, he is able freely to utter his heart's sentiments and indulge his tastes, like that æsthetic and wicked Giovanni Malatesta whose life Yriarte has written.

I do not think that I could ever place so lofty an estimate upon the poet's work, however, as you give — although no doubt rests in my mind as to your critical superiority. I think that Genius must have greater attributes than mere creative power to be called to the front rank — the thing created must be beautiful; it does not satisfy me if the material be rich. I cannot content myself with ores and rough jewels. I want to see the gold purified and wrought into marvellous fantastic shapes; I want to see the jewels cut into roses of facets, or turned as by Greek

TO W. D. O'CONNOR

cunning into faultless witchery of nude loveliness. And Whitman's gold seems to me in the ore: his diamonds and emeralds in the rough. Would Homer be Homer to us but for the billowy roar of his mighty verse — the perfect cadence of his song that has the regularity of ocean-diapason? I think not. And did not all the Titans of antique literature polish their lines, chisel their words, according to severest laws of art? Whitman's is indeed a Titanic voice; but it seems to me the voice of the giant beneath the volcano — half stifled, half uttered — roaring betimes because articulation is impossible.

Beauty there is, but it must be sought for; it does not flash out from hastily turned leaves: it only comes to one after full and thoughtful perusal, like a great mystery whose key-word may only be found after long study. But the reward is worth the pain. That beauty is cosmical — it is world-beauty; — there is something of the antique pantheism in the book, and something larger too, expanding to the stars and beyond. What most charms me, however, is that which is most earthy and of the earth. I was amused at some of the criticisms — especially that in the "Critic" — to the effect that Mr. Whitman might have some taste for natural beauty, etc., *as an animal has!* Ah! that was a fine touch! Now it is just the animalism of the work which constitutes its great force to me — not a brutal animalism, but a *human* animalism, such as the thoughts of antique poets reveal to us: the inexplicable delight of being, the intoxication of perfect health, the unutterable pleasures of breathing mountain-wind, of gazing at a blue sky, of leaping into clear deep water and drifting with a swimmer's dreamy confidence down the current, with strange thoughts that drift faster. Communion with Nature teaches philosophy to those who love that communion; and Nature imposes silence sometimes, that we may be forced to think: — the men of the plains say little. "You don't feel like talking out there," I heard one say: "the silence makes you silent." Such a man could not tell us just what he thought under that vastness, in the heart of that silence: but Whitman tells us for him. And he also tells us what we ought to think, or to remember, about things which are not of the wilderness but of the city. He is an animal, if the "Critic" pleases, but a human animal — not a camel that weeps and sobs at the sight of the city's gates. He is rude, joyous, fearless, artless — a singer who knows nothing of musical law, but whose voice is as the voice of Pan. And in the violent magnetism of the man, the great vital energy of his work, the rugged and ingenuous kindliness of his speech, the vast joy of his song, the discernment by him of the Universal Life — I cannot help imagining that I perceive something of the antique sylvan deity, the faun or the satyr. Not the distorted satyr of modern cheap classics: but the ancient and godly one, "inseparably connected with the worship of Dionysus," and sharing with that divinity the powers of

TO W. D. O'CONNOR

healing, saving, and foretelling, not less than the orgiastic pleasures over which the androgynous god presided.

I see great beauty in Whitman, great force, great cosmical truths sung of in mystical words; but the singer seems to me nevertheless *barbaric*. You have called him a bard. He is! But his bard-songs are like the improvisations of a savage skald, or a forest Druid: immense the thought! mighty the words! but the music is wild, harsh, rude, primæval. I cannot believe it will endure as a great work endures: I cannot think the bard is a creator, but only a precursor — only the voice of one crying in the wilderness — *Make straight the path for the Great Singer who is to come after me!* ... And therefore even though I may differ from you in the nature of my appreciation of Whitman I love the soul of his work, and I think it a duty to give all possible aid and recognition to his literary priesthood. Whatsoever you do to defend, to elevate, to glorify his work you do for the literature of the future, for the cause of poetical liberty, for the cause of mental freedom. Your book is doubly beautiful to me, therefore: and I believe it will endure to be consulted in future times, when men shall write the "History of the Literary Movement of 1900," as men have already written the "Histoire du Romantisme."

I don't think you missed very much of my work in the "Times-Democrat." I have not been doing so well. The great heat makes one's brain languid, barren, dusty. Then I have been making desperate efforts to do some magazine work. Thanks for your praise of "The Pipes of Hameline." I wish, indeed, that I could drag myself out of this newspaper routine — even though slowly, like a turtle struggling over uneven ground. Journalism dwarfs, stifles, emasculates thought and style. As for my translation of Gautier, it has many grave errors I am ashamed of, but it is not castrated. My pet stories in it are "Clarimonde" and "Arria Marcella."

Victor Hugo was indeed the Arthur of the Romantic Movement, and Gautier was but one of his knights, though the best of them — a Lancelot. I think his "Emaux et Camées" surpass Hugo's work in word-chiselling, in goldsmithery; but Hugo's fancy overarches all, like the vault of the sky. His prose is like the work of Angelo — the paintings in the Sistine Chapel, the figures described by Emilio Castelar as painted by flashes of lightning. He is one of those who appear but once in five hundred years. Gautier is not upon Hugo's level. But while Hugo wrought like a Gothic sculptor, largely, weirdly, wondrously, Gautier could create mosaics of word-jewelry without equals. The work is small, delicate, elfish: it will endure as long as the French language, even though it figure in the Hugo architecture only as arabesque-work or stained glass or inlaid pavement.

Oh, yes! you will catch it for those articles! you will have the fate of every champion of an unpopular

TO JOHN ALBEE

cause — thorns at every turn, which may turn into roses.

I hope to see you some day. Will always have time to write. Sometimes my letter may be short; but not often. Believe me, sincerely

LAFCADIO HEARN

TO JOHN ALBEE

NEW ORLEANS, 1883

DEAR SIR, — Your very kind letter, forwarded to me by Mr. Worthington, was more of an encouragement and comfort than you, perhaps, even desired. One naturally launches his first literary effort with fear and trembling; and at such a time kind or unkind words may have a lasting effect upon his future hopes and aims.

The little stories were translated five years ago, in the intervals of rest possible to snatch during reportorial duty on a Western paper. I was then working fourteen hours a day. Subsequently I was four years vainly seeking a publisher.

Naturally enough, the stories are not even now all that I could wish them to be; but I trust that before long I may escape so far from the treadmill of daily newspaper labour as to produce something better in point of literary execution. It has long been my aim to create something in English fiction analogous to that warmth of colour and richness of imagery hitherto peculiar to Latin literature. Being of a meridional race myself, a Greek, I *feel* rather

LAFCADIO HEARN

with the Latin race than with the Anglo-Saxon; and trust that with time and study I may be able to create something different from the stone-grey and somewhat chilly style of latter-day English or American romance. This may seem only a foolish hope — unsubstantial as a ghost; but with youth, health and such kindly encouragement as you have given me, I believe that it may yet be realized. Of course a little encouragement from the publishers will also be necessary. Believe me very gratefully yours

LAFCADIO HEARN

TO H. E. KREHBIEL

NEW ORLEANS, *September*, 1883

DEAR KREHBIEL, — I trust you will be able to read the hideously written music I sent you in batches — according as I could find leisure to copy it. The negro songs are taken from a most extraordinary book translated into French from the Arabic, and published at Paris by a geographical society. The author was one of those errant traders who travel yearly through the desert to the Soudan, and beyond into Timbuctoo occasionally, to purchase slaves and elephants' teeth from those almost unknown Arab sultans or negro kings who rule the black ant-hills of Central Africa. I have only yet obtained the great volume relating to Ouaday; the volume on Darfour is coming. Perron, the learned translator, in his "Femmes Arabes" (published at Algiers), gives

H. E. Krehbiel

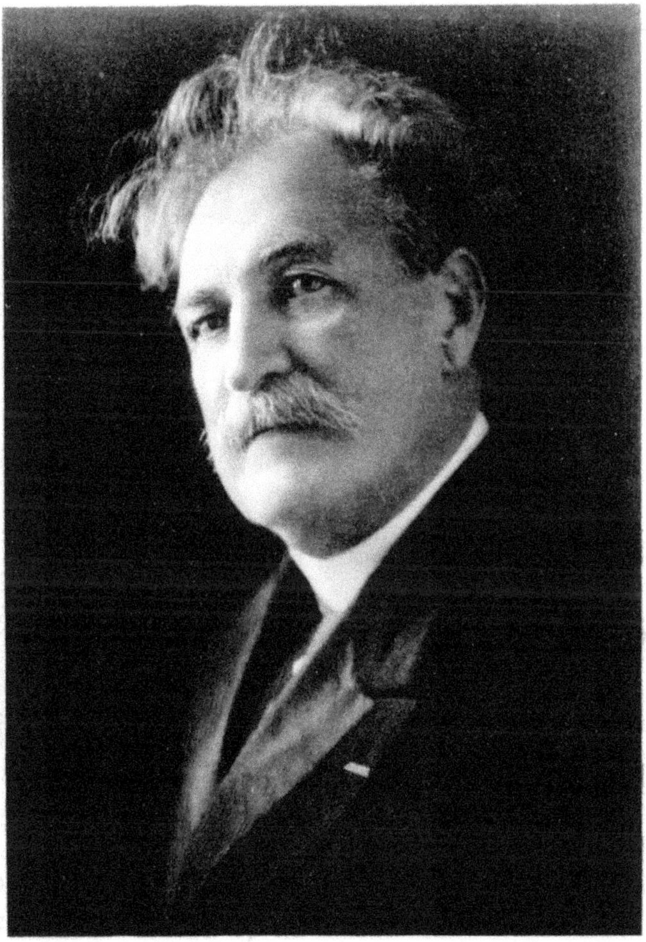

TO H. E. KREHBIEL

some curious chapters on ancient Arab music which I must try to send you one of these days. The Japanese book — a rather costly affair printed in gold and colours — is rapidly becoming scarce. I expect soon to have some Hindoo music; as I have a subscription for a library of folk-lore and folk-lore music of all nations, of which only seventeen volumes are published so far — Elzevirians. These mostly relate to Europe, and contain much Breton, Provençal, Norman, and other music. But there will be several volumes of Oriental popular songs, etc. Some day, I was thinking, we might together get up a little volume on the musical legends of all nations, introducing each legend by appropriate music.

I have nearly finished a collection of Oriental stories from all sorts of queer sources — the Sanscrit, Buddhist, Talmudic, Persian, Polynesian, Finnish literatures, etc. — which I shall try to publish. But their having been already in print will militate against them.

Could n't get a publisher for the Fantastics, and I am, after all, glad of it; for I feel somewhat ashamed of them now. I have saved a few of the best pieces, which will be rewritten at some future time if I succeed in other matters. Another failure was the translation of Flaubert's "Temptation of Saint Anthony," which no good publisher seems inclined to undertake. The original is certainly one of the most exotically strange pieces of writing in any language, and weird beyond description. Some day

I may take a notion to print it myself. At present I am also busy with a dictionary of Creole Proverbs (this is a secret), four hundred or more of which I have arranged; and, by the way, I have quite a Creole library, embracing the Creole dialects of both hemispheres. I have likewise obtained favour with two firms, Harpers', and Scribners' — both of whom have recently promised to consider favourably anything I choose to send in. You see I have my hands full; and an enormous mass of undigested matter to assimilate and crystallize into something.

So much about myself, in reply to your question. ...Your Armenian legend was very peculiar indeed. There is nothing exactly like it either in Baring-Gould's myths ("Mountain of Venus") or Keightley's "Fairy Mythology," or any of the Oriental folk-lore I have yet seen. The ghostly sweetheart is a universal idea, and the phantom palace also; but the biting of the finger is a delightful novelty. Many thanks for the pretty little tale.

I don't think you will see me in New York this winter. I shudder at the bare idea of cold. Speak to me of blazing deserts, of plains smoking with volcanic vapours, of suns ten times larger, and vast lemon-coloured moons — and venomous plants that writhe like vipers and strangle like boas — and clouds of steel-blue flies — and skeletons polished by ants — and atmospheres heavy as those of planets nearer to the solar centre! — but hint not to me of ice and slush and snow and black-frost winds. Why

TO H. E. KREHBIEL

can't you come down to see me? I'll show you nice music: I'll enable you to note down the musical cries of the Latin-faced venders of herbs and gombo fève and calas and latanir and patates.

If you can't come, I'll try to see you next spring or summer; but I would rather be whipped with scorpions than visit a Northern city in the winter months. In fact few residents here would dare to do it — unless well used to travelling. Some day I must write something about the physiological changes produced here by climate. In an article I wrote for "Harper's" six months ago, and which ought to appear soon (as I was paid for it), you will observe some brief observations on the subject; but the said subject is curious enough to write a book about. By the way, I have become scientific — I write nearly all the scientific editorials for our paper, which you sometimes see, no doubt. Farney ought to spend a few months here: it would make him crazy with joy to perceive those picturesquenesses which most visitors never see.

I thought I would go to Cincinnati next week or so; but I'm afraid it's too cold now. If I do go, I'll write you.

As to your protests about correspondence, I think you're downright wrong; but I won't renew the controversy. Anyhow I suppose we keep track of each other, with affectionate curiosity. I am quite sorry you missed my friend Page Baker: he is a splendid type — you would have become fast friends

LAFCADIO HEARN

at once. Never mind, though! if you ever come down here, we'll make you enjoy yourself in earnest. Please excuse this rambling letter.

Your Creolized friend   LAFCADIO HEARN

P.S. By the bye, have you the original music of the Muezzin's call — as called by the first of all Muezzins, Bìlâl the Abyssinian, to whom it was taught by Our Lord Mohammed? Bìlâl the black Abyssinian, whose voice was the mightiest and sweetest in Islam. In those first days, Bìlâl was persecuted as the slave of the persecuted Prophet of God. And in the "Gulistan," it is told how he suffered. But after Our Lord had departed into the chamber of Allah — and the tawny horsemen of the desert had ridden from Medina even to the gates of India, conquering and to conquer — and the young crescent of Islam, slender as a sword, had waxed into a vast moon of glory that filled the world — Bìlâl still lived with that wonderful health of years given unto the people of his race. But he only sang for the Kalif. And the Kalif was Omar. So, one day, it came to pass, that the people of Damascus, whither Omar had travelled upon a visit, begged the Caliph, saying: "O Commander of the Faithful, we pray thee that thou ask Bìlâl to sing the call to prayer for us, even as it was taught him by Our Lord Mohammed." And Omar requested Bìlâl. Now Bìlâl was nearly a century old; but his voice was deep and sweet as ever. And they aided him to ascend the

TO H. E. KREHBIEL

minaret. Then, into the midst of the great silence burst once more the mighty African voice of Bìlâl — singing the Adzan, even as it has still been sung for more than twelve hundred years from all the minarets of Islam:

> God is Great!
> God is Great!
> I bear witness there is no other God but God!
> I bear witness that Mohammed is the Prophet of God!
> Come to Prayer!
> Come to Prayer!
> Come unto Salvation!
> God is Great!
> God is Great!
> There is no other God but God!

And Omar wept and all the people with him.

This is an outline. I'd like to have the music of that. Sent to London for it, and could n't get it.

L. H.

TO H. E. KREHBIEL

NEW ORLEANS, 1883

I'M so delighted with that music that I don't know what to do.

First, I went to my friend Grueling, the organist, and got him to play and sing it. "It is very queer," he said; "but it seems to me like chants I've heard some of these negroes sing." Then I took it to a piano-player, and he played it for me. Then I went to a cornet-player — I think the cornet gives the best idea of the sound of a tenor voice — and he played it exquisitely, beautifully. Those arabesques

LAFCADIO HEARN

about the name of Allah are simply divine! I noticed the difference clearly. The second version seems suspended, as a song eternal—something never to be finished so long as waves sing and winds call, and worlds circle in space. So I thought of Edwin Arnold's lines:

> Suns that burn till day has flown,
> Stars that are by night restored,
> *Are thy dervishes*, O Lord,
> *Wheeling* round thy golden throne!

I believe I'll use both songs. The suspended character of the second has a great and pathetic poetry in it. Please tell me in your next letter what kind of voice Bìlâl ought to have — being a woolly-headed Abyssinian. I suppose I'll have to make him a tenor. I can't imagine a basso making those flourishes about the name of the Eternal.

Next week I'll send you selections of Provençal and other music which I believe are new. My library is very fine. I have a collection worth a great deal of money which you would like to see.

If you ever come down here, you could stay with me nicely, and have a pleasant artistic time.

LAFCADIO HEARN

TO H. E. KREHBIEL

NEW ORLEANS, October, 1883

MY DEAR KREHBIEL, — I have been too sick with a strangling cold to write as I had wished, or to copy for you something for which I had already obtained the music-paper. Nevertheless I am going to ask

TO H. E. KREHBIEL

another favour. I hope you can find time to copy separately for me the Arabic words of the Adzan: I prefer Villoteau. As for Koran-reading, it would delight me; but please give me the number of the sura, or chapter, from which the words are taken. My article on Bìlâl is progressing: the second part being complete. I am dividing it into four sections. But I do not feel quite so hopeful now as I did before. Magazine-writing is awful labour. Six weeks at least are required to prepare an article, and then the probability is that the magazine editor will make beastly changes: my article on Cable suffered at his hands. The Harpers change nothing; but they keep an article over for twelve months and more. One of mine is not yet published. I have been hoping that if my "Bìlâl" takes, you might follow it up with an article on Arabic music generally: the open letter department of "Scribner's" pays well, and the Harpers pay even better. I would like to see you with a series, which could afterward be united into a volume: you could copyright each one. This is only a suggestion.

I will not make much use of the Koran-reading in "Bìlâl": I want to leave that wholly to you. I feel even guilty for borrowing your pithy and forcible observation upon the cantillado.

If you have a chance to visit some of your public libraries, please see whether they have Maisonneuve's superb series: "Les Littératures populaires de toutes les nations." I have fourteen volumes of it, rich in musical oddities. If they have it not, I will send you extracts from time to time. Also see if they have "Mélusine": my volume of it (1878) contains the music of a Greek dance, older than the friezes of the Parthenon. Of course, if you can see them, it will be better than the imperfect copying of an ignoramus in music like me.

I grossly offended a Creole musician the other day. He denied in toto the African sense of melody. "But," said I, "did you not tell me that you spent hours trying to imitate the notes of a roustabout-song on your flute?" "I did," he replied, "but not because it pleased me — only because I was curious to learn why I could not imitate it: it still baffles me, but it is nevertheless an abomination to my ear!" "Nay!" said I, "it hath a most sweet sound to me; and to the ethnologist a most fascinating interest. Verily, I would rather listen to it, than hear a symphony of Beethoven!" ... Whereupon he walked away in high fury; and now ... he speaketh to me no more!

   Yours very thankfully L. HEARN

TO H. E. KREHBIEL[1]

TO H. E. KREHBIEL

NEW ORLEANS, 1883

MY DEAR KREHBIEL, — There is nothing in magazine-work in the way of profit; for the cent-a-word pay does not really recompense the labour required: but the magazines introduce one to publishers, and publishers select men to write their books. Magazine-work is the introduction to book-work; and book-work pays doubly — in money and reputation. I hope to climb up slowly this way — it takes time, but offers a sure issue. You could do so much more rapidly.

I find in my Oriental catalogues "Villoteau — 'Mémoire sur la Musique de l'antique Egypte.' — Paris: Maisonneuve & Cie, 1883 (15 fr.)." Wonder if you have the work in any of your public libraries. If you have not, and you would like to get it, I can obtain it from Paris duty-free next time I write to Maisonneuve, from whom I am obtaining a great number of curious books.

You must have noticed in the papers the real or pretended discovery of an ancient Egyptian melody — the notes being represented by owls ascending and descending the musical scale. Hope you will get to see it. I have been thinking that we might some day, together, work up a charming collection of musical legends: each legend followed by a specimen-melody, with learned dissertation by H. Edward Krehbiel. But that will be for the days when we shall be "well-known and highly esteemed authors." I think I could furnish some singular folk-lore.

Meanwhile "Bìlâl" has been finished. I wrote to "Harper's Magazine"; — the article was returned with a very complimentary autograph letter from Alden, praising it warmly, but recommending its being offered to the "Atlantic," as he did not know when he could "find room for it." Find room for it! Ah, bah!... I am sorry: because I had written him about your share in it, and hoped, if successful, it would tempt him to write you. It is now in the hands of another magazine. I used your Koran-fragment in the form of a musical footnote.

I notice you called it a "brick." Are you sure this is the correct word? Each sura (or chapter) indeed signifies a "course of bricks in a wall"; but also signifies "a rank of soldiers" — and the verses, which were never numbered in the earlier MSS., are so irregular that the poetry of the term "brick" could scarcely apply to them. However, I may be wrong.

I was delighted with your delight, as expressed in your beautiful letter upon the Hebrew ceremonial. Hebrew literature has been my hobby for some time past: I have Hershon's "Talmudic Miscellany"; Stauben's "Scènes de la Vie Juive" (full of delicious traditions); Kompert's "Studies of Jewish Life," which you have no doubt read in the original German; and Schwab's French translation of the be-

TO H. E. KREHBIEL

ginning of the Jerusalem Talmud (together with the Babylonian Berachoth), 5 vols. I confess the latter is, as a whole, unreadable; but the legends in it are without parallel in weirdness and singularity. Such miscellaneous reading of this sort as I have done has given new luminosity to my ideas of the antique Hebrew life; and enabled me to review them without the gloom of Biblical tradition — especially the nightmarish darkness of the Pentateuch. I like to associate Hebrew ceremonies rather with the wonderful Talmudic days of the Babylonian rabbonim than with the savage primitiveness of the years of Exodus and Deuteronomy.

There are some queer things about music in the Talmud; but they are sometimes extravagant as that story about the conch-shell blown at the birth of Buddha — "whereof the sound *rolled on unceasingly for four years!*" The swarthy fishermen of our swampy lakes do blow conch-shells by way of marine signalling; and whenever I hear them I think of that monstrous conch-shell told of in the Nidānakathā.

As I write it seemeth to me that I behold, overshadowing the paper, the most Dantesque silhouette of one who walked with me the streets of the far-off Western city by night, and with whom I exchanged ghostly fancies and phantom hopes. Now in New York! How the old night-forces have been scattered! But is it not pleasant to observe that the members of the broken circle have been mounting higher and higher toward the supreme hope? Perhaps we may all meet some day in the East; whence as legendary word hath it — "lightning ever cometh." Remember me very warmly to my old comrade 'Tunison.

But I think it more probable I shall see you here than that you shall see me there. New York has become something appalling to my imagination — perhaps because I have been drawing my ideas of it from caricatures: something cyclopean without solemnity, something pandemoniac without grotesqueness — preadamite bridges — superimpositions of iron roads higher than the aqueducts of the Romans — gloom, vapour, roarings and lightnings. When I think of it, I feel more content with my sunlit marshes — and the frogs — and the gnats — and the invisible plagues lurking in visible vapours — and the ancientness — and the vast languor of the land.

Even our vegetation here, funereally drooping in the great heat, seems to dream of dead things — to mourn for the death of Pan. After a few years here the spirit of the land has entered into you — and the languor of the place embraces you with an embrace that may not be broken; — thoughts come slowly, ideas take form sluggishly as shapes of smoke in heavy air; and a great horror of work and activity and noise and bustle roots itself within your soul — I mean brain. Soul = Cerebral Activity = Soul.

TO H. E. KREHBIEL

I am afraid you have read the poorest of Cable's short stories. "Jean-ah Poquelin," "Belles-Demoiselles," are much better than "Tite Poulette." There is something very singular to me in Cable's power. It is not a superior style; it is not a minutely finished description — for it will often endure no close examination at all: nevertheless his stories have a puissant charm which is hard to analyze. His serial novel — "The Grandissimes" — is not equal to the others; but I think the latter portion of "Dr. Sevier" will surprise many. He did me the honour to read nearly the whole book to me. Cultivate him, if you get a chance.

Baker often talks with me about you. You would never have any difficulty in obtaining a fine thing here. Perhaps you will be the reverse of flattered by this bit of news; but the proprietors here think they can make the "Times-Democrat" a bigger paper than it is, and rival the Eastern dailies. For my part I hope they will do it; but they lack system, experience, and good men, to some extent. Now good men are not easily tempted to cast their fortunes here at present. It will be otherwise in time; the city is really growing into a metropolis — a world's market for merchants of all nations — and will be made healthier and more beautiful year by year.

Good-bye for the present.

Your very sincere friend

L. HEARN

LAFCADIO HEARN

TO W. D. O'CONNOR

NEW ORLEANS, 1883

MY DEAR O'CONNOR, — I felt the same regret on finishing your letter that I have often experienced on completing a brief but delightful novelette: I wanted more — and yet I had come to the end!... Your letters are all treasured up; — they are treats, and one atones for years of silence. My dear friend, you must never trouble yourself to write when you feel either tired or disinclined: when I think I have the power to interest you, I will always take advantage of it, without expecting you to write. I know what routine is, and what weariness is; and some day I think we shall meet, and arrange for a still more pleasant intimacy.

Your preference for Boutimar pleases me: Boutimar was my pet. There is a little Jewish legend in the collection — Esther — somewhat resembling it in pathos.

Your observation about my knowledge is something I cannot accept; for in positive acquirements I am even exceptionally ignorant. By purchasing queer books and following odd subjects I have been able to give myself the air of knowing more than I do; but none of my work would bear the scrutiny of a specialist; I would like, however, to show you my library. It cost me only about two thousand dollars; but every volume is *queer*. Knowing that I have nothing resembling genius, and that any ordinary

TO W. D. O'CONNOR

talent must be supplemented with some sort of curious study in order to place it above the mediocre line, I am striving to woo the Muse of the Odd, and hope to succeed in thus attracting some little attention. This coming summer I propose making my first serious effort at original work — a very tiny volume of sketches in our Creole archipelago at the skirts of the Gulf. I am seeking the Orient at home, among our Lascar and Chinese colonies, and the Prehistoric in the characteristics of strange European settlers.

The trouble kindly taken by you in transcribing the little words of praise by a lady was more than compensated by the success of its purpose, I fancy. The only pleasure, indeed, that an author derives from his labours is that of hearing such commendations from appreciative or sympathetic readers. Your sending copies "hither and thither" was too kind; I could scold you for it! Still, the consequences indicated that the book may some day reach a new edition; and I receive nothing until the publisher pockets one thousand dollars.

Have you seen the exquisite new edition of Arnold's "Light of Asia"? It has enchanted me — perfumed my mind as with the incense of a strangely new and beautiful worship. After all, Buddhism in some esoteric form may prove the religion of the future. Is not the cycle of transmigration actually proven in the vast evolution from nomad to man — from worm to King through innumerable myriads of brute form? Is not the tendency of all modern philosophy toward the acceptance of the ancient Indian teaching that the visible is but an emanation of the Invisible — a delusion — a creature, or a shadow, of the Supreme Dream? What are the heavens of all Christian fancies, after all, but Nirvana — extinction of individuality in the eternal interblending of man with divinity; for a bodiless, immaterial, non-sensuous condition means nothingness, and no more. And the life and agony and death of universes, are these not pictured forth in the Oriental teachings that all things appear and disappear alternately with the slumber or the awakening, the night or the day, of the Self-Existent? Finally, the efforts of Romanes and Darwin and Vignoli to convince us of the interrelation — the brotherhood of animals and of men were anticipated by Gautama. I have an idea that the Right Man could now revolutionize the whole Occidental religious world by preaching the Oriental faith.

Very affectionately, LAFCADIO HEARN

If Symonds praises Whitman, I stand reproved for my least doubts; for he is the very apostle of *classicism* and *form*.

TO H. E. KREHBIEL

NEW ORLEANS, *December*, 1883

DEAR KREHBIEL, — I greatly enjoyed that sharp, fresh, breezy letter from Feldwisch, which I reënclose

TO H. E. KREHBIEL

with thanks for the pleasure given. While I am greatly delighted with his success, I cannot say I have been surprised: he possessed such rare and splendid qualities of integrity and manliness — coupled with uncommon quickness of business perception — that I would not have been astonished to hear of Congressman Feldwisch — always supposing it were possible to be a politician and an upright member of modern American society — which is doubtful. Please let me have his exact address; — I would like to write him once in a while.

After all, I believe you are right in regard to magazine-work. I fully appreciated the effect upon a thoroughbred artist of being asked to write something flimsy — ask Liszt to play Yankee Doodle! Our magazines — excepting the "Atlantic" — do not appear to be controlled by, or in the interest of, scholars. Fancy how I felt when asked (indirectly) by the "Century" to write something "SNAPPY"! — even I, who am no specialist, and if anything of an artist, only a word-artist in embryo!... I also suspect you are correct in your self-interest: your forte will never be *light* work, because your knowledge is too extensive, and your artistic feeling too deep, to be wasted upon puerilities. It has always seemed to me that your style gains in solid strength and beauty as the subject you treat is deeper. To any mind which has grasped the general spirit and aspect of a science, isolated facts are worthy of consideration only in their relation to universal and, perhaps, eternal laws: anecdote

LAFCADIO HEARN

for the mere sake of anecdote is simply unendurable. Five years of hard study here have resulted in altogether changing my own literary inclinations — yet, unfortunately, to no immediate purpose that I can see; for I must always remain too ignorant to succeed as a specialist in any one topic. But a romantic fact — the possession of which would have driven me wild with joy a few years ago, or even one year ago, perhaps — now affects me not at all unless I can perceive its relation to some general principle to be elucidated. And the mere ideas and melody of a poem seem to me of small moment unless the complex laws of versification be strictly obeyed. Hence I feel no inclination to attempt a story or sketch unless I can find some theme of which the treatment might do more than gratify fancy. Unless a romance be instructive — or inaugurate a totally novel style — I think it can have no lasting value. The old enthusiasm has completely died out of me. But meanwhile I am trying to fill my brain with unfamiliar facts on special topics, believing that some day or other I shall be able to utilize them in a new way. I have thought, for example, of trying to write physiological novelettes or stories — based upon scientific facts in regard to races and characters, but nevertheless of the most romantic aspect possible: natural but never naturalistic. Still, I am so fully conscious that this idea has been suggested by popular foreign novelists, that I fear it may prove merely a passing ambition.

TO H. E. KREHBIEL

Another great affliction is my inability to travel. I hate the life of every day in connection with any idea of story-writing: I would give anything to be a literary Columbus — to discover a Romantic America in some West Indian or North African or Oriental region — to describe the life that is only fully treated of in universal geographies or ethnological researches. Won't you sympathize with me?... If I could only become a Consul at Bagdad, Algiers, Ispahan, Benares, Samarkand, Nippo, Bangkok, Ninh-Binh — or any part of the world where ordinary Christians do not like to go! Here is the nook in which my romanticism still hides. But I know I have not the physical qualifications to fit me for such researches, nor the linguistic knowledge required to make such researches valuable. I suppose I shall have to settle down at last to something horribly prosaic, and even devoid of philosophic interest.... Alas! O that I were a travelling shoemaker, or a player upon the sambuke!

I have two — nay three — projects sown: the seed has not yet sprouted. I expressed to Harpers' a little Dictionary of Creole Proverbs — a mere compilation, of course, from many unfamiliar sources; "Bîlâl" is under consideration at the "Century" (where, I fear, they will cut up every sentence which clashes with Baptist ideas on the sinfulness of Islam); and my compilation of Oriental stories is being "seriously examined" by J. R. Osgood & Co....

This letter is getting wearisome; but I don't know

LAFCADIO HEARN

how soon I can again snatch time to write.... Ah, yes! — for God's sake (I suppose you believe just a small bit in God) don't try to conceive how I could sympathize with Cable! Because I never sympathized with him at all. His awful faith — which to me represents an undeveloped mental structure — gives a neutral tint to his whole life among us. There is a Sunday-school atmosphere.... But Cable is more liberal-minded than his creed; he has also rare analytical powers on a small scale.... Belief I do not think is ridiculous altogether; — nothing is ridiculous in the general order of the world: but at a certain point it prevents the mind from expanding; — its horizon is solid stone and its sky a material vault. One must cease to believe before being able to comprehend either the reason or beauty of belief. The loss is surely well recompensed by the vast enlargement of vision — the opening up of the Star-spaces — the recognition of the Eternal Life throbbing simultaneously in the vein of an insect or the scintillations of a million suns — the comprehension of the relations of Infinity to human existence, or at least the understanding that there are such relations — and that the humblest atom of substance can tell a story more wondrous than all the epics, romances, legends, or myths devised by ancient or modern fancy. — Now I am getting long-winded again. I conclude with a promise soon to forward another little bit of queer music. Hope you like the last. Come down here and I will turn you loose in my library. I need hardly specify

TO H. E. KREHBIEL

that if you come, your natural expenses will be represented by zero — that is, if you condescend to live in my neighbourhood. It is not romantic; but it is comfortable. I'm sick of Creole Romance — it nearly cost me my life.
Bye, my friend.
Your old goblin
LAFCADIO HEARN

TO H. E. KREHBIEL
NEW ORLEANS, *February*, 1884

DEAR KREHBIEL, — I hope you may prove right and I wrong in my judgment of ——. As you say, I have a peculiar and unfortunate disposition; nevertheless I had better reasons for my suggestions to you than it is now necessary to specify.

Your syrinx discoveries seem to me of very uncommon importance. What is now important to learn is this: Is the syrinx an original instrument in those regions whence the American and West Indian slave-elements were drawn? — an account of which slave-sources is to be found in Edwards's "History of the West Indies." The Congo dances with their music are certainly importations from the West Coast — the Ivory Coast. Have you seen Livingstone's account of the multiple pipe (chalumeau, Hartmann calls it in French) among the Batokas? I would like to know if it is a syrinx. We have no big public libraries here; but if you have time to make some West African researches, one could perhaps trace out the whole history of the syrinx's musical migration. I send you the latest information I have been able to pick up. Just so soon as I can get the material ready, will send also information regarding the various West Indian dances in brief — also the negro-Creole bottle-dance, danced over an upright bottle to the chant —

>   Ça ma coupé —
>   Ça ma coupé —
>   Ça ma coupé —
>   Ça!
>
>   Ça ma coupé —
>   Ça ma coupé —
>   Ça ma coupé —
>   Ça!

I've reopened the envelope to tell you something I forgot — a suggestion.

I was quite pleased to hear you like my Chinese paragraph; and I have a little proposition. Do you know that a most delightful book was recently published in France, consisting wholly of odd impressions about strange books and strange people exchanged between friends by mail. Each impression should be very brief. Why could n't we do this: Once every month I'll write you the queerest and most outlandish fancy I can get up — based upon fact, of course — not more than two hundred words; and you write me the most awful thing that has struck you in relation to new musical discoveries. In a year's time we would have twenty-four little pieces between us, which would certainly be original

TO H. E. KREHBIEL

enough to elaborate into more artistic form; and we could plot together how to outrage the public by printing them. I would contribute a hundred dollars or so — if we could n't find an enthusiastic printer. The book would be very small.

Everything should be perfectly monstrous, you know — ordinary facts, or ideas that could by any chance occur to commonly balanced minds, ought to be rigidly excluded.

I don't think I can go North till April. March would be too cold for me. The temptation of hearing grand singers is not now strong — I'm sorry to say — for I never go to the theatre on account of the artificial light, never read or write after dark; and I anticipate no special pleasure except that of seeing an old friend, and talking much monstrous talk about matters which I but half understand.

Yours very affectionately

L. HEARN

TO H. E. KREHBIEL

NEW ORLEANS, *February*, 1884

EXTRA volume of the series: Price, five hundred dollars. Large folio.

THE BATTLE-CRIES OF ALL NATIONS. With accompaniment of Barbaric instruments. Arranged for modern Orchestral reproduction.

> I. ARYAN DIVISION. — Battle-Shouts of Gothic Races — Teutoni and Cimbri — Frank and Alleman — Merovingian — The Roar of Pharamond

LAFCADIO HEARN

— Iberian — The Triumph of Herman — Viking War-Chants — The Song of Roland as sung by Taillefer — Celtic and Early British War-Cries, etc., etc.

II. SEMITIC DIVISION. — Hebrew War-Cries — "God is gone up with a shout, the Lord with the sound of the Trumpet" — Arabs and Crusaders — "Allah — hu-u-u Akbar!" etc. — Berber Cries — The Numidian Cavalry.

(The work also contains Ancient Egyptian, Babylonian, and Scythian war-cries; war-cries of the Parthians and Huns, of the Mongols and Tartars. Sounds of the Battle of Châlons; Cries of the Carthaginian mercenaries; Macedonian rallying-call, etc., etc. In the modern part are included Polynesian, African, Aztec, Peruvian, Patagonian and American. A magnificent musical version of the chant of Ragnar Lodbrok will be found in the Appendix: "We smote with our swords.")

(This is not intended as a part of our private extravaganzas: but is written as a just punishment for your silence.)

Vol. I. MONOGRAPH UPON THE POPULAR MELODIES OF EXTINCT RACES. XXIII and 700 pp.

Vol. II. MUSIC OF NOMAD RACES. Introduction. "Men of Prey; the Falcon and Eagle Races of Mankind." Part I. The Arabs. Part II. The Touareg of the Greater Desert. Part III. The Turkish and Tartar Tribes of Central Asia. With 1600 examples of melodies, engravings of musical instruments, etc.

Vol. III. MANIFESTATION OF CLIMATIC INFLUENCE IN POPULAR MELODY. In Two Parts. Part I.

TO H. E. KREHBIEL

Melodies of Mountain-dwellers. Part II. Melodies of Valley dwellers and inhabitants of low countries. (3379 Ex.)

Vol. IV. RACE-TEMPER AS EVIDENCED IN THE POPULAR MUSIC OF VARIOUS PEOPLES. Part I. The Melancholy Tendency. Part II. The Joyous Temperament. Part III. Ferocity. Part IV. etc., etc. — 2700 ex.

Vol. V. PECULIAR CHARACTERISTICS OF EROTIC MUSIC IN ALL COUNTRIES. (This volume contains nearly 7000 examples of curious music from India, Japan, China, Burmah, Siam, Arabia, Polynesia, Africa, and many other parts of the world.)

Vol. VI. MUSIC OF THE DANCE IN THE ORIENT. (3500 pp.)

Chap. I. The Mussulman Bayaderes of India (17 photolith).

Chap. II. The Bayaderes of Hinduism — especially of the Krishna and Sivaite sects.

Chap. III. Examples of Burmese Dance — music (with 25 photographic plates).

Chap. IV. The Tea-house dancers of Japan; and Courtesans of Yokohama. (34 Photo-Engrav.)

Chap. V. Chinese dancing melodies. (23 Photo-Engrav.)

Chap. VI. Tartar dance-melodies: the nomad dancing girls. (50 beautiful coloured plates.)

Chap. VII. Circassian and Georgian Dances, with Music. Examples of Daghestan melodies (49 plates).

Chap. VIII. Oriental War-Dances (480 melodies).

LAFCADIO HEARN

Vol. VII. THE WEIRD IN SAVAGE MUSIC (with 169 highly curious examples).

Vol. VIII. HISTORY OF CREOLE MUSIC IN THE OCCIDENTAL INDIES.

Part I. Franco-African Melody, and its ultimate development. (298 ex.)

Part II. Spanish. Creole music and the history of its formation (359 examples of Havanese and other West Indian airs are given).

Vol. IX-X-XI. MELODIES OF AFRICAN RACES. (This highly important work contains no less than 5000 different melodies, and a complete description of all African musical instruments known, illustrated with numerous engravings.) Price per vol., $27.50.

Vol. XII. RECONSTRUCTION OF ANTIQUE MELODIES AFTER THE IRREFUTABLE SCIENTIFIC SYSTEM OF THE GERMAN SCHOOL OF MUSICAL EVOLUTIONISTS. (By this new process of anthropological research, it is now possible to reconstruct a lost melody, precisely as it was previously possible to affirm the existence of an extinct species of mammal which left no fossil record of which we know.)

Vol. XIII. MAGICAL MELODIES. The music of Apollo and Orpheus. — The Melodies of Wäinamöinen. — The Harp-playing of Merlin the Great. — Exhumation of the extraordinary Wizard-music referred to in the Kalewala. — Melodies that petrify. — Melodies that kill. — Melodies which evoke storms and tempests. — The Hávamál of Odin. — Scandinavian be-

TO H. E. KREHBIEL

lief in chants which seduce female virtue. — The Indian legend of Amaron. — Polynesian magic song. — The thief's song that lulls to sleep: a musical "hand-of-glory." — The invocation of demons by song. — Examples of the melodies which fiends obey. — Songs that bring down fire from heaven. — Strange Hindoo legend of the singer consumed by his own song. — The melodies of the greater magic. — The chants that change the colour of the Moon. — Deva-music: the conch-shells sounded at the birth of Buddha. — Notes on the Kalewala legends of singers who made the sun and moon to pause in heaven and changed the courses of the stars.

Vol. XIV. THE MELODIES OF MIGHTY LAMENTATION. Isis and Osiris. — Demeter and Persephone. "By the Rivers of Babylon." — Jeremiah's knowledge of music. — Lamentation of Thomyris. — The musicians of Shah Jehan, etc.
Apocalyptic music of the Bible.

Vol. XV. MOURNING FOR THE DEAD. History of cries of mourning in all nations. — Description of ancient writers. — Howling of the women of the Teutoni and Cimbri. — Terror of the Romans at the hideous sounds. (With 1300 examples of musical wailing among ancient nations.) — Modern wailing. — Survival of the Ancient Mourning Cry among modern peoples. — The Corsican voceri. — African funeral-chants. — Negro-Creole funeral-wail. (Tout pití çabri — ça Zoé non yé)! — Irish keening. — Gradual development of funeral-music, etc., etc.

LAFCADIO HEARN

Vol. XVI. SONGS OF TRIUMPH. — "Up to the everlasting Gates of Capitolian Jove." — Triumphal Chants of Rameses and Thotmes. — Assyrian triumphal marches. — A Tartar triumph. — Arabian melodies of war-joy, etc., etc.

KOROL AR C'HLEZE (The Sword-Dance)
Ancient dialect of Léon (Bretagne)

Goad, gwin, ha Korol.
D'id Heol!
Goad, gwin, ha Korol.
Tan! tan! dir! oh! dir! tan! tan! dir ha tan!
Tann! tann! tir! ha tonn! tonn! tir ha tir ha tann!

Ha Korol ha Kan,
Kan, ha Kann!
Ha Korol ha Kan.
Tan! tan!...

Korol ar c'hleze,
Enn eze;
Korol ar c'hleze.
Tan! tan!...

Kan ar c'hleze glaz
A gar laz;
Kan ar c'hleze glaz.
Tan! tan!...
Kann ar c'hleze gone
Ar Rone!
Kann ar c'hleze gone.
Tan! tan!...

Kleze! Rone braz
Ar stourmeaz!
Kleze! Rone braz!
Tan! tan!...

TO H. E. KREHBIEL

Kaneveden gen
War da benn!
Kaneveden gen!

*Tan! tan! dir! oh! dir! tan! tan dir ha tan!
Tann! tann! tir! ha tonn! tonn! tann! tir ha tir ha tann!*

LITERAL TRANSLATION

Blood, wine, and dance to thee, O Sun! — blood, wine and dance!
And dance and song, song and battle! dance and song!
The Dance of Swords, in circle! — the dance of swords.
Song of the Blue Sword that loves murder! — song of the blue sword!
Battle where the Savage Sword is King! — battle of the savage sword!
O Sword! — O great King of the fields of battle! — O Sword! O great King!
Let the Rainbow shine about thy brow! — let the rainbow shine!

(The chorus is literal in my own translation, or rather metrification!)

(Rude metrical translation by your most humble servant.)

CELTIC SWORD-SONG

Dance, battle-blood, and wine,
O Sun, are thine!
Dance, battle-blood, and wine!
*O Fire! — O Fire!
O Steel! — O Steel!
O Fire! — O Fire!
O Steel and Fire!
O Oak! — O Oak!
O Earth! — O Waves!
O Waves! — O Earth!
O Earth and Oak!*

' LAFCADIO HEARN

The dance-chant and the death-lock
    In battle-shock! —
The dance-chant and the death-lock!
      O Fire! — O Fire!
      O Steel! — O Steel! . . .

The Sword-dance, circling
    In a ring! —
The Sword-dance, circling!
      O Fire! O Fire!
      O Steel! O Steel! . . .

Sing the Slaughter-lover blue
    Broad and true!
Sing the Slaughter-lover blue!
      O Fire! — O Fire!
      O Steel! — O Steel! . . .

Battle where the savage Sword
    Is sole Lord, —
Battle of the savage Sword!
      O Fire! — O Fire!
      O Steel! — O Steel! . . .

O Sword! mighty King!
    Battle-King!
O Sword! mighty King! . . .
      O Fire! — O Fire!
      O Steel! — O Steel! . . .

Let the Rainbow's magic rays
    Round thee blaze! —
Let the Rainbow round thee blaze!
      O Fire! — O Fire!
      O Steel! — O Steel!
      O Fire! — O Fire!
        O Steel and Fire!
      O Oak! — O Oak!
      O Earth! — O Waves!
      O Waves! — O Earth!
        O Earth and Oak!

TO H. E. KREHBIEL

TO H. E. KREHBIEL

NEW ORLEANS, *February*, 1884

DEAR K., — Charley Johnson's coming down to spend a week with me. I shall be soon enjoying his Rabelaisian mirth, and his Gargantuesque laughter. He is going to Havana, and I shall ask him to get, if possible, the music of the erotic mime-dance — the Zamacueca of the Creoles.

I see they are offering prizes for a good opera. Why don't you compose an opera? I can suggest the most tremendous, colossal, Ragnarockian subject imaginable — knocks Wagner endwise and all the trilogies: "THE WOOING OF THE VIRGIN OF POJA," from the "Kalewala." The "Kalewala" is the only essentially *musical* epopea I know of. Orpheus is a mere clumsy charlatan to Wainamoinen and the wooers. The incidents are more charmingly enormous than anything in the Talmud, Ramayana, or Mahabharata. O! the old woman who talks to the Moon! — and the wicked singer who turns all that hear him to stone! — and the phantoms created by magical chant! — and the songs that make the stars totter in the frosty sky! — and the melodies that melt the gates of iron! And then, too, the episode of the Eternal Smith, by whose art the blue vault of heaven was wrought into shape; and the weird sleigh-ride over the Frozen Sea; and the words at whose utterance "the waters of the great deep lifted a thousand heads to listen!" And the story of the Earth-giant, aroused

LAFCADIO HEARN

by magical force from his slumber of innumerable years, to teach to the Magician the runes by which all things are created — the enchanted songs by which the Beginning was made to Begin. If you have not read it, try to get a *prose* translation: no poetical version can preserve the delightful goblinry and elfishness of the original, whereof the metre rings even as the ringing of a mighty harp.

I have also a delightful Malay poem which would make a much finer operatic subject or dramatic subject than the European féeries modelled upon the Hindoo drama of Sakuntala, or, as my French translator writes it, Sacountala. I have an inexhaustible quarry of monstrous and diabolical inspiration.

Yours truly, etc.

I spend whole days in vocal efforts — vain ones — to imitate those delicious arabesques about the Name of Allah in the Muezzin's Song — and do suddenly awake by night with a Voice in my ears, as of a Summons to Prayer. Bismillah! — enormous is God!

(Punishment No. 2)
Monograph upon the Music of the Witches' Sabbath.
Dictionary of the Musical Instruments of all Nations.
With 50,000 wood engravings.
The Musical Legends of All Nations.
By H. Ed. Krehbiel and Lafcadio Hearn. Seven Vols. in 8vo, with 100 chromolithographs and 2000 eaufortes. Price $300 per vol. 24th edition.
On the Howling Dervishes, and on the melodies of the six other orders of Dervishes. With music.

TO H. E. KREHBIEL

The Song of the Muezzin in All Moslem Countries.
From Western Morocco to the Chinese Sea. Nine hundred different Notations of the Chant — with an Appendix treating of the Chant in the Oases and in the Soudan, as affected by African influence. Price $8000.
Dance-Music of the Ancient Occident, 1700 Ex.
Temple-Melodies of the Ancient and Modern World. Vol. I, China. Vol. II, India. Vol. III, Rome. Vol. IV, Greece. Vol. V, Egypt, etc.

(To be continued.)

TO H. E. KREHBIEL

NEW ORLEANS, *February*, 1884

˙DEAR KREHBIEL, — Please don't let my importunacy urge you to write when you have little time and leisure. I only want to hear from you when it gives you pleasure and kills time. Never mind if I take a temporary notion to write every day — you know I don't mean to be unreasonable.

Now, as I have your postal card I'll cease the publication of my imaginary musical library, and will reserve that exquisite torture for some future occasion when I shall think you have treated me horribly. Just so soon as this beastly weather changes I'll go to New York, and hope you'll be able — say in April — to give me a few days' loafing-time.

I'm afraid, however, I shall have to leave my Ideas behind me. I know I could never squeeze them under or over the Brooklyn Bridge. Furthermore, I'm afraid the Elevated R.R. cars might run over my

Ideas and hurt them. In fact, 't is only in the vast swamps of the South, where the converse of the frogs is even as the roar of a thousand waters, that my Ideas have room to expand.

Your banjo article delighted me — of course, there is a great deal that is completely new to me therein. By the way, have you noticed the very curious looking harps of the Niam-Niams in Schweinfurth? They seem to me rather nearly related to the banjo in some respects. I am glad my little notes were of some use to you. I will take good care of the proof. Every time I see anything you'd like, I'll send it on. The etymology of the banjo is a very interesting thing; perhaps I may find something fresh on the subject some day.

Yours enthusiastically
L. Hearn

I know you would not care to hear about "the thousand different instruments to which the daughter of Pharaoh introduced King Solomon on the day he married her," because the names of the instruments and the melodies which were performed upon them and the various chants to all the idols of Egypt which the daughter of Pharaoh taught Solomon are utterly forgotten. Yet, by the Kabbalistic rules of Gematria and Temurah might they not be exhumed?

In treatise Shekalim of Seder Mo'ed of the Talmud of Jerusalem it is related on the authority of Rabbi

TO H. E. KREHBIEL

Aha, that Hogrus ben Levi, who directed the singing in the temple, "knew a vast number of melodies, and possessed a particular talent for modulating them in an agreeable voice. *By thrusting his thumb into his mouth he produced many and various sorts of chants, so that his brethren, the Cohanim, were utterly amazed thereat.*"

Hast read in Chapter XII of the Treatise Shabbat (Seder Mo'ed) concerning that lost Hebrew musical instrument, unlike any other instrument known in the history of mankind?...

TO H. E. KREHBIEL

NEW ORLEANS, *March*, 1884

DEAR KREHBIEL, — I was quite glad to get your short letter, knowing how busy you are. Johnson changed his mind about Havana, as the season there has been very unhealthy; and for the time being I am disappointed in regard to the Spanish-Creole music. But it is only a question of a little while when I shall get it. I sent you the other day some Madagascar music. You will observe it is arranged for men and women alternately. By the way, speaking of the refrain, I think you ought to find it scientifically treated in Herbert's Spencer's "Sociology"; for in that giant summary of all human knowledge, everything relating to the arts of life is considered comparatively and historically. I have not got it: indeed I could not afford so immense a series as a mere work of reference, and life is too short. But you can easily refer to it in your public libraries. This reminds me of a curious fact I observed in reading Tylor — the similarity of an Australian song to a Greek chorus at Sparta — at least, the construction thereof. You remember the lines, sung alternately by old men, young men, and boys:

>(OLD MEN) We once were stalwart youths.
>(YOUNG MEN) We are: if thou likest, test our strength.
>(BOYS) We shall be, and far better too!

Now Tylor quotes this Australian chant:

>(GIRLS) Kardang garro. — Young-brother again.
>(OLD WOMEN) Manmal garro. — Son again.
>(BOTH TOGETHER) Mela nadjo Nunga broo. — Hereafter I shall see never.

And it is also odd to find in Jeannest that in certain Congo tribes there is a superstition precisely like the Scandinavian superstition about the "hell-shoon" — a strange coincidence in view of the fact that these negroes do not allow any save the king and the dead to wear shoes.

I am happy to have discovered a new work on the blacks of Senegambia — home of the Griots; and I expect it contains some Griot music. I have sent for it. It is quite a large volume. I am beginning to think it would be a pity to hurry our project. The subject is so vast, and so many new discoveries are daily being made, that I think we can afford to gain material by waiting. I believe we can pick up a great deal of queer African music this summer; and I feel convinced

TO H. E. KREHBIEL

we ought to get specimens of West Indian Creole music.

I am afraid my imagination may have outstripped human knowledge in regard to negro physiology. You remember my suggestion about the possible differentia in the vocal chords of the two races. I feel more than ever convinced there *is* a remarkable difference. I heard a negro mother the other day calling her child's name — a name of two syllables — Ella; — the first syllable was a low but very loud note, the second a very high sharp one, with a fractional note tied to its tail; and I don't believe any white throat could have uttered that extraordinary sound with such rapidity and flexibility. The Australian *Coo-eee* was nothing to it! Well, I have been since studying Flower's "Hunterian Lectures on the Comparative Anatomy of Man"; and I find that the science of comparative anatomy is scarcely yet well defined — what then, can be said about the Comparative Physiology of Man? Nevertheless Flower is astonishing. He indicates extraordinary race-differences in the pelvic index (the shape of the pelvis), the length and proportion of the limbs, etc. I have been thinking of writing to him on the subject. Tell me — do you approve of the idea?

I have also sent to Europe for some works on Oriental music.

Your affectionate friend   L. H.

Charley Johnson spent a week with me. He is the

same old Charley. We had lots of fun and talk about old times. He was quite delighted with my library; nearly every volume of which is unfamiliar to ordinary readers. I have now nearly five hundred volumes — Egyptian, Assyrian, Indian, Chinese, Japanese, African, etc., etc. Johnson seems to have become a rich man. The fact embarrassed me a little bit. Somehow or other, wealth makes a sort of Chinese wall between friends. One is afraid to be one's self, or even to be as friendly as one would like toward somebody who is much better off. You know what I mean. Of course, I only speak of my private feelings; for Charley was just the same to me as in the old days.

TO W. D. O'CONNOR

NEW ORLEANS, *March*, 1884

MY DEAR O'CONNOR, — What a delicious writer you are! — you do not know what pleasure your letter gave me, and how many novel combinations of ideas it evoked. I like your judgment of the Musée Secret; and yet . . . I do not find it possible to persuade myself that the "mad excess of love" should not be indulged in by mankind. It is *immemorial* as you say; — Love was the creator of all the great thoughts and great deeds of men in all ages. I felt somewhat startled when I first read the earliest Aryan literature to find how little the human heart had changed in so many thousand years; — the women of the great Indian epics and lyrics are not less lovable than the ideal beauties of modern romance. All the great po-

TO W. D. O'CONNOR

ems of the world are but so many necklaces of word-jewelry for the throat of the *Venus Urania;* and all history is illuminated by the *Eternal Feminine,* even as the world's circle in Egyptian mythology is irradiated by Neith, curving her luminous woman's body from horizon to horizon. And has not this "mad excess" sometimes served a good purpose? I like that legend of magnificent prostitution in Perron's "Femmes Arabes," according to which a battle was won and a vast nomad people saved from extinction by the action of the beauties of the tribe, who showed themselves unclad to the hesitating warriors and promised their embraces to the survivors — of whom not over-many were left. Neither do I think that passion necessarily tends to enervate a people. There is an intimate relation between Strength, Health, and Beauty; they are ethnologically interlinked in one embrace — like the *Charities.* I fancy the stout soldiers who followed Xenophon were far better judges of physical beauty than the voluptuaries of Corinth; — the greatest of the exploits of Heracles was surely an amorous one. I don't like Bacon's ideas about love: they should be adopted only by statesmen or others to whom it is a duty to remain passionless, lest some woman entice them to destruction. Has it not sometimes occurred to you that it is only in the senescent epoch of a nation's life that love disappears? — there were no grand loves during the enormous debauch of which Rome died, nor in all that Byzantine orgy interrupted by the lightning of Moslem swords. . . . Again, after all, what else do we live for — ephemeræ that we are? Who was it that called life "a sudden light between two darknesses"? "Ye know not," saith Krishna, in the Bhagavad-Gita, "either the moment of life's beginning or the moment of its ending: only the middle may ye perceive." It is even so: we are ephemeræ, seeking only the pleasure of a golden moment before passing out of the glow into the gloom. Would not Love make a very good religion? I doubt if mankind will ever cease to have faith — in the aggregate; but I fancy the era *must* come when the superior intelligences will ask themselves of what avail are the noblest heroisms and self-denials, since even the constellations are surely burning out, and all forms are destined to melt back into that infinite darkness of death and of life which is called by so many different names. Perhaps, too, all those myriads of suns are only golden swarms of ephemeræ of a larger growth and a larger day, whose movements of attraction are due to some "mad excess of love."

The account your friend gave you of De Nerval's suicide is precisely like the details of M. de Beaulieu's picture exposed in 1859 — and, I *think*, destroyed by the police for some unaccountable reason. It is described in Gautier's "Histoire du Romantisme," pp. 143-4 (note). . . . I am glad you notice my hand once in a while, and that you liked my De Nerval sketch and the "Women of the Sword." You

TO W. D. O'CONNOR

speak of magazine-work. I think the magazines are simply inabordables. My experiences have been disheartening. "Very good, very scholarly — *but not the kind* we want"; — "Highly interesting — sorry we have no room for it"; — "I regret to say we cannot use it, but would advise you to send it to X——"; "Deserves to be published; but unfortunately our rules exclude" — etc. I have an article now with the "Atlantic" — an essay upon the Adzan, or chant of the muezzin; its romantic history, etc. This has already been rejected by other leading magazines. Another horrible fact is that after your article is accepted, the editor rewrites it in his own way — and then prints your name at the end of the so-created abomination. This is the plan of——. I would like to see the ideal newspaper started we used to talk about: then we could write — eh?

So you think Doré's Raven a failure! I hope you are not altogether right. I thought so when I first looked at the plates; but the longer I examined them, the more strongly they impressed me. There is ghostly power in several. What do you think of "The Night's Plutonian Shore"; and the "Home by Horror haunted"? I must say that the terminal vignette with its Sphinx-death is one of the most terrible ideas I have ever seen drawn — although its force might be augmented by larger treatment. I would like to see it taken up by that French artist who painted that beautiful "Flight into Egypt," where we see the Virgin and Child (in likeness of an

Arab wanderer with her baby), slumbering between the awful granite limbs of the monster.

Your Gautier has just arrived. If you had sent me a little fortune you could not have pleased me so much. I never saw the photo before: it not only pleased, it excelled anticipation. You know our preconceived ideas of places we should like to visit and people we should like to know, usually excel the reality; but the head of Gautier seems to me grander than I imagined. One can almost hear him speak with that mellow, golden, organ-toned voice of his which Bergerat described; and I like that barbaric luxury of his attire — there is something at once rich and strange about it, worthy some Khan of the Golden Horde.... I really feel quite enthusiastic about my new possession.

I am glad to hear you dislike Matthew Arnold. He seems to me one of the colossal humbugs of the century: a fifth-rate poet and unutterably dreary essayist; — a sort of philosophical hermaphrodite, yet lacking even the grace of the androgyne, because there is neither enough of positivism nor of idealism in his mental make-up to give real character to it. Don't you think Edwin Arnold far the nobler man and writer? I love that beautiful enthusiasm of his for the beauties of strange faiths and exotic creeds. This is the spirit that, in some happier era, may bless mankind with a universal religion in perfect harmony with the truths of science and the better nature of humanity.

TO W. D. O'CONNOR

You ask about this climate. One who has lived by the sea and on the mountain-tops, as I have, must spend several years here to understand how this intertropical swamp-life affects the unacclimated. The first year one becomes very sick — fevers of unfamiliar character attack him; the appetite vanishes, the energies become enfeebled. The second summer one feels even worse. The third summer one can just endure without absolute sickness. The fourth, one begins to gain flesh and strength. But the blood has completely changed, the least breath of really cool air makes one shiver, and energy never becomes quite restored. After a few years in Louisiana, hard work becomes impossible. We are all lazy, enervated, compared with you Northerners. When my Northwestern friends come down here, it seems to me like a coming of Vikings and Berserkers; they are so full of life and blood and vital electricity! But when it is cold to me, it seems frightfully warm to them; and yet we used once to work together as reporters with the thermometer twenty below zero.

Sorry to say that Leloir died before completing the illustrations; and I suppose the subscribers to the edition will be the losers. It was to be issued in parts. Perhaps ten numbers were out. But I am not sure whether any of the engravings were printed. I based my error upon the critique of Leloir's work in "Le Livre." It is dangerous to anticipate!

I believe I have the very latest edition of W. W. [Walt Whitman] — 1882 (Rees, Welsh & Co.), which

I like very much. You did not quite understand my allusion to the Bible. I wished to imply that it was when W. W.'s verses approached that Biblical metre in form, etc., that we most admired him. I agree with all you say about slang — especially nautical slang; also about the grand irregularity of the wave-chant. Still I'll have to write some examples of what I refer to, and will do so later.

Yours very warmly and gratefully
L. HEARN

TO H. E. KREHBIEL

NEW ORLEANS, March, 1884

DEAR KREHBIEL, — I am sorry to be in such a hurry that I have to write a short letter; but I must signal my pleasure at seeing you coming out in public, and I have a vision of future greatness for you. As for myself, I trust I shall in a few years more obtain influence enough to be able to return some of your many kindnesses in a literary way. Eventually we may be able to pull together to a very bright goal, if I can keep my health.

I think that Osgood will announce the book about the 1st of April, but I am not sure. It would hardly do to anticipate. I send you his letter. The terms are not grand; but a big improvement on Worthington's. Next time I hope I will be able to work *to order.* You can return letter when you are done with it, as it forms a part of my enormous collection of letters from publishers — 199 rejections to 1 acceptation.

TO H. E. KREHBIEL

I expect I shall have to postpone my visit until the book is out, as I must wait here to receive and correct proofs. I have dedicated the book to Page Baker, as it was entirely through his efforts that I got a hearing from Osgood. The reader *had already rejected* the MS. when Baker's letter came. From the "Atlantic" I have not yet heard. If I have good luck (which is extremely improbable) I would make the Muezzin No. 1 in a brief series of Arabesque studies, which would cost about two years' labour — at intervals. I have several subjects in mind: for example, the lives of certain outrageous Moslem Saints, and a sketch of the mulatto and quadroon slave-poets of Arabia before Mahomet; "The Ravens," as they were called from their colour; — also the story of the *Ye monnat*, or those who died of love.... But these are beautiful dreams in embryo!

Yours affectionately

L. HEARN

TO H. E. KREHBIEL

NEW ORLEANS, *March*, 1884
[Postal-card]

... IT is related by Philostratus in his life of Apollonius of Tyana, that when Apollonius visited India, and asked the Brahmins to give an example of (musical) magic, the Brahmins did strip themselves naked and dance in a ring, each tapping the earth with a staff, and singing a strange hymn. Then the earth within the ring rose up, quivering, even as fermenting dough — and rose higher — and undulated and was lost in great waves — and elevated the singers unto the height of two cubits....

TO H. E. KREHBIEL

NEW ORLEANS, *April,* 1884

DEAR KREHBIEL, — I read your leader with no small interest; and "the gruesome memories" were revived. The killing of the man in the Vine Street saloon, however, interested me most as a memory-reviving interest. That murderer was the most magnificent specimen of athletic manhood that I ever saw — I suspect he was a gipsy; for he had all the characteristics of that race, and *was not a regular circus-employee* — only a professional rider, now with one company, now with another. Did you see him when you were there? He was perhaps six feet four; for his head nearly touched the top of the cell. He had a very regular handsome face, with immense black eyes; and an Oriental sort of profile: — then he seemed slender, in spite of his immense force — such was the proportion of his figure. A cynical devil, too. I went to see him with the coroner, who showed him the piece of the dead man's skull. He took it between his fingers, held it up to the light, handed it back to the coroner and observed; "Christ! — *he must have had a d——d rotten skull.*" He was ordered to leave town within twenty-four hours as a dangerous character. It is a pity such men should be vulgar murderers and ruffians; — what

TO H. E. KREHBIEL

superb troopers they would make! I shall never forget that splendid stature and strength as long as I live. . . .

I don't know whether I shall ever be living in that terrible metropolis of yours. It will be impossible for me ever again to write or read by night; and hard work has become impossible. If I could ever acquire reputation enough to secure a literary position on some monthly or weekly periodical where I could take it easy, perhaps I might feel like enduring the hideous winters. But I am just now greatly troubled by the question, What shall I work for? — to what special purpose? Perhaps some good fortune may come when least expected.

Now I want to talk about our trip. I think it better not to go now. Page wants me to take a good big vacation this summer — a long one. If I wait till it gets warm, I will be able to escape the feverish month; and if you should be in Cincinnati at the Festival, or elsewhere, I would meet you anyhow or anywhere you say. Were I to leave now I could not do so later; and I am waiting for some curious books and things which I want to bring you so that we can analyze them together. A month or so won't make much difference.

Will write you soon.

Had to quit work for a few days on account of eye-trouble.

                Yours very truly

                            L. HEARN

LAFCADIO HEARN

TO H. E. KREHBIEL

NEW ORLEANS, *May*, 1884

DEAR KREHBIEL, — I have been so busy that I have not been able to answer your last. They are sending me proofs at the rate of twenty pages a day; and you can imagine this keeps me occupied in addition to my other work. Alas! I find that nothing written for a newspaper — at least for an American newspaper — can be perfect. My poor little book will show some journalistic weaknesses — will contain some hasty phrases or redundancies or something else which will mar it. I try my best to get it straight; but the consequences of hasty labour are perpetually before me, notwithstanding the fact that the collocation of the material occupied nearly two years. I am thinking of Bayard Taylor's terrible observation about American newspaper-work. It seems to be generally true. Still there *are* some who write with extraordinary precision and correctness. I think you are one of them.

What troubles my style especially is ornamentation. An ornamental style must be perfect or full of atrocious discords and incongruities; and perfect ornamentation requires slow artistic work — except in the case of men like Gautier, who never re-read a page, or worried himself about a proof. But I think I'll improve as I grow older.

I won't be away till June. Then I'll have some queer books in my satchel, and we'll talk the book

TO H. E. KREHBIEL

over. I fear it is no use to discuss it beforehand, as I shall be overwhelmed with work. Another volume of the Talmud has come, and some books about music containing Chinese hymns. By the way, in Spencer's last volume there is an essay on musical origination. I have had only time to glance at it. Your Creole music lecture cannot fail to be extremely curious; wish I could *hear* and see it. The melodies will certainly make a sensation if you have a good assortment. Did you borrow anything from Gottschalk? — I hope you did: the Bamboula used to drive the Parisians wild.

Thanks for the musical transcription. I'm afraid the project won't pan out, however. Trübner & Co. of London made an offer, but wanted me to guarantee the American sale of a hundred copies — that means pay in advance. I would not perhaps have objected, if they had mentioned a low price; but when I tried to get them to come down to about five shillings per copy they did not write me any more.

Then I abandoned the pursuit of the Ignis Fatuus of Success, and withdrew into the Immensities and the Eternities, even as the rhinoceros withdraweth into the recesses of the jungle. And I gave myself up to the meditation of the Vedas and of the Puranas and of the Upanishads, and of the Egyptian Ritual of the Dead — until the memory of magazines and of publishers faded out of my mind, even as the vision of demons.

    Yours very truly   L. HEARN

LAFCADIO HEARN

TO W. D. O'CONNOR

NEW ORLEANS, *May*, 1884

MY DEAR O'CONNOR, — I did not get time until to-day to drop you a line; and just at present I am enthusiastically appreciating your observations regarding The Foul Fiend Routine. I wish I could escape from his brazen grip; and nevertheless he has done me service. He has stifled my younger and more foolish aspirations, and clipped the foolish wings of my earlier ambition with the sharp scissors of revision. It is true that I now regret my inability to achieve literary independence; but had I obtained a market for my wares in other years, I should certainly have been so ashamed of them by this time, that I should fly to some desert island. These meditations follow upon the incineration of several hundred pages of absurdities written some years back, and just committed to the holy purification of fire....

I am not, however, sorry for writing the fantastic ideas about love which you so thoroughly exploded in your letter; they "drew you out," and I wanted to hear your views. I suppose, however, that the mad excess is indulged in by every nation at a certain period of existence — perhaps the Senescent Epoch, as Draper calls it. What a curious article might be written upon "The Amorous Epochs of National Literatures" — or something of that sort; dwelling especially upon the extravagant passionateness of Indian, Persian, and Arabic belles-lettres —

TO W. D. O'CONNOR

and their offshoots! Not to bore you further with theories, however, I herewith submit another specimen of excess from the posthumous poetry of Gautier. It has been compared to those Florentine statuettes, which are kept in shagreen cases, and only exhibited, whisperingly, by antiquaries to each other....

There is real marmorean beauty in the lines — their sculpturesqueness saves them from lewdness. I think them more beautiful than Solomon's simile, or the extravagances of the Gita-Govinda.

June 29

You see how busy I have been. And my brain seems so full of dust and hot sun and feverish vapours that it is hard to write at all.... I am thinking of what you said about Arnold's translating the Koran. There are two English translations besides Sale's — one in Trübner's Oriental Series, and one in Max Müller's "Sacred Books of the East" (Macmillan's beautiful edition). Sale's is chiefly objectionable because the suras are not versified: the chapters not having been so divided in early times by figures. But it is horribly hard to find anything in it. The French have two superb versions: Kazimirski and La Beaume. Kazimirski is popular and cheap; the other is an analytical Koran of eight hundred quarto pages with concordance, and designed for the use of the Government bureaux in Algeria. I have it. It is unrivalled.

LAFCADIO HEARN

My book is out; and you will receive a copy soon. If you ever have time, please tell me if there is anything in it you like. It is not a gorgeous production — only an experiment. I have a great plan in view: to popularize the legends of Islam and other strange faiths in a series of books. My next effort will be altogether Arabesque — treating of Moslem saints, singers, and poets, and hagiographical curiosities — eschewing such subjects as the pilgrimage to the ribath (monastery) of Deir-el-Tiu in the Hedjaz, where fragments of the broken aidana of Mahomet are kissed by the faithful. . . .

I'm sorry to say I know little of Bacon except his Essays. Those surprised and pleased me. I started to read them only as a study of Old English; but soon found the ideas far beyond the century in which they were penned. You will be shocked, I fear, to know that I am terribly ignorant of classic English literature — of the sixteenth, seventeenth, and eighteenth centuries. Not having studied it much when at college, I now find life too short to study it — except for style. When I want to clear mine — as coffee is cleared by the white of an egg — I pour a little quaint English into my brain-cup, and the Oriental extravagances are gradually precipitated. But I think a man must devote himself to one thing in order to succeed: so I have pledged me to the worship of the Odd, the Queer, the Strange, the Exotic, the Monstrous. It quite suits my temperament. For example, my memories of early

TO W. D. O'CONNOR

Roman history have become cloudy, because the Republic did not greatly interest me; but very vivid are my conceptions of the Augustan era, and great my delight with those writers who tell us how Hadrian almost realized that impossible dream of modern æsthetes, the resurrection of Greek art. The history of modern Germany and Scandinavia I know nothing about; but I know the Eddas and the Sagas, and the chronicles of the Heimskringla, and the age of Vikings and Berserks — because these were mighty and awesomely grand. The history of Russia pleaseth me not at all, with the exception of such extraordinary episodes as the Dimitris; but I could never forget the story of Genghis Khan, and the nomad chiefs who led 1,500,000 horsemen to battle. Enormous and lurid facts are certainly worthy of more artistic study than they generally receive. What De Quincey told us in his "Flight of a Tartar Tribe" previous writers thought fit to make mere mention of. . . . But I'm rambling again.

I don't know whether I shall be able to go North as I hoped — I have so much private study before me. But I do really hope to see you some day. Could n't you get down to our Exposition? . . .

Did you ever read Symonds's "Greek Poets"? The final chapters on the genius of Greek art are simply divine. I mention them because of your observation about our being or not being ephemeral. I feel fearful we are. But Symonds says what I would

LAFCADIO HEARN

have liked to say, so much better, that I would like to let him speak for me with voice of gold.
Very truly your friend
LAFCADIO HEARN

TO H. E. KREHBIEL

NEW ORLEANS, *June*, 1884

DEAR KREHBIEL, — I'm expecting every day to get some Griot music and some queer things, and have discovered an essay upon just the subject of subjects that interests Us: — the effect of physiological influences upon the history of nations, and "the physiological character of races in their relation to historical events." Would n't it be fine if we could write a scientific essay on Polynesian music in its manifestations of the physiological peculiarities of the island-races? Nothing would give me so much pleasure as to be able some day to write a most startling and stupefying preface to some treatise of yours upon exotic music — a preface nevertheless strictly scientific and correct. By the way, have you any information about Eskimo music? If you have, tell me when I see you. I have some singular songs with a *double-refrain* — but no music — which I found in Rink. Why the devil did n't Rink give us some melodies?

I am especially interested just now in Arabic subjects; but as I am following the Arabs into India, I find myself studying the songs of the bayaderes. They are very strange, and sometimes very pretty

TO H. E. KREHBIEL

— sweetly pretty. Maisonneuve promised to publish some of this Indian music, but that was in '81, and we have n't got it yet. I have found curious titles in Trübner's collection; but I'm afraid the music is n't published — "Folk-Songs of Southern India," etc.

I want you to tell me how long you will stay in New York, as I would like to go there soon. The vacations are beginning. Don't fail to keep me posted as to your movements. How did you like the sonorous cry of the bel-balancier man?

Am writing in haste; excuse everything excusable.
Yours affectionately
L. HEARN

A man ignorant of music is likely to say silly things without knowing it when writing to a professor; so you must excuse my faults on the ground of good will to you. I have just destroyed two pages which I thought might be waste of time to read.

TO H. E. KREHBIEL

NEW ORLEANS, *June*, 1884

DEAR K., — I want you to let me hear about old Bilâl for the following reasons:

1. I have discovered that a biography of him — the only one in existence probably — may be found in Wüstenfeld's "Nawawi," for which I have written. If the text is German I can utilize it with the aid of a bouquiniste here.

LAFCADIO HEARN

2 I have been lucky enough to engage a copy of Ibn Khallikan in twenty-four volumes — the great Arabic biographer. It containeth legends. The book is dear but invaluable to an Oriental student — especially to me in the creation of my new volume, which will be all Arabesques.

And here is another bit of news for you. My Senegal books have thrown a torrent of light on the whole history of American slave-songs and superstitions and folk-lore. I was utterly astounded at the revelation. All that had previously seemed obscure is now lucid as day. Of course, you know the slaves were chiefly drawn from the West Coast; and the study of ethnography and ethnology of the West Coast races is absolutely essential to a knowledge of Africanism in America. As yet, however, I have but partly digested my new meal.

Siempre á V.

LAFCADIO HFARN

NEW ORLEANS, *June*, 1884

DEAR K., — Your letter has given me unspeakable pleasure. In making the acquaintance of Howells, you have met the subtlest and noblest literary mind in this country — scarcely excepting that prince of critics, Stedman; and you have found a friend who will aid you in climbing Parnassus, not for selfish motives, but for pure art's sake. Cultivate him all you can. . . .

I got a nice letter from Ticknor. He actually

TO H. E. KREHBIEL

promises to open the magazine-gates for me. And a curious coincidence is that the book is published on my birthday, next Friday.

I will write you before I start for New York in a few weeks more....

I will bring my African books with me, and other things.

Yours sincerely
LAFCADIO HEARN

TO H. E. KREHBIEL

NEW ORLEANS, *October*, 1884

DEAR KREHBIEL, — I sit down to write you the first time I have had leisure to do justice to the subject for a month.

Now I must tell you what I am doing. I have been away a good deal, in the Creole archipelagoes of the Gulf, and will soon be off again, to make more studies for my little book of sketches. I sent you the No. 2, as a sample. These I take as much pains with as with magazine work, and the plan is philosophical and pantheistic. Did you see "Torn Letters" — (No. 1) about the Biscayena. The facts are not wholly true; I was very nearly in love — not quite sure whether I am not a little in love still — but I never told her so. It is so strange to find one's self face to face with a beauty that existed in the Tertiary epoch — 300,000 years ago — the beauty of the most ancient branch of humanity — the oldest of the world's races! But the coasts here are just as I described them, without exaggeration — and I am so enamoured of those islands and tepid seas that I would like to live there forever, and realize Tennyson's wish:

I will wed some savage woman; she shall rear my dusky race:
Iron-jointed, supple-sinewed, they shall dive and they shall run —
Catch the wild goat by the hair, and hurl their lances in the sun,
Whistle back the parrot's call — leap the rainbows of the brooks —
Not with blinded eyesight poring over miserable books.

The islanders found I had one claim to physical superiority anyhow — I could outswim the best of them with the greatest ease. And I have disciplined myself physically so well of late years, that I am no longer the puny little fellow you used to know.

All this is sufficiently egotistical. I just wanted, however, to tell you of my wanderings and their purpose. It was largely inspired by the new style of Pierre Loti — that young marine officer who is certainly the most original of living French novelists.

All this summer Page could not get away; so you will not have the pleasure of seeing my very noble and lovable friend — a tall, fine, eagle-faced fellow, primitive Aryan type. I only got away on the pledge to give the results to the "Times-Democrat," which is giving me all possible assistance in my literary undertakings.

I was glad to receive Creole books, as I am working on Creole subjects. Several new volumes have appeared. I have some Oriental things to send

TO H. E. KREHBIEL

you — music, if you will agree to return in one month from reception. But you need not have expressed those other things — made me feel sorry. I expressed them to you for other reasons entirely.

I have a delightful Mexican friend living with me, and teaching me to speak Spanish with that long, soft, languid South American Creole accent that is so much more pleasant than the harsher accent of Spain. His name is José de Jesus y Preciado, and he sends you his best wishes, because he says all my friends must be his friends too.

Now, I hope you'll write me a pretty, kind, forgiving letter — not condescendingly, but really nice — you know what I mean.

Your supersensitive and highly suspicious friend
LAFCADIO HEARN

TO H. E. KREHBIEL

NEW ORLEANS, *January*, 1885

DEAR FRIEND KREHBIEL, — Many, many happy New Years. Your letter came luckily during an interval of rest — so that I can answer it right away. I have not been at all worried by your silence — as your former kind lines showed me you had fully forgiven my involuntary injustice and my voluntary, but only momentary *malice*. (Please give this last the French accent, which takes off the edge of the word.)

In a few days my Creole Dictionary will be published in New York; and I will not forget to send you a copy, just as soon as I can get some myself. I do not expect to make anything on the publication. It is a give-away to a friend, who will not forget me if he makes money, but who does not expect to make a fortune on it. This kind of thing is never lucrative; and the publication of the book is justified only by Exposition projects. As for the "Stray Leaves" I have never written to the publishers yet about them — so afraid of bad news I have been. But I have dared to try and get a good word said for it in high places. I succeeded in obtaining a personal letter from Protap Chunder Roy, of Calcutta, and hope to get one from Edwin Arnold. This is cheeky; but publishers think so much about a commendation from some acknowledged authority in Oriental studies.

The prices are high; the markets are all "bulled"; and for the first time I find my room rent here (twenty dollars per month) and my salary scarcely enough for my extravagant way of life. Money is a subject I am beginning to think of in connection with everything except — art. I still think nobody should follow an art purpose with money in view; but if no money comes in time, it is discouraging in this way — that the lack of public notice is generally somewhat of a bad sign. Happily, however, I have joined a building association, which compels me to pay out twenty dollars per month. Outside of this way of saving, I save nothing — except queer books imported from all parts of the world.

Very affectionately yours
HEARN

TO H. E. KREHBIEL

TO H. E. KREHBIEL
NEW ORLEANS, *January*, 1885

MY DEAR KREHBIEL, — I fear I know nothing about Creole music or Creole negroes. Yes, I have seen them dance; but they danced the Congo, and sang a purely African song to the accompaniment of a dry-goods box beaten with sticks or bones and a drum made by stretching a skin over a flour-barrel. That sort of accompaniment and that sort of music, you know all about: it is precisely similar to what a score of travellers have described. There are no harmonies — only a furious contretemps. As for the dance — in which the women do not take their feet off the ground — it is as lascivious as is possible. The men dance very differently, like savages, leaping in the air. I spoke of this spectacle in my short article in the "Century."

One must visit the Creole parishes to discover the characteristics of the real Creole music, I suspect. I would refer the "Century" to Harris's book: he says the Southern darkies don't use the banjo. I have never seen any play it here but Virginians or "upper country" darkies. The slave-songs you refer to are infinitely more interesting than anything Cable's got; but still, I fancy his material could be worked over into something really pretty. Gottschalk found the theme for his Bamboula in Louisiana — Quand patate est chinte, etc., and made a miracle out of it.

LAFCADIO HEARN

Now if you want any further detailed account of the Congo dance, I can send it; but I doubt whether you need it. The Creole songs, which I have heard sung in the city, are Frenchy in construction, but possess a few African characteristics of method. The darker the singer the more marked the oddities of intonation. Unfortunately most of those I have heard were quadroons or mulattoes. One black woman sang me a Voodoo song, which I got Cable to write — but I could not sing it as she sang it, so that the music is faulty. I suppose you have seen it already, as it forms part of the collection. If the "Century" people have any sense they would send you down here for some months next spring to study up the old ballads; and I believe that if you manage to show Cable the importance of the result, he can easily arrange it. . . .

You answered some of my questions charmingly. Don't be too sarcastic about my capacity for study. My study is of an humble sort; and I never knew anything, and never shall, about acoustics. But I have had to study awful hard in order to get a vague general idea of those sciences which can be studied without mathematics, or actual experimentation with mechanical apparatus. I have half a mind to study medicine in practical earnest some day. Would n't I make an imposing Doctor in the Country of Cowboys? A doctor might also do well in Japan. I'm thinking seriously about it.

This is the best letter I can write for the present,

TO H. E. KREHBIEL

and I know it's not a good one. I send a curiosity by Xp to you.

The Creole slaves sang usually with clapping of hands. But it would take an old planter to give reliable information regarding the accompaniment.

Yours very truly

L. HEARN

TO H. E. KREHBIEL

NEW ORLEANS, 1885

DEAR KREHBIEL, — I regret having been so pressed for time that I was obliged to return your MS. without a letter expressing the thanks which you know I feel. I scribbled in pencil — which you can erase with a bit of bread — some notes on the Cajan song, that may interest you.

The Harpers are giving me warm encouragement; but advise me to remain a fixture where I am. They say they are looking now to the South for literary work of a certain sort — that immense fields for observation remain here wholly untilled, and that they want active, living, opportune work of a fresh kind. I shall try soon my hand at fiction; — my great difficulty is my introspective disposition, which leaves me in revery at moments when I ought to be using eyes, ears, and tongue in studying others rather than my own thoughts.

I find the word "Banja" given as African in Bryan Edwards's "West Indies." My studies of African survivals have tempted me to the purchase of a great many queer books which will come in useful some day. Most are unfortunately devoted to Senegal; for our English travellers are generally poor ethnographers and anthropologists, so far as the Gold Coast and Ivory Coast are concerned. You remember our correspondence about the comparative anatomy of the vocal organs of negroes and whites. A warm friend of several years' standing — a young Spanish physician and professor here — is greatly interested in this new science: indeed we study comparative human anatomy and ethnology in common, with goniometers and Broca's instruments. He states that only microscopic work can reveal the full details of differentiation in the vocal organs of races; but calls my attention to several differences already noticed. Gibb has proved, for instance, that the cartilages of Wrisberg are larger in the negro; — this would not affect the voice especially; but the fact promises revelations of a more important kind. We think of your projects in connection with these studies.

I copied only your Acadian boat-song. What is the price of the slave-song book? If you have time to send me during the next month the music of "Michié Preval," and of the boat-song, I can use them admirably in "Mélusine.". . .

Your friend

L. H.

TO W. D. O'CONNOR

TO W. D. O'CONNOR
NEW ORLEANS, *March*, 1885

Big P. S. No. 1.

I forgot in my hurried letter yesterday, to tell you that if you ever want a copy of "Stray Leaves," don't go and buy it, as you have been naughty enough to do, but tell me, and I'll send you what you wish. I hope to dedicate a book to you some day, when I am sure it is worth dedicating to you.

I am quite curious about you. Seems to me you must be like your handwriting — firmly knit, large, strong, and keen; — with delicate perceptions, (of course I know *that*, anyhow!) well-developed ideas of order and system, and great continuity of purpose and a disposition as level and even as the hand you write. If my little scraggy hand tells you anything, you ought to recognize in it a very small, erratic, eccentric, irregular, impulsive, variable, nervous disposition — almost exactly your antitype in everything — except the love of the beautiful.

Very faithfully

L. H.

Big P. S. No. 2.

I did not depend on "Le Figaro" for statements about Hugo; but picked them up in all directions. What think you of his refusal to aid poor blind Xavier Aubryet by writing a few lines of preface for his book? What about his ignoring the services of his greatest champion, Théophile Gautier? What about his studied silence in regard to the works of the struggling poets and novelists of the movement which he himself inaugurated? I really believe that the man has been a colossus of selfishness. One who prejudiced me very strongly against him, however, was that eccentric little Jew, Alexander Weill, whose reminiscences of Heine made such a sensation. Perhaps after all literary generosity is rare. Flaubert and Gautier possessed it; but twenty cases of the opposite kind, quite as illustrious, may be cited. In any event I am glad of your rebuke. Whether my ideas are right or wrong, I believe we ought not to speak of the weaknesses of truly great men when it can be avoided; — therefore I cry peccavi, and promise to do so no more.

Yours very sincerely
LAFCADIO HEARN

TO H. E. KREHBIEL

NEW ORLEANS, 1885

DEAR KREHBIEL, — I have been away in Florida, in the track of old Ponce de Leon — bathing in the Fount of Youth — talking to the palm-trees — swimming in the great Atlantic surf. Charley Johnson and I took the trip together — or to be strictly fair, it was he that induced me to go along; and I am not sorry for the expense or the time spent, as I enjoyed my reveries unspeakably. For bathing — sea-bathing — I prefer our own Creole islands in the Gulf to any place in Florida; but for scenery

TO REV. WAYLAND D. BALL

and sunlight and air — air that is a liquid jewel — Florida seems to me the Garden of Hesperus. I'll send you what I have written about it. . . . Charles Dudley Warner, whose acquaintance I made here, strikes me as the nicest literary personage I have yet met. . . . Gilder of the "Century" was here — a handsome, kindly man. . . . A book which I recently got would interest you — Symonds's "Wine, Women, and Song." I had no idea that the Twelfth Century had its literary renascence, or that in the time of the Crusades German students were writing worthy of Horace and Anacreon. The Middle Ages no longer seem so Doresquely black.

Your friend
LAFCADIO HEARN

TO REV. WAYLAND D. BALL

NEW ORLEANS, 1885

MY DEAR BALL, — I regret my long silence, now broken with the sincere pleasure of being able to congratulate you upon a grand success and still grander opportunities. The salary you are promised is nearly double that obtained by the best journalist in the country (excepting one or two men in highly responsible positions of managers); it far exceeds the average earnings of expert members of the higher professions; and there are not many authors in the United States who can rely upon such an income. So that you have a fine chance to accumulate a nice capital, as well as ample means to indulge scholarly tastes and large leisure to gratify them. I feared, sensitive as you are, to weigh too heavily upon one point before, but I think I shall not hesitate to do so now. I refer to the question of literary effort. Again I would say: Leave all profane writing alone for at least five years more; and devote all your talent, study, sense of beauty, force of utterance to your ministerial work. You will make an impression, and be able to rise higher and higher. In the meanwhile you will be able to mature your style, your thought, your scholarship; and when the proper time comes be able also to make a sterling, good, literary effort. What we imagine new when we are young is apt really to be very old; and that which appears to us very old suddenly grows youthful at a later day with the youth of Truth's immortality. None, except one of those genii, who appear at intervals as broad as those elapsing in Indian myth between the apparition of the Buddhas, can sit down before the age of thirty-five or forty, and create anything really great. Again the maxim, "Money is power" — commonplace and vulgar though it be — has a depth you will scarcely appreciate until a later day. It is power for good, quite as much as for evil; and "nothing succeeds like success," you know. Once you occupy a great place in the great religious world of wealth and elegance and beauty, you will find yourself possessed of an influence that will enable you to realize any ambition which inspires you. This is the best answer I can now give to your

TO REV. WAYLAND D. BALL

last request for a little friendly counsel, and it is uttered only because I feel that being older than you, and having been knocked considerably about the world, I can venture to offer the results of my little experience.

As you say, you are drawing nearer to me. I expect we shall meet, and be glad of the meeting. I shall have little to show you except books, but we will have a splendid time for all that. Meanwhile I regret having nothing good to send you. The story appeared in "Harper's Bazar."

Sincerely your friend
LAFCADIO HEARN

TO REV. WAYLAND D. BALL

NEW ORLEANS, *July*, 1885

MY DEAR BALL, — Your welcome letter came to me just at a happy moment when I had time to reply. I would have written before, but for a protracted illness. I am passionately fond of swimming; and the clear waters of that Florida spring seduced me into a plunge while very hot. The water was cold as death; and when I got back to New Orleans, I had the novel experience of a Florida fever — slow, torpid, and unconquerable by quinine. Now I am all right.

The language of "Stray Leaves" is all my own, with the exception of the Italic texts and a few pages translated from the "Kalewala." The Florida sketch I sent you, although published in a newspaper, is one of a number I have prepared for the little volume of

LAFCADIO HEARN

impressions I told you about. I sent it as an illustration of the literary theory discussed in our previous correspondence, which I am surprised you remember so well.

Apropos of your previous letter, I must observe that I do not like James Freeman Clarke's work — immense labour whose results are nullified by a purely sectarian purpose. Mr. Clarke sat down to study with the preconceived purpose of belittling other beliefs by comparison with Christianity — a process quite as irrational and narrow as would be an attempt in the opposite direction. My very humble studies in comparative mythology led me to a totally different conclusion — revealing to me a universal aspiration of mankind toward the Infinite and Supreme, so mighty, so deeply sincere, so touching, that I have ceased to perceive the least absurdity in any general idea of worship, whether fetish or monotheistic, whether the thought of the child man or the dream of hoary Indian philosophy. Nor can I for the same reason necessarily feel more reverence for the crucified deity than for that image of the Hindoo god of light, holding in one of his many hands Phallus, and yet wearing a necklace of skulls — symbolizing at once creation and destruction — the Great Begetter and the Universal Putrifier.

A noble and excellently conceived address that of yours on Thomas Paine — bolder than I thought your congregation was prepared for. Yes, I certainly think you are going to effect a great deal in a good

TO REV. WAYLAND D. BALL

cause, the cause of mental generosity and intellectual freedom. I almost envy you sometimes your opportunities as a great teacher, a social emancipator, and I feel sure what you have already done is nothing to be compared with what you will do, providing you retain health and strength.

I don't know just what to say about your literary articles; but I can speak to the editor-in-chief, who is my warm personal friend. The only difficulty would be the bigotry here. Even my editorials upon Sanscrit literature called out abuse of the paper from various New Orleans pulpits, as "A Buddhist Newspaper," an "Infidel sheet," etc. If published first in the Boston paper, I could get the lecture reproduced, I think, in ours. If you expect remuneration you would have to send the MS. first to us and take the chances. I think what you best do in the interim would be to write on the subject to Page M. Baker, Editor "Times-Democrat," mentioning my name, and await reply.

You asked me in a former letter a question I forgot to answer. I have no photograph at present, but will have some taken soon and will send you one.

Very sincerely yours
LAFCADIO HEARN

TO REV. WAYLAND D. BALL

NEW ORLEANS, 1885

DEAR BALL, — I regret extremely my long delay in writing you — due partly to travel, partly to work,

LAFCADIO HEARN

for I have considerable extra work to do for the Harpers, and for myself. You ask me about literary ventures. I suppose you have seen the little book Osgood published for me last summer — "Stray Leaves from Strange Literature," a volume of Oriental stories. Since then I have had nothing printed except a dictionary of Creole proverbs which could scarcely interest you — and some Oriental essays, which appeared in newspapers only, but which I hope to collect and edit in permanent form next year. Meantime I am working upon a little book of personal impressions, which I expect to finish this summer. Of course I will keep the story you want for you, and mail it; and if you have not seen my other book I will send it you.

Your project about a correspondence is pleasant enough; but I am now simply overwhelmed with work, which has been accumulating during a short absence in Florida. In any event, however, I do not quite see how this thing could prove profitable. I doubt very much if Christ is not a myth, just as Buddha is. There may have been a teacher called Jesus, and there may have been a teacher Siddartha; but the mythological and philosophical systems attached to these names have a far older origin, and represent only the evolution of human ideas from the simple and primitive to the complex form. As the legend of Buddha is now known to have been only the development of an ancient Aryan sun-myth, so probably the legend of Jesus might be

TO W. D. O'CONNOR

traced to the beliefs of primitive and pastoral humanity. What matter creeds, myths, traditions, to you or me, who perceive in all faiths one vast truth — one phase of the Universal Life? Why trouble ourselves about detailed comparisons while we know there is an Infinite which all thinkers are striving vainly to reach by different ways, and an Infinite invisible of which all things visible are but emanations? Worlds are but dreams of God, and evanescent; the galaxies of suns burn out, the heavens wither; even time and space are only relative; and the civilization of a planet but an incident of its growth. To those who feel these things religious questions are valueless and void of meaning, except in their relation to the development of ethical ideas in general. And their study in this light is too large for the compass of a busy life.

In haste, your friend
LAFCADIO HEARN

I read your sermon with pleasure and gave a copy to our editor-in-chief.

TO W. D. O'CONNOR

NEW ORLEANS, *July*, 1885

MY DEAR O'CONNOR, — Your kind little surprise came to me while I was very ill, and, I believe, helped me to get better; for everything which cheers one during an attack of swamp-fever aids convalescence. As you know, I made a sojourn in East

LAFCADIO HEARN

Florida; and I exposed myself a good deal, in the pursuit of impressions. The wonderful water especially tempted me. I am a good swimmer, and always crazy to enjoy a dive, so I yielded to the seduction of Silver Spring. It was a very hot day; but the flood was cold as the grip of old Death. I did n't feel the effect right away; but when I got back home found I had a fever that quinine would take no effect upon. Now I am getting all right, and will be off to the sea soon to recruit.

Well, I thought I would wait to write until I could introduce myself to you, as you so delicately divined that I wanted you to do to me; but I delayed much longer than I wished or intended. Photographs are usually surprises; — your face was not exactly what I had imagined, but it pleased me more — I had fancied you a little stern, very dark, with black eyes — partly, perhaps, because others of your name whom I knew had that purplish black hair and eyes which seems a special race-characteristic — partly perhaps from some fantastic little idea evolved by the effort to create a person from a chirography, as though handwriting constituted a sort of *track* by which individuality could be recognized. I know now that I should feel a little less timid in meeting you; for I seem to know you already very well — for a long time — intimately and without mystery.

I send a couple of little clippings which may interest you for the moment — one, a memory of

TO W. D. O'CONNOR

Saint Augustine; the other, a translation which, though clumsy, preserves something of a great poet's weird fancy.

I am sorry that I have so little to tell you in a literary way. As you seem to see the "Times-Democrat" very often, you watch me tolerably closely, I suppose. I have been trying to complete a little volume of impressions, but the work drags on very, very slowly: I fear I shan't finish it before winter. Then I have a little Chinese story accepted for "Harper's Bazar," which I will send you, and which I think you will like. Otherwise my plans have changed. With the expansion of my private study, I feel convinced that I know too little to attempt anything like a serious volume of Oriental essays; but my researches have given me a larger fancy in some directions, and new colours, which I can use hereafter. Fiction seems to be the only certain road to the publishers' hearts, and I shall try it, not in a lengthy, but a brief compass — striving as much as possible after intense effects. I think you would like my library if you could see it — it is one agglomeration of exotics and eccentricities.

And you do not now write much? — do you? I would like to have read the paper you told me of; but I fear the "Manhattan" is dead beyond resurrection — and, by the way, Richard Grant White has departed to that land which is ruled by absolute silence, and in which a law of fair play, unrecognized by our publishers, doth prevail. Do you never take

LAFCADIO HEARN

a vacation? If you could visit our Grande Isle in the healthy season, you would enjoy it so much! An old-fashioned, drowsy, free-and-easy Creole watering-place in the Gulf — where there is an admirable beach, fishing extraordinary, and subjects innumerable for artistic studies — a hybrid population from all the ends of heaven, white, yellow, red, brown, cinnamon-colour, and tints of bronze and gold. Basques, Andalusians, Portuguese, Malays, Chinamen, etc. I hope to make some pen drawings there.

Have you seen the revised Old Testament? How many of our favourite and beautiful texts have been marred! I almost prefer the oddity of Wickliffe. ... And, by the way, I must tell you that Palmer's Koran is a fine book! ("Sacred Books of the East," Macmillan.) Sale is now practically obsolete.

Hoping I will be able, one of these days, to write something that I can worthily dedicate to you,
  Believe me
            Very affectionately
                    LAFCADIO HEARN

TO H. E. KREHBIEL
              NEW ORLEANS, *October*, 1885

DEAR KREHBIEL, — I would suggest as a title for Tunison's admirably conceived book, "The Legends of Virgil," or, better still, "The Virgilian Legend" (in the singular), as it is the custom among folklorists to assemble a class of interrelated myths or

TO H. E. KREHBIEL

fables under such a general head. Thus we have "The Legend of Mélusine, or Mère Lusine"; "The Legend of Myrrdlium, or Merlin"; "The Legend of Don Juan" — although each subject represents a large number of myths, illustrating the evolutional history of one idea through centuries. This title could be supplemented by an explanatory sub-title.

Of course you can rely on me to praise, sincerely and strongly, what I cannot but admire and honourably envy the authorship of. I wish I could even hope to do so fine a piece of serious work as this promises to be.

I am exceedingly grateful for your prompt sending of the Creole songs, which I will return in a day or two. Some Creole music of an *inedited* kind — just one or two fragments — I would like so as to introduce your rôle well. I now fear, however, that I shall not be able to devote as much time to the work as I hoped.

As for my "thinkings, doings, and ambitions," I have nothing interesting to tell. I have accumulated a library worth two thousand dollars; I have studied a great deal in directions which have not yet led me to any definite goal; I have made no money by my literary outside work worth talking about; and I have become considerably disgusted with what I have already done. But I have not yet abandoned the idea of evolutional fiction, and find that my ethnographic and anthropologic reading has enabled me to find a totally new charm in character-analysis, and suggested artistic effects of a new and peculiar description. I dream of a novel, or a novelette, to be constructed upon totally novel principles; but the outlook is not encouraging. Years of very hard work with a problematical result! I feel pretty much like a scholar trying hard to graduate and feeling tolerably uneasy about the result.

Since you have more time now you might drop a line occasionally. I hope to hear you succeed with the Scribners; — if not, I would strongly recommend an effort with Houghton, Mifflin & Co., the most appreciative publishers on this side of the Atlantic.

Yours very affectionately
LAFCADIO HEARN

TO H. E. KREHBIEL

NEW ORLEANS, 1885

DEAR K., — I was in hopes by this time to have been able to have sent you for examination a little volume by La Selve, in which a curious account is given of the various negro-Creole dances and songs of the Antilles. The book has been ordered for a very considerable time, but owing to some cause or other, its arrival has been delayed.

I find references made to Duveyrier ("Les Touaregs du Nord") in regard to the music of those extraordinary desert nomads, who retain their blue eyes and blonde hair under the sun of the Timbuctoo country; and to Endemann (by Hartmann) as a preserver of the music of the Basutos (South Africa).

TO H. E. KREHBIEL

Hartmann himself considers African music — superficially, perhaps, in the smaller volume — in his "Peuples d'Afrique"; and in his "Nigritiens" (Berlin: in 2 vols.). I have the small work ("Peuples d'Afrique") which forms part of the French International Scientific Series, but has not been translated for the American collection. Hartmann speaks well of the musical "aptitudes" of the African races, while declaring their art undeveloped; and he even says that the famous Egyptian music of Dendera, Edfu, and Thebes never rose above the orchestration at an Ashantee or Monbuttoo festival. He even remarks that the instruments of the ancient Egyptian and modern Nigritian peoples are almost similar. He also refers to the negro talents for improvisation, and their peculiar love of animal-fables — the same, no doubt, which found a new utterance in the negro myths of the South. The large work of Hartmann I have never seen, and as it is partly chromolithographed I fear it is very expensive. The names Hartmann and Endemann are very German: I know of the former only through French sources — perhaps you have seen the original. He supports some of his views with quotations you are familiar with, perhaps — from Clapperton, Bowdich, and Schweinfurth.

It is rather provoking that I have not been able to find any specimens of Griot music referred to in French works on Senegal; and I fancy the Griot music would strongly resemble (in its suitability to improvisation especially) the early music of the negroes here. Every French writer on Senegal has something to say about the Griots, but none seem to have known enough music to preserve a chant. The last two works published (Jeannest's "Au Congo" and Marche's "Afrique Occidentale") were written by men without music in their souls. The first publishes pictures of musical instruments, but no music; and the second gives ten lines to the subject in a volume of nearly four hundred pages. Seems to me that a traveller who was a musician might cultivate virgin soil in regard to the African music of the interior. All I can find relating to it seems to deal with the music of South Africa and the west and north coasts; — the interior is unknown musically. I expect to receive La Selve soon, however — and if his announcement be truthful, we shall have something of interest therein regarding the cis-Atlantic Africa.

L. H.

I saw a notice in the "Tribune" regarding the negro Pan's pipe described by Cable. I never saw it; but the fact is certainly very interesting. The cane is well adapted to inspire such manufacture.

TO H. E. KREHBIEL
NEW ORLEANS, 1885

DEAR K., — Just got a letter from you. Hope my reply to your delightful suggestion was received. I

TO H. E. KREHBIEL

fear I write too often; but I can only write in snatches. Were I to wait for time to write a long letter, the result would be either zero or something worse.

I have already in my mind a little plan. Let me suggest a long preface, and occasional picturesque notes to your learning and facts. For example, I would commence by treating the negro's musical patriotism — the strange history of the Griots, who furnish so singular an example of musical prostitution, and who, although honoured and petted in one way, are otherwise despised by their own people and refused the rites of burial. Then I would relate something about the curious wanderings of these Griots through the yellow desert northward into the Moghreb country — often a solitary wandering; their performances at Arab camps on the long journey, when the black slaves come out to listen and weep; — then their hazardous voyaging to Constantinople, where they play old Congo airs for the great black population of Stamboul, whom no laws or force can keep within doors when the sound of Griot music is heard in the street. Then I would speak of how the blacks carry their music with them to Persia and even to mysterious Hadramaut, where their voices are held in high esteem by Arab masters. Then I would touch upon the transplantation of negro melody to the Antilles and the two Americas, where its strangest black flowers are gathered by the alchemists of musical science, and the perfume thereof extracted by magicians like Gottschalk. (How is that for a beginning?)

I would divide my work into brief sections of about one and a half pages each — every division separated by Roman numerals and containing one particular group of facts.

I would also try to show a relation between negro *physiology* and negro music. You know the blood of the African black has the highest human temperature known — equal to that of the swallow — although it loses that fire in America. I would like you to find out for me whether the negro's vocal cords are not differently formed, and capable of *longer* vibration than ours. Some expert professor in physiology might tell you; but I regret to say the latest London works do not touch upon the negro vocal cords, although they do show other remarkable anatomical distinctions.

Here is the only Creole song I know of with an African refrain *that is still sung:* — don't show it to C., it is one of *our* treasures.

(Pronounce "Wenday," "makkiyah.")

>   *Ouendé, ouendé, macaya!*
>   Mo pas barassé, *macaya!*
>   *Ouendé, ouendé, macaya!*
>   Mo bois bon divin, *macaya!*
>   *Ouendé, ouendé, macaya!*
>   Mo mangé bon poulet, *macaya!*
>   *Ouendé, ouendé, macaya!*
>   Mo pas barassé, *macaya!*
>   *Ouendé, ouendé, macaya!* —
>   *Macaya!*

TO H. E. KREHBIEL

I wrote from dictation of Louise Roche. She did not know the meaning of the refrain — her mother had taught her, and the mother had learned it from the grandmother. However, I found out the meaning, and asked her if she *now* remembered. She leaped in the air for joy — apparently. Ouendai or ouendé has a different meaning in the eastern Soudan; but in the Congo or Fiot dialect it means "to go" — "to continue to," "to go on." I found the word in Jeannest's vocabulary. Then macaya I found in Turiault's "Etude sur la Langage Créole de la Martinique": ça veut dire "manger tout le temps" — "excessivement." Therefore here is our translation:

    Go on! go on! *eat enormously!*
    I ain't one bit ashamed — *eat outrageously!*
    Go on! go on! *eat prodigiously!*
    I drink good wine — *eat ferociously!* —
    Go on! go on! — *eat unceasingly*[1] —
    I eat good chicken — gorging myself! —
        Go on! go on! etc.

How is this for a linguistic discovery? The music is almost precisely like the American river-music — a chant, almost a recitative until the end of the line is reached; then for your mocking-music!

And by the way, in Guyana, there is a mocking-bird more wonderful than ours — with a voice so sonorous and solemn and far-reaching that those Creole negroes who dwell in the great aisles of the forest call it zozo mon-pè (l'oiseau mon-père), the "My father-bird." But the word father here signifieth a spiritual father — a *ghostly* father — the "Priest-bird"!

Now dream of the vast cathedral of the woods, whose sanctuary lights are the stars of heaven!

L. H.

TO H. E. KREHBIEL

NEW ORLEANS, 1885

DEAR KREHBIEL, — You are a terribly neglectful correspondent: I have asked you nearly one hundred questions, not a single one of which you have ever deemed it worth while to answer. However, that makes no matter now — as none of the questions were very important, certainly not in your estimation. I think you are right about the negro-American music, and that a Southern trip will be absolutely essential — because I have never yet met a person here able to reproduce on paper those fractional tones we used to talk about, which lend such weirdness to those songs. The naked melody robbed of these has absolutely no national characteristic. The other day a couple of darkeys from the country passed my corner, singing — not a Creole song, but a plain negro ditty — with a recurrent burthen consisting of the cry:

Oh! Jee-roo-sa-le-e-em!

I can't describe to you the manner in which the syllable *lem* was broken up into four tiny notes, the utterance of which did not occupy one second —

TO H. E. KREHBIEL

all in a very low but very powerful key. The rest of the song was in a regular descending scale: the *oh* being very much prolonged and the other notes very quick and sudden. Wish I could write it; but I can't. I think all the original negro-Creole songs were characterized by similar eccentricities. If you could visit a Creole plantation — and I know Cable could arrange that for you — you would be able to make some excellent studies.

Cable told me he wanted you to treat these things musically. I am *sure*, however, that his versions of them lack something — as regards rhythm (musical), time, and that shivering of notes into musical splinters which I can't describe. I have never told him I thought so; but I suggest the matter to you for consideration. I think it would be a good idea to have a chat with him about a Southern trip in the interest of these Creole studies. I am also sure that one must study the original Creole-ditty among the full-blooded French-speaking blacks of the country — not among the city singers, who are too much civilized to retain originality. When the bamboulas were danced there was some real "Congo" music; but the musicians are gone God knows where. The results of your Southern trip might be something very important. There is a rage in Europe for musical folk-lore. Considering what Gottschalk did with Creole musical themes, it is surprising more attention has not been paid to the ditties of the Antilles, etc. I am told there are stunning treasures of such curiosities in Cuba, Martinique — all the Spanish and French possessions, but especially the former. The outlook is delightful; but I think with you that it were best to rely chiefly upon *personal* study. It strikes me the thing ought to be scientifically undertaken — so as to leave as little as possible for others to improve upon or even to glean. If you care for names of French writers on African music, I can send.

Didst ever hear the music of the Zamacueca?

L. H.

TO H. E. KREHBIEL

NEW ORLEANS, *February*, 1886

DEAR KREHBIEL, — Your very brief note was received almost simultaneously with my first perusal of your work in the "Century." But the Cala-woman's song is, I really think, imaginary. I have the real cry — six notes and some fractions — which I will send you when I get a man to write it down. The patate-cry is less African, but very pleasing. I have been somewhat surprised to discover that the word Voudoo is not African, but the corruption of a South-American mythological term with a singular history — too long to write now, but at your service whenever you may need it.

Plympton has been here on his way to the W. Indies via Florida — a white shadow, a ghost, a Voice — utterly broken down. I fear his summers are numbered. He will return to his desk only to

TO H. E. KREHBIEL

die, I fancy. A good, large-minded, frank, eccentric man — always a friend to me.

If you are interested in Provençal literature and song, and are not acquainted with Hueffer's "Troubadours" (Chatto & Windus), let me recommend the volume as one of the most compact and scholarly I have yet seen. It is not exactly *new*, but new in its popularity on this side. His theories are original; his facts, of course, may be all old to you.

Houssaye is not a New Orleans favourite, like Albert Delpit, the Creole — or Pierre Loti — or Guy de Maupassant — or the leaders of the later schools of erudite romance, such as Anatole France — or the psychologists of naturalism. Finally, I am sorry to say, the same material saw light months ago in the "Figaro," and is now quite ancient history to French-speaking New Orleans. However, I have to leave the matter entirely to Page, and the greatest obstacle will be price — as we usually only pay five dollars for foreign correspondence. Picayunish, I know; but Burke will pay seventy-five dollars for a note from Loti, or a letter from Davitt, just for the name.

Try Roberts Bros. for Tunison. Chatto & Windus, of London, might also like the book; — the only trouble is that in England there is a lurking suspicion (not without foundation) of the untrustworthiness of American work of this kind — so many things have been done hastily in this country, without that precision of scholarship and leisurely finish indispensable to solid endurance. If they can only be induced to *read* the MS., perhaps it would be all right. Rivington of London is another enterprising firm in the same line.

I expect to see you this summer — also to send you a volume of Chinese stories. Material is developing well. Won't write again until I can tear and wrench and wring a big letter out of you.

    Affectionately
        L. HEARN

TO H. E. KREHBIEL
    NEW ORLEANS, *February*, 1886

MY DEAR MUSICIAN, — Your letter delighted me. Strange as it may seem to you, the books and papers you sent me, I never received!

I feel a somewhat malicious joy in telling you that the translations you considered so abominable are printed without the least alteration, and also in assuring you that if you can spare time to read them you will like them. Still, I must say that the book is not free from errors, and that were I to do it all over again to-day, I should be able to improve upon it. It is my first effort, however, and I am therefore a little anxious; for to commence one's literary career with a collapse would be very bad. I think I shall see you in New York this summer. I have a project on foot — to issue a series of translations of archæological and artistic French romance — Flaubert's "Tentation de Saint-Antoine"; De Nerval's "Voy-

TO H. E. KREHBIEL

age en Orient"; Gautier's "Avatar"; Loti's most extraordinary African and Polynesian novels; and Baudelaire's "Petits Poëmes en Prose." If I can get any encouragement, it is not impossible that I might stay in New York awhile; but there is no knowing. I am working steadily toward the realization of one desire — to get rid of newspaper life.

No: I am not writing on music now — only book reviews, French and Spanish translations, and an occasional editorial. The musical reviews of the "Times-Democrat" are the work of Jean Augustin — one of the few talented Creoles here, who is the author of a volume of French poems, and is personally a fine fellow. We are now very busy writing up the Carnival. I have charge of the historical and mythological themes — copies of which I will send you when the paper is printed. One of the themes will interest you as belonging to a novel and generally little known subject; but I have only been able to devote two days apiece to them (four in all), so you will make allowance for rough-and-ready work.

I am very happy to hear you are cozy, and nicely established, and the father of a little one, which I feel sure must inherit physical and mental comeliness of no common sort.

I cannot write as I wish to-day, as Carnival duties are pressing. So I will only thank you for your kindness, and conclude with a promise to do better next time.

Your friend and admirer   L. Hearn

LAFCADIO HEARN

By the way, would you like a copy of De l'Isere's work on diseases of the voice, and the rapports between sexual and vocal power? I have a copy for you, but you must excuse its badly battered condition. I have built up quite a nice library here; and the antiquarians bring me odd things when they get them. This is one, but it has been abused.

L. H.

TO W. D. O'CONNOR

NEW ORLEANS, *April*, 1886

MY DEAR O'CONNOR, — Your dainty little gift was deeply appreciated. By this mail I send you a few papers containing an editorial on the subject — rather hastily written, I much regret to say, owing to pressure of other work — but calculated, I trust, to excite interest in the nobly written defence of Mrs. Pott's marvellous commentary.

I have not written you because I felt unable to interest you in the condition I have been long in — struggling between the necessities of my *trade* and the aspirations of what I hope to prove my *art*. I have a little Chinese book on Ticknor & Co.'s stocks: if it appear you will receive it, and perhaps enjoy some pages. The volume is an attempt in the direction I hope to make triumph some day: *poetical prose*. I send also some cuttings — leaves for a future volume to appear, God knows when, under the title "Notebook of an Impressionist." Before completing it I expect to publish a novelette, which

TO W. D. O'CONNOR

will be dedicated to you — if I think it worthy of you. I will work at it all this summer.

I may also tell you that since I last wrote a very positive change has been effected in my opinions by the study of Herbert Spencer. He has completely converted me away from all 'isms, or sympathies with 'isms: at the same time he has filled me with the vague but omnipotent consolation of the Great Doubt. I can no longer give adhesion to the belief in human automatism — and that positive skepticism that imposes itself upon an undisciplined mind has been eternally dissipated in my case. I do not know if this philosophy interests you; but I am sure it would, if you are not already, as I suspect, an adept in it. I have only read, so far, the First Principles; but all the rest are corollaries only.

Now I have been selfish enough with my *Ego;* — let me trust you are well, not over-busy, and as happy as it is possible to be under ordinary conditions. I may run away to the sea for a while; I may run up North, and take the liberty of spending a few hours in Washington on my way back from New York. But whether I see you or not, believe always in my sincere affection.

Your friend   LAFCADIO HEARN

TO W. D. O'CONNOR

NEW ORLEANS, *April,* 1886

DEAR O'CONNOR, — I had not received your letter when I wrote mine. It pained me to hear of your having been ill, and especially ill in a way which I am peculiarly well qualified to understand — having been almost given up for dead some eight years ago. The same causes, the same symptoms — in every particular. Luckily for me I found a warmer climate, a city where literary competition was almost nothing, and men of influence who took an interest in my work, and let me have things my own way. Rest and cultivation of the *animal* part of me, and good care by a dear good woman, got me nearly well again. I am stronger than I ever was in some ways; but I have not the same recuperative vitality — I cannot trust myself to any severe mental strain. "Sickness is health," they say, for those who have received one of Nature's severe corrections.

I mention my own case only to show that I understand yours, and to give you, if possible, the benefit of my experience. Long sleep is necessary, for two or three years. Do not be afraid to take ten, eleven or twelve hours when you so feel inclined. I observe that the mind accomplishes more, and in a shorter time, after these protracted rests. Never work when you feel that little pain in the back of the head. Rare beefsteaks — eggs just warmed — and claret and water to stimulate appetite as often as possible, are important. Doctors can do little; you yourself can do a great deal. I think a few months, or even weeks, at the sea, would astonish you by the result. It did me. The abyss, out of which all mundane life is said to have been evolved — the vast salt gulf of Crea-

TO W. D. O'CONNOR

tion — seems still to retain its mysterious power: the Spirit still hovers over the Face of the Deep — and the very breath of the ocean gives new soul to the blood.

You will already know what I think of your beautiful book, with all of which I heartily concur. But do not attempt to overwork any more. You ought not to trust yourself to do more than three or four hours' work a day — and even this application ought to be interrupted at intervals. I take a smoke every hour or so. The main thing — *please do not doubt it* — is plenty of nourishment, cultivation of appetite, and much sleep. Then Nature will right herself — slowly, though surely.

Do not write to me if it tires you. I know just how it is; I know also that you feel well toward me even if you have to keep silence. I will write whenever I think I can interest you — and never fail to drop me a line if I can do anything to please you — just a line. I would not have been silent so long, had I even suspected you were ill. My own illness of eight years back was caused by years of night-work — sixteen hours a day. Several of my old comrades died at it. I quit — took courage to attempt a different class of work, and, as the French say, I have been able to remake my constitution. I trust it won't bore you, my writing all this: I understand so exactly how you have been that I am anxious to give all the suggestions I can. I remain, dear O'Connor

Very affectionately

LAFCADIO HEARN

LAFCADIO HEARN

TO H. E. KREHBIEL

NEW ORLEANS, *May*, 1886

DEAR KREHBIEL, — I think I shall soon be able to send you a Hindoo. Yes, a Hindoo — with Orientally white teeth, the result of vegetal diet and Brahmanic abstemiousness — rather prognathous, I am sorry to say, and not therefore of purest Aryan breed. He may be a Thug, a Sepoy deserter, a Sikh drummed out of the army, a Brahmin who has lost caste, a Pariah thief, a member of the Left-hand or of the Right-hand caste (or other sections too horrible to name), a Jain, a half-breed Mongol Islamite from Delhi, a Ghoorkha, a professional fraud, a Jesuitic convert on trial ... I know not; — I send him to you with my best regard. You are large and strong; you can take care of yourself! I send him to the "Tribune" — fearing the awful results of his visit to 305 West Fifty-Fifth Street.

How did I find him? Well, he came one day to our office to protest about some of my editorials on Indian questions. I found he talked English well, wrote with sufficient accuracy to contribute to the "Times-Democrat," and had been in the Indian civil service. I questioned him on Hindoo literature: found him somewhat familiar with the Mahabharata and Ramayana, the Bhagavad-Gita and the Vedantas — heard him reiterate the names of the great Sanscrit poets and playwrights — Kalidasa, Vyasa, Jayadeva, Bhartrihari. He first taught me

TO H. E. KREHBIEL

accurately to pronounce the awful title "Mricchakatikâ," which means "The Chariot of Baked Clay"; and he translated for me, although with great effort and very badly, one of the delicious love-lyrics of the divine Amaron. Therefore I perceived that he knew something vaguely about the vast Mother of Languages.

And he sang for me the chants of the temples, in a shrill Indian tenor, with marvellously fine splintering of notes — melancholy, dreamy, drowsy, like the effect of monotonous echoes in a day of intense heat and atmospheric oppression.

Why, then, did not my heart warm toward him? Was it because, in the columns of the "Times-Democrat," he had boldly advocated the burning of widows and abused the Government of which I remain a loving subject? Was it because he made his appearance simultaneously with that of that colossal fraud, the "North, South, and Central American Exposition"? Nay: it was because of his prognathism, his exceedingly sinister eye, like the eye of a creature of prey, his shaky suppleness of movement; and his mysterious past. How might I trust myself alone with a man who looked like one of the characters of the "Moonstone"? And yet I regret ... what a ridiculous romance I might have made!

Never mind, I send him to you! He says he is a Brahman. He says he can sing you the chants and dirges of his sun-devoured land. Let him sing! —

LAFCADIO HEARN

let him chant! If he merit interest in the shape of fifty cents, give it to him, and watch him slip it into his swarthy bosom with the stealthy gesture of one about to pull forth a moon-shaped knife. Or tell him where to get, or to look for work. He worked here in a moss-factory and in a sash-factory and other factories; living upon rice and beans more cheaply than a Chinaman. Yet beware you do not smite him on the nostrils without large and solid reason.

I give him a letter to you. Amen!

(P S His alleged name is Sattee or Suttee — perhaps most probably the *latter*, as he advocates it.)

I received your book — a charming volume in all that makes a volume charming: including clear tinted paper, not too glossy; fascinating type; broad margins; tasteful binding. Thanks for dear little phrase written in it. I will send first criticism of contents in shape of a review. Have something else to talk of later.

I hope you received photograph sent by Baker through me — and paper. The translation does not convey original force of style; but it may serve to reveal something of the author's *intensity*. His power of impressing and communicating queer sensations makes him remarkable.

        Affectionately
                      L. Hearn

TO H. E. KREHBIEL

TO H. E. KREHBIEL

NEW ORLEANS, 1886

DEAR KREHBIEL, — I was waiting to write you in the hope of being able to send you some literary news. I have my little Chinese book in Ticknor's hands; but the long silence is still unbroken. The omen is not a bad one, yet I am disappointed in not being able now, when replying to your delightful letter, to tell you everything is O. K. — because the book is dedicated to you. There are only six little stories; but each of them cost months of hard work and study, and represent a much higher attempt than anything in the "Stray Leaves." The dedication will, I think, amuse you if the book appears — and will be more or less mysterious to the rest of the world. I fear now it cannot be published in time to reach you before you leave for Europe.

Well, dear old fellow, I think I must try to see you at New York anyhow. At all events I must have a change. The prolonged humidity and chilliness of our winter is telling on me; I have been considerably pulled down in spite of an easy life, and must try the sea somewhere. I fear the Eastern beaches are too expensive; but I could run North, and spend the rest of the time allowed me after my visit at some obscure fishing village. Europe, I fear, must be given up this summer. I could visit Spain in company with a dear friend, Dr. Matas; but I feel it a duty to myself to stick at literary work this summer in order to effect a new departure.

Now, I must tell you about it. I am writing a novelette. It will require at least twelve months to finish — though it will be a tiny book. It will be all divided into microscopic chapters of a page or half-a-page each. Every one of these is to be a little picture, with some novel features. Some touches of evolutionary philosophy. I want to make something altogether odd, novel, ideal in the best sense. The theme, I fear, you will not like. The story of a somewhat improper love — a fascination developed into a sincere but vain affection — an effort to re-create what has been hopelessly lost — a seeking after the impossible. I am not quite sure yet how I shall arrange the main part; — there will be much more of *suggestion* than of real plot. ... I do, indeed, remember your advice; but I am not sorry not to have followed it before. My style was not formed; I did not really know how to work; I am only now beginning to learn. Ticknor writes that if I should undertake a novelette, he is certain it would succeed. So I shall try. In trying I must study from real material; I must take models where I can find them. Still the work will be ideal to the verge of fantasy.

So much for that. If I have been selfish enough to talk first about myself, it is partly because I cannot answer your question without giving some of my own experience. You ask about style; you deem yours unsatisfactory, and say that I overestimated

TO H. E. KREHBIEL

it. Perhaps I may have overestimated particular things that with a somewhat riper judgment I would consider less enthusiastically. But I always perceived an uncommon excellence in the tendency of your style — a purity and strength that is uncommon and which I could never successfully imitate. A man's style, when fully developed, is part of his personality. Mine is being shaped for a particular end; yours, I think, is better adapted to an ultimately higher purpose. The fact that you deem it unsatisfactory shows, I fancy, that you are in a way to develop it still further. I have only observed this, that it is capable of much more polish than you have cared to bestow upon it. Mind! I do not mean *ornament;* — I do not think you should attempt ornament, but rather force and sonority. Your tendency, I think, is naturally toward classical purity and correctness — almost severity. With great strength — ornament becomes unnecessary; and the general cultivation of strength involves the cultivation of grace. I still consider yours a higher style than mine, but I do not think you have cultivated it to one fourth of what it is capable. Now, let me say why.

Chiefly, I fancy, for want of time. If you do not know it already, let me dwell upon an art principle. Both you and I have a *trade:* journalism. We have also an *art:* authorship. The same system of labour cannot be applied to the one as to the other without unfortunate results. Let the trade be performed as mechanically as is consistent with preservation of one's reputation as a good *workman:* any more labour devoted to it is an unpaid waste of time. But when it comes to writing a *durable* thing — a book or a brochure — every line ought to be written at least twice, if possible *three* times. Three times, at all events, to commence with. First — roughly, in pencil: after which correct and reshape as much as you deem necessary. Then rewrite *clean* in pencil. Read again; and you will be surprised to find how much improvement is possible. Then copy in ink, and in the very act of copying, new ideas of grace, force, and harmony will make themselves manifest. Without this, I will venture to say, fine literary execution is *impossible.* Some writers need the discipline less than others. You, for example, less than I. My imagination and enthusiasm have to be kept in control; my judgments to be reversed or amended; my adjectives perpetually sifted and pruned. But my work is ornamental — my dream is poetical prose: a style unsuited to literature of the solid and instructive kind. Have you ever worked much with Roget's "Thesaurus"? — it is invaluable. Still more valuable are etymological dictionaries like those of Skeat (best in the world), of Brachet (French), of Dozy and Engelmann (Spanish-Arabic). Such books give one that subtle sense of words to which much that *startles* in poetry and prose is due. Time develops the secret merit of work thus done. . . . These, dear K., are simply my own experiences, ideas, and

TO H. E. KREHBIEL

impressions. I now think they are correct. In a few years I might modify them. They may contain useful suggestions. Our humblest friends may suggest valuable things sometimes.

Talking of change in opinions, I am really astonished at myself. You know what my fantastic metaphysics were. A friend disciplined me to read Herbert Spencer. I suddenly discovered what a waste of time all my Oriental metaphysics had been. I also discovered, for the first time, how to apply the little general knowledge I possessed. I also learned what an absurd thing positive skepticism is. I also found unspeakable comfort in the sudden and, for me, eternal reopening of the Great Doubt, which renders pessimism ridiculous, and teaches a new reverence for all forms of faith. In short, from the day when I finished the "First Principles" — a totally new intellectual life opened for me; and I hope during the next two years to devour the rest of this oceanic philosophy. But this is boring you too much for the nonce.

Believe me, dear friend, affectionately
LAFCADIO HEARN

TO H. E. KREHBIEL
NEW ORLEANS, 1886

DEAR KREHBIEL, — I must drop you another line or two; for you must let me hear from you again before you go to Europe.

I have completely recovered from the nervous

LAFCADIO HEARN

shock which the sudden return of my tiny volume produced in spite of myself; and all my scattered plans are being re-crystallized. I know my work is good in some respects; and if it bears reading over well, next winter I may take a notion to publish a small edition at my own expense. In fact, I believe I will have to publish several things at my own expense. Even if my art-ideas are correct (and I sincerely believe they are) — in their most mature form they would represent a heterodox novelty in American style, and literary heterodoxies no publisher will touch. I am going to give up the novelette idea — it is too large an undertaking at present — and will try short stories. My notebooks will always be useful. Whenever I receive a new and strong impression, even in a dream, I write it down, and afterwards develop it at leisure. These efforts repay me well in the end.

There are impressions of blue light and gold and green, correlated to old Spanish legend, which can be found only south of this line. I obtained a few in Florida; — I must complete the effect by future visits: therefore I shall go to the most vast and luminous of all ports known to the seamen of the South — the Bay of the Holy Ghost (Espiritu Santo) — in plainer language, Tampa. So I shall vegetate a while longer in the South. I have some six hundred dollars saved up; but, I fear, under present circumstances, that I would be imprudent to expend it all in a foreign trip, and will wait until

TO H. E. KREHBIEL

I can make some sort of impression with some new sort of work. The "Times-Democrat" will save expenses for me on Florida trip, and instead of roar and rumble of traffic and shrieking of steam and dust of microbes, I shall dream by the shores of phosphorescent seas, and inhale the Spirit that moveth over the face of the Deep.

I forgot in my last to thank you for little notice in the playbill of my Gautier stories; but you were mistaken as to their being paraphrases. They were literal translations, so far as I was able to make them at the time. I am sorry that they now appear full of faults: especially as I cannot get any publisher to take them away from Worthington. If I succeed some day, I may be able to get out a more perfect edition in small neat shape. "Stray Leaves" also has several hideous errors in it. I never dare now to look at them for fear of finding something else worse than before.

By the way, last year I had to muster up courage to condemn a lot of phantasmagoria to the flames.
Very affectionately

LAFCADIO

DEAR K., — Like a woman I must always add a P.S.

Something that has been worrying me demands utterance. A Paris correspondent of the "Tribune," grossly misinformed, has written an error to that paper on "Lakme." "Lakme" may have been

LAFCADIO HEARN

drawn from "Le Mariage de Loti" — the weirdest and loveliest romance, to my notion, ever written; — but that novel has nothing to do with India or English officers. It is a novel of Polynesian life in Tahiti. It is unspeakably beautiful and unspeakably *odd*. I translated its finest passages in a so-and-so way when it first came out, and won the good will of its clever author, Julien Viaud, who sent me his portrait and a very pretty letter. I have collected every scrap "Loti" wrote, and translated many things: will send you a rough-and-ready translation from his new novel on Sunday. No writer ever had such an effect upon me; and time strengthens my admiration. I hold him the greatest of living writers of the Impressionist School; and still he is something more — he has a spirituality peculiarly his own, that reminds you a little of Coleridge. I cannot even think of him without enthusiasm. Therefore I feel sorry to hear of him being misrepresented. He is a great musician in the folk-lore way, too; and in one of my letters to him I mentioned your name. Some day you might come together; and he could sing you all the Polynesian and African songs you want. He has lived in the Soudan. I sent you once a fragment by him upon those African improvisors, called Griots. If the "Tribune" ever wants anything written about Loti, see if you can't persuade them to apply to me. I know all about his life and manners, and I would not ask any remuneration for so delightful a privilege as that of being able to do him justice in a great

TO H. E. KREHBIEL

paper. His address is 141 Rue Saint Pierre, Rochefort-sur-Mer. You might see him in Europe, perhaps.
LAFCADIO H.

TO H. E. KREHBIEL

NEW ORLEANS, *October*, 1886

DEAR KREHBIEL, — While in hideous anxiety I await the decision of my future by various damnably independent censors, I must seize the moment of leisure — the first calm after a prolonged storm of work — to chat with you awhile, and to thank you for your musical aid. Alden is, of course, deliberating over the "Legend of l'Ile Dernière"; Roberts Bros. are deliberating over "Chinese Ghosts"; I am also deliberating about a voyage to Havana, the Mystical Rose of a West Indian dawn — with palms shaking their plumes against the crimsoning. What are you deliberating about? Something that I shall be crazy to read, no doubt, and will have the delight of celebrating the appearance of in the editorial columns of the provincial "Times-Democrat"! O that I were the directing spirit of some new periodical — backed by twenty million dollar publishing interests — and devoted especially to the literary progression of the future — the realization of a dream of poetical prose — the evolution of the Gnosticism of the New Art! Then, would n't I have lots to say about The Musician — *my* musician — and the Song of Songs that is to be!

For my own purpose now lieth naked before me,

without shame. I suppose we all have a purpose, an involuntary goal, to which the Supreme Ghost, unknowingly to us, directs our way; and when we find we have accomplished what *we* wished for, we also invariably find that we have travelled thither by a route very different from that which we laid out for ourselves, and toward a consummation not precisely that which we anticipated — although pleasing enough. Well, you remember my ancient dream of a poetical prose — compositions to satisfy an old Greek ear — like chants wrought in a huge measure, wider than the widest line of a Sanscrit composition, and just a little irregular, like Ocean-rhythm. I really think I will be able to realize it at last. And then, what? I really don't know. I fancy that I shall have produced a pleasant effect on the reader's mind, simply with pictures; and that the secret work, the word-work, will not be noticed for its own sake. It will be simply an eccentricity for critics; an originality for those pleased by it — but I'm sure it will be grateful unto the *musical* ear of H. E. K.!

Now I remember promising to write about going to New York.

Br-r-r-r-r-r-r-r-r-r!

'T is winter. My lizard blood freezes at the thought. In my room it is 71°: that is cold for us. New York in winter signifieth for such as me — Dissolution — eternal darkness and worms. Transformation of physical and vital forces of L. H. into the forces of innumerable myriads of worms! "And

TO H. E. KREHBIEL

though a man live many years, and rejoice in them all — yet let him remember the Days of Darkness — for they shall be many!" No: March, April, or May! But you say — "Then it will be the same old story, and seasons will cycle, and generations pass away, and yet he will not come." Yet there are symptoms of my coming: little spider-threads of literary weaving with New York are thickening. When the rope is strong, I can make my bridge. — Think of the trouble I would have with my eighteen hundred dollars of books, and all my other truck. Alas! I have an anchor!

My friend Matas has returned. He tells me delightful things about Spanish music, and plays for me. He also tells me much concerning Cuban and Mexican music. He says these have been very strongly affected by African influence — full of contretemps. He tried to explain about the accompaniments of Havanen and Mexican airs having peculiar interresemblances of a seemingly *dark* origin — the bass goes all the time something like Si, Mi, Si — si, mi, si. "See me? — see?" that's how I remembered it. But he has given me addresses, and I will be able to procure specimens.

Affectionately

LAFCADIO